GLOW OF DEATH

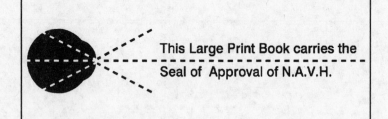

This Large Print Book carries the Seal of Approval of N.A.V.H.

A JOSIE PRESCOTT ANTIQUES MYSTERY

GLOW OF DEATH

JANE K. CLELAND

THORNDIKE PRESS
A part of Gale, a Cengage Company

Farmington Hills, Mich • San Francisco • New York • Waterville, Maine
Meriden, Conn • Mason, Ohio • Chicago

LIBRARY OF CONGRESS CATALOGING-IN-PUBLICATION DATA

Names: Cleland, Jane K., author.
Title: Glow of death / by Jane K. Cleland.
Description: Large print edition. | Waterville, Maine : Thorndike Press, a part of Gale, a Cengage Company, 2017. | Series: A Josie Prescott Antiques mystery | Series: Thorndike Press large print mystery
Identifiers: LCCN 2017028683| ISBN 9781432844097 (hardcover) | ISBN 1432844091 (hardcover)
Subjects: LCSH: Prescott, Josie (Fictitious character)—Fiction. | Antiques—Expertising—Fiction. | Murder—Investigation—Fiction. | New Hampshire—Fiction. | Large type books. | BISAC: FICTION / Mystery & Detective / Women Sleuths. | GSAFD: Mystery fiction.
Classification: LCC PS3603.L4555 G58 2017b | DDC 813/.6—dc23
LC record available at https://lccn.loc.gov/2017028683

Published in 2017 by arrangement with Macmillan Publishing Group, LLC / St. Martin's Press

Printed in the United States of America
1 2 3 4 5 6 7 21 20 19 18 17

This is for Joe.

AUTHOR'S NOTE

This is a work of fiction. While there is a Seacoast Region in New Hampshire, there is no town called Rocky Point, and many other geographic liberties have been taken.

CHAPTER ONE

Hank, my Maine coon cat, pranced over to say hello. I wedged the phone receiver between my ear and shoulder so I could pat my lap. He jumped up.

"It's a mystery," Edwin Towson said on the other end of the line, his voice confident and urbane. "Grandma Ruby swore her mother never mentioned owning a Tiffany lamp."

"I don't know whether we'll be able to figure out how it ended up in your great-grandmother's attic, but for sure we can determine if it's genuine."

"That's all I'm asking. I'm leaving for Europe in the morning, but Ava will be around. She's home today if you have time to get started right away."

"Perfect. Are you interested in selling the lamp?"

"I haven't thought about it. The urgency has to do with insurance. If it's an actual

Tiffany, I need to get it covered."

I thanked him for the opportunity, grabbed my tote bag, and rushed downstairs. A Tiffany lamp!

Hank trotted beside me as I jogged across the warehouse toward the front office. I pushed open the heavy door. Hank came along.

Fred, one of Prescott's antiques appraisers, was on the phone, discussing Chippendale-style furniture with a curator in Virginia. Sasha, our chief appraiser, was out on a call — Victor and Sue O'Hara were downsizing, and I'd just signed off on her recommended bid for the lot. The O'Haras planned on making a decision within a week or two, probably in early July.

I sat at our guest table and invited Hank onto my lap for a pet-pet. While I waited for Fred to finish his call, I gave Hank a cheek rub. Jowlies, I called it.

Fred replaced the receiver in its cradle, pushed up his super-cool, black square-framed glasses, and said, "You win some. You lose some. Looks like all we have is a good repro of a Chippendale chair."

"Emphasis on the repro," I said.

"Exactly."

All in a day's work, I thought. "I bet I can cheer you up. I just got off the phone with a

10

man named Edwin Towson," I said, glancing at Cara, our grandmotherly receptionist. "Husband of Ava, who is a friend of Cara's."

"Ava and I are in the same book club," Cara said. "She's a lovely woman."

"What does Edwin do?" I asked her.

"He runs an investment company. I don't know much about it."

"Towson?" Fred said. "They're big in renewable energy."

"He wants us to appraise his Tiffany lamp."

Fred's eyes communicated his skepticism. "Everyone thinks their pretty stained glass lamp is a Tiffany."

"True." I smiled, my sassy one. "Still . . . you've got to admit that it's a nice way to start a Monday."

"One of the best." He leaned back, lacing his hands behind his head, and grinned. "In fact, you ought to let me take charge of the appraisal. I know how busy you are."

I chuckled. Fred was an antiques snob, disdainful of mere collectibles. A Tiffany lamp was right up his alley. I wasn't going to turn over the job, though. As part of Prescott's Antiques & Auctions protocol, we video-record all objects before we begin the authentication process. I like to do as many

11

of the recordings myself as I can. It's a good way for me to stay on top of the business.

"That's awfully thoughtful of you, Fred," I said, ever the diplomat. "I'll get us started, and we'll see after that."

Gretchen, Prescott's office manager, sat at her desk, smoothing out the red, white, and blue star-decked bunting we hung every year on every window a week before July Fourth. I asked her to fax over our standard contract and rattled off the number Edwin had given me.

While we waited for him to sign and return the contract, Fred asked, "What's known about the lamp?"

"Nothing before it was found wrapped in an old army blanket, packed in a trunk in Edwin's great-grandparents' attic. That was in 1983 when his folks cleaned out the family house after his great-grandmother died. No one had ever heard of it or seen it before, and everyone who might know about it was dead. When they found it they assumed it was a knock-off. Everyone did, including Edwin and Ava."

"What happened to change their minds?" Fred asked.

"My TV show. They watched the episode of *Josie's Antiques* where I talk about how the colors in a Tiffany lampshade change when the light is on, how it glows. Their lamp does that, so they figured it was worth the appraisal fee to find out what they have."

"Completely credible," Fred said, intrigued. "How about receipts or letters or insurance policies from before they found the lamp. Do they still exist?"

"No. Edwin went through everything himself after his dad died — boxes of papers from his grandparents and great-grandparents. There was nothing that referred to the lamp."

"No surprise," Fred said.

"Is that a problem?" Gretchen asked, listening in, her emerald eyes focused on Fred's face.

"It's helpful to have proof of provenance," Fred explained, "which as you know is a documentary record of ownership, from manufacture or creation to today — but we rarely do."

"How come? If I bought a Tiffany lamp, I'd sure as shooting keep the receipt."

"Maybe it was a wedding gift," I suggested.

Gretchen laughed. "And they didn't like it, so they stashed it in the attic."

The fax machine whirred to life.

"That was fast," Gretchen said, taking the sheets from the paper tray. She checked that

Edwin had signed and dated the agreement, smiled, and said, "You're good to go."

I gave a small air pump. "Excellent!"

I had Eric, Prescott's operations manager and jack-of-all-trades, load my trunk with packing material. Tiffany lamps were fragile, so delicate, in fact, that only a small percentage had survived the hundred-plus years since their creation. Those that did were culturally and artistically significant, scarce, and popular, a hat trick of value.

Fred was correct — people always thought their pretty stained glass lamps were the real deal, but usually the lamps were among the legions of excellent reproductions on the market. As I walked to my car, warmed by the strong June sun, a trill of excitement sped my pace. What Fred neglected to mention was that sometimes they were right.

CHAPTER TWO

The Towsons' waterfront mansion sat at the ocean end of a cul-de-sac in the ritzy Garnet Cove section of Rocky Point, a private community surrounded by a two-hundred-year-old fieldstone wall and an ancient forest. I drove down empty streets, past deserted manicured lawns. Mingled with the roar of thundering surf were sounds of distant fun — laughter, splashing, and music, some too-loud hip-hop from near the end of the block, and a dissonant jazz tune I didn't recognize from across the street.

The only person I saw was a woman kneeling in the garden of the house to the left of the Towsons'. She waggled her hand, and I raised a palm acknowledging her hello. She looked to be about seventy-five. From the small wrinkle lines on either side of her mouth, I suspected she'd spent a lot of her life laughing. She wore a raspberry pink visor, a seashell pink T-shirt, and bright turquoise capri pants. Very snazzy.

To the right of the house, a knot of bushes and ferns melded into a dense thatch of woods. The fieldstone wall that separated Garnet Cove from the rest of Rocky Point was barely visible through the lush summer growth. I parked in the driveway behind a red Mercedes sedan. The vanity plate read MYLV. *Sweet,* I thought: *My Love.* As I made my way to the stoop, I counted three chimneys. The shutters and front door were painted a rich colonial blue that went well with the mellowed red brick. Beds of yellow and white flowers, thimbleweed, St. John's wort, and petunias lined the walkway. A red maple stood in the middle of the lawn, its crimson leaves luminous in the early summer sun. Neatly organized patches of white and lavender phlox carpeted the ground. Stands of lilac and forsythia, their blossoms long gone, their leaves verdant and full, separated the Towson property from the one next door.

The door opened before I reached it. An elegantly dressed and coiffed woman greeted me with a cool hello.

"I'm Ava Towson," she said. "Thanks for coming so quickly."

"You're more than welcome. I'm eager to get started."

She led the way across the expansive entryway, a soaring space almost as big as my first New York City apartment. Ava exuded wealth and assurance from the tips of her Gucci horsebit loafers to the top of her expertly cut blond-highlighted hair. Her sterling silver cuff featuring an olive leaf cutout pattern was, I was certain, a Paloma Picasso original. Her tortoiseshell eyeglasses had Chanel's interlocking *C*'s logo near the hinge, a perfect frame for her cornflower blue eyes. I saw a flash of diamonds when she moved, teardrop earrings mostly hidden by her hair.

"How are you holding up in the heat wave?" she asked.

Three days in a row over ninety degrees, an anomaly for New Hampshire.

"It makes me wish I was at the beach."

She smiled politely. "Me, too."

I followed her into the living room, decorated with an appealing mix of modern furniture and antiques. My eye was drawn to a still life framed in gilt, a pair of ornate silver candlesticks on the mantel, and a magnificent Victorian walnut and rosewood hinged chess table in the corner.

The painting showed a red table against a gold stucco wall. A stack of unremarkable books sat on the table, and a tarnished silver goblet filled with half a dozen paintbrushes of various sizes was perched on top of the books.

"That's striking," I said, pointing at it. "Is it a William Nicholson?"

"You obviously know your art. Is that a specialization?"

"My taste — and so our business — is diverse. I value beauty and craftsmanship in all their forms." I turned toward the chess table. "Like this table . . . it's fabulous." The top was narrow, only about a foot wide, and flanked by two side pieces. "Are there drawers?"

"Yes, one on either side, for the chess pieces. The flaps lift and swivel. When the top is in place, it's an oval."

"It's spectacular," I said.

"Thank you."

I paused, transfixed by the view. An undulating expanse of hundred-year-old lawn led to an appealing welter of lady ferns, purple Canterbury bellflowers, and lavender mistflower, their leaves and blossoms glimmering in the sun. Frills of whitecaps and opalescent sequins dotted the midnight blue ocean.

"Wow," I said.

"Some people take views like this for granted. I never do."

"I could stand here all day."

"Me, too." She laughed, a pleasant, high-bred tinkling. "But duty calls. Please have a seat."

I sat on the ivory twill sofa; she chose a pale blue and grass green club chair angled to one side.

A professionally groomed apricot toy poodle lay curled like a comma in a basket by Ava's chair.

"This sweet thing is Eleanor," Ava said, bending over to pat the dog's head. Eleanor sat up, her tail wagging furiously. "Eleanor, this is Josie."

"Hello, Eleanor," I said.

Eleanor gave a chirpy yelp, then settled down and curled up again.

Ava stroked her back. "She's old."

"You wouldn't know."

"She's a good girl, aren't you, Eleanor?" She sat back in her chair. "Edwin and I enjoy your TV show."

I flushed, disconcerted, as always, at acclaim. "Thank you . . . so . . . as far as you know, no one has ever had the lamp appraised. Is that right?"

"That's correct. I'm not even sure what's involved in an appraisal."

"It's a two-step process. First we authenticate the object. Then we assess its value."

"And you can do that even though we don't know how the lamp ended up in the attic?"

"Many antiques lack provenance. People don't expect an object to gain value, so they don't keep records. Things get lost. Life isn't a business, after all."

She smiled, pleased. "Would you like to see it?"

"I'd love it."

"It's in the study." She stood. "This way."

The study was attached to the far side of the living room, accessed through French doors.

The walls were painted celery green. The carpet was gray. The curtains featured green ferns against a lavender background. Bookshelves lined the inside walls, with the books, mostly modern firsts, artfully arranged for show. And there, next to a dark green leather club chair, perched on a mahogany end table, was a Tiffany-style wisteria-patterned lamp.

"Yowzi," I said.

"I'll take a 'yowzi' at first glance as a good omen."

I extracted my iPad from my tote bag. "There's no way to tell if it's a replica until we examine it. Some astonishingly good fakes have been on the market for nearly

fifty years. That's why appraising a pur-
ported Tiffany lamp is one of the most
complex challenges we face."

"But you will be able to tell, right?"

I grinned, my feisty one. "Oh, yeah." I
walked to the back of the table, assessing
the object from the rear. "You don't see
many of them out in the open."

"We like to use it, and the housekeeper
knows not to touch it." She fixed her eyes
on the lamp. "I heard some Tiffany lamps
have sold for more than a million dollars."

"That's true. A wisteria lamp similar to
yours sold for one and a half million not
long ago. Others have sold for even more,
but that's probably a fluke — a specific
buyer with unlimited resources determined
to acquire a specific lamp."

"Like a drug kingpin."

"Or an oil mogul."

"A million dollars," she said, her eyes on
the lamp. "It's hard to believe."

"Keep your fingers crossed!"

She held up crossed fingers. "What happens now?"

"The first step is creating an annotated
video recording of what I see."

"Will I be in the way if I listen in?"

"Not a bit."

I measured the lamp's height and the top

and bottom diameters of the lampshade. I asked Ava to pick up the lamp, squatting so I could measure the base's diameter. I tapped through my apps and brought up the video recorder we'd had configured for our specific needs.

"We video-record all objects before we remove them for appraisal," I explained. "It's all part of documenting provenance. Here we go." I tapped the START button and held the device steady. "I'm in the Towsons' study. This is a Tiffany-style table lamp, twenty-six and three-quarters inches high. The bottom diameter of the shade is eighteen inches." I stated the other measurements. "It has irregular upper and lower borders. The upper aperture is the typical openwork crown designed to showcase tree branches. The branches on the shade are dark." I leaned in for a closer view. "Dark brown. The wisteria blossoms are formed of intricately cut pieces of variously shaded purple glass connected by what appears to be solder. The coloration shifts from pale lavender to deep purple, through the use of what appears to be confetti glass. Specks of various hues are visible to the naked eye." I paused the video and lifted the lamp. Genuine Tiffany lamps were made of hollow bronze tubes, filled with lead. It was appropriately heavy. I turned to Ava. "Would you hold it for me sideways? I want to record the base bottom."

"Sure," she said.

I inspected the bottom carefully, using the miniflashlight I kept attached to my belt, then had her readjust her grip so her hands wouldn't show in the video and reactivated the recorder.

"On the base bottom is a stamp reading 'Tiffany Studios New York,' followed by the numerals one-eight-one." I paused recording again and smiled at her. "Thank you. You can put it back on the table." I waited until she got it situated and backed away before continuing. "The base is designed to look like a tree trunk, with irregular patterns of grooves and nubs resembling bark." I gazed at the lamp, wondering if I'd missed anything, then nodded, satisfied that I hadn't, and saved the video. "I think that's it. We'll let you know as soon as we have news."

"You said earlier that you thought you could complete the appraisal in a few days, right?"

"God willing and the creek don't rise, as the saying goes."

I uploaded the recording to Dropbox, then IM'd Gretchen to prepare a receipt and attach the form authorizing me to use the lamp on my TV show.

I brought my tote bag out to my car and returned with a lamp box, padded blankets, and bubble wrap. Ten minutes later, Gretchen e-mailed the documents.

Ava read through the two pages. "I'm not comfortable allowing you to film the lamp or appear on camera with it."

"That's fine. We often film an antique at our location, but of course, if you'd prefer that I don't use the lamp at all, that's okay, too. Your husband said you hadn't discussed whether you want to sell it, but if you ever do, the fact that it was featured on my show should boost its sales price."

"Really?"

"It's called 'association.' That this lamp is worthy of being shown on TV adds allure to some potential buyers."

"And we'd stay anonymous?"

"Yes, but the lamp wouldn't. The best of both worlds!"

Ava used the electronic signature function on my device to sign off on it, and within another few minutes, the meticulously packed lamp and I were out the door.

As I gentled the box into place, the next-door neighbor I'd seen earlier greeted me.

"Hello there," she said. "Gorgeous day,

isn't it?"

"Heavenly," I agreed.

She tied a hearty tomato plant to a four-foot-tall wrought-iron trellis and snipped off excess twine.

"Those are some beautiful tomato plants you've got there," I added.

"I'm a tomato fiend," she said.

"Me, too. My dad used to grow them when I was a kid."

"Nothing like tomatoes off the vine."

"I have always wondered why scientists can't get them to taste good all year round," I said. "Whoever succeeds in doing that will make a fortune."

"I doubt they ever will. Mother Nature always has the last word." Another knot, another snip. "I'm Sylvia, by the way. Sylvia Campbell."

"I'm Josie Prescott. Nice to meet you."

"You, too."

"I didn't know you could harvest them so early in the season."

"You've got to pick the right variety. These are called Fourth of July. Want to guess why?"

I laughed. "I'm betting it's not because they explode."

Sylvia chuckled. "Nope. They're all-American and have an early harvest."

We chatted for another moment, and then I left. Driving back to work, I recalled those long hot summer days spent with my dad eating tomatoes plucked fresh from the plant, talking about our days. My dad died more than a dozen years ago, yet I felt his presence like a friendly ghost. He was with me, except he wasn't. I shook off the melancholy reflection and turned on Vivaldi's *Four Seasons,* a surefire way to improve my mood. I couldn't wait to get started on the appraisal. I thought there was a real chance that we were about to join one of the rarest of clubs — antiques appraisers who'd authenticated a Tiffany lamp.

CHAPTER THREE

The lamp's base was bronze, filled with lead. The materials showed an age-appropriate patina, the kind of wear and shine that comes from 110 years of use. The turn-paddle off-on knob and General Electric–made socket were as expected. The maker's stamp was accurate. When the shade was gently tapped, the glass rattled, suggesting that the solder that held the glass in place had dried out over time, another indicator that the lamp was authentic. When illuminated, the shade glowed. The intricacy of the pattern and the luminescence of the translucent lavender and purple blossoms took my breath away.

"Wow," I whispered to the air. "It's real."

The absence of documentary proof of ownership was a disappointment, but not a problem. There were no reports of stolen wisteria-patterned Tiffany table lamps that I needed to investigate. I took a step back to gain a wider view of the lamp and smiled in private celebration of another milestone reached. A minute later, I was ready to get back to work. I reached for a phone.

I asked Fred to do his own assessment, specifically, to confirm that the material under the soldering was copper, and he eagerly went to work.

A day later, he concurred with my evaluation and started the write-up.

I called Timothy Brenin, the director-producer of *Josie's Antiques,* and told him that if he could get to New Hampshire right away, we could include a genuine Tiffany lamp in next season's episodes.

"I'll be there at eight tomorrow with a crew," he said.

I laughed. "No one could ever accuse you of being indecisive."

"You snooze, you lose."

"I'm so lucky to work with you, Timothy."

"I'm the lucky one! See ya in the morning."

At seven Thursday morning, three days after Ava and Edwin Towson entrusted the lamp to me, and an hour before Timothy was due to arrive, I signed the appraisal, estimating that the lamp, if sold at auction, would fetch as much as $1.5 million. I texted the number listed on the contract, Ava's cell, and asked if I could drop off the lamp later that afternoon. She texted back saying that would be fine. Ava was going to be a very happy woman.

Timothy's limo, followed by two trucks, arrived shortly before eight. I opened the front door and stood in the entryway to greet the team. Timothy stepped out and called hello.

He pointed to the bunting that adorned all the windows. "Will you look at that? Bunting. I haven't seen bunting in . . . I don't know . . . forever."

"We're all dressed up for the Fourth." I gave him a hug. "I'm so glad you were able to come up on such short notice."

"When your show is number one in its time slot, the powers that be facilitate rare opportunities happily."

He used his thumbs and index fingers to frame the American flag mounted over the front door, creating a mock camera lens. He peered through it, viewing the picture with a professional eye. "What a great opening shot."

I greeted Starr, the makeup girl with pink hair and star-shaped tattoos, and Mack and Vinnie and the rest of the crew, escorting them into the section of warehouse I'd had cleared for their use. I stood off to the side while they wheeled in equipment, set up a baby blue backdrop, raised the light mounts, and tested everything from ambient sound to light density.

Just before noon, they were ready to start filming. Starr gave my nose a final swipe with her feathery powder puff and nodded. I was ready to go. Wardrobe had selected a peach silk shirtwaist dress. The lights flashed on, brighter than the sunniest day.

"Action!" Timothy called.

"This," I said, raising my open palm toward the lamp, speaking to the camera as if it were my friend, "is a genuine Tiffany lamp. The pattern is known as Wisteria, and it's made from what's called confetti glass. Let me show you how you can tell the actual from a reproduction — or a counterfeit."

We took three takes, two of which Timothy said weren't needed because I got it right the first time.

"You know me," he said. "I'm a belt-and-suspenders sort of guy."

"Expect the best, but prepare for the worst."

"Exactly. Who's to say that when we look at the recording you won't have blinked at exactly the wrong moment."

"With three takes you can snip and tuck

and make me look better than I am."

"I can't do that . . . but I can darn well make certain you look as good as you are."

I loved working with Timothy.

I asked Gretchen, a fan of celebrity gossip, to be on hand for the teardown and packing-up process in case anyone needed something, and she eagerly agreed. I went upstairs to wash off the thick makeup, then went back down to pack up the lamp.

As I turned into the Towsons' driveway, I smiled and nodded at Sylvia. She stood on her lawn, watering her tomatoes. Today's visor was white with blue polka dots, her T-shirt was white, and her capris featured narrow blue and white stripes.

"Another gorgeous day!" Sylvia called.

"We must be living right."

"That's what I think, too!"

"Come on in," Ava said, as soon as I reached the stoop. "I can't stand the suspense!"

"It's real," I told her, relishing one of my favorite parts of my job.

She raised her hands to her chest as if in prayer and clapped softly, a quiet celebration as befits a dignified woman. When I get good news, I do a half disco, half old-style rock 'n' roll happy dance. When she heard the appraised value, she gasped and pressed her fingertips to her cheeks.

"I was hopeful," she said, her eyes alight, "but this is beyond anything."

"Some insurance agents prefer to get appraisals directly from the source. If yours is in that category, we're glad to cooperate."

I unpacked the lamp, placing it on the table by the leather chair. The curtains were drawn, and the room was dim. When I switched on the lamp, the room took on a delicate lavender hue. By today's standards, the light was barely adequate, but the ambience was sumptuous.

"I feel like I'm in a different time and place," I said, unwilling to take my gaze off the lampshade.

"A more civilized place," she said with a tinge of bitterness. "A time of refinement, when beauty was truly valued."

"You appreciate it," I said.

"George Bernard Shaw said, 'Youth is wasted on the young.' I say, 'Beauty is wasted on the rich.' They almost never appreciate it."

I ignored what seemed to me to be an unwarranted generalization, focusing instead on a value we shared. "I became an antiques appraiser because I wanted to be surrounded by beauty."

"I grew up poor. It leaves a mark."

"Which beauty can't erase."

"Not completely." She extended her hand. "Thank you, Josie."

"It's been a pleasure."

Outside, I waved good-bye to Sylvia, still watering her tomatoes.

My best friend, neighbor, and landlady, Zoë Winterelli, and I take turns each year hosting a Fourth of July barbecue. This year was my turn. We hoped to begin by late afternoon, but our actual start time was up in the air since we didn't know when Ty, my boyfriend, would make it home. Ty, a training guru with Homeland Security, was in the field leading an exercise involving intercepting illicit fishing trawlers as they tried to land surreptitiously along the remote and craggy Maine coastline. I hated it that he conducted training exercises on Sundays and holidays, but I understood his reasoning — it was far less disruptive than running them during standard business hours.

At about eleven that morning, I was deep in dicing potatoes when Zoë popped into the kitchen.

"Come to the movies with us," she said. "We're going to make a noon show."

"What are you going to see?"

"I forget its name. Some kids' supernatural animated zombie flick. Jake picked it out."

Zoë had two children, fourteen-year-old Jake and eleven-year-old Emma.

"Tempting, but I'll pass. Is Ellis going?"

Her boyfriend, Rocky Point police chief Ellis Hunter, appeared behind her. "No. He's decided to stay home and offer to be your sous chef."

"How can you possibly resist a zombie movie?" I asked in a tone brimming with faux amazement.

He raised his chin. "I'm a man of iron will."

"You guys," Zoë said, laughing. She waggled her fingers good-bye and kissed Ellis, a quick one, then left.

"I'm all yours," Ellis said as he walked toward me. "What's my first task?"

"Mincing onions and chopping celery for the potato salad." I pointed my knife at a wicker basket near the sink. "Onions are there. Celery is in the fridge. Half a Vidalia. Four stalks."

He'd finished the onion when his smart phone rang. He glanced at the display, then answered with a crisp "Hunter." He listened for a long time, two minutes, maybe longer, grunting periodically and jotting notes on a small spiral-bound notebook he extracted from his shirt pocket. "I'm on my way," he said as he punched the off button. "Sorry to bail, but duty calls. There's been a murder in Garnet Cove."

I spun to face him, knife in hand. "I was just there, appraising a Tiffany lamp. A week ago. The Towson family."

His eyes held mine for a moment. "You'd better come along."

CHAPTER FOUR

A patrol car with its lights flashing blocked the street. I recognized the uniformed officer standing watch. His name was Griff, and he was close to retirement. Right now he was facing Wes Smith, a twenty-something reporter for our local newspaper, the *Seacoast Star*.

Ellis parked behind a black SUV. The gold Crime Scene Investigation Team insignia stenciled on the side door sparkled in the sun.

"Nope," Griff said to Wes, sounding more amused than irritated.

Wes looked shocked. "I can't believe you're keeping a journalist out. What do you have to hide?"

The medical examiner drove up. I hopped down from Ellis's SUV in time to see Griff shake his head at Wes, an indulgent smile on his face.

"Chief!" Wes called, hurrying in our direction.

Ellis smiled. "Nice to see you, Wes. No comment."

Leaving Wes sputtering, Ellis approached Griff.

"Anything I should know?" Ellis asked.

"CSI is inside."

Ellis thanked him, then turned to greet the medical examiner, Dr. Graham.

Dr. Graham said something I couldn't hear. I took a step in their direction, hoping to listen in, but her words were lost amid the crashing waves. I'd seen her before, but I didn't know her. She was petite and young, and she had a reputation as a stickler for protocol.

Ellis nodded, his expression grave. He replied. I couldn't hear him, either, and after a few seconds, I stopped trying. Instead, I shut my eyes and turned my face toward the sun. From the ferocious ocean sounds, I could picture the waves pummeling the boulders that edged the shore. A seagull screeched, fighting for food or maybe complaining that there wasn't any. An air horn from a faraway tugboat blared, its sound low and mournful, like a widow's wail. Griff's in-car radio squawked. I could feel someone staring at me, and I opened my eyes.

It was Wes.

Griff turned his back on us as he reached in through the open window to answer the call. Wes took advantage of Ellis's concentration and Griff's inattention to send me a silent message. He held his right index finger and thumb to his ear, miming talking into a phone, and mouthed, "Call me."

I nodded, one quick up-and-down motion, then looked away.

Wes and I had our own sort of quid pro quo — if I wanted information, I had to give information. I was an uneasy, albeit willing, participant in our exchange since Wes, who made a swarm of killer bees look lazy, was always in the know.

Griff hung up his radio, turned toward Ellis, and said, "Detective Brownley just picked up Edwin Towson at his company."

Dr. Graham started off toward the Towson house.

"When they get here," Ellis told Griff, "send them in." He turned to me. "Let's go."

Wes shouted, "I have a right to observe the police."

Ellis ignored him.

Sylvia nodded as we passed her house. I nodded back. She was dressed for the holiday, wearing a stars-and-stripes-patterned T-shirt with a matching visor.

A police officer I'd never seen before stood on the Towsons' front stoop. He was young and thin with a crew cut, and I wondered if he was ex-military. Dr. Graham listened to something he said, then disappeared inside the house. The officer's brass name tag read OFFICER A. KILEY. The door was open. I heard a dog barking, desperate, panicky yelps.

"That's Eleanor," I said. "The dog. Where is she?"

"Upstairs," Officer Kiley said. "We locked her in a bathroom to keep her safe."

"She sounds upset."

Kiley was unmoved. "We brought up bowls of food and water."

I tried to ignore Eleanor's yaps.

"Anything I should know?" Ellis asked Officer Kiley.

Ellis stood under the peaked porch overhang. Out of direct sunlight, his jagged scar looked darker than it did in bright sunlight, almost brown. I'd never asked Ellis where he got the scar, but I suspected he'd been wounded in a bar fight, against someone wielding a beer bottle or a knife. He never talked much about any aspect of his life before taking on the chief's job, but I knew he'd been a New York City homicide detective for more than twenty years, until shortly after his dancer wife died of lung cancer. He'd told me once that he'd moved to Rocky Point to find out if Norman Rockwell had it right about small towns.

"Nothing, sir," Officer Kiley said.

I followed Ellis into the living room.

"Did I hear Griff right?" I asked. "Edwin was at work? On the Fourth of July?"

"It's July fourth everywhere, but it's only a holiday in America."

"That's some kind of work ethic."

"Or ambition," Ellis said.

"Or zeal."

"Wait here," Ellis said. "I won't be long."

The house was fresh-smelling. A light breeze swirled in through the open windows. I rested my brow against the cool wood frame and gazed out over the ocean. Golden dots danced along the ocean surface. I watched a gull nosedive into the water, then soar toward the sun and fly away.

A few minutes later, Ellis called my name from the entryway. I turned to face him.

"Come into the kitchen," he said. "I need you to ID the body."

"Me? I thought Edwin was on his way."

"I like to have independent confirmation."

"What about whoever discovered the body?"

"That was the dog walker, a fourteen-year-old girl named Merry. She saw the corpse through a kitchen window and ran home, screaming like a banshee. Her mother called it in. Merry was — and is — hysterical. All she noticed was rivers of blood. She's too upset to do an ID, and her mom won't leave her side. Understandable, but it means we need another set of eyes."

"Poor kid," I said, thinking that Ava's murder would stay with Merry forever, coloring her view of the world, changing her in ways she couldn't anticipate and might never understand.

As we walked down a short corridor that led to the back of the house, I girded myself for the grim task waiting for me at the end of the hall. I dreaded seeing what a violent death had done to the elegant woman I'd only just met. Goosebumps dimpled my arms.

The kitchen was painted lemon yellow. The white cabinets had been finished with an antiquing glaze to add a distressed look. A woman's body was sprawled across a small rug in front of the sink. She lay on her stomach, her face turned toward the cabinets, toward the ocean. She wore navy blue linen shorts and a sleeveless orange and blue paisley blouse. She was barefoot. Her short brown hair was stiff with congealed blood. Brown hair. She must have colored it. Her blouse was saturated with it. Rivulets of the copperish brown liquid ran toward the back door, drying in the sun that streamed in through the windows.

Dr. Graham stood near the woman's feet, tapping notes into a tablet. "No info yet," she said without looking up.

"Can we do an ID?" Ellis asked.

"Sure."

She finished a note, then joined Ellis by the body. They squatted near the woman's head and rotated her face toward me.

My mouth fell open. I stepped back, bumping into the center island. I couldn't drag my eyes from her face. She looked to be in her thirties, and it was easy to see she'd been a knockout. Her eyes were open. Her mouth was closed. She looked relaxed, as if she were thinking beautiful thoughts. I blinked, then blinked again, trying to understand what I was seeing — a gorgeous woman, a stranger.

CHAPTER FIVE

I stood there staring at the bloody and battered corpse, my mouth agape.

Ellis eased his hands from under the woman's head and stood up. "Josie?"

I transferred my gaze to his face. Dr. Graham moved a few steps away and resumed typing on her tablet.

"What is it?" Ellis asked.

"That's not Ava."

"Who is it?"

"I don't know. I've never seen her before."

He looked down at the body, then touched my arm and led the way into the living room.

"Are you okay?" he asked.

"I'm close to speechless."

Ellis glanced around. "You were in this room before, right?"

"Yes."

"Is everything the same?"

I closed my eyes for a moment and let the

picture come, then opened them and compared my memory to what I saw in front of me.

"Look," I said, pointing at the mantel. Four silver-framed photographs stood in a symmetrical row. In all of them, a smiling brunette in her thirties stood next to a stern-looking bald man in his fifties. He was half a head shorter than she was. One photo showed them standing in front of a pyramid. Another had them bundled in parkas on a snowy mountaintop. In the third, they were nestled together on a porch swing. In the last one, the woman cradled an apricot toy poodle, Eleanor, I presumed.

I shivered as my blood turned to ice. "If that's Ava Towson, the woman I met must be an imposter."

"Work the logic for me," Ellis said. "What's the point?"

I gasped. "Oh, God! The Tiffany lamp." I dashed across the room toward the study, skittered on the threshold, and grasped the doorjamb to steady myself. The lamp was in place, the wisteria petals gleaming where the sun hit the glass. "It's here. It's safe."

Ellis joined me at the door. "So that's a Tiffany lamp." He cocked his head. "How rare is it?"

"Very. The shades are super fragile."

"Isn't it . . . I guess the word is 'unusual' . . . that it's here, out in the open?"

"Yes, but it's not unique. The lamp wasn't designed as a decorative object. Tiffany intended it to be used. Lots of people share that utilitarian attitude."

"Is this Tiffany the same guy who started the jewelry store?"

"No. That was his dad, Charles Lewis Tiffany. The lamp fellow is Louis Comfort Tiffany."

"He didn't join the family business?"

"No. He was trained as a painter but got into glassmaking in his early twenties. He figured out how to create three-dimensional effects in glass — he received a patent for his opalescent glass."

"What's this one worth?"

"I just appraised it at one-point-five million dollars."

He whip-turned to face me, his eyes wide, ready to laugh. He thought I was joking. "Are you serious?" he asked.

"Yes."

"That's nuts."

I shrugged. "That's business."

He did a 360, taking in the desk, the walls, and the bookshelves. "Does anything look different?"

I glanced around. "No." We walked back

to the living room. I stopped in front of the fireplace. "Those photos weren't here before."

"What was in their place?"

"Candlesticks. Silver candlesticks." I scanned the tabletops. "Those." I pointed to a pair of tall, elegantly gadrooned candlesticks sitting on a side table. "I noticed the scalloped rim and reeded feet. It's a remarkable set."

"So someone replaced the photographs with candlesticks. Why?"

"Because it's odd to have a bare mantel. The fake Ava made sure that nothing would call attention to the fact that she was impersonating Ava Towson. She played me."

"Looks that way. Don't take it personally. If a clever con man — or woman — wants to play you, you get played."

"That's unacceptable. I'm experienced and knowledgeable. I should have smelled a scam."

"Chief?" a woman called from the front.

We turned. Detective Claire Brownley, a woman I'd known for years, stood next to the man in the photos on the mantel. She'd cut her blacker-than-black hair into an asymmetrical wedge, very au courant. The man had aged some since the photographs had been taken, and he'd gained some weight.

"What's going on?" he asked, sounding more like an executive out of patience than a husband worried about his wife. "This detective won't tell me anything."

I heard a faint hint of some Slavic language in his voice.

"Wait here," Ellis told me.

I hung back as Ellis explained that he had bad news, news he'd wanted to deliver personally. Ellis asked to see the man's ID, and after a brief protest, Edwin Towson slapped open his wallet, showing his driver's license. Ellis thanked him, calling him by name, Mr. Towson.

"A woman has been killed. I'm hoping you can identify the body so we can proceed with the investigation."

"Killed?" Edwin repeated, as if he were unfamiliar with the word.

"This way."

Ellis guided him into the kitchen. Detective Brownley stayed close. I trailed along, reaching the kitchen door in time to see Edwin Towson kneel by the corpse.

"Oh, my darling," he murmured, his voice cracking. "Ava, Ava, Ava."

I swallowed unexpected tears and turned away. Edwin's grief was palpable, his anguish raw, and I was touched.

I hurried outside and took in a deep breath, glad for the warmth, glad for the fresh, sea-scented air. Officer Kiley stood with his back to me near the driveway, reading something on his smart phone. I sat on the stoop. A small brown bird flew by, low and straight, perching on a forsythia bush. It wiggled its tail feathers for a few seconds, then took off toward the ocean. It was about eighty with low humidity, a perfect summer day, a perfect day to celebrate our nation's independence. The sun was partially hidden by the red maple, its rays dappling the front lawn with amber lace, the backlit crimson leaves glowing with an iridescent sheen. I heard a lawn mower, a big one, but I couldn't see it. A car backfired. I couldn't see the car, either. Laughter floated through the still air from somewhere down the block. I thought about the woman who'd hired me, replaying our conversations, seeking out anomalies, trying to identify anything that should have warned me that I was being conned. I was so mad I could spit.

I took my tablet from my tote bag and did an image search for Ava Towson. An array of photos appeared. The most recent came from the July issue of Rocky Point Hospital's newsletter. The article described last

June's annual fund-raising gala, which Ava had helped organize. The photo showed her in an off-the-shoulder celery green gown standing next to Edwin, in a tux. Ava looked regal; Edwin looked bored. I'd never met Ava. I'd never spoken to Edwin. Prescott's always verified the identity of people who walked in wanting to sell antiques, but we never did when appraising objects in the client's home. Now, staring into Ava's sloe-colored eyes, I wondered if we should. I navigated back to the search results page and clicked on the link to a community blog. Ava used the blog like a diary. There were annotated photos of thatched cottages and verdant gardens from a recent walking tour in Wales; the ballroom at the Austin Arms, Rocky Point's finest hotel, where her high school class planned to hold its twentieth-year reunion; Ava posing with a woman named Janet Chirling, the chair of the high school reunion committee, with a note saying how excited she was to be asked to serve on it; Ava and Edwin dancing at a New Year's Eve party on a cruise ship; and Ava and Edwin lying on chaise lounges in their backyard, raising flutes of champagne in a silent toast to the unseen photographer or someone standing nearby. I went back to the photos from Wales and checked the dates embedded in the postings. Ava had been in Wales during the week I'd been appraising the Tiffany lamp.

Ellis came out and sat beside me. Officer Kiley slipped his phone into his pocket. He began a slow walk around the yard.

"That has to be one of the worst parts of your job," I said to Ellis.

"It is." He raised and then lowered his shoulders in what I suspected was a futile effort to ease tension. "So this woman we'll refer to as Ms. Doe calls your office."

"Mr. Doe called. I spoke to him at some length." I shielded my eyes with the side of my hand, blocking the sun, so I could see into Ellis's eyes. I kept my voice low. "He's an imposter, too. Way different voices."

Ellis's eyes rounded. "Are you sure?"

"Yes."

He stared into the middle distance for a moment, then said, "Tell me about it."

I recounted our conversation and explained about faxing the contract. "Edwin signed it within minutes, and I drove here right away."

"Why the hurry?"

"Insurance. If the lamp was real, he wanted to update his policy."

"I'll need the fax number. And the fax. Also, the phone numbers."

"Of course."

"While you were here getting the lamp, did she touch anything?"

"The doorknob, when she let me in and out. And the lamp. She held it while I recorded the bottom. The dog. The chair arms." I paused, checking my mind's eye to see if I'd missed anything. I hadn't. "That's it."

"I'm going to have one of the police officers take you to the station, to sit down with a sketch artist, okay?"

"Can he take me home first, so I can get my own car?"

"Sure."

Ellis passed along his instructions to Officer Kiley, then turned back to me. "When you sit with the sketch artist —" He broke off and spun toward the street at the sound of Griff shouting, "Stop. Police. Stop."

A woman ran down the street with Griff in pursuit. She veered to the right, zigzagged past Officer Kiley, and aimed directly at us. I leapt up, astonished. She kept coming. I backed away, onto the lawn, out of the line of attack.

"Is it Ava?" the woman shrieked, her eyes fixed on Ellis's face.

"Whoa!" Ellis said, thrusting out his arm

51

like a tollgate, stopping her. "What's going on?"

Tears streamed down her cheeks. "My sister."

She wore a white diaphanous cover-up over a gold and black leopard print one-piece bathing suit and gold sandals. She looked to be somewhere around forty.

"What's your name?"

"Jean Cooper."

"Do you have any ID, ma'am?"

Her fingers trembled as she patted her pockets. She found what she was looking for, a small gold metallic zippered case, and handed it over. Ellis opened it and looked in, then handed the purse back.

Her chest heaved. "I just heard . . . on the radio . . . there was a murder at this address. Was it Ava?"

"Yes. I'm sorry."

She swept her tears away. "He killed her. Edwin. Her husband."

"Why do you say that?"

"She was afraid he would." Her shoulders bowed. "And he did."

Ellis told me to wait for my ride and escorted Jean Cooper inside.

I shut my eyes for a moment, half shocked, half numb, then looked around. Sylvia stood amid her tomato plants in mute sympathy.

"Are you all right?" she asked in a stage whisper.

"About as you'd expect."

"Is it Ava?"

I glanced at Officer Kiley. He stood facing the street, speaking into a mic attached to his collar. I walked across the lawn and joined Sylvia at one of the forsythia bushes that separated the properties.

"Yes," I said.

She shook her head.

"Do you have any idea who might have wanted Ava dead?" I asked.

"I don't like to say."

"It's not gossip."

She sighed. "I did hear an argument about a month ago."

"Between Edwin and Ava?"

She pressed her lips together, her eyes on her sneaker-clad feet. "I was watering my tomatoes."

"And the Towsons' windows were open."

Sylvia nodded and lowered her voice to a whisper. "Ava accused Edwin of cheating, then Edwin accused Ava of being as warm and loving as an iceberg." Sylvia raised her eyes to my face. "Ava told Edwin not to touch her. I heard a slap, then a scream. I thought about calling the police, but then she ran to her car and drove away." Sylvia looked over my shoulder into the distant woods. "It was awful."

"Frightening and awkward all at once," I said. "No one wants to hear neighbors arguing."

I turned back toward the Towson house. Ellis stood by the front door. He was on his phone, glowering at me, no doubt irritated at what he perceived as my messing with a potential witness. He kept his eyes on me as he finished his call.

"Your ride's ready," he said coldly.

I told Sylvia good-bye and walked across to join him, shaken to realize that two women in the know — Jean and Sylvia — both assumed Edwin was the killer.

CHAPTER SIX

Wes was still standing next to Griff, and when I breezed past him, he gave me a fish-eyed glare. I shook my head, a tiny shake, then looked away. I was going to fill him in, but I wasn't going to say a word in front of a cop, and he should have known that.

Daryl Lucher, a police officer with a blond crew cut, drove me home.

"Are you going to the fireworks tonight?" he asked as he turned onto Main Street.

Rocky Point organized the display from a pair of barges a hundred yards out in the ocean. You could see the show from anywhere along the three-mile stretch of beach. We brought blankets to sit on and baskets filled with nibblies.

"I was, but now I don't know. How about you?"

"Like you. I was, but now I'll have to see. The chief might need us. We were going to have a barbecue."

"And I bet you're the magic man in your family."

He grinned. "You got that right. I'm the only one who knows the recipe to the barbecue sauce. I invented it."

"Ketchup, brown sugar, and spices?"

His sly grin told me his recipe went far beyond the ordinary. "Nope. You use ketchup, you're using someone else's flavors."

"I'm intrigued," I said. "Fess up."

"I won't tell you everything, but I'll let you know some. I start with a jar of last year's tomatoes my wife and I put up. Then I add vinegar, honey, brown sugar, and onion juice. And lots of spices: allspice, cloves, red pepper. Garlic. And salt. You've got to let it simmer for a full day so it tastes right, something to do with the flavors coming together. But you'll never guess the secret ingredient."

"Is it sweet or savory?"

He chuckled but didn't answer.

I smiled. No way was Daryl spilling the beans. "How long did it take you to perfect it?"

"Years," Daryl said as he rolled to a stop in front of my house. "My grandpa got me started on the quest. He challenged me to make one better than his. I'm still trying."

Daryl walked me to my door. I thanked him for the lift, and he touched his cap with old-world courtesy. Even though it was only a momentary respite, it was a relief to talk about normal things, not murder, to picture a fun backyard barbecue celebrating America's birthday, not a woman covered in blood.

Zoë and the kids weren't back yet. Neither was Ty. I left him a voice mail telling him what was going on and that I loved him. I left Zöe a message, too, explaining why the barbecue had to be postponed. I suggested rescheduling on the ninth, next Sunday.

Before heading to the police station, I remoted into my work computer from my home office and opened the Towson folder on my desktop. As per Prescott's protocol, we had scanned in the contract that the fake Edwin had faxed back. He'd listed two phone numbers, one to reach him, the other to reach Ava. Both started with 617 area codes, which meant they'd originated in Boston. I zoomed in so I could read the fax's header. The fax had been sent locally, from somewhere with a 603 area code. I used a reverse directory to locate the owner, Rocky Point Chemists. I knew the shop. It was a family-owned, old-style drugstore on

Main Street that so far, at least, had resisted being gobbled up by a chain. The time stamp matched my recollection — the fax had arrived just after ten last Monday, June 26. I e-mailed the contract to Ellis, as promised.

Before leaving, I took a few minutes to steady my still-shaky nerves. I walked around my house, finding comfort in the familiar. I rearranged the small jewel-colored bottles on the windowsill over my kitchen sink, moving the ruby one forward, pushing the cobalt one back. I touched the shimmering rim of the antique cut-glass Waterford bowl I'd bought for myself to celebrate my first year in business, a private acknowledgment of my business success, and of my personal success, too. The bowl sat beside my mother's favorite Lunt silver candlesticks. I walked into my study and picked up the photo I kept on a corner of my desk. My dad. He'd been a handsome man, confident and competent, loving and kind, smart and determined. After my mom's ghastly cancer death when I was only thirteen, we'd looked to each other for solace, and we'd found it. We'd been a team until the day he died. I didn't want to think about that. I replaced the photo and headed back to the kitchen.

I stepped outside my back door. My hair ruffled by the soft breeze, I shut my eyes, the aroma from the pale pink rambling roses that twirled up the porch column easing my tension, nature's aromatherapy. I opened my eyes and gazed out over the goldenrod, purple loosestrife, orange hawkweed, and Queen Anne's lace that dotted the open field, into the hardwood forest.

New Hampshire was beautiful in all seasons, from the fiery colors of autumn to the pristine whites of winter to the red buds and unfurled green leaves of spring, but it was summer I liked the most. The buttercups and violets and honeysuckle that line the winding country roads. The feathery grasses and wild roses along the sandy dunes. The wildflowers that spread like rainbows across the meadows. The easy breezes. I was a sucker for a breeze.

I inhaled deeply. "All right then," I said aloud.

Halfway to the Rocky Point police station, I slipped in my earpiece and called Wes.

"Tell me," he said, skipping preliminaries, par for his course.

"Have you heard anything about the victim?" I asked, using a trick I'd learned from him years earlier: If you don't want to answer a question, ask one.

"Yeah. It's Ava Towson, all right. She and her husband just got back from the U.K. He stayed in London, working. She went on a walking tour in Wales."

From Ava's blog postings, I already knew about her trip, but hearing it from Wes made it real.

"Wales," I said.

"Doesn't that sound lame? Who goes on a walking tour? Jeesh!"

"Lots of people. You need to get out and about more, Wes. I think a walking tour sounds wonderful. Relaxing. Why didn't Edwin go?"

"Maybe they were fighting."

"Why would you think that?" I asked.

"Because his secretary says he's a workaholic like you read about, and my police source tells me there have been two reports of domestic violence over the last year. Evidently, Edwin is a slapper."

"How awful!"

"How stupid. First time, shame on you. Second time, shame on me, right? She should have walked."

"Maybe she had nowhere to walk to."

"She had a sister."

"There might have been reasons she

couldn't go to her sister's. We shouldn't judge."

"I don't buy that," Wes said. "Everyone has somewhere to go — even if it's a homeless shelter or a church or the police station."

"I hear what you're saying, but when someone's been beaten down, sometimes they lack the inner strength to leave."

"And look what it got her. Dead."

"Do they know what killed her?" I asked to change the subject. I knew Wes was right, but I knew I was right, too.

"Yeah — a cast-iron frying pan, one of a set hanging over the center island. I figure Edwin got mad and whacked her upside the head."

"You're saying it was a crime of passion."

"All I'm saying is cherchez l'homme, baby. Cherchez l'homme. So what ya got for me?"

"Something bizarre." I told him about my meeting with the woman calling herself Ava and my conversation with the man calling himself Edwin.

"How can you tell that it was a different man you spoke to? Maybe he just disguised his voice."

"Pitch, timbre, pace, and accent — all were different. Plus, the man I spoke to on the phone was younger."

"You're right," Wes said. "It's bizarre."

"I can think of three things to check out, but nothing the police aren't already looking into."

"Shoot," Wes said.

"One, does Rocky Point Chemists, the shop that faxed over the contract, have any security cameras? They must, right? I know they have a fax machine they let customers use. Two, the man who isn't Edwin called me — who owns that phone number? And three, I called the mystery woman on her cell phone. Who owns that number?"

"Want to bet that those phones are disposables?"

"No bet. Still, we need to know. Hold on a sec." I pulled into the breakdown lane, set my flashers, and read off the two phone numbers and the fax number.

"Thanks, Joz! Anything else?"

"No."

"Catch ya later," he said, and just like that, he was gone.

CHAPTER SEVEN

The Rocky Point Police Department sketch artist was young, fresh out of college, and earnest. His name was Bryan. He was medium-sized with short sandy hair and a pale, thin mustache that he probably thought made him look older.

We started on the computer with some fancy software program, but I couldn't translate my memory into a realistic portrait using computer renderings of noses and chins, so he extracted a pad of drawing paper from under a stack of files, took an artist's pencil from a drawer, and told me to shut my eyes.

"What does she look like?" he asked.

What a good question, I thought. "Elegant. When I first saw her, that's the word that came to mind. Normal height."

"Was her face round like a ball?"

"No. More like an oval."

"Tell me about her eyes. Were they round

or slanted like almonds?"

"I couldn't see them, not really. She was wearing Chanel glasses."

He asked me to take a look at Chanel's eyeglass designs from the company's Web site, and I recognized them easily.

"What color were her eyes?"

"Blue. At the time, I thought of them as cornflower blue. They were beautiful. Vivid."

"Good," he said. "How about her eyebrows?"

I shut my eyes again and tried to get the picture into focus. Nothing came to me. "Sorry. I don't remember."

"That's okay. What do you remember?"

"Her hair. It was highlighted, blond on blond. Shoulder length. She wore it parted on the right, then swept across to the other side, covering her cheek. Now that I think of it, I bet that's why I can't recall her eyebrows — between her hairstyle and the glasses, they were hidden."

Bryan nodded, used a dark gray kneaded eraser on something, smudged something else with his pinkie, then asked, "What did her hair look like on the right side? Did she tuck it behind her ear?"

"No. It hung straight down, framing her face."

"Was her chin pointy?"

"No. Normal."

"Any dimples?"

I thought for a moment. "I don't think so. I don't remember."

"Could you see her ears?"

"Just an occasional flash. I noticed her earrings. Diamond drops. Teardrop shaped."

"What were her lips shaped like?"

"I don't remember."

"Did she have high cheekbones? Like a model?"

"I'm sorry. I have no idea."

He went on for half an hour, asking questions I couldn't answer, then told me to open my eyes.

I stared at Bryan's drawing, then raised my eyes to his. "I wish I could have done a better job. This doesn't really look like her."

"Take a close look at each feature and tell me what to change."

I did as he instructed, then shook my head helplessly. I knew it wasn't right, but I couldn't tell him what was wrong.

"The hair and glasses are dead-on," I said.

He nodded. "When you see a beard and hat, that's all you remember. You registered the hair and glasses, so that's what you recall."

"I wish I could help more."

"Don't feel bad. Eyewitness testimony is

dicey at best."

It was nice of him to say, but I felt terrible. I'd spent half an hour with her, but I hadn't really noticed her at all.

I came home to an empty house.

Ty had left me a voice mail saying he was sorry to hear about the murder and asking me to text him that I was okay. His work wasn't going well, he said, and he didn't know when he'd be back. The first time he ran the exercise, two of five boats slipped through the barricades. He insisted on restaging it with unexpected variations until the team got it 100 percent right, twice running.

I called Zoë, and she invited me over for leftover lasagna and a Rouge Martini, our new favorite.

"You okay?" Zoë asked as I walked up her porch steps.

"No. I feel awful about that woman, Ava Towson. I feel ashamed, too. I'm so stupid. I don't think there's a worse feeling than realizing you've been had, that you were a mark."

"Tell me what happened."

Zoë was the best listener I knew, and I trusted her absolutely. I told her what had happened and how I felt and what I feared.

Talking about a problem always made me feel as if I were doing something about it, an illusion, I knew, but comforting nonetheless.

"Thanks for letting me talk," I said when I was done. "I wish I knew what was going on."

"You will," she said confidently, without hesitation.

I raised my glass. "Here's to you, the best friend anyone ever had, ever." We clinked glasses.

"Ditto to you," she said.

We clinked again.

"And to silver light in the dark of night," I said, quoting my dad's favorite toast.

We clinked a third time and ate and talked some more, and by seven, when I was ready to go home, I felt better, not good, but better. Ellis was right — if a con man or woman wants to take you, you get taken.

"We're going to leave for the beach around eight," she said, "if you change your mind."

"Thanks. Maybe. I doubt it, though."

I brought a portion of Zoë's lasagna home with me for Ty, made a salad, and got garlic bread ready for the oven, then curled up with *Three for the Chair,* my current Rex Stout mystery, and a cup of black currant tea.

Just after nine, as I was rinsing the teapot and listening to the distant cracks of fireworks, Ty stepped into the kitchen. Ty was tall with broad shoulders and narrow hips. Since he'd been spending so much time outside with his training job, his face had darkened to nut brown. His features were craggy. His hair was cut short. His eyes were dark brown, and when he looked at me, they emanated love. I adored him.

"You're a sight for sore eyes," he said, smiling, his radiant one, the one no one but me ever saw.

"Why are your eyes sore?"

"I'm tired, annoyed, hungry, and grimy. But then I see you, the love of my life, the most beautiful woman on earth, and I feel just fine."

I touched his cheek, streaked with dirt. "I love you, Ty."

He enveloped me in a full-on hug and held me close, and I felt myself relax for the first time since Ellis had asked me to join him at the scene of a murder.

Ellis texted me just before eleven to ask me to come into the station first thing in the morning. He added a single word at the end: *URGENT.* I stared at my phone, seeking out the meaning behind the words and coming up empty. I replied that I would be there and went to bed.

I didn't sleep, although I must have dozed, at least, because I awoke with a gasp, wispy threads of a wrenching nightmare fading away like fog in the sun. I sat up and forced myself to breathe calmly. I felt shocked, as if I'd touched a live wire, and confused. I looked at the clock beside the bed — 5:37. Shards of light crisscrossed the wooden floor, the sun streaming in through gaps in the blinds. Sunrise comes early in New Hampshire. I heard a voice from far away. Ty.

I slipped into my pink chenille bathrobe and fuzzy slippers and padded downstairs.

"I'll leave within half an hour," Ty said from the kitchen.

I stood in the hall, out of sight, so I wouldn't distract him. When his call ended, I stepped into the room. "Bad news?"

He looked beat, the kind of weary you get after a hard day of physical labor followed by not enough sleep.

Ty fussed with the coffee machine for a moment before replying. "I need to go to D.C." He reached across the counter and touched my cheek. "I can't tell you why."

The aroma of the dark French blend we preferred drifted across the room.

"Security issue?" I asked, my heart sink-ing at the thought of the kind of emergency that would drag him out of bed and catapult him from his post in northern New England to Washington, D.C., on a moment's notice.

"I don't know how long I'll be gone," he said, doing a good job of avoiding answering my question.

"Are you in trouble?"

"No." He flicked his finger against my cheek. "I'm the white knight."

I smiled. "I've known that all along."

He leaned in to kiss me, and I kissed him back.

"There's been a breach," I said, meeting his eyes, my arms circling his waist. "A leak traced back to one of your guys."

"Stop prying."

"They know there's a leak," I continued, thinking aloud, "but not who's responsible. It's *not* in your department. Because they don't know who's the snake, they can't trust anyone in that line of command." I spread my arms wide. "They need a person of unimpeachable integrity, someone knowledgeable about the agency who is also a top investigator . . . and they picked you."

Ty kissed me again, a short one. "I've got to get packed. I'm catching a plane out of Boston." He turned back at the door. "You're not such a bad detective yourself."

I tapped my temple with my index finger. "It's all logic. Logic and experience."

"I'll call you from the airport."

Twenty minutes later, he walked out the door.

Chapter Eight

The Rocky Point police station looked more like an oceanfront cottage than a government office. The wood shingles had weathered to a soft dove gray. The trim was crisp white. The heavy wooden door was painted forest green. I was glad to get inside. It wasn't even eight in the morning, and the temperature was already over eighty, and the air was dank. Cathy, the longtime civilian admin, stood in the open office area, her eyes on the ceiling.

I followed her gaze. "You're counting dots on the acoustic tile."

Cathy was in her forties, big-boned, full-figured, and well proportioned, a doubtful blonde with an easy smile. She glanced over her shoulder, and when she saw it was me, she grinned.

"Hi, Josie!" She turned back to the ceiling. "I'm worried we have a leak in the air-conditioning system. Or a pipe is cracked.

Or something. I've called the maintenance guys. Maybe it's my imagination, but I swear I can hear a drip. There's nothing I can do until they get here. It's always something, right? Chief Hunter said you'd be coming in. I'll let him know you're here."

While I waited, I walked to the community bulletin board and read the notices. The annual sand castle competition was slated for the first Saturday in August. Academy Brass, my favorite group, was playing a program called "Star-Spangled Music" on an upcoming Sunday in the gazebo on the village green. The town was offering free sailing lessons to teens.

"Josie," Ellis said from his office door. "Thanks for coming in."

He nodded toward an armchair at his round guest table and waited until I sat before taking a chair across from me. He reached for a manila folder on his desk.

"Bryan tells me you had some trouble with the sketch," he said.

"That's an understatement."

He opened the folder and placed Bryan's drawing on the table in front of me.

"What's wrong with it?" he asked.

I drew it toward me and studied it. The woman's face was pretty, the eyes alive. The glasses were exactly right, and so was the hair. Yet the drawing looked nothing like the imposter, or only a bit like her.

"I don't know." I kept my eyes on the drawing. "I'm sorry."

"You have nothing to apologize for." He replaced the drawing in the folder, then extracted another sheet of paper from the folder and squared it up. "Take a look."

Three color photographs of a pretty woman with delicate features were printed side by side on an 8 1/2″ × 11″ sheet of paper, oriented the long way, landscape. The first one showed her full face. The next two showed each profile. Her hair was the way I described it, blond-on-blond highlighting and swept to the side. The Chanel glasses were the same, too.

"What am I looking at?" I asked.

"Bryan used photo-editing software on a photo we got from a security camera. Is this the fake Ava?"

A ding of recognition flustered me. "This is Jean," I said. My throat closed, and I coughed, choked, really. Ellis thought Ava might have been killed by her sister. I raised my eyes to his face. As always, his expression revealed nothing about what he was thinking. I looked back at the photographs. "The fake Ava's face was thinner."

"Good," he said, writing in his notebook.

"What else?"

"Jean is too short. Maybe five-two."

"How tall was the imposter?"

"Five-four. Maybe five-five. A few inches taller than me."

He wrote in his notebook.

"It's easier than you think to create an illusion of size. Elevator shoes so subtly canted, you don't even notice the rise. Form-fitting, padded undergarments." He touched the paper. "What else is different?"

"The nose. The imposter's nose had a little upturn at the end."

He jotted something in his notebook. "How about the cheeks?"

I stared at the photos for a moment before answering. "Something's different, but I don't know what." I looked up. "It's silly, but she seems to be wearing more blush than the fake Ava, so I can't tell if the contours of her cheeks are actually different or not. Another example of not trusting your own eyes."

"Good stuff." Ellis selected another sheet of paper from the folder and slipped it in front of me. "Do you recognize this woman?"

Another Photoshopped image, featuring the same hair, glasses, and eye color. This woman was built on a larger scale, though.

Wide cheekbones. Brows set far apart. Rounded chin. Broader nose. Bushier brows, too.

"This is so interesting, Ellis. Seeing different versions of the same thing makes it clearer what I know and what I don't." I tapped the paper. "This woman looks pleasant, friendly, you know, accessible. The fake Ava looked glamorous, but not particularly warm. More like Jean in style than this woman. But to answer your question, I've never seen her before."

Ellis looked at the photos, upside down to him. "What — specifically — makes you perceive one as friendly and the other as glamorous?"

"Does that matter? Since I'm comparing apples to apples — my own perceptions — I'm not sure it does."

"I don't know . . . but take a crack at answering."

"Jean has more delicate features." I pointed to the photo array. "Who is she?"

"The Towsons' housekeeper, Tori Andrews." He rubbed the side of his nose. "On paper, she meets the specs." He took out the first sketch again, the one Bryan drew based on my recollections, and the photos of Jean, and lined up all three sheets in front of me. "What's reassuring is that when we track down the real fake Ava, I think you'll recognize her."

"Are you going to release my sketch to the media?"

"Yes," Ellis said, "with a caveat that the image is not exact. We've already drafted the news release."

"Can I have an advance copy?"

Ellis tilted his head, considering. "You in touch with Wes much?"

I met Ellis's impenetrable gaze. "Some."

"I'll e-mail the sketch to you. Along with the news release draft."

"Thanks."

I looked again at Bryan's rendering of the fake Ava. The hair was right. The glasses were right. But the face was all wrong, and I couldn't explain why. Frustration gnawed at my insides like hunger, then intensified into anger, expanding and darkening as it took hold until finally searing fury tore through my veins like fire blazing along a gasoline-soaked wick. I shoved the drawing aside.

No one could play me for a sucker and expect me to sit still and take it. No one.

CHAPTER NINE

I parked near my company's loading dock in the shade of an ancient chestnut tree. It was nine forty. I'd been with Ellis in the police station for nearly ninety minutes. As I trudged through the sultry air to the front door, I scanned my text messages and listened to my voice mails. Ty had left a voice mail that he'd made it to D.C. and would let me know where he was staying once he got situated. Wes left me two sigh-filled messages. His sighs were code, Wesian for his profound disappointment in me. He also sent a text, short and not so sweet: *You promised.*

He was right.

I stopped under the canopy of a weeping willow tree, a favorite hiding place, and called him back.

"Wes," I said when I had him on the line, "I got your messages."

"I can't believe you didn't call me yesterday," he said, his voice rippling with righteous outrage.

"I was busy," I said. Wes was work.

"Whatcha got?"

"Nothing."

He sighed again. "Josie. What did you see?"

"Blood. Too much blood."

"Did you take photos for me?"

"God, Wes. Don't be crass. I have to go. I'll talk to you later."

I pushed the END CALL button, cutting off his sputtering protests.

Inside my company, cheered by the familiar, merry tinkle of Gretchen's wind chimes jangling as I opened the front door, I glanced around. Everyone was busy, a good thing.

Cara was on the phone giving someone directions to the weekly tag sale. Her eyes were puffy and rimmed in red. Gretchen was also on the phone, asking Eric whether she should sign off on the asphalt company's invoice — were the pothole repairs finished? Fred was reading from his monitor. So was Sasha. Hank meowed with superior disdain, demanding to know where I'd been.

"Sorry, baby. I had to make a stop." I squatted and drew my fingernails lightly along his spine, a move known to give him blissed-out jelly-legs. "Does that feel good, sweetie?"

He mewed.

"What a good boy."

I scooped him up and kissed the top of his silvery little head. He rested his cheek against my shoulder. His purring was world class.

As soon as Cara was off the phone, I said, "I'm so sorry about Ava, Cara. Being in a book club . . . you really get to know people well."

"Thank you, Josie." Her eyes watered, and she swallowed hard. "Everyone here has been wonderful. So kind."

Gretchen, still talking to Eric, stretched out her arm and patted Cara's shoulder, her expressive eyes communicating empathy and concern.

"If you feel up to it," I said, settling into a nearby chair, "I'd love to hear about Ava. If you don't want to talk about her, of course, I'll understand."

"Thank you. It's good to talk about her, to remember her many wonderful qualities."

"People live on in the stories we tell about them."

"Yes." She gazed out the window for a moment, then turned back to me. "Ava cherished beauty. She never put a mere stick

80

of butter on the table, for example. She created butter flowers and floated them in a low bowl of water with bay leaves, a kind of faux lily pond." She sighed, remembering. "She was caring and generous and smart. I never heard her say a bad word about anyone."

"How long was Ava in the book club?"

"About five years. I don't remember exactly. She replaced Dottie after she moved to Hilton Head. Diane keeps the group small — there are only four of us. No one joins unless someone leaves. We're only three, now."

Cara pulled a tissue from the box on her desk. She'd crocheted the tissue-box cover last winter. She patted her eyes.

"If your book club is like mine," I said, still nuzzling Hank, "you spend as much time talking about your own lives as you do about the book."

Cara half-smiled through her tears. "We're the same." She smiled, a tremulous one. "Each of us takes a turn hosting our quarterly meeting. Whoever is the host chooses the book and cooks a dinner based on the book's setting. We focus on novels set in foreign locations." Cara lovingly patted a hardback resting on her desk, *The Lantern,* by Deborah Lawrenson. "This is the book

Ava picked for our next meeting. It's set in Provence. She already told us her menu — salade Niçoise, bouillabaisse, and ratatouille."

"Oh, Cara. I'm so sorry."

She dabbed her eyes again. "It's so awful."

"If you need some time off," I said, "I hope you'll take it."

"Thank you, Josie. When her funeral is scheduled, I'll let you know."

"Of course. It's so jarring. Someone you care about is here, and then they're not."

"Exactly."

"You mentioned Diane. Who is she?"

"Diane Hawkins. She's a librarian. It's her book club, actually. She's run it for more than a dozen years. The other member is Olive Winslow, the principal of Rocky Point Elementary School. She's the newbie. She's only been a member for three years."

"I don't think I know them."

"You know Diane from Rocky Point Community Theater. She's a regular player there. She has a wonderful voice."

Recognition dawned. "Of course! She's terrific. She played the mother in *Gypsy*, right? She can sure belt out a tune."

"That's her. And Olive volunteers at Oceanside Music School, and she's very involved in crew. She was all-state when she was in college, at Hitchens, and now she attends all the regattas." Cara tried another smile, this one a bit less shaky. "We almost always go together. My grandson, Patrick, is on the team now."

The phone rang again, and Gretchen said, "I'll take it." She picked up the receiver.

"Did Ava ever tell you about any problems she might have had?" I asked, lowering my voice. "Any issues? Marriage? Money? Health? Anything?"

"I don't feel comfortable talking about it." Cara twisted her tissue into a screw, then smoothed it out. "We thought of our conversations as confidential."

"I understand. But it may well help catch her killer. How about her marriage? Anything there?"

Cara kept her eyes on her frayed tissue and shook her head.

"Really?"

She raised her eyes. "Just normal griping. It was all in good fun."

"How can you be sure? A lot of truth is hidden in jokes."

"I know what you mean, but that's not this. Let me give you an example: Ava laughed as she told us that she was tempted to hang a wooden plaque she found at a gift store over the kitchen sink. It read 'No man was ever murdered while washing dishes.' Do you see what I mean? It was cute. Not bitter or anything. I think she loved Edwin very much."

"I understand. That is cute."

"I thought so, too."

Hank hopped down, and I stood up.

I knew Cara well enough to know that she always thought the best of people. It wasn't that her head was in the sand; it was that she truly saw the glass as half full. It made her a joy to be around, but an unreliable character witness.

CHAPTER TEN

I went to the *Seacoast Star*'s Web site, hoping Wes had posted some news. With his web of sources, he might have learned anything, but there were no updates. I checked my e-mail. Ellis had sent Bryan's sketch and the news release. I downloaded them, then drafted an e-mail to Wes with a note reading *You're getting these first. You're welcome.* I saved it, determined to get a little quid for my pro quo before sending it. I dialed his number.

"Whatcha got?" Wes demanded, as brusque as usual.

I never took his brusqueness personally because it wasn't personal. It was just Wes.

"We need to meet. I have news."

"Good. How's an hour?"

I glanced at my computer monitor to see the time. It read 10:50. "Let's call it noon. At our dune?"

"Perfect," he said, and hung up without

another word.

I poked through the stacks of papers littering my desk. I needed to review Eric's capital budget request for the fourth quarter. I had accounting reports to go over. I couldn't focus on any of it. I was stewing and impatient. I went downstairs again.

A pale pink foam egg carton containing a dozen multicolored glass marbles sat atop a pile of papers on Sasha's desk.

"What do you have here?" I asked.

"Potential treasures," Sasha said, her eyes alight.

Sasha was normally shy and reserved, so any flicker of enthusiasm always got my heart pumping. I dragged a guest chair over to her desk.

"Evidently, we won the O'Hara bid."

"We did indeed."

"Yay!" I said, clapping. It's always harder to buy antiques than it is to sell them, so acquiring an entire houseful of antiques and collectibles was a cause for celebrating.

"What you see here is one of Mr. O'Hara's collections, as he stored them. Each of the marbles is more than an inch in diameter, with no pits, cracks, dings, or chips."

"The bigger the marble, the more valuable."

"Exactly. There are no pontil marks or

signs of grinding, yet they're smooth as satin, so the pontil marks must have been ground off. Melting wouldn't do this fine a job. I've been working on identifying the designs. Then I'll move on to authentication. Look at this one." She pointed to a brick red matte marble with a thin band of white twirling on the diagonal, smiling as if she had a secret, a good one she couldn't wait to share. "I think it's a Banded Oxblood Swirl." She tucked her fine brown hair behind her ear, her already expansive smile widening. "If so, we really have something. A sale of an undamaged example has never been recorded. Never ever."

"Never ever," I repeated, awed. "Are they antiques?"

We used a conservative definition of an antique — a hundred years. If an object wasn't more than a hundred years old, it was, at Prescott's, a collectible.

"I think so. Mr. O'Hara had excellent taste."

"Did he keep records?"

"Notes, but no records. He bought all of them at flea markets in the 1960s. He called this one a 'red and white swirl.' He paid a dollar for it in 1964."

"A dollar."

Sasha smiled. "It's worth more now."

I laughed. "I should think so. Keep me posted." I turned toward Fred, who was absorbed by whatever he was reading. "Hey, Fred — sorry to interrupt. What are you working on?"

Fred stared at me for several seconds, coming back to the here and now from wherever he'd been. Fred always worked with laserlike focus.

"A writing desk. Mrs. O'Hara got it from her aunt Louise, who got it from a man she didn't marry."

"Come again?"

"Aunt Louise was quite a gal. Ahead of her time. She was a big-cheese magazine editor in New York. She never married, but she always had a man in her life." He swiveled his monitor so I could see the image. The desk was a beauty, a huge wooden globe.

"It's a globe," I said, my excitement apparent.

Fred grinned. "The gods are with us."

Prescott's ran monthly themed auctions, and we were in the middle of gathering objects for a spring auction called "The World as Seen Through the Eyes of Explorers, Travelers, and Cartographers."

I moved my chair nearer his desk so I could get a closer look. Fred had uploaded a series of photographs, standard operating procedure for an object under review.

Two quarter doors opened sideways, exposing a black leather writing surface and a series of handsome arched compartments and small drawers framed by miniature Doric columns.

"This was a birthday gift from one of Aunt Louise's fellas, but Mrs. O'Hara doesn't remember his name, if she ever knew it, which she probably didn't because Aunt Louise never brought men around." Fred chuckled. "Mrs. O'Hara was a little upset that she had to tell me about Aunt Louise's love life. Apparently, Aunt Louise scandalized the family while she was alive by having one affair after another from the day she graduated Vassar to the day she died — a span of more than sixty years — and here she is scandalizing them after she's dead. I had to promise we wouldn't publicize that she had serial relationships before she would reveal Aunt Louise's past."

"I look forward to seeing which euphemisms you'll come up with for the catalogue copy."

Fred pushed his glasses up. "Me, too."

I laughed. "Times sure have changed, haven't they? When did Aunt Louise die?"

"In 2008. She was eighty-two. She got the

gift in the midfifties, as best as Mrs. O'Hara can place it."

"When she was roughly thirty. Any chance we can track down the gentleman who gave it to her?"

"I was thinking it would take some knocking on doors to find someone who knew Aunt Louise. I can't imagine many of her contemporaries are still alive, but there's nothing to say she might not have been friends with a neighbor or co-worker or someone who was younger."

"If so, that person would be too young to have seen anything relevant to us, but he or she could have been told about the various love affairs." I paused, thinking. "Aunt Louise didn't keep a diary, I suppose?"

"No. Mrs. O'Hara recalled that Aunt Louise always kept a datebook in her purse, but she doesn't have them, and has no idea where they might be."

"Too bad. It's worth a call to the magazine, though, and maybe a trip to New York." I turned my attention back to Fred's monitor. The desk was magnificent. "Mahogany and ebony?"

"Maybe. I need to confirm it. There are lots of exotic woods that look similar. From comparable examples owned by museums, I think it's English, circa 1800, which means it could have been made in a British colony."

"Like India or Jamaica, where the maker might have had easy access to exotic woods. Got it." I leaned back. "Did I hear you say museums?" If a museum bought an object, it had value.

He pushed up his glasses and smiled. "Three so far."

I turned back to his monitor, studying the image. Round pulls glimmered in the light.

"Gilt-covered bronze?" I asked.

"Looks that way," Fred said.

The globe sat on four ornately carved legs, which rested on griffin feet.

"Any marks?" I asked. A maker's signature or seal or a company's name or logo can jump-start a hunt for ownership records.

"Not so far."

"Condition?"

"Pristine."

I smiled. "Where is it?"

"Seventy-nine," he replied, referring to a roped-off section of the warehouse.

"What does your gut tell you?"

"It's good."

"I want to see it."

Fred stood and grinned. "I want to see it again."

Fifteen minutes later, I concurred with Fred's preliminary assessment. From the

91

peg-and-dowel craftsmanship to the expertly curved planks of wood, and from the gilt fleur-de-lis etched onto the leather writing surface to the fit and finish of the drawers, all signs pointed to the piece being genuine. I couldn't wait to see what Fred would learn about the maker — and the man who gave it to Aunt Louise.

"Let's get an estimate of value first, then decide if it's worth the investment to try to track the provenance."

"Josie!" Cara's voice crackled over the PA system. "Pick up, please."

I reached for a wall phone.

"Jean Cooper is here to see you. She's hoping you can give her a few minutes."

I looked at the closest wall clock. I had half an hour before I needed to leave to meet Wes. I told Cara to bring her in.

Jean Cooper looked like what my father pictured when he described a woman as a lady. She walked with effortless grace. Her shoulder-length dark hair shone. Her makeup was expertly applied and subtle. She wore a peach and white floral print sleeveless belted dress and off-white open-toe pumps.

Upstairs, she sat on the yellow brocade love seat with her hands resting in her lap. I sat across from her on a matching Queen Anne wing chair. She didn't want anything to drink.

"I'm sorry to barge in on you like this. I'm rarely so impulsive."

"I'm glad you did. It gives me an opportunity to tell you how sorry I am for your loss."

Her eyes filled, and she didn't speak for a moment, a masterful example of self-control.

"Thank you. You didn't know Ava."

"No."

"The police chief explained it to me. He said they're looking into whether Ava interrupted a robbery."

"You don't think so."

"I don't know." Her fingers ran along the pleat fold, smoothing the satiny fabric. "My first reaction — well, you saw me yesterday. I assumed it was Edwin." She laced her fingers together. "Do you think someone was trying to steal the Tiffany lamp?"

"It looks that way."

"Isn't it hard to sell such a rare object?"

"Yes, especially if you hope to get top dollar."

She pressed her fingertips against her forehead for a moment.

"Do you have a headache?" I asked. "Can

I get you something?"

"Thank you, no. I'm just so confused."

"Me, too."

Jean looked aside, taking in my rooster collection. A minute passed, then another. When she finally spoke, her tone was low and dreamy, as if she were alone and thinking aloud.

"Ava was weak, so she stayed in a loveless marriage. I adored her, but she was weak."

"You're not."

"No, I'm not." Jean turned back to face me. "Ava was always worried about money. Even though she didn't need to be, not now, she was."

"She didn't want to leave Edwin because she'd lose his lifestyle."

"She signed a prenup."

"You're thinking she organized the theft so she could leave him and keep the lifestyle."

"Ava would never steal. She just wouldn't." She stood up. "The police showed me your sketch. I didn't recognize the woman."

"It's not a good reproduction. It's not the sketch artist's fault. He was terrific. It's me. I simply have no picture in my head. It's frustrating."

"Maybe you'll remember more later."

"That's what the police think."

"I loved my sister very much." Her eyes filled again, and she used the sides of her index fingers to press under them. "Edwin isn't going to have a funeral. I think that's just cruel. Ava was loved by the community."

"Did he explain why?"

"No."

"I'm sorry. I wish I could help."

When she'd regained her composure, I walked her downstairs.

I turned to Cara. "Cara, this is Ava's sister, Jean." To Jean, I added, "Cara was in Ava's book club."

"Of course," Jean said. "Ava spoke of you often. She was very fond of you."

Cara wiped away a tear. "I felt the same."

Jean opened her bag and eased a business card from an inside pocket. She handed it to me, and I took it. Her name was in the center in raised burgundy lettering. A phone number and e-mail address were below. The area code was 603, New Hampshire. The e-mail was a Gmail account.

"If you think of anything, please call."

I said I would.

"She's lovely," Cara said, after she'd gone.

"And lost," I said, watching Jean walk to her car. "She seems all at sea."

Cara made a tchich-tchich sound. "The poor soul."

As I drove out of the lot to keep my appointment with Wes, I tried to focus on the O'Hara marble collection and Aunt Louise's extraordinary desk, and for a few fleeting moments, my emotional turmoil quieted. I'd never seen anything like that desk, and that fact alone made me think we were dealing with a very special object indeed. Soon, though, the grim reality of Ava's murder and Jean's grief crept back into my mind, souring my mood. Ava was dead, and I didn't have a clue what was going on.

CHAPTER ELEVEN

I got to the dune first and clambered up the shifting sand to the top. Along that stretch of coast, the shore was more tumbled rocks and jumbled seaweed than sandy beach. It was a good spot for a private conversation. Clouds had blown in from the west, and only slivers of weak sunlight shone through. A wind-driven white frothy chop charged toward shore. To my left, tall grass shuddered in the light, hot breeze. It was a tease. Even though I wore a lightweight cotton sundress, I felt like a limp dishrag.

Wes rolled to a stop in his shiny Ford Focus. Maggie, Wes's wife, had executed a campaign to change his image from scruffy upstart to polished professional, and so far, it was working. He was wearing khakis and a blue button-down oxford shirt, with the sleeves rolled up, not dirty jeans and a torn T-shirt. He carried a pocket-sized notebook, not a ratty piece of lined paper. And the

Focus had replaced a rusty old rattletrap.

"Talk to me," Wes said as he sidestepped up the dune.

I did. I told Wes what I knew about the Towsons, sharing my sadness that Ava had been killed, my fury at being conned, my confusion about why someone would undertake such a project, and my frustration at being unable to remember much about the fake Ava's appearance.

"I'll send you the sketch," I said, "but I have questions."

Wes grinned. "Now who's negotiating?"

I kept my expression neutral and didn't reply.

"Okay, okay," he said.

I sent the e-mail I'd previously drafted. "I just e-mailed you the sketch along with a draft of the press release the police are sending out later today. You're getting the first look."

"You're one hot banana, Joz!" He pulled his smart phone from his pocket and brought up my e-mail sketch. "I need to get this on our Web site."

"Read the news release first," I warned him. "The image is only a rough approximation, so the police are asking anyone who thinks the woman looks even a little bit familiar to contact them."

"Got it."

I turned toward the ocean while Wes worked. A few faint orange streaks of light deckled the water. The chop was rougher and less organized than when I'd arrived only minutes earlier. The entire ocean surface bubbled like a witch's cauldron.

I tousled my hair at the back of my neck, hoping for a break from the sticky oppressiveness, but it was useless. While I waited, I patted around in my tote bag until I found the velvet pouch containing the antique bronze hairpins I used to put my hair up on hot days. They were, I thought, adorable, with an etched bee design at the top of each spear. They'd started life as hatpins, but I'd repurposed them years earlier. I removed the mushroom-shaped protective tips, twirled my hair into a loose French twist, threaded the hairpins through, and popped the tips back into place. Far off to the south, a man and a black Lab were playing ball near the water's edge. The Lab wore a red and white bandana knotted around his neck. His tail wagged so fast, it was a blur. The air was electric, full of barely repressed rage.

"Okay," Wes said. "Done." He smiled like he meant it. "Thanks."

"You're welcome. What have you found out?"

"Those two phone numbers you had me check? Disposables."

"As expected."

"Right. They were sold at a small electronics store in the North End section of Boston four months ago, for cash. The shop only keeps security videos for three months, so that's a dead end. Rocky Point Chemists is a dead end, too. My police source says the shop's security camera shows a tall thin man wearing a denim jacket, jeans, sunglasses, and a Red Sox baseball hat with the visor pulled down low. All you can see is that he's white."

"A tall, thin white man who knew where the cameras were positioned."

"Right."

"I'm assuming the Towsons have an alarm system," I said. "Have they checked with the company? Maybe it's an inside job — whatever 'it' is."

"The system doesn't include cameras, so that's a bust. None of the security company's employees has skipped out. Besides, they don't have keys. If the system is breached in any way, the company gets an electronic alert, and they call the owner and the cops. It wasn't, so whoever the fake Ava is, she had a key, and she knew the security code."

"The fake Ava has to be someone who knew the dog's name."

"Like who?"

"The girl who walked the dog — Merry. Maybe she's not a teenager."

Wes chuckled. "You're in hot-petunia mode today, Joz! I met with Merry myself. She's a kid, all right, nothing like your sketch."

"How about her mother?"

"She's shorter than you."

"No one is shorter than me."

"Except Merry's mom. There's no grand-mother around. Plus, Merry swears the key was never out of her pocket and she didn't tell anyone the alarm code."

I shrugged, unimpressed. "Security systems can be hacked."

"You're crossing over to the dark side, Joz. The conspiracy is growing."

Safety is an illusion, I thought. "You're right. It's probably not some tech whiz hacking into the system. It's someone who knew them well enough to have access to their alarm codes."

"A relative or a good friend."

"Be careful who you trust, Wes. It's the people you trust the most who pose the biggest risk. No one else can get close enough to do much damage."

"Jeez, Joz. You're in rare form today."

"Well, it's true, and Ava's murder proves it. Someone she knew and trusted, or someone Edwin knew and trusted, killed her."

"Maybe the murder is unrelated to the scam that you got caught up in."

"I didn't get caught up in anything. I got conned." I waved it aside. I'd learned over our decade-long relationship that Wes liked to twitch the cat. I resisted the urge to respond by showing my claws. "A murder and a con happening at the same time, and they're unrelated? That would be quite a coincidence. For the sake of argument, let's assume there's cause and effect at work. Which brings us back to Edwin. Have the police covered the basics? Money trouble? An affair? Recently fired employees?"

"Yup. Nothing that raised a red flag. His staff reports he's a slave driver, but they don't care, because he pays them so much. I wish my boss paid me so much I wouldn't care that he's a slave driver. Anyway, Edwin has money up the wazoo. The police checked his credit card receipts, phone logs, and personal e-mail account — all with his permission. No unusual charges. No sign of a mistress."

"Maybe he has a disposable cell, a separate e-mail account, and pays in cash."

"Good one, Joz! If so, they haven't got a whiff of it. They asked to search his office and his car, but he refused, saying he has countless sensitive and confidential documents, which he can't allow them to paw through, and they don't have enough evidence to get a search warrant. They were able to search his house because it's a crime scene, but they didn't turn up anything incriminating."

"I wonder if Edwin is telling the truth. You know how it is — rumors can take on a life of their own. It's possible that Ava was the one having the affair, not him, and it was her guilty conscience that led her to accuse him. Or maybe her accusation was an attempt to deflect attention from herself onto him. After all, everyone knows that a good offense is the best defense." I opened my palms. "There's no way to know."

Wes turned to a fresh page in his notebook and scratched a note, intrigued. He looked up for a moment to add, "Did you know that Jean, Ava's sister, hates Edwin? 'Loathes' is the word she used to the police."

"I'm not surprised. She accused him of murder in front of them. Do you know why she hates him so much?"

"Protective of her kid sister, maybe. Jean is forty-three, five years older than Ava. If there's any truth to the rumors of domestic violence, that would do it, right? Jean says Edwin's temper was escalating, and there's a neighbor who heard some pretty nasty fights, but Ava never reported anything. The two calls to the cops came from other people, and neither Edwin or Ava acknowledged any trouble. What do you think of her?"

"Jean? I just met her. She seems in shock."

"Did you get a photo?"

"Of course not! God, Wes! What do you know about her?"

"Not much. She's a longtime divorcée who lives in a ritzy condo and has a boyfriend with a good job who's nice to her. She volunteers at stuff." He slid his notebook into his shirt pocket. "The medical examiner says the murder weapon, the cast-iron frying pan, had been bleached, so there's no meaningful forensic evidence. They found a half-empty jug of bleach in the laundry room and traces of Ava's blood on the lip of the dump sink. It looks like the killer balanced the frying pan on the edge of the sink while he bleached it. From the blood coagulation, she pegs the time of death as between eight and eleven that morning. No fingerprints that stand out. The Tiffany lamp had been thoroughly wiped. No prints at all."

"Does Edwin have an alibi?"

"Yeah, fair to middling. He gave a video presentation from eight thirty to eleven thirty the day Ava was killed for a group of potential investors. His secretary swears he was already in his office when she arrived at eight, but he has a private entrance, and she was busy getting ready for the video conference, so that means nothing. Once the conference started, Edwin was in plain sight of everyone on the video feed the whole time, except for a ten-minute scheduled break in the middle and another five-minute break that came up unexpectedly when one of the participants had to take a call — and ten minutes wouldn't be enough time for Edwin to get home and back. But he could have whacked Ava before he left home. It's cutting it close, but it's doable. He kills Ava at eight and takes, what, five minutes to clean up? Ten? It's a ten-minute drive to his office. He sneaks in through his private entry. His secretary insists it didn't happen, but she doesn't really know, and she's been with him for years. She's loyal. She's the only employee he brought with him when he relocated from New York."

"When was that?"

"Nine years ago. Right after he and Ava got married."

"Why would the secretary lie?" I asked. "Loyalty alone wouldn't explain it."

"You don't bite the hand that feeds you. You know that. You see it all the time. A guy lies because his boss told him to. Or because even though his boss didn't tell him to, or didn't even ask him to, he sees which way the wind is blowing, and he's no fool. He needs the income more than he needs lofty ideals like justice. Or maybe the secretary plans on blackmailing Edwin down the road. Regardless, if you believe her, he's out of it. The police are taking it slow."

I closed my eyes for a moment, processing the information. "No one in Garnet Cove saw the imposter or her car?"

"Nope. The police are still checking security cameras along likely routes, you know, banks on Main Street, and so on, but so far, nothing that rings any bells."

Exclusive communities like Garnet Cove prided themselves on providing privacy for their residents, but it was a double-edged sword. The same woods that sheltered them allowed bad guys unfettered access once they were over the outside wall.

"Either the fake Ava got lucky or she snuck in through the forest," I said.

"If the thief was planning to escape through a forest and climb a wall, he was going for cash and jewelry, stuff he could carry."

"I keep coming back to the fact that whoever was trying to steal the lamp knew details about Edwin and Ava they could only have learned from them. Who was Ava closest to?"

"Jean. She says so, and Edwin agrees."

My dress swooped up as a sudden blast of wind tore across the ocean and the dunes. I smoothed it down.

"Something's out of whack," I said.

Wes started down the dune. "If you think of what it is, let me know."

I crab-walked down the dune after him.

I wanted to know more about Ava. Jean was closest to Ava. Jean might not know all the answers, but she was clearly the place to start.

CHAPTER TWELVE

Jean didn't answer her phone. Since I planned on asking questions, not offering answers, I didn't leave a message. She'd visited me unannounced. I decided I would return the favor.

A simple online search got me Jean's address. She lived in a chichi condo complex called the Grey Gull that overlooked Old Mill Pond. I'd been there once, years earlier, appraising a Minton dinnerware set. The complex was surrounded by an eight-foot-high, elegantly designed black wrought-iron fence. Mature landscaping precluded easy peeking. Garnet Cove was private; Grey Gull was fortified.

There were two ways in, three if you counted boating across Old Mill Pond as an option. If you were staff or making a delivery, you turned into the Grey Gull from Grove Boulevard, a pretty tree-lined street with a well-groomed center median that dead-ended at the water. Residents and guests used a private entry road, a turnoff from a mansion-lined street named Tucker. That's how I'd entered when I'd come to assess the china, and this time, I anticipated as easy an entry as then. I passed a neatly planted garden, complete with a waterfall and koi pond. A huge American flag flew overhead. It was flanked by a small triangular Grey Gull flag and a New Hampshire state flag. I rolled to stop at the guardhouse.

The uniformed guard on duty looked like an ex-NFL player, big and wide and tall. At a guess, he was close to sixty. A gold-tone pin-on badge gave his name as A. Henderson. A small microphone was clipped to his collar. He smiled with professional indifference and asked how he could help me.

"Jean Cooper, please," I said.

"One moment."

He disappeared into the small enclosure — nearer a shack than a building in size, but elegantly appointed with shutters and decorative trim — and reappeared two minutes later to report Ms. Cooper wasn't available.

"She's not home?"

"She didn't answer her phone, which might mean she's not home, or it might mean she doesn't want to be disturbed."

"Or the ringer was turned off so she could nap, or she turned it off so she could sleep late and she forgot to turn it on. How about if I go knock on her door?"

"That's not allowed, miss."

"It's important."

"Sorry," he said in a tone that didn't invite argument.

"Would you go? Or send someone?"

"Also not allowed."

"Let's slip a note under her door."

"You're going to have to try later. Or call and make an appointment."

"There has to be a way."

"Sorry."

He wasn't surly, exactly, but he was clearly losing patience, so I thanked him, which felt silly since he hadn't been the least bit helpful, and with no options left, I followed the circular turnaround and drove out.

I backtracked to Tucker and turned right onto Grove. At the pond end, I executed a three-point turn that would have made my driving instructor proud and parked with my back to the water. I had a clear view of the Grey Gull staff entrance.

There was no guard, but there was an iron gate as tall as the fence that blocked vehicle access. I was certain it opened and closed slowly enough that I could easily scoot through when a vehicle entered, assuming I could dodge whatever surveillance they had in place.

I lowered my window so I could see clearer, and sticky air whooshed in. I couldn't see any cameras. I examined the top of the fence inch by inch. If I were planning security, that's where I'd attach cameras — high enough to be out of reach and low enough to capture detailed images. I didn't see a thing. Inside the compound, mature trees nearly blocked my view, but when I tilted my head to the left, I could see a modern streetlight, a replica of an old-style flickering gas lamp. If a security camera was attached to it, it was camouflaged.

I got out of my car and stepped onto the median. I looked around inside the Grey Gull and at the nearby houses. No one was out and about. This wasn't that kind of neighborhood. This section of Rocky Point was too dignified for block parties, or even casual conversations. I was glad I didn't live there. I called Jean again, and again the phone went to voice mail. This time, I left a message.

"Hi, Jean," I said. "This is Josie Prescott. I was hoping we could get together. I'm in the neighborhood if you're available." I stated my phone number and rang off. In case she was checking e-mail but not voice mail, I sent a quick note duplicating my phone message.

I assumed I'd hear from her soon. If I were Jean, I'd be curious. I was too impatient to wait, though. If I could get into the complex, I would.

I resumed my study of the gate as I considered how to gain access. A camera was attached to a standing intercom system aimed to see the driver of a car or truck. I could just make out a list of residents and codes. Someone who wanted in would look up the code that corresponded to the name and punch it in on the keypad. No doubt there was a code to reach the guard house at the main entry, too. Owners, looking at an image of who had rung, could push a button to activate the gate. To the left, there was a hundred-year-old walnut tree with big knurly roots that would be perfect to hide behind. When the gate opened, I could scurry in, staying low to avoid the camera. I nodded, plan made.

Locking my tote bag in my trunk, I pocketed the key and my phone. As I stepped behind the tree, I hoped I wouldn't have too long to wait.

No such luck.

■ ■ ■ ■

Ellis called an hour into my vigil, just as I was deciding how much longer I should wait. I was hot and frustrated and bored. The only person I'd seen was a man in a blue pickup pulling out of a driveway and heading farther into the complex.

"We've been going through Ava's laptop," Ellis said, "and there's an inventory labeled 'Insurance List.' It includes those candlesticks you mentioned and some paintings and so on. I'm hoping you can stop in to tell me if there's anything there for me to look into."

"Can you e-mail it to me?"

"Not at this point. We're not releasing anything from her computer."

"I understand. I'll come now."

He thanked me, and I gave one last look around inside the complex. From this vantage point, I had an unobstructed view of the lampposts that lined the road.

My lips went dry.

A camera had been placed inside the ornate finials that topped the lamps. From the familiar iridescent reddish glow, I concluded they were the same kind that I used at my company. They snapped photos every three seconds, which were sent digitally to the security company charged with monitoring activity. There was no way to disable them unless you were already inside and had a tall ladder, at which point, it was too late.

A bird cawed, startling me. I looked up. He was settling into his nest. I gasped, not believing what I was seeing. A security camera mounted in a branch twenty feet above my head was aimed at the intersection of Grove and Tucker, a perfect way to monitor who was driving in. I had been tracked since I turned onto Grove. No one had come to question me, which meant the complex hadn't bought the same Platinum level service package as I had. They would only go to the footage as needed.

Now that I knew what I was looking for, it didn't take me long to find two more cameras. One was tucked into a pine tree branch on the other side of the entryway. A second camera was cleverly hidden in my tree. This one was angled toward the pond. I'd been joking when I'd thought of rowing over, but whoever set up the Grey Gull's security was one step ahead of me.

I gave up. There was no way in.

I sat in Ellis's office sipping iced tea and

skimming through the inventory Ava had prepared for the insurance company.

"We've confirmed that everything on this list is included in their insurance policy," Ellis said. "What I'm hoping you can tell me is whether anything seems undervalued or overvalued, or anything else that strikes you."

"Got it."

The inventory was three pages long and included nearly $500,000 worth of jewelry. The chess table was valued at $15,000, which seemed about right. The Nicholson was listed at $250,000. There was also a small painting by Irene Rice Pereira, which was insured for $5,200. A set of Lunt sterling silver flatware was assessed at $7,000, a bargain. The Towsons had eclectic taste. It was impossible to judge pricing accuracy on even the most cursory level without viewing the objects.

"I'd like to see photos," I said.

"I don't know anything about photos."

"I'm sure they exist. I would expect there to be a document that includes appraisals, too."

"Let me get Katie down here."

"I can search the computer."

"Protocol." He picked up the phone and dialed.

I'd met Katie before. She was the Rocky Point police's IT whiz.

"We need to check for photos and apprais-als on Ava Towson's computer," Ellis said once he reached her. "How long, do you think? . . . Did you make a backup? . . . Okay then, thanks."

He hung up and said, "She's tied up, but she's backed everything up, so you can search away. Wait here. I'll go get the laptop out of the evidence room."

While I waited, I reviewed the rest of the inventory. The candlesticks were listed at $225, the least valuable objects included in the policy. There was a Marie Bracquemond painting I hadn't seen, several rare books, and other pieces of furniture. I was intrigued that the Towsons owned a Bracquemond. Marie Bracquemond was a highly respected Impressionist artist, but she wasn't well known.

Ellis returned with the computer and set it up for me on the guest table. He went back to his desk and started typing some-thing. I started with the picture section of the library but didn't find any images that corresponded to the inventory. I opened Adobe and navigated to recent documents. The first one listed was called "Prenup."

The second was labeled "June bank statement."

I opened the search function and typed "insurance." The top item listed was a PDF filed in a folder called "Other." The document's name was "Updated ins." It ran twenty pages and included photos and appraisals, in addition to the master list.

I glanced at Ellis. He was absorbed in his work, reading something on his monitor. I went back to the Recent list and clicked on the document called "Prenup."

The PDF was only one page long. I skimmed it quickly. If Edwin and Ava divorced before their tenth anniversary for any reason except infidelity, a felony conviction, or any conviction related to a domestic violence charge, Ava would get a lump sum payout of $500,000. If those exceptions came into play on Edwin's end, the prenup would be null and void. If Ava was the guilty party, she'd get nothing. The next paragraph stated that they agreed not to have any children.

I wondered why they'd include a clause like that, then answered my own question. Edwin loved his life — lots of international travel with a beautiful, younger wife on his arm. He had no interest in domesticity. Ava must have felt the same — after all, she signed it.

The document went on to state that Edwin had had a vasectomy, so if Ava got pregnant, she agreed to allow a paternity test. If it proved Edwin wasn't the father, they would divorce and Ava would get nothing. I clicked on the x, and the document disappeared.

Ellis was still working on his computer, so I opened Ava's bank statement. It was a regular savings account in her name only. The only transactions in June were the addition of a small amount of interest and the withdrawal of the balance, more than $125,000, in cash. Ava closed the account on June thirteenth.

Ava was getting ready to leave Edwin.

New Hampshire isn't a community property state. She was worried that Edwin's income was so much larger than hers, the court would toss her savings into the marital pot.

The question was, why would she leave him with only a few months before the prenup was scheduled to go away? Maybe Edwin had been beating her, and the attacks were getting worse, unbearable. She figured she could get the prenup tossed out for cause, but in case he cut her off without a dime, canceling all her credit cards and so on before a judge ruled, at least she'd have some cash to fall back on. Or Ava wanted to buy Edwin a special gift like a Rolex or a Porsche and didn't feel right using his money to do it. Or she got in trouble gambling. Or with drugs.

Ellis stood up. "Any luck?"

I closed the bank statement and brought up the inventory.

"Yes. I found it. Everything looks right. Someone should confirm that each of these items is in the house."

He looked over my shoulder at the monitor. "Great. Thanks, Josie."

As I walked to my car, I called Jean again. Still no answer. I didn't leave another message.

There has to be a way into the Grey Gull, I thought. When in doubt, ask Wes. If anyone knew how to reach Jean, he would.

I called and got his voice mail. "Any chance you have Jean's cell phone number?" I asked it.

As I waited for a break in the traffic so I could turn onto Ocean, I considered what to do next.

Cara said Diane, the librarian who organized her book club, had selected Ava as a member. Cara had been glad for the op-

portunity to talk about Ava. Maybe Diane
would feel the same.

CHAPTER THIRTEEN

The Rocky Point Library was housed in a century-old edifice constructed of local granite, mottled gray flecked with sparkling mica.

A huge circular customer service desk sat in the middle of the ground-floor atrium. Countertop racks held community event notices and flyers. Reference librarians and checkout staff were at the ready. On the right, a reading room, furnished with the kind of chairs you'd find in a modern living room, overlooked Old Mill Pond. The chairs were upholstered in an eggplant and sage geometric print. I gazed across the water. The Grey Gull's fence was partially blocked by scrub oaks and pussy willows.

A "Happy Birthday, America!" display was positioned near the entry to the reading room. The table was covered with a plastic July Fourth–themed tablecloth. A framed copy of the Declaration of Independence rested on a nearby easel. A computer setup played a video of a docudrama telling the story of the Revolution, and six pairs of headphones allowed multiple people to listen to the movie at once. A dozen books on the subject were available for checkout. I recognized Ruth Chessman's *Bound for Freedom,* a middle school mystery set in colonial America. It had been one of my favorites. On the left, a row of individual computer stations flanked shelves of books, a sampling of all sorts of genres, selected to entice readers into the upstairs stacks. Toward the rear, an oversized spiral staircase led to the turret that housed the children's department. I smiled. I loved libraries.

I stood behind a PLEASE WAIT HERE sign attached to a black and gold stanchion, waiting my turn. A man in a conservative navy blue suit told a woman behind the counter that he needed information about using a Monte Carlo simulation, which told me he was working on enterprise risk management, a subject I knew well. One of my most important responsibilities as Prescott's CEO was minimizing risk in all its forms.

I recognized Diane from her theater program photo and stepped out of line.

Diane was a pretty woman in her forties, with short black hair, gelled into trendy spikes, and big honey-brown eyes. She wore summer-weight Dockers trousers with a pale blue sleeveless linen blouse and black Tom's espadrilles. My work required me to wiggle under furniture and crawl through dusty, sometimes stifling attics, so most of the time I dressed in jeans and T-shirts. The cotton pink-flowered sundress and thin-strapped sandals I wore today was, for me, going formal.

Diane stood near the staircase, nodding at something an older woman was saying. The older woman leaned on a silver walker. I didn't want to break into their conversation, so I stood about ten feet away, but facing them, hoping Diane would notice me. After a few seconds, as if she could feel my eyes on her, she looked in my direction. I smiled and nodded. She did the same, then turned her attention back to the older woman.

Two minutes later, the woman using the walker touched Diane's arm, a friendly thank-you, and lumbered off toward the reading room. Diane smiled again, took a step in my direction, and raised her eyebrows, silently inviting me to join her.

"Hi," I said, extending a hand for a shake as I walked up. "I'm Josie Prescott. Cara, my company's receptionist, speaks very highly of you. She loves being in your book club."

"How nice to meet you, Josie," Diane said. "I love Cara!"

"Do you have a minute to talk? I'm hoping you can help me."

"Of course," she said, not allowing her surprise, if she felt any, to show. "If you don't mind sitting amid mile-high stacks of books, we can talk in my office."

"It sounds heavenly. I love books."

She led the way across the hall toward a closed, unmarked door.

"Me, too," she said, laughing a little. "Which is a good thing, since I'm a librarian. Cara's told me a bit about your business, some of the delicious-sounding antiques you sell. Do you deal in many books?"

She opened the door, and I followed her down a long hallway full of administrative offices. Some doors were open, providing a clear view of people sitting at desks and tapping into computers or talking on the phone. Brass signs on the closed doors read HUMAN RESOURCES and ACCOUNTING.

"We sometimes sell nice but undistinguished books during the weekly tag sale," I said, "what we call reading copies. Rare books wind up in our high-end auctions. We run those monthly. They're all themed, so the books are merely one element in a multifaceted collection. For instance, we're gathering objects right now for an auction next spring called 'The World as Seen Through the Eyes of Explorers, Travelers, and Cartographers.' We'll be including some rare travel and exploration books we're just now cataloguing."

Diane unlocked a door toward the rear of the hall using a key attached to a curly plastic bracelet she wore on her left wrist. Her name was on the brass plaque, which told me she was pretty high up in the library pecking order. Private offices make a statement.

Her lady's desk was charming, old-school, but the double monitor all-in-one computer setup showed she was also high-tech. The *Seacoast Star*'s Web site was up, and I saw the familiar red lightning bolt, alerting viewers to a news flash.

I pointed at it. "I recognize the symbol. What's going on?"

She glanced at the monitor, then hit RE-FRESH. "The sky looked so ominous, I was checking the weather report." She met my eyes. "They've just posted a storm warning. Have a seat and I'll see what they say."

I took the chair across from her desk as

she turned back to the monitor.

"It looks like we're in for a thunderstorm, maybe with hail." She smiled. "I like a good rainstorm, don't you?"

"I love them — if I'm home, all curled up with a good book. Do they say when the rain will start?"

While she read on, I took a look around. The whitewashed shelving that covered three walls held scores of books. Additional stacks sat on the floor and covered her desk. Two silver-framed photos hung on the back wall. In the first photo, Diane was standing in an outdoor market under a scorching sun. With her arms thrust upright in a perfect V, she looked like a gymnast who'd nailed her dismount. She wore a fuchsia and yellow sundress and a big floppy straw hat. She was smiling as if she'd just won the lottery. The second photo showed a younger Diane with her arms linked around a younger Ava. Two young men stood in back of them. Diane wore a blue satin minidress. Ava's was longer and rose colored. The men wore tuxes. All four of their expressions brimmed with promise and hope.

"Sometime after six. Good, we can get ourselves all cozy."

"Those photos are terrific," I said, pointing.

"Senior prom. And Nassau. My honeymoon."

"You went to high school with Ava."

She nodded, her eyes on the photo. "She was a dear friend."

"Everything I've heard about her has been positive. I'm sorry I never met her." My eyes went to the other photo, then to her ringless finger. "I didn't know you were married."

"I'm not. Thank God."

I turned back to the photo. "You look ecstatic."

"Which proves that looks can be deceiving. The marriage lasted longer than the flight home, but not by much. Never mind . . . water under the bridge. Nassau — my biggest adventure." She laughed devilishly. "So far. I'm a nut about travel. That's why I created the book club. So tell me about some of your special travel books. Let a girl dream."

"We have a first edition of *Sketches of Japanese Manners and Customs,* by J. M. W. Silver. It was published in 1867 and rebound thirty years later. Red leather with gilt stamping. Twenty-eight chromolithographs, including a vignette title page."

"Why would someone rebind it?"

"Either it was so well used the binding

showed signs of wear, or, what's just as likely, the owner redesigned his library and wanted the binding to match the color scheme. Times change, but people don't. Interior designers routinely buy leather-bound books by the yard."

"That's a hoot! So don't keep me in suspense. How much will it sell for?"

"Are you sitting down?" I asked.

She clutched her chair's arms and made a funny face.

"Around nine hundred."

Her eyes widened. "I had no idea."

"Supply and demand." I glanced around her office. "You weren't kidding when you said you had miles of books."

"So many books. So little time."

She paused for a moment, waiting for me to explain why I was there. I hesitated, deciding how to phrase my question. Diane waited me out, a sign of a good listener, a good friend.

"I was hoping you would talk to me about Ava."

Her brows came together. She looked mystified. "Because . . ."

"In connection with an appraisal, I need more information about Ava."

"I read about your appraising their Tiffany lamp. It's all so horrible."

"Very. That's why I'm asking about her."

"I'm sick about her death."

"What was she like?"

"She was kind. Intelligent. Calm."

"How did she come to join the book club?"

"I knew her from high school, of course. We were best buds for a while; then we drifted apart the way you do. I happened to be working at the checkout desk when she borrowed a stack of travel guides to South Africa, and we got talking. We just picked up where we left off. I was so glad to reconnect with her. Then, of course, she'd traveled all over, and she loved the idea of the book club. She was so knowledgeable and articulate, I invited her to sit in with us a couple of times." The corners of Diane's mouth turned up, a sort-of smile. "Ava's stories brought the places we read about to life. We were lucky to have her. When one of our members retired and moved south, I asked her to join. Knowing her schedule, I didn't think she'd be able to fit us in, but she did."

"When did you last see her?"

"Just before she left for Europe. She came in for some books to take on the trip. I was surprised by one of her picks. Are you familiar with *The Walking Tour*? By Kathryn

Davis? A woman disappears while on a walking tour in Wales. I thought it was an odd choice for someone about to embark on a walking tour in Wales."

"I wonder if she was thinking about disappearing," I said.

"I hadn't thought of that."

"That day, did she seem the same as always?"

"I guess. She was excited about her trip and looking forward to hosting our next get-together. Nothing struck me as off."

"Was she happy?"

"Is anyone?"

Yes, I thought. *Lots of people.*

"Was Ava less happy than most people?" I asked.

Diane eased a metal paper clip out of a magnetic holder on her desk. She unfolded the smaller section, then folded it back in. Out and in. Out and in.

"I think she had her struggles," she said.

"With Edwin?"

"There was quite an age difference between them."

"Had Ava fallen in love with a younger man?"

"Whoa! Where did that come from?"

"I was just reacting to your comment about their age difference. It happens."

"I guess . . . but I have no reason to think Ava was anything but loyal to Edwin. All I meant was . . . well . . . as you say, you never know, and Ava was a beautiful woman." She tossed the paper clip aside. "Tell me again how these questions relate to your appraisal?"

I smiled back. "Fair question. I can't go into details except to say that someone seems to be taking advantage of me — and the Towsons. It's important that I discover what happened regarding the lamp. I'm sorry I can't be more open."

"Ava was a friend. Anything I can do to help, I will."

"Thank you. Did you know Edwin, too?"

"I met him a couple of times when Ava was hosting."

"What do you think of him?"

"I don't know him well enough to venture an opinion. I can only go by what Ava told us. She had expressed some discontent in the last few months. She said that Edwin was driving her crazy, always wanting to know where she was, hounding her about little things. Ava never said anything negative about him, but I could tell that beneath her lighthearted grumbles, something darker was going on." She eased another paper clip from the container and began the unfolding process. "I hate to talk about other people's business."

"Me, too. You're not repeating rumors for no reason or to stir up trouble, though. You're helping me figure out what is going on."

"No mean-girl snark?" she asked with a crooked smile.

"None."

"To tell you the truth, I got the impression Ava was afraid of Edwin." She raised a hand, anticipating my next question. "I can't tell you anything in particular. She never confided in me. There was a tension that came over her when his name came up. Not anger. Apprehension. As if she felt the need to watch her back." Diane leaned forward and rested her elbows on the desk. "May I ask you something?"

"Of course."

"I read in the *Seacoast Star* that Edwin was at work — on July Fourth. Does that sound like a loving husband to you?"

I thought of all the Sundays and holidays Ty worked. I didn't like it, but I didn't resent it, and I never took it personally, any more than Ty resented it that I worked at our tag sale almost every Saturday.

"We can't know how Ava felt about Edwin's schedule," I said. "Lots of folks work off-hours."

"Maybe."

"Do you think there's any chance she was considering leaving him?"

She pressed her lips together for a moment. "Yes. I'm sad to say I do think she'd reached that point. I don't know whether she would have had the courage, though. While I did have a strong sense that she was afraid of him, I also had a sense she was afraid of what he might do if she tried to leave him."

I shook my head and clucked sympathetically. I couldn't think of anything else to ask, so I stood and thanked her. She walked me out, chatting about the storm.

My mind was in a whirl. Edwin's alibi was apparently imperfect, and Diane, who seemed to be a straight shooter, brought to mind something my dad always said. No matter what you think you know about a couple's relationship, you're probably wrong. You can't ever know what goes on behind closed doors.

CHAPTER FOURTEEN

The rain started slowly, a misty drizzle — mizzle, my mom used to call it. I ran for my car, my stomach rumbling. I was starving. While I waited for the air-conditioning to kick in, I checked my messages.

Wes had texted Jean's cell phone number, adding: *Why?*

I texted back: *Thx.* Wes would be mega-irritated with me, but I didn't want to take the time to explain now. If I connected with Jean and got anything Wes could use, all would be forgiven.

I called Jean's cell. After six rings, her voice mail kicked in. I didn't leave a message.

"Grrr," I said, frustrated. "Oh, well. Talking to Jean today is clearly not meant to be."

I was backing up, preparing to head back to work, when a call came in. I didn't recognize the number, but from the 603 area code, I could tell it was local. I answered with my usual "This is Josie!" greeting.

A woman's voice asked, "Josie Prescott?"

"Yes. Who is this, please?"

"Mr. Towson's executive assistant. Hold, please, for Mr. Towson."

Her tone indicated she wasn't used to anyone declining to hold for Mr. Towson.

Half a minute later, he was on the line.

"I'm glad I got you," he said. "Any chance you're available for a private chat?"

"Sure," I said, my curiosity meter whipping onto high alert. I glanced at the dash clock. It read 1:45. "Now?"

We settled on two thirty, at his company.

As I ate a premade chopped salad from a local deli, I tried to imagine what Edwin was feeling. Grief-stricken. Stunned. Confounded. Horrified. Desperate to know the truth. Terrified of the truth. All of the above. If he'd killed her, add panicked. The windows fogged up, and I toggled to DEFROST.

Before heading out to Towson's, I opened up a browser on my phone, navigated to the *Seacoast Star*'s Web site, and read Wes's latest update. The police, he wrote, had shown my sketch to everyone they could think of. They started with the couple's neighbors and staff — both Edwin's employees at Towson's, and Ava's domestic workers, including Tori Andrews, the housekeeper; Sonny Russo, the handyman/ gardener; and Merry Wagner, the dog walker. They moved on to members of the Rocky Point Hospital fund-raising committee where Ava volunteered, her high school reunion committee, and the gourmet grocery store, wine shop, and butcher where she shopped. They even ran it by all Ava's doctors and their staffs. No one expressed even a glimmer of recognition. No one.

As I tossed the empty salad bowl into the trash bin, an unwelcome thought came to me. If Edwin had killed Ava, he hadn't asked to see me to discover what I might know that could help him find answers or manage his grief. He was interested in learning if I knew anything that made me a threat.

The Towson Company corporate headquarters was housed in a contemporary stone structure on Ocean Avenue. I parked in a visitor spot. The double-wide front doors were fashioned from cedar and stained a rich cordovan. The door pulls were large hammered-iron rectangles. I ran through the drizzle to the entry, fluffed my hair to try to counteract the humidity and dampness, and climbed the stairs to the first floor.

A young woman, possibly right out of high school, smiled as I stepped into the reception area. She had straight, strawberry blond hair and round blue-framed glasses. Her desk was made of teak. A brass tented sign read JUDI DAVIDSON. A small American flag was attached to the top of her monitor. The reception area was designed to impress. The muted brick red and midnight blue Oriental carpet was plush. The indirect lighting was diffuse and free of glare. The art was modern, from the Abstract Expressionism school. A wall of windows to Judi's right offered a dazzling view of the ocean.

"With this view," I said, "I'd never get any work done."

She giggled. "Work? No one works around here."

I smiled. "I don't believe you." I stepped forward. "I'm Josie Prescott. Mr. Towson is expecting me."

She called someone and passed along my message, listened for a moment, then told me it would only be a minute or two.

I thanked her and walked to what looked like a Willem de Kooning, the red and gold hues similar to his *Woman V*. Another painting appeared to be a Franz Kline *Nijinsky*, the dancer's cherry red eyes glowing like the devil's. A third canvas featured a deceptively simple red line running vertically down a narrow bone-colored canvas. The image was similar to Barnett Newman's *The Wild.* If they were genuine, and I had every reason to suppose they were, I was looking at more than a hundred million dollars' worth of art.

I crossed the lobby to the window wall. The view was awe-inspiring. On a sunny day, I bet you could see clear to Portugal. The rain was still more mist than water, but I could tell a major storm was coming. The sky had darkened to a solid Payne's gray, and the ocean seethed with tumultuous frenzy.

A woman called my name, and I turned toward her. She was tall, maybe five-nine, and elegant. She wore a navy blue cowl-neck dress with a skinny black leather belt and matching pumps. Her golden blond hair was styled in an old-fashioned chignon.

"I'm Miranda Dowle, Mr. Towson's executive assistant. We spoke earlier. He's just finishing a video call to London and asked me to get you settled in his office." She opened the door and waved me in.

Edwin's office was big enough for badminton.

"Would you like a cup of coffee?" she

asked. "Some water? Anything?"

"Thank you, no. I'm good."

Miranda left me, and I settled into a sensible blue upholstered chair at the far end of the oversized oak desk. Nice but unremarkable nineteenth-century British landscapes hung on the walls. One depicting a thatched cottage near a pond was reminiscent of Robert Gallon. We'd sold one of his landscapes not long ago for $4,800. Another painting showed cattle grazing near a lake. I could just make out the signature: D. Sherrin. Daniel Sherrin's paintings routinely sold for around $3,500.

Edwin strode into the room like a man on a mission. I stood and extended my hand for a shake. His grip was firm, his shake practiced. He wore a gray suit, crisp white shirt, and red tie, the uniform of his profession. I was still in my sundress, and still damp from the oppressive humidity and light rain. I felt massively underdressed.

"Thank you for coming," he said, walking behind his desk.

"My pleasure. I'm terribly sorry for your loss."

He acknowledged my comment with one quick nod. "Have a seat."

He waited for me to sit, then took his place behind his desk. He leaned forward, his hands clasped tightly together, resting on an old-style desk blotter. He stared at them for a moment, then raised his eyes to mine.

"You didn't know my wife."

"No."

"I thought she was an angel."

I couldn't think of anything to say, so I stayed silent.

"I haven't cooked for myself in nine years. Can you imagine? Nine years. That's how long we were married. Ava handled everything. The bulb in my bedside lamp went out yesterday, and it took me half an hour to find a spare. Never was there a dirty dish in the sink. I didn't even know the housekeeper's name or how much we paid her. I don't like feeling helpless." He resumed studying his hands. "I left a note on the kitchen counter asking the housekeeper to call me. She said she could help with the grocery shopping and would even cook a little something for me." He closed his eyes for a moment. When he opened them again, he pinned me with his gaze. "I'm hoping you can help me understand what happened. This man you talked to. The police told me he recounted what he claimed was my family history."

"I know all about your Grandma Ruby

and how she found the Tiffany lamp in a trunk in her mother's attic."

"How could he know that? How could he possibly know that?"

"He's either someone you know well or he's associated with someone you know well."

He shook his head. "No one knows me well. Even Ava didn't know —" He broke off midsentence. His gaze became distant, his demeanor introspective. I wondered what had come into his mind.

"You've thought of something," I said, hoping he'd tell me.

He shifted his eyes back to mine. "Not thought of, exactly. That happened last night, while I wasn't sleeping. What I realized just now is that I'm tired of keeping secrets. Ava asked about Grandma Ruby a month or so before we left for Europe. She knew of her, of course, but we'd never talked about my family much beyond the basic facts." He looked down at his hands again. "I was flattered. We'd been having a little trouble in our marriage. I thought her interest was a sign that she was trying her best to make things better."

"Maybe it was."

He shook his head, and when he raised his eyes, I saw the determined glare of an avenger. Edwin would make a fearsome enemy.

"Wouldn't it be nice to think so. The only explanation that accounts for Ava's behavior is that she was planning to leave me — and had been for some time. That's what I realized overnight." He crossed his arms and raised his chin, a gladiator ready for battle. "She intended to sell the Tiffany lamp to fund her new life. She saw your TV show, and it got her wondering whether the lamp was real. In order to sell the lamp, she needed an appraisal, and in order to get an appraisal, she needed to be able to recount the lamp's history."

He folded his lips together until they formed a long, thin, angry line.

"Maybe someone overheard you telling her about it," I said.

"Or maybe she told someone. A lover."

"I'm sorry. I didn't know."

"I don't know, either. I'm speculating. Ava got someone to pretend to be her so she could keep an eye on me and make certain I didn't interfere. Damn her." He slapped his desk. "She had to have a reason to leave. We weren't unhappy. At least . . . I wasn't unhappy." He raised a hand, stopping himself. Edwin, I suspected, wasn't a man often given to emotional displays. "That's neither here nor there, but it brings me to the primary reason I asked to see you. I'm moving to London. We lived here in Rocky Point because Ava wanted to be near her sister. Rocky Point means nothing to me. I want to sell the Tiffany lamp. I never liked it as much as Ava did, and given the situation, it will only represent deceit and failure going forward. I've researched you and your company. You're supposed to be the best. Are you?"

"Yes."

"Will you take the lamp on consignment?"

My pulse quickened. It would be unseemly to celebrate Edwin's loss and disillusionment with a happy dance, so I kept my feet firmly planted, my tone even, and my expression neutral.

"Of course," I said.

"Good. Let's do it."

While I texted Gretchen to prepare the consignment agreement, Edwin had Miranda call Merry to see if she was around and could let me in, then lock up after I'd left with the Tiffany lamp. When the two-page contract arrived, Edwin printed it out and read it slowly, then read it again, flipping back from page two to page one, reviewing the wording in some earlier paragraph.

"Is there any wiggle room on your commission?" he asked.

"No," I said. "My fee structure rewards us for developing a marketing plan that results in the highest possible sales price. If you make more, we make more."

"Fair enough," he said. He signed with a flourish.

His phone rang. Miranda had arranged with Merry to meet me at the house in thirty minutes. Edwin and I shook hands, and I left.

As I sprinted through the now lashing rain to my car, I considered the possibility that Ava was having an affair. If so, it seemed likely that her lover was the man who'd impersonated Edwin on the phone, but the question remained — who was the fake Ava? Someone her lover had deputized? Perhaps Ava hadn't even known the woman's identity. Ignorance in the face of accusations could be a powerful defense. Had Ava planned out the scheme so thoroughly that she had even prepared for getting caught?

Had her lover killed her? Had the fake Ava?

What drove her to the affair in the first place, if she'd been having one? Had she been motivated by loneliness? Lust? Love? Revenge?

Or was she motivated by bald avarice? If Ava needed a man to pretend to be her husband in order to sell the Tiffany lamp without fielding awkward questions about its pedigree, she might have negotiated a deal that satisfied both parties. She got a willing partner. He got her body. Merely thinking such a sordid thought made me sad, and to make matters worse, I knew that idle speculation didn't get me any closer to understanding what was going on. Was Ava simply greedy — or desperate?

CHAPTER FIFTEEN

As I latched my seat belt, a crack of thunder startled me.

"Wow," I exclaimed, looking up through the windshield at the pewter sky.

Jagged lines of lightning ran along the shoreline. The storm was blowing in from the east. Within seconds, hail began pelting the roof and hood, and gossamer fog rolled in off the ocean.

I called Cara and arranged for Eric to meet me at the Towson house with packing material.

I sat for a few minutes watching the whitecaps leap along the high chop, thinking about how I could best market the Tiffany lamp. When it comes to selling high-end antiques for top dollar, buzz is key. You need to create a groundswell of excitement, the sooner the better. I scrolled through my photos and found a terrific one of the Towson lamp, the multihued wisteria aglow. I e-mailed it to Wes, then called him. He answered on the first ring.

"Did you reach Jean?" he asked as soon as he realized it was me, skipping hello and how are you, as always.

"No, just her voice mail. Have you spoken to her?"

"No," he said, sounding chagrined. "Her condo's like a fortress."

"With a moat — the pond."

"You were there?" he asked, his tone implying I'd gone rogue.

"I told you. I want to talk to her."

"When you do, I'm your first call, all right?"

Wes was half steamroller. Luckily for our relationship, the other half was adorable kid brother.

"So let me tell you why I called," I said, avoiding a commitment. "You know how I appraised the Towson Tiffany lamp?"

"Sure. It's worth megabuckos."

"I'm giving you a heads-up. Edwin Towson is selling it. I'm handling the sale. I e-mailed you a photo. You can announce all that, including my involvement, but only if you attribute it to an anonymous source in the antiques world."

"Why?" Wes whined. "I need to quote you."

147

Give Wes an inch and he wants a football stadium. "It's better this way. You're making a hush-hush announcement that will rock the art and antiques world. All the big magazines, including *Antiques Insights,* will be annoyed, to say the least, that you scooped them. No joke, Wes. This is a big deal. Be prepared to field dozens of calls from reporters who are über-annoyed."

"Really?" he asked, sounding skeptical. "If you say so. When will the sale be?"

"I don't know. I'm picking up the lamp today. Now. Edwin is moving to London, soon, I think, and he wants it gone. It takes time to organize a sale like this. Three months at least. Remember — you didn't get this from me. Promise?"

"Jeesh, Josie! I already said okay. What else you got?"

"Nothing."

"Catch ya later!" he said.

I touched the END CALL button, smiling to myself. I checked messages. Nothing urgent. My accountant wanted to discuss his quarterly report, all good news, he said. Sasha had sent an e-mail about the marbles. Nothing specific yet, but the early signs looked good. She was scheduled to talk to a man named Franklin Colby, based in Oklahoma City. He was, by all accounts, the top-dog marble man. Ty had left a sweet I-love-you message.

I called Ty and said, "We're now officially playing phone tag. Let's set a phone date. I want to chat, just like we would if you were home." I added an "I love you" and hung up, holding the phone to my chest for a moment, keeping him close.

The rain was steady, pounding, the ocean, a deadly vortex. The distant horizon was nearly black. Slashes of lightning shot into the water, sending ten-foot sprays exploding upward. There was anger in the air.

I clicked open the *Seacoast Star*'s Web site. Wes had exceeded my expectations. His article was laced with innuendo about his mysterious source, describing the person as a high-ranking, world-class expert. I blushed. He referred to Edwin Towson as one of the world's leading financiers who was downsizing in anticipation of his move to London. He added that I was refusing to confirm the story — thank you, Wes — but his source told him I was picking up the lamp today. If I knew anything about people, gossip would soon be rocketing through the art, antiques, and financial worlds. I refreshed the site. Already there were three comments, two people wondering how much the lamp would sell for and one asking Wes how he — a potential buyer — could get more information. Buzz.

I turned the wipers to high and set off. The rain swept across the windshield, and I could only see a few feet in front of me.

While I waited at the light to make the turn from Islip Street into Garnet Cove, a flash of silver from inside the fog-and-rain-shrouded woods caught my eye. I leaned in closer to the window, trying to see through the rivulets of water running down the glass, hoping to discern a shape, a better sense of color, anything to explain the unexpected glint. The light changed. It was probably nothing. I turned into the community.

I was the first to arrive, and I parked at the curb. Ava's Mercedes was in the same place as last time, taking up the left side of the driveway, leaving the right side available for Eric. I wiggled my umbrella out from the passenger-door cubbyhole and stepped out into the rain. The humidity was, if anything, worse. It was a good day to be inside. When I reached the front door, I stood under the overhang, my umbrella dripping by my side.

Sylvia's tomato plants looked content. My dad always said that the secret to tomatoes is to water them every day, even when it rains. I wouldn't be the least bit surprised to see Sylvia come outside with a hose in her hand.

A sharp muted crack startled me, and I whirled, trying to locate the source. An engine revved somewhere down the street. *A car backfiring,* I thought. Another bang, this one louder, closer. *Kids shooting off firecrackers left over from the Fourth.* A third blast hit a window frame a foot from where I stood, splintering the wood. I gasped as the truth dawned on me — someone was shooting at me.

I dropped my umbrella and tote bag and squatted, trying to make myself small.

The shooter had to be in the forest, which meant there was only one way out — I had to reach Sylvia's house, a sanctuary if she was home, a barricade if she wasn't.

If I could survive the run across open lawn.

In one motion, I stood, grasped the cold, wet, metal handrail, and catapulted myself into the garden, wrenching my knee as I landed on sodden mulch. The next shot shattered a brick inches from my head, and chunks of masonry rained down on me. I scooted along the perimeter of the house, trouncing the phlox, scraping my hands and knees on twigs and gravel, ignoring the stabbing pain that radiated from my knee to my calf, and had almost made it to the end of the house when I heard an engine. I turned to look, terrified the shooter had called for backup.

My company's van slid into view. Eric, driving directly into the line of fire.

Before I could warn him, another shot landed in the bricks over my head.

"Run!" I yelled. "Eric! Run!"

Tears of frustration blurred my vision. No way could he hear me through the unremitting rain.

The van slowed, then stopped. Eric was peering through the driver's window. When he spotted me, he gawked. I could only imagine what I looked like, a drowned rat.

I risked sitting up a bit and flapped my hand like a third-base coach signaling the runner to go for it, to try to make it home. *Please, God,* I thought as I scampered away, *keep Eric safe.* Our van backed up, tires screeching. Another shot sounded, this one farther away. Glass shattered.

I pushed through one of the forsythia bushes that ran along the property line, my arms out straight, hands pressed together, as if I were about to dive. Spiky bits on the branches tore at my arms and neck. A siren sounded, then another, almost in sync, but not quite. I stopped moving, using the bush as cover. Help was on the way. The rain pummeled me. The sirens' faint whine became a blaring keen, then abruptly stopped.

The cavalry had arrived, and I was safe.

CHAPTER SIXTEEN

"Nothing's broken. I'm fine," I told Ty, grating nutmeg into simmering squash soup. I wedged the phone between my ear and my shoulder. "I'm making soup."

"I don't like that answer. How are you really feeling?"

I placed the wooden spoon on a little plate near the soup pot and glanced at Zoë, sitting on the bench that ran under my kitchen window, her eyes clouded with fear. I slid onto the cushion beside her.

"The truth?" I asked, leaning my head against Zoë's shoulder for a moment. "A little battered."

"Zoë's there, right?"

"Yup. With the kids, who are watching yet another zombie movie as we speak. This one is animated."

"I know you, Josie. You joke to reassure the people who love you that you're okay."

"Truly, I'm okay," I said.

"Put me on speaker."

I tapped the button. "Ty?"

"I'm here. Can you hear me, Zoë?"

"Loud and clear," she said.

"How does Josie look?"

"Rumpled and a little banged up. But she's clean. Before, she looked like she got caught in a downpour, then rolled around in mud-covered twigs and rocks and such."

"Guess why?" I interjected.

"Because you got caught in a downpour and rolled in mud-covered twigs and rocks and such?" Ty asked, sounding less worried.

"Yes." I laughed. "I'm shocked that Zoë didn't describe me as a hottie-tottie wrapped in a soft pink chenille robe. Nothing was hurt except the house, but the shooter got away. Three bricks. One window. And one window frame. Eric is my hero. He got out of Dodge and called the cops. They were there in like a minute. Two, tops. Even Merry is fine. Eric saw her walking up and chased her away."

"Who shot at you?" Ty asked.

"I don't know."

"How many shots were there?"

"Five, I think. Maybe six."

"Spaced how far apart?" he asked.

"Ellis asked me that." I closed my eyes for a moment, trying again to recall, but I couldn't. All I remembered was the fear and the dank, musty smell of the soaked mulch and sticky mud. And the rage. I was growing angrier by the minute. "I don't know."

"Someone shot at you, Josie. It's got to be related to the Towsons, either the lamp or the murder. Did anything out of the ordinary happen in the last day or so? I mean, obviously, this whole situation with Ava's murder is out of the ordinary — but what got someone jumpy *now*?"

I sat up with a start. "Oh, my God! Edwin decided to sell the Tiffany lamp today. Wes publicized it. He wrote that I'd be picking it up immediately. I came along and interrupted the robbery. They shot at me to give themselves time to get it. I have to check if Eric went back for it, if it's safe. I'll call you back as soon as I know something."

"What can I do?" Zoë asked as soon as I ended the call.

"Stir the soup," I said, scrolling through my contacts until I got to Eric's home number. Ten seconds later, I had the answer. The police questioned him at the scene, then sent him home.

"The police said I couldn't go inside," he said. "I'm sorry."

"You have nothing to be sorry about. I just needed to check. Don't worry, Eric."

I called Edwin, and he answered with a curt "Towson."

"I'm checking on the lamp." I explained my concern, that I might have interrupted a burglary. "Are you home?"

"Yes. Are you all right?"

"Yes. Just a little dinged up. Can you see if the lamp is there?"

"I'm walking to the study now. That noise you hear in the background is Sonny, the fellow who helps around the house, boarding up the broken window."

"Did anything get ruined with the rain pouring in?"

"No. Luckily it was just a pane in the kitchen door, so only the floor got wet. I'm in the study . . . The lamp is here."

I fell back against the cushions and breathed. "Thank goodness. If it's all right, Edwin, I'd like to send someone to pick it up now. I'll feel better when it's in our safe."

"Good. I decided after you left that I'm moving into a hotel. There's no reason why I should stay here, but I'll wait for whoever you send."

I tried the office, thinking I might reach Fred. It was only seven, and Fred was a night owl, often coming in close to noon and working until eight or nine, or even later. He often took time off in the late afternoon to have an early dinner with his girlfriend, Suzanne. She was the general manager of my favorite restaurant, the Blue Dolphin, so her late-night hours matched Fred's. If we had an early morning appraisal, Fred mainlined coffee.

Fred wasn't there. I tried his cell phone, but he didn't answer. I called Sasha, too, but her phone went to voice mail as well. I called Eric back.

I apologized for bothering him and explained why I was calling. He said he'd go to the Towson house right away, stopping at the office for packing materials.

I called Edwin back and told him Eric was on his way to pick up the lamp.

"That's fine. In case you need me, I'll be at the Austin Arms until I leave for London."

"You're moving out permanently?"

"Yes. I'll be glad to be out of here. The house is riddled with ugliness and lies."

"I'm sorry about all your trouble."

"Thank you. It's been quite a week. I'll be glad when the killer and shooter are caught and the house is sold and I'm settled in London. I need to decide what I want to keep. Not much. Some of the books in the study have sentimental value for me. My dad gave them to me as gifts. Ava chose the furnishings. Do you buy household goods?"

"Yes. We can buy everything outright or take it on consignment."

"I'll be in touch in a week or two about selling the household furnishings," Edwin said.

"And I'll be in touch about the lamp."

Why now? I thought as I placed the handset in the cradle. That's what Ty had wanted to know. The Tiffany lamp had been in the news since Ava's murder. If someone wanted to steal it, they'd had days to do so. Why hadn't they?

Thursday morning, I slept late and awakened stiff. I e-mailed Cara that I'd be in by noon, then decided to treat myself to a hot bath and a big breakfast, eggs Benedict, my favorite. I'd texted Ty before I went to bed, then crashed, and I'd awakened to an I-love-you reply text. Lying in orange-blossom suds, with my head resting on my blue terrycloth-covered waterproof pillow, I tried to imagine what Ava's life had been like. From all reports, she was not in any way a bubblehead. She read literary novels. She went on walking tours in historic districts. She had decorated her home with taste and refinement. I wanted to know more about her, and that meant talking to Jean. As soon as I was dressed, I called both numbers I had for her, without luck. I left a simple message, just giving my name and number.

Ellis called while I was poaching eggs.

"We've checked surveillance cameras everywhere around Garnet Cove," he said. "There are eighteen attached to private houses, but their aim is on the owners' driveways and property, so the only footage we might garner is a car passing by. We tracked you and Eric as you passed by three houses, but no one else. Garrison Bank has two, covering their parking lot and part of Islip Street, but nothing rang a bell. The community maintains two as well, one at each of the turn-ins to the property. No unexplained vehicles were parked anywhere near either entrance to Garnet Cove, at least not within the cameras' range."

"I didn't know there were two entrances," I said.

"The one off Islip and another off Hastings."

"Hastings . . . that's that little road off Ocean, right?" I asked, picturing the turnoff. Just before the Portsmouth line, Ocean Avenue drifted inland, wrapping around a no-man's-land of craggy cliffs and desolate stretches of seaweed-strewn rocky shoreline until it merged with Route 1. A mile farther on, it broke off again, wending its way back to the coast. At the point where Ocean first turned inland, a secondary road snaked along the coast for a quarter mile or so before dead-ending at a rocky precipice. That was Hastings, the shortest road in Rocky Point. The road had been cut into the stone by a real estate developer with big dreams of creating another condo community like Garnet Cove, but the land won. The developer learned the hard way that it was too expensive and time-consuming to tame the wild coast. "What's the point of looking at camera footage? Anyone trying to sneak in would know enough not to park near an entrance. You could park anywhere along the perimeter and climb over the stone wall. What is it? Three feet high?"

"About that. And once you're over the wall, you've got perfect cover. You're surrounded by thick woods and five feet from the hiking path."

"What hiking path?" I asked.

"It runs through the woods surrounding Garnet Cove."

"The flash I saw — the shooter had a gun in his hand. He was on the hiking path."

"Who carries a gun in the rain?" Ellis asked.

I looked out my window. The rain had

stopped overnight, and pale sunlight dappled the patio. The thermometer mounted to the window frame read 62.

"Someone about to use it."

Between the bath, my hearty breakfast, and the ibuprofen, I was feeling almost as good as new, or at least mobile enough to work. I got into the office earlier than I'd expected and greeted everyone.

Fred pushed up his glasses. "I have news."

"I love news. News is progress."

"Aunt Louise worked for *News and Views* for more than twenty years." He leaned back and grinned. "They're old-school. They have an archivist on staff."

I slid into a guest chair. "Do they, now?"

"She and I have become pals. Her name is Karla. There's thousands of photos taken during Aunt Louise's tenure showing her at various parties, meetings, and events. Karla is going through them, trying to identify the men in the pictures."

"That sounds impossible."

"She's loving it."

"Amazing." I turned to Cara and asked if anything demanded my attention. She said no, so I headed straight for the safe.

Hank came running up, mewling and dragging a rainbow-colored felt banner, wanting to play. The banner was attached to a long clear plastic wand. To see Hank balance the wand in his mouth, carefully navigating his way around obstacles, the banner trailing behind him, was a sight to behold. He dropped the banner at my feet, expecting me to hurl it as far as I could.

"Hi, baby," I said. "Not now, Hank. Later. I promise."

He mewed.

"I know, baby, I know. It's not fair. You need someone to play with."

He nuzzled my leg, assuring me he understood.

I punched in my personal security code. When the green light appeared, I pressed my thumb against the fingerprint reader and waited for the click that told me I'd been cleared. I lugged open the heavy metal door. It wasn't usually so heavy. Yesterday's attack had taken a toll on me.

I logged out the lamp and carried it to a worktable near Hank's basket. I plugged it in and turned it on, ready to repeat the appraisal Fred and I had completed just days earlier. I booted up the computer and checked the records. Eric signed the lamp in at twenty after eight last night. Fred entered the safe at ten but didn't log anything in or out. No one had been in the safe yet today. I signed the lamp out to myself.

The barklike trunk was familiar, but the purple glass was less confetti-like than I recalled. The solder that held the glass in place was more worn than I remembered. On the inside of the shade, I saw a wink of copper and something that might be wax.

My heart plunged to my knees.

In making the lampshades, Tiffany's artisans used all three materials, solder, copper, and beeswax, and after a hundred years, wear and dryness were the norm; however, the wear pattern here was not the same. I lifted the lamp high above my head and used my small flashlight to examine the bottom. The stamp read TIFFANY.

"Oh, no," I whispered.

I lowered the lamp to the table and stared at the delicate glass shade, the muted lavender and lilac wisteria blossoms, the pale and dark green leaves, the brown branches. I switched off the light, walked to the green nubby carpet that marked Hank's territory, eased myself down to the ground, and leaned back against the cold concrete wall. I stretched my legs out straight and kept my eyes on the lamp. Hank climbed onto my lap and curled up. I stroked his cheek, and he started purring. I concentrated on my breathing, and just like always, crisis-calm came over me. I was good in an emergency, able to focus with absolute clarity. Once a crisis passed, I fell apart, at least a little, but that was something I'd worry about later. Now, I had to navigate the disaster confronting me.

Eric hadn't videotaped the Tiffany lamp before removing it from the Towson house, which meant there was no way to prove the lamp I was staring at was the same one Eric had packed up. If Edwin sued, he'd win. I considered my options, none of them appealing, some of them appalling.

I scooched Hank into his basket and got myself upright. He grumbled. I used the computer on the closest worktable to bring up the lamp's record, then called Fred and asked him to join me.

"What's up?" Fred asked, unaware of the quagmire looming in front of us.

"I need you to do a full appraisal on this lamp. It's the one Eric brought in from the Towson house."

Fred shot it a glance. "What's the matter?"

"I want to ensure we have an unbroken chain of possession," I said, ignoring his question. "When you check the computer file, you'll see that he placed it in the safe and entered it into our log. I entered the safe and checked it out just now. If necessary, we can confirm this with the security cameras." I typed into the computer. "I'm now signing it over to you."

Fred tapped the screen, activating his electronic signature. "Is there anything I should know?"

"No." I started up the spiral stairs that led to my private office, pausing halfway up I looked over my shoulder. "Hurry. Let me know the minute you determine anything. The second."

Fred, picking up on my gravitas, nodded solemnly.

I sat behind my desk and swiveled to face my window. The leaves on my old maple were as large as my hand. I wandered into my private bathroom and looked at the scratches on my face and neck. They were red and tender to the touch. I returned to my desk. I waited.

Three minutes later, I heard Fred bounding up the stairs, and I swiveled to face him.

"It's a fake," he said.

"What can you tell me about it?"

"It looks to be a good reproduction, probably mid-twentieth century, based on the age-appropriate patina and wear patterns. At a guess, it's worth about fifty thousand dollars."

"You entered the safe last night."

"Yeah. To check on the lamp."

"Is the lamp we're examining now the same one you looked at last night?"

Fred held my gaze, his eyes stony. I understood. I'd just asked him if he'd switched out the genuine Tiffany lamp for this nice fake. A vein in his neck throbbed.

"Yes."

"Okay. Find out everything you can about that lamp. Who made it. When. Who owned it. I'll work on figuring out who sold it during the last couple of months — and who they sold it to." Fred started off, then paused when I called his name. "I had to ask."

He met my gaze. "No, you didn't."

"You're right — you wouldn't work here if I couldn't trust you absolutely. But this is a legal issue."

His eyes softened a bit, and his shoulders lowered. "I know."

"It isn't Eric's fault. He didn't know he was supposed to video-record it. I shouldn't have sent him alone."

"Will you tell him?"

"No. He has no need to know. It will just upset him."

"You're right."

"One more thing — don't tell anyone. Not yet."

"Understood."

After Fred left, I sat and stared out the window, thinking it through. I'd interrupted a burglary, all right, but they weren't after the genuine Tiffany lamp. That one had been stolen earlier, probably immediately after my appraisal. This break-in was to prevent me from discovering they'd switched out the real lamp for a replica. Their plan was clear to me now. With any luck, Edwin, a man who didn't care about domestic issues, would never have noticed the difference, so the real lamp would never have been reported stolen. As soon as the thief learned I was picking up the lamp, the die was cast — the fake lamp had to be removed.

Anyone looking at me or talking to me would see a woman in complete control, but on the inside I was ready to explode, I was so angry.

CHAPTER SEVENTEEN

I called Ellis, and Cathy said he was unavailable.

"Tell him it's an emergency."

He came on the line.

"I have bad news," I said. "The Tiffany lamp we took from the Towsons' house yesterday is a fake. Sometime between the time I returned the real lamp and yesterday, someone pulled off a switch."

Ellis didn't respond right away. I could hear him breathing. I could hear him thinking.

"How?" he asked, his tone as unperturbed as always.

"I don't know, but I guarantee you, I'm going to find out."

"Don't do anything stupid."

I chortled, one unamused chuckle. "I'm done being stupid."

I hung up, sat, and stewed.

■ ■ ■ ■

Ten minutes later, I knew my next step.

Edwin didn't answer his cell phone, and Judi, Towson's receptionist, told me he was unavailable, so I called Miranda Dowle, his assistant, explaining that I needed to see him urgently, that it would only take five or ten minutes, and she squeezed me in. I considered asking my lawyer, Max Bixby, to join the meeting, but didn't. There would be time enough for lawyers if it ever came to that.

I arrived at Edwin's company to find Judi behind the reception desk. She greeted me like an old friend.

"I'm so glad it worked out that you can meet with Mr. Towson."

I smiled as best I could. I wasn't in a smiling mood. "Thanks, Judi. Me, too."

"Yesterday when you were here it was pouring," she said, "and you still loved the view. What do you think now?"

I turned to face the ocean. Sun-sparked diamonds skipped along the sapphire water with the same hop-and-a-jump motion as the flat rocks I'd flicked across the ocean surface when I was a kid. Five skips was my record. The tide ebbed, then flowed, like a

170

gently rocking cradle.

"It's stunning," I said.

"Josie?" Miranda said, her tone both refined and welcoming. She stood at the entry to the office wing.

I waved at Judi as I passed. Miranda led the way into Edwin's office. He was on the phone. I took the same chair as before.

"Coffee?" Miranda whispered.

"No, thanks," I whispered back.

She left.

"Do it," Edwin said in a tone that made ice seem warm. "Do it now."

He hung up and looked at me, and just like that, his mood shifted. "What can I do to help?"

"I'm the bearer of bad news. Someone switched out the Tiffany lamp. The one I picked up yesterday is a fake."

His gaze became electrified, dangerous. "You're certain?"

"Yes. It's a good reproduction, probably from the mid-twentieth century, worth about fifty thousand dollars."

"Okay, then. I have the confirmation I didn't want about how Ava planned to support herself. She stole the lamp, probably with help from her bitch-queen sister. Can you get it back?"

"Maybe. I hope so. If she sold it to a

reputable dealer, I'll find it by the end of the day. If it was a private sale or if she sold it to someone who knew it was stolen, it will be harder to locate. The FBI has a team dedicated to stolen art and artifacts. We may need to bring them in."

"I hope not. That kind of notoriety is good for no one. Let me think about it before you report it stolen."

"I already have. Because of the lamp's possible connection to Ava's murder, I had to alert the local police," I said.

"Understood." He pinched his lips together and swiveled toward the window, fixing his gaze on the distant horizon.

"I recommend that you let me report it as stolen, to alert dealers."

"Bad publicity."

"We can do it anonymously. It's done all the time. No one wants to admit to losing a valuable object."

He swung back to face me. "Think of all the stolen objects that never turn up. I figure they're in the hands of Colombian drug lords or oil sheikhs, don't you? There's no point in reporting it stolen if the thief is out of reach."

"Whoever stole your lamp isn't a professional, which means they have no way to reach a Colombian drug lord or oil sheikh.

172

It's someone close to you, or someone who was close to Ava. They expect to get more than a million dollars. Let's say they get lucky and find a fence with deep pockets. On the black market, they might get half a million — tops. I think they'd be stunned at that low offer and walk out to regroup."

"Jean."

"It's possible."

Edwin nodded slowly, listening well, thinking hard. "All right. Do it." His fingertips tapped on his desk for a moment; then he adjusted his position, leaning back. "If tracking the thief down requires cash, let me know. I want you to do everything you can to find out who's behind this — and to find the lamp — and I don't want you to consider the cost."

"Thank you."

Edwin stood up, so I did, too.

"There's one more thing," I said. "At some point, you might wonder whether I pulled a fast one. I want to assure you, I didn't."

"Of course not. You wouldn't be in business if you pulled fast ones. You'd be in jail. I bet you feel nearly as bad about this as I do."

I'd been braced for his condemnation and contempt, not empathy. The relief was physical. My knees shook for a moment. "Maybe more."

"Not possible. Close, I'll grant you. More — no way."

"We can leave it that we both feel awful."

"Catch the son of a bitch and I'll feel hunky-dory, and I bet you will, too."

"I'll do my best. Thank you for your confidence."

He nodded his dismissal, and I showed myself out.

I called to Hank as I crossed to the staircase that led to my office, and he sauntered in my direction.

"Do you want to keep me company while I work?" I asked.

He mewed and scampered up the steps. As soon as I got settled in my chair, he sprang into my lap, but he didn't settle down. He sat up and looked at me expectantly.

"I'm sorry, baby. I told you — I need to work."

He huffed and curled up.

I e-mailed Ellis:

Hi Ellis,

I spoke to Edwin about the theft. He's

eager to keep his name out of it.

I'll go ahead and post a call for sightings anonymously.

I'll list my name as the antiques contact and your name as the law enforcement contact.

If I hear anything, I'll let you know right away, and I hope you'll do the same for me.

Thanks, Ellis.

Best, Josie

I sent another e-mail to Fred, asking him to take care of the postings, then reached for my water bottle. Hank complained about the disruption.

"Sorry, baby," I said, stroking his back.

He settled down again, and I brought up *Antiques Insights'* online marketplace, the most respected outlet for private sales of high-end antiques in the country. Anyone able to afford the hefty fee could buy a listing, and the cost might be worth it since you saved the buyer's and seller's premiums that auction houses, including Prescott's, routinely charged. For objects that required complex marketing plans, you were usually better off going the conventional route, but if you had a low-ticket item that didn't require a certified appraisal, or if you knew potential buyers frequented the site and you had an appraisal in your pocket, it might be a smart way to go.

I entered "wisteria Tiffany lamp" in the advanced search field, and four ads popped up. Three touted high-quality reproductions; the fourth offered a genuine Tiffany lamp. The ad, which referenced an appraisal from an IAAA-certified professional, had been posted the day Ava was killed, then withdrawn a day later. I clicked through the various menus, trying and failing to find a way into the original listing. I did another search looking for replica Tiffany lamps sold in the last two months. None turned up. Progress of a sort. At least I knew one place where the thieves hadn't bought the fake lamp.

I called the customer service number listed on the banner that ran along the bottom of the Web page and got a perky young woman who explained they never released seller information when ads were withdrawn. I didn't bother to try to convince her. She was working off a script, and that was that. I thanked her and pressed the END

CALL button, releasing it a moment later to call a staff writer I knew at the magazine. Madge Garcia and I had worked together a few years back when the magazine selected Prescott's for inclusion in an article called "Five Small Antiques Auction Houses to Watch," still one of my greatest honors.

"*Antiques Insights*. Madge speaking."

"Madge! It's Josie. Josie Prescott. Long time no speak."

"Sheesh! No kidding, Josie, I was just thinking of you. I'm writing an article on vintage clothing from the forties, and I remembered you added a specialization a few years back, am I right?"*

"Yes, we bought out a shop. We have some beautiful pieces in stock now, an unbelievable Mainbocher pale pink satin gown. You know him, right? He horrified the world with his corset lacing up the back. The lacing on this one is black. Very sexy against the pale pink. We also have a color-block Bonnie Cashin day dress. It's fabulous. Suede, in muted fall colors." I laughed. "You can tell how much I love vintage fashion — but before I just keep rambling on . . . tell me, how can I help?"

"Those dresses sound to die for. I'm still

* Please see *Deadly Threads*.

in the planning stages, but I may call on you for tips on authentication."

"With pleasure, Madge — anytime."

"So what can I do for you?" Madge asked.

"I need to know who posted an online ad and then withdrew it."

"I'm sorry, Josie. I'm on the magazine side, and never the twain shall meet."

"Darn. Can you give me a name?"

"I really can't. I know some of the content folks over there, but no one on the business side. We don't commingle. We're not even in the same location — I'm in New York, as you well know, and they're in Phoenix. The two entities operate as separate businesses."

"I guess I didn't know that. Isn't that kind of inefficient? I mean, aren't you each reinventing the wheel?"

"Not really. They have access to all our material. They rejigger things to suit the different medium. We probably share all sorts of backroom stuff I'm unaware of, like accounting systems, mailing lists, that sort of thing."

"Interesting. Well, back to the drawing board for me. Thanks anyway, Madge."

She told me she wished she could help and promised to get in touch soon about the vintage clothing article, and I thanked her again. I was spending a lot of time thanking people for nothing. My next call was to Shelley, my pal from my days at Frisco's in New York.

Shelley and I met when we were both fresh out of college, thrilled to land jobs at Frisco's, one of the largest and most prestigious antiques auction houses in the world. During the dark days when I'd been shunned for doing the right thing — I was a whistle-blower, turning in my boss for his complicity in a price-fixing scheme — Shelley had been one of the few people who hadn't acted like I had a contagious disease. Now, a dozen years later, Shelley still worked for Frisco's and was still my friend. Calling her was a risk, though. She was intuitive and so clever in slyly drawing me out that I had to be constantly on guard lest I reveal more than I intended.

"Hey, pal," I said when I had her on the line. "I'm surprised you're at work. Shouldn't you be lounging in the Hamptons?"

"I should, shouldn't I? It's appalling to think my boss won't let me take the entire summer off."

I laughed. "Shocking."

"Are you calling me from New Hampshire? Has the snow melted yet?"

"You're going to have to come up here

sometime, Shelley. You've never seen anything so beautiful as New Hampshire in the
summer."

"You're such a card, Josie. I saw that
you're selling a Tiffany lamp. Lucky girl!"

"How did you possibly know that?" I
asked, thinking that luck had far less to do
with my success than hard work. "It got one
small mention in a local paper."

"We keep our eyes out. Is it as good as it
sounds?"

"Better. Listen, Shelley, I'm hoping you
can help me. I need some info on the QT."

"I smell a hot deal," Shelley said. "Count
me in."

"Not so hot. Who do you know at the
Antiques Insights Web site who'll give me
some semiconfidential information?"

"No one you don't know. You made the
mag cover, remember? 'Five Small Houses,'
but it was Prescott's they put on the cover.
Call your contact."

"She's on the editorial side of the magazine. I need someone on the business end
of the Web site."

"Why?"

I swiveled to face my window, stroking
Hank. A small dark blue bird was perched
on a nearby branch. I decided to fib. Since
what Shelley didn't know wouldn't hurt her,

I felt no guilt, not even a twinge.

"There's an ad I want to follow up on," I said, "but the sale is completed. You know what that means. They mark the object sold and remove all the details but the sales price."

"Don't you hate that? What's the object?"

Shelley reminded me of Wes, inquisitive and persistent. I turned back to my computer and hit the PAGE DOWN button until I found an object that had sold — a set of nineteenth-century jewel-encrusted gold dueling pistols.

"Some guns," I said, drawing out the words, hoping Shelley would conclude that my delayed and begrudging response indicated only that I didn't want to tell her but knew I had to in order to get her help, not that I was making it up on the fly. "Dueling pistols. I have a client who's hot for them. I want to see if I can convince the buyer to let them go."

I heard tapping in the background. "Got it. They're beauties, aren't they? Deadly beauty. Hmm, that would be a pretty good name for an auction, don't you think? 'Deadly Beauty.' Call Cormac McKenna at extension 1438. He goes by Mac. Nice guy. Knows everything. Use my name."

"Thanks, Shelley. You're the best."

We chatted for another few minutes about men and line dancing and beaches and bikinis and drinks with small umbrellas in them. Then I called Mac.

"I love Shelley," Mac said.

"Me, too. We've been friends since we both worked at Frisco's a thousand years ago."

"You're a Frisco's alum, are you? How long ago for real?"

"Twelve years. Hard for me to believe."

"Not so long. I've heard of Prescott's, of course. You have a wonderful reputation."

I smiled, gratified. "You just made my day. Thank you. So . . . Shelley tells me you might be able to help me." I explained my request — a client hot after the Tiffany wisteria lamp.

"We're not supposed to give out that info. Withdrawn is withdrawn."

"I understand, and if you can't, you can't. You'd be doing the seller a favor, though. Between you and me and the gatepost, my client is willing to pay top dollar. The worst that will happen is the seller says no. I won't ever say where I got his name."

"I'd hate to have someone miss out on an opportunity like this," he said.

I assured him again that I'd never tell

where I got the info, and he gave me the name — Orson Thompkins. The phone number started with a 603 area code, New Hampshire. The credit card used was a Visa in Thompkins's name. The address was 19 Sonille Road in Portsmouth.

"Portsmouth . . . that's close to you, isn't it? Hard to believe you're both from the same area."

"And my client is from Los Angeles," I said, hoping to deflect his attention. "Antiques is a cosmopolitan business."

"No question about that."

"Any idea why Mr. Thompkins withdrew the listing?"

"There's nothing in the notes section. Withdrawals are usually seller's remorse, though."

I agreed that was probably the reason, thanked him again, and ended the call.

No doubt the phone would prove to be a disposable, and the Visa card the kind you get when you lay out cash and can refill if you choose. The address, though, was a genuine lead. Time to reconnoiter.

CHAPTER EIGHTEEN

If Orson Thompkins had used his home address in the *Antiques Insights* listing, he lived in the left half of a two-family house around the corner from a small grocery store. The neighborhood was decent, but that was about all you could say about it. It was stable, homely, and working class.

I parked four houses down and across the street from the address. I had a clear view of the house, the driveway, and part of the backyard. The house looked empty. No lights were on. The shades were drawn. A rolled-up newspaper lay on the front porch.

Nothing happened. No one went in or out. I wondered if I could see inside through a back window. I scolded myself for the thought. Going to the house alone had been foolish to the point of recklessness. What if Thompkins had seen me drive up? Did I plan to confront him on my own? I knew better. Cornered rats jump high and strike fast. I was lucky no one was home. Five minutes after I arrived, I drove to the nearby grocery store, parked facing the street, and called Ellis.

I looked down at my hands. I was sitting in Ellis's office, avoiding meeting his unforgiving gaze. I didn't want to be here. I didn't want to talk to him. I wanted to handle this myself. Knowing that I couldn't, that I shouldn't, further soured my already bitter mood.

Ellis sat at his desk, waiting for me to speak.

"I promised you I wouldn't be stupid," I said.

"I remember."

"I think I know who stole the Tiffany lamp, and I went to his house. I didn't see him or anyone. I didn't do anything. But I know it was stupid."

"That sounds like an understatement. He might be a killer."

"I know."

"Tell me."

I did. When I finished, Ellis rolled a yellow pencil back and forth across his desk for a few seconds, thinking, then tossed it aside and raised his eyes to my face.

"Who told you he has the lamp?" Ellis asked.

"I can't tell you. I gave my word."

"This is a murder investigation."

"Do you think I don't know that?"

He stood up, unsmiling, patently annoyed. "From what I can tell, you think it's your own personal vendetta. I'm officially asking you to cooperate."

"I am. I came in voluntarily."

"With half a story."

I bit my tongue to stop myself from giving a flip answer. *That's better than no story,* I wanted to say, but I didn't. I pushed back my chair. "I did what I thought was right."

Ellis opened the door, shooing me out. "If you reconsider, you know where to find me."

Detective Brownley pulled into the lot as I reached my car. She smiled and waved, and I waved back. Guilt is a funny thing. I'd felt none in the face of Ellis's disapproval, but I felt it now. If Claire Brownley knew that I was refusing to reveal a source, she'd be as upset with me as Ellis. I was relieved to turn onto Ocean and drive away. I wasn't having second thoughts, but even so, censure from people you admire and respect weighs you down.

Back at my company, I ran upstairs to my private office. I paced from my desk to the display cabinet where I kept my rooster collection, and back again. Three laps in, Wes called.

"I've got a complete info-bomb," he said, his voice pulsating with excitement. "Two of them. Our dune. Ten minutes."

I glanced at the time display on my computer monitor. It showed 2:47. "I'll be there at three."

Wes's excitement was contagious, and I ran for the door.

CHAPTER NINETEEN

Wes was standing on the top of the dune with his back to me. He was wearing what I now took to be his uniform, khakis and a long-sleeved shirt, with the sleeves rolled up. Today's shirt was pale pink. The sun was strong, not scorching, like yesterday, but hot enough to make me glad I was wearing sandals and a spaghetti-strapped sundress.

"Aren't you hot?" I asked as I scrambled up the dune.

"I'm okay," Wes replied, turning. He took in my face and arms. "You're not as banged up as I expected."

"Don't sound so disappointed."

"I'm not disappointed. I'm surprised."

"How come you don't wear short-sleeved shirts?" I asked, eager to turn the subject away from my bumps and bruises.

"Maggie says it's more professional-looking to wear long sleeves and roll them up."

"She's a banker. Maybe a journalist can dress a little less formally."

"It's not formal like a suit. Anyway, I like the look."

I reached the summit and planted my feet on the shifting sand, then play-punched his arm. "So do I. You look terrific."

"So do you."

I clasped my right hand to my chest and threw out my left arm, pretending I was about to keel over. "Did I hear a compliment, Wes?"

He grinned. "You always look good. I just forget to say it."

"Maggie's done wonders for you."

"She's great, isn't she?" he asked, coloring a bit, as if talking about his love for her disconcerted him.

"Yes. So tell me your info-bombs."

"I shouldn't," he said, morphing from awkward kid brother to stern professional in a heartbeat. "One of them is about that Orson Thompkins guy you turned up. You told the police, but not me."

"I would have told you, Wes. You know that."

"When? I'm in the *news* business, Josie, not the it-doesn't-matter-if-I-tell-him-later business."

"Don't yell at me, Wes. I'm having a hard

189

time with all this. I'm so mad I can't think straight."

"Yeah, I can understand that. You got snookered good this time around."

"I didn't get snookered, Wes. I got mixed up with a thief who's maybe a killer." I stared at him, feeling fierce and letting it show. "Talk."

"Okay, okay . . . According to my police source, Orson Thompkins doesn't exist. Whoever is behind the scam piggybacked on the guy who lives in that house. Isn't that a hoot? The real tenant's name is Cal Miller. He's a long-distance truck driver, oil and liquid propane, and he's often gone for two weeks at a time, sometimes three. Someone commandeered his address for the ad listing, probably figuring that a single guy who's on the road a lot wouldn't pay much attention to odd mail, and that's exactly what happened."

"So it's someone who knows him."

"It's got to be. The police reached Miller in his rig — they got his cell phone number from the property manager. He's in Illinois en route to Tennessee. He said he has a dim memory about an antiques magazine arriving about a week or ten days ago, but he couldn't pin down the date. All he remembers is thinking it was weird, since he's not an antiques kind of guy. At first he assumed the post office messed up, but when he looked at the label, he saw it was the magazine that got it wrong. The address was right; it was the name that was wrong. He didn't recognize it, so he tossed the magazine. He doesn't remember the subscriber's name. The police checked with *Antiques Insights.* When someone who isn't already a subscriber to the magazine places an online ad, they send a complimentary issue."

"I can't believe the police learned all that so fast."

"There's more," Wes said, milking the suspense. "No surprise — the Visa Thompkins used is the kind you can refill for cash, and the phone was a throwaway, bought at a convenience store in Manchester. The place he got it from is a hole in the wall. They only have one security camera, and it's been busted for a year."

"I'm kind of dazzled at how simple it was to pull off," I said. "Thompkins didn't need a Social Security number or any credit history. He didn't even need an address that matched his name. Amazing. So now the police are trying to locate someone named Orson Thompkins."

"Who probably doesn't exist. Orson sounds like a made-up name, doesn't it?"

"I think it sounds distinguished," I said.

"You do? Anyway, there's more. The alarm at the Towsons' house was turned off and on multiple times each day while they were in London."

"That makes sense. Merry walked Eleanor. The housekeeper probably came in. Maybe the handyman, too."

"Right. On the days you were there, the alarm was turned off about an hour ahead of your visit. Someone was getting ready for you."

"I can see that. They had to take the pictures off the mantel and arrange the candlesticks. For something this complicated, you leave plenty of time for triple-checking your work and for unforeseen events."

"Right. That security info doesn't get us anywhere . . . but this might." Wes lowered his voice, his eyes on fire. "Ava was pregnant. Almost five months."

I opened my mouth, then closed it. Ideas spun through my head like a whirling dervish, but none resolved themselves into words.

"That changes everything, huh?"

I nodded, speechless, and turned toward the ocean. Gold specks twinkled across the surface like fairy dust.

"Do you think Edwin knew?" Wes asked.

"No. Given what he said, he couldn't."

"Unless he's playing deep."

"Unless that."

"You have to be a good poker player to be an investment banker."

"We keep coming back to his alibi," I said. "The police haven't cracked it yet."

"Maybe he wrapped Ava's body in ice or something to throw the medical examiner off."

"Do you really think so?"

"No, she probably would have found some trace. Maybe Edwin hired it out."

"Hitting someone over the head with a frying pan isn't exactly what hired killers do."

"Which means it would be a clever way to throw the cops off your trail."

"Maybe," I said, unconvinced.

"So what do you have for me?"

"What you'd probably call a shockeroonie. I'll tell you, but only if you promise not to quote me."

After our usual tussle in which he insisted he needed to be able to cite a source and I held firm that he was welcome to cite any source but me, he agreed to my terms, and I explained about the switch of lamps.

Wes's eyes were ablaze. "Yowza, howza,

mala-gadowzer. Do you think Jean is on the lam with the Tiffany lamp?"

"It's possible."

"Maybe she and this Orson guy hit the highway together."

"Also possible."

"Do the police know?" Wes asked.

"Yes."

"Where are you with finding the real lamp?"

"Nowhere yet."

Wes chuckled. "I bet you hate that."

"You have no idea."

"What else ya got?"

"Nothing."

"Catch ya later!"

He shimmied down the dune. Seconds later I heard his engine whirr to life. I stayed a while longer, my eyes fixed on a sailboat whizzing along toward Maine. Ava was having a baby. As the initial shock dulled, sadness settled over me like a veil.

"Now what?" I asked the breeze.

I shuffled down the dune, found my phone in my tote bag, and tried each of the numbers I had for Jean again. No answer.

I leaned against my car. Pink and white wild roses lined the road. I'd talked to Sylvia about Edwin and Ava, but not about what she might have seen in the hours before my visits to the fake Ava. She'd been on her lawn, watering her plants, when I arrived. Maybe she'd been working in her garden all morning. Certainly there was no harm in asking if she noticed who arrived about an hour before me.

I executed a three-point turn so I was heading toward Garnet Cove. After a mile, I had to slow down. A van painted to resemble a yellow school bus rolled to a stop at the curb. MAXWELL DAY CAMP was painted in black on the back and sides. Hexagonal red stop signs unfolded, and the door swung open. A cute little girl in lime green shorts hopped out and waved to the driver, then ran up the walkway to her house.

Seeing the grammar-school-aged girl got me wondering if Olive Winslow, the principal of Rocky Point Elementary School, might know more about Ava than Cara or Diane had, and if she worked over the summer. I bet she did. Teachers had time off, but administrators were on a different schedule.

The van stopped again about a half mile farther down Ocean. Three children jumped out at this stop, two boys and a girl. All three were laughing. The two boys high-fived, then tore off to their own houses. The girl cartwheeled her way across her lawn to her stoop.

I turned onto Pleasant Street, then, a mile farther on, pulled into the Rocky Point Elementary School parking lot. There were a dozen cars and three dozen empty spaces.

The front door was locked, but a sign affixed to a silver metal box mounted on the left read IF THE DOOR IS LOCKED, PLEASE USE THIS PHONE TO REACH THE OFFICE. Inside the box was a handset. I picked up the receiver, and a phone started ringing.

"This is Lucy. May I help you?"

Her voice was low and rumbly, like distant thunder. I suspected Lucy was a longtime smoker.

"Hi, Lucy. I'm Josie Prescott, and I was hoping I could talk to Ms. Winslow."

"I'm so sorry. She's in a curriculum meeting, and you know what that means."

She laughed, a jolly low-pitched chortle.

"I'm afraid I don't."

"Sorry. Curriculum is always a contentious subject. She won't be done until close to five, and then she'll be leaving for the day. Is there something I can help you with? I'm her executive assistant."

"Thanks, no. It's about her book club."

"How nice! She loves books, no doubt about that! She has time tomorrow if you'd like to make an appointment."

"Let me think about that," I said, not wanting to delay, thinking I might be able to catch Olive on her way out. I thanked Lucy and hung up.

Sitting in my car, I wiggled my tablet out of my tote bag and Googled the school's Web site. A welcome letter from the principal was on the home page. It included a standard-issue photo. Olive Winslow looked to be about fifty. She had shoulder-length salt-and-pepper hair and blue eyes. I knew her face. She was a frequent customer at our weekly tag sale, collecting, if I remembered right, English bone china teacups and saucers, the more ornate, the better. We'd exchanged pleasantries for years, but I'd never known her name.

While I waited, I brought up photos of the Tiffany lamp. I could look at it for hours. I was congratulating myself on having arranged for Timothy to film it when a realization hit me like a tsunami — I had no right to use the lamp on my show. The authorization had been signed by the fake Ava, not the rightful owner.

"Oh, God," I whispered, thinking of the money the network had invested, the time the team had put in, all for nothing.

I stared at my tablet, the implications

ricocheting through my brain like bumper cars at an amusement park. Starring in *Josie's Antiques* wasn't a lark, although it started that way. Now we'd found an audience and were an established hit. The crew was no longer a pickup band. There were dozens of employees under contract, all of whom counted on the job. If I messed up, my show might get canceled, and they'd be out of work.

This wasn't idle speculation or paranoia. There was a morals clause in my contract and another specifying that all objects shown on air would have an unimpeachable pedigree, unless my using a certain object was cleared by the network's lawyers. They'd explained that they were fine with my showcasing repros and counterfeits as part of my authentication process, but they didn't want me using stolen objects, no matter what point I hoped to make.

I had to get Edwin to allow us to use the footage; I just had to. Then I had to call Timothy. If I could get Edwin to sign off on it, my call to Timothy would be easier.

I called Edwin and reached Miranda. I explained I needed two minutes, urgently.

"I'm sorry, Josie. He's booked solid."

The best she could offer was one minute at eleven forty-five tomorrow morning. I accepted and thanked her for fitting me in.

I was tempted to wait until after my meeting with Edwin to call Timothy, but I couldn't justify it.

"I have some less than comfortable news," I said once he was on the line.

"Time for me to talk to the lawyers," he said after I explained the situation.

"Can you wait until after I meet with Edwin?"

"No, I think I'd better give them a heads-up. They don't like surprises."

"I understand. I wish I'd thought of this before."

"You and me both. Will you call me the minute you get the owner to sign the release? Or heaven forbid, if he refuses?"

I promised I would.

Quashing my impatience, I resumed my drive to Garnet Cove. Sylvia wasn't an eavesdropper or a Peeping Tom, but she was in her garden a lot — which meant there was a good chance she might have seen something relevant, whether she recognized its significance or not.

CHAPTER TWENTY

Sylvia was watering her tomatoes. I parked in front of her house and crossed the lawn to join her. She wore a denim skirt and a sleeveless blouse with a pretty red and blue flowered pattern. No weeding today, not in a skirt.

"You're going to think all I do is water my tomatoes," Sylvia said, smiling. Her smile dimmed as she took in my face. "I heard you were fine."

"I am. Just a few nicks and bruises."

"And scratches."

"Which are healing nicely."

Sylvia turned a dial on the nozzle and gave the plants a gentle shower.

"I'm hoping you'll help me," I said.

She shot me a glance. "What do you have in mind?"

"Have you talked to the police?"

"Several times." She kept her eyes on the plants and lowered her voice. "I told them about the fight I overheard between Edwin and Ava. I had to."

"Of course. What about people coming and going while the Towsons were in Europe? Did that come up?"

"A woman detective took me through it one day at a time. She got me remembering more than I would have thought I could."

"Detective Brownley?" I asked.

"Yes. Do you know her?"

"A little. She's smart."

"And those eyes! Cobalt."

"What did you remember?"

She lowered the nozzle, redirecting the spray to the dirt. I counted a dozen tomatoes almost ripe enough to harvest. Sylvia didn't say anything else, so I had to. Sometimes all it took was a nudge.

"I know Merry came in several times a day to walk the dog."

"At least three times a day. She's a very responsible young lady."

"Did the housekeeper come in at all?"

"A couple of times. I think Ava liked Tori to do thorough cleanings while they were away."

"How about the handyman?"

"Sonny? I saw him splitting logs outside and mowing the grass and so on."

"Did you see Ava's sister, Jean?"

"Yes, but I can't be sure about the day."

"I know the police showed you my sketch. The one of the woman I met with — the fake Ava. You didn't recognize her?"

"No, I'm sorry. I did see a woman entering the house before you both days, but I simply can't recall what she looked like beyond saying she was white and young — in her forties."

I smiled, amused that to a woman in her seventies, like Sylvia, forty is young.

"Was she tall?"

Sylvia opened her palms, a gesture of helplessness. Water sprayed sideways.

"Old eyes can't be trusted."

"I understand," I said, disappointed but not surprised. I talked to the woman — twice — and I couldn't describe her worth a cup of beans, and I was a trained observer.

Sylvia turned off the water. "Wait here a minute, will you?"

"Of course."

She dropped the hose on the lawn and hurried toward the back of her house, reappearing two minutes later carrying a medium-sized wicker basket with a big loopy handle.

"Here," she said, handing me the basket. "I picked some this morning. I want you to have a few."

The basket was brimming with scrumptious-smelling, bright red tomatoes. "Thank you so much, Sylvia. They're gorgeous!"

Her easy smile broadened. She reached for the hose and began coiling it around her arm.

"Let me help," I offered.

"No, thanks. I have a system."

I thanked her again for the tomatoes and walked back to my car.

As I wedged the basket between my toolbox and a picnic blanket, a young girl, maybe a teenager, but not by much, opened the Towsons' front door. Cornsilk yellow hair poked out from under the brim of a red cotton hat. Her features were delicate, creating an overall impression of sweetness. Eleanor stood nearby, her tail wagging. She yelped and bounced and hopped all around the girl, perhaps trying to leap into her arms. The girl giggled and dropped to her knees. Eleanor lapped her cheek noisily as the girl cuddled and stroked her back.

"She loves you," I said, walking up the path.

"And I love her right back, don't I, Eleanor?" She unsnapped the harness, and Eleanor ran inside. "We're good friends, aren't we, sweetheart?"

Eleanor barked her agreement.

"I think you must be Merry, the Towsons' dog walker." She glanced at me covertly. I smiled. She smiled back, a small one, as if she weren't sure how friendly she should be. "I'm Josie Prescott, an antiques appraiser. I'm doing some work for Mr. Towson."

"Hi," Merry said. She tossed the harness inside, then closed the door, calling, "I'll see you later, Eleanor!"

"Eleanor's got a lot of pep for an old dog."

"She's not old," Merry said. "She's only two."

Another lie the fake Ava told me.

"I'm just leaving," I continued. "Can I give you a lift?"

"No, thanks. I like the walk."

I lowered my voice. "Please? I want to ask you something."

"What?"

I glanced over my shoulder. Sylvia was walking toward the back, the neatly coiled hose draped over her shoulder.

"About a timeline," I said, lowering my voice, "related to Mr. Towson's project. It's nothing complicated, just who you saw in or around the house while the Towsons were overseas."

Merry looked at her feet, and when she

spoke, I could barely hear her. "No one."

The gauge on my truth-meter swung toward zero. Merry was lying, but I couldn't for the life of me see why unless she was protecting the fake Ava.

"Are you sure?" I asked softly, aiming for empathy, not criticism.

She nibbled on a hangnail. "Uh-huh."

"I'm pretty good at reading people, and I'm getting the sense that there's something you know that you don't want to talk about."

No response.

"Did someone ask you to fib?" I asked as gently as I could.

Her eyes flew to my face. "I'm helping," she whispered, "not fibbing."

"How is that?"

"I'm not supposed to say."

"Did the police ask you to keep quiet?"

"No."

"Mr. Towson?"

"No."

"It's always best to tell the truth, Merry. You know that."

She nodded, then looked down again.

"Was it Ms. Cooper? Mrs. Towson's sister?"

"Ms. Cooper didn't want the police to waste their time on stupid distractions."

"I can see that," I said, keeping my tone neutral. "The police are pretty savvy about avoiding distractions, though."

"I wondered about that."

"And you haven't felt good about keeping quiet, have you?"

"No, but I told Ms. Cooper I wouldn't say anything. I know you're supposed to tell the truth, but you're supposed to keep promises, too."

"I'll tell you what I think. I think it's outrageous that Ms. Cooper put you in this situation. No one should ask you to lie. Period. End of discussion."

"It makes sense when you say it."

"Good. So who was in and out?"

"Tori came twice to clean."

"That's the Towsons' housekeeper."

"Right. And Sonny came lots of times. He helps out around the house, you know, watering the plants and stuff. He chopped up an apple tree branch that fell last winter. The Towsons don't use their fireplace, so they told my mom we could take the wood. Sonny loaded it into the back of his pickup and drove it over."

"That was nice of him. And Ms. Cooper?"

"Yes."

"Once?"

"Uh-huh."

"When was that?"

She shrugged. "I don't know."

"Was it the same day the Towsons left?"

"No. They'd been gone a while."

"Was it the day before they got back?"

"It was way before then." Merry's eyes lit up as a memory came to her. "It was the Monday before July Fourth. I mean, the week before."

The day of my first visit, I thought. "What did you remember?"

"It was really hot and humid, totally icky. That is so crazy for seven in the morning, right? Anyway, I always take Eleanor for her first walk around then. After we got home, Eleanor and I played ball in the backyard. Eleanor likes to chase a tennis ball. We normally play after her noontime walk, but I thought we should do it early, before the heat of the day. Eleanor doesn't like the heat. Ms. Cooper carried in a box. I saw her through the living room window."

"Did she see you?" I asked.

"Yeah, that's why she asked me not to tell the police. She didn't want them to waste their time questioning her."

"Did you talk through the window?"

"No. She came outside."

"What was in the box?"

"Shoes and boots." Merry giggled. "I said

207

I wished I had that many shoes and boots. She said she was a complete nut for shoes."

"It sounds like a big box."

"It was. Really big."

"Like a refrigerator?"

She giggled again. "No. Like an amp. My brother bought an amp to take to gigs." She smiled proudly. "He plays guitar with a band named Rifle Jocks."

I smiled. "Very cool. Who else came to the house?"

"The woman next door." She dropped her voice again. "The one who's always fussing with her tomatoes. Ms. Campbell."

"Sylvia?" I asked, stunned.

"Uh-huh."

"She has a key?"

"I don't know. The day I saw her, Sonny let her in."

"Which day was that?"

She pressed her lips together, turned toward the ocean, and stared into the far distance. I kept my eyes on her face. She swung back toward me, smiling.

"The sixth. It was the Thursday of that week. I remember because Nana, my grandmother, surprised us all with tickets to a play at the York Theater the night before. In Maine, you know? We saw *Guys and Dolls*. Have you seen that play? It's a musical."

"You bet! I love it."

"Me, too. It was awesome. Anyway, Eleanor and I left by the kitchen door and had just reached the hiking trail when I looked back, I don't know why. Maybe I heard something. I don't know . . . but I saw Sonny letting Ms. Campbell in."

"Was she carrying anything?"

Merry scrunched up her nose. "Avocados. I remember because I hate avocados. She had a crate bungeed to a kind of wheeled cart. Sonny was working in the front yard. He carried it in for her."

"And she followed him in?"

"Uh-huh."

"How long was she in there?"

"I don't know. Eleanor was sniffing around for long enough for me to see that much, but then she tugged on her leash and off we went."

"How did you know the crate contained avocados?"

"The word 'avocado' was stamped on the side in really big letters."

"How big was the crate?" I asked. "About the same size as the box Ms. Cooper was carrying?"

Merry pulled in her lips in and puffed out her cheeks, an "I haven't got a clue" face if I ever saw one. Her shoulders lifted an inch, then lowered. "I don't know. Maybe."

"You're doing a great job, Merry. Who else did you see at the house?"

She thought for a moment, then shook her head. "I think that's it, unless you mean like the mailman or something."

"You've been very helpful, Merry," I said. "I'll be sure to tell Mr. Towson."

Her teeth clamped her lower lip for a moment. "Will you have to tell Ms. Cooper?"

"No, but I do have to share what you told me with the police, and I can't promise they won't tell her. You know, Merry, what Ms. Cooper asked you to do wasn't fair. Or right. You don't owe her anything. Not your loyalty. Not an explanation. Nothing."

"I guess."

I couldn't think of what else to say to reassure her. She'd learn, probably the hard way, like most of us.

"Are you sure I can't drive you home?"

"No, thanks," she said.

Watching Merry mosey along the sidewalk, I shivered as a long-ago memory of betrayal came to me and the anger and hurt whiskered through my veins. A girlfriend, a real pal, I'd thought, asked me to cover for her so she could go out. We were fourteen. Her name was Robin. She wanted to go to a party, and her mom said no way since the boy throwing it was a senior and his parents were off skiing in Aspen. Robin asked me to say she was with me if it ever came up, and of course I agreed. I didn't think anything of it. I wished I could have gone to the party, too, but my dad and I had tickets to a comedy show, just the two of us. After my mom died, he started making fun plans for us on Saturday nights, his way of helping us overcome the wrenching loss. Even at thirteen, I understood his intentions, and I loved him for them.

Robin's mother came over the next morning around ten hoping to surprise Robin, my dad, and me by taking us to breakfast. When she discovered that Robin wasn't there, that she hadn't been there all night, the color drained from her face. I'd never seen anything like it. She was smiling and joking around, and then, within seconds, she was tottering, bloodless.

I knew where the boy hosting the party lived, and we found Robin passed out on the living room floor along with half a dozen other kids. She was groggy and tearful and resentful toward me. Later she told me and anyone else who'd listen that I'd betrayed her. I said that from where I sat, she was the one doing the betraying. After that last shattering argument, I never saw her again.

Her mom sent her to live with some cousins in North Carolina, then moved down herself a few months later. My dad used my too-easy acquiescence as what he called a teachable moment. Live your life as if you're running for political office, he told me. Never lie. Never help anyone else lie. Always do the right thing. *Oh, Dad,* I thought, wishing he were here, wishing I could ask him what I should do now.

Sylvia, now dressed in her turquoise capris, was in a different part of her garden, on her knees, weeding. I was tempted to ask her if she grew avocados, but I didn't. If I didn't report this new discovery to Ellis pronto, I'd be in real trouble.

CHAPTER TWENTY-ONE

I drove out of Garnet Cove and parked in a grocery store lot, then dialed Ellis. I was relieved to get his voice mail. Delivering a message spared me a real-time scolding.

"As promised," I said, "I'm letting you know what I learn." I repeated what Merry had observed, explaining why she hadn't come forward before now, ending with a friendly "Talk to you later." Knowing that if Wes picked up the call, he would demand more information than I wanted to give, I updated him via e-mail, providing only the facts, not my source.

"Good," I said aloud, glad those obligations were behind me.

I pulled into the Rocky Point Elementary School parking lot for the second time that day. It was 4:53 P.M. Three minutes later, Olive Winslow stepped out of a side door and tugged on the handle, confirming it was locked.

I got out of my car and called, "Ms. Winslow?" She turned toward me, her brows raised, and I added, "We've never formally met, but we've seen each other a lot at my company's tag sale. I'm Josie Prescott."

Her features relaxed, and she smiled as she walked toward me. "Of course. How nice to finally meet you. I love your tag sale. I've found some real treasures there!"

She wore a pale blue seersucker A-line skirt that fell below her knees, sensible navy blue pumps, and a short-sleeved pink silk blouse. A small blue purse dangled from her shoulder. She carried a brown leather briefcase.

"You collect cups and saucers, if I remember right."

"What a memory!"

" 'The true art of memory is the art of attention.' "

"Samuel Johnson."

"That's right," I said. "My dad used to quote him all the time. His favorite was 'The law is the last result of human wisdom acting upon human experience for the benefit of the public.' "

"That's wonderful. Insightful." She tilted her head, her eyes steady on mine. "Is it a coincidence that you're here?"

"No," I said, smiling. "Lucy told me when you'd be leaving. I hear from Cara — she's our receptionist — that you're in her book club. I was hoping I could buy you a cup of coffee and ask you about Ava."

Olive placed her briefcase on the ground. "I wish I could, but I can't. I'm on the board of Oceanside Music School, and our quarterly meeting starts in a few minutes. What did you want to ask?"

"Nothing in particular. I'm just trying to understand what happened. As you probably know, I was doing an appraisal for the Towsons when she was killed."

"I heard something about that on the news. Ava was charming. She'll be sorely missed."

Hoping to move beyond platitudes, I said, "I heard Ava was upset with her husband, Edwin."

"Really? I wouldn't know anything about that. I wasn't in her confidence."

"I'm just shooting in the dark here . . . Did you notice a change in her over the last few months?"

"What's your interest exactly?"

"It involves a Tiffany lamp I'm trying to trace. I don't know what might be helpful, which is why I'm asking anything I can

215

think of."

"Ava was a bit somber the last time I saw her."

"And that was unusual for her?"

"Very. As a rule, Ava always seemed quite chipper. Outgoing."

"And that day she was sad."

"Quiet, yes, as if she had a lot on her mind."

"And you don't know why?"

"No. I'm sorry."

I believed her, which only added to my frustration. It seemed the more I asked, the less I learned.

"Have you spoken to Diane?" Olive asked. "Diane Hawkins? She runs our book club. I'll be talking to her in the morning — I want to make a donation to the library in Ava's honor . . . so sad." She sighed and shook her head a little. "Anyway . . . probably Diane knew Ava better than any of us, and I'll be glad to ask for her take on Ava's mood."

"Thank you so much, but there's no need. I spoke to Diane the other day, and she was just as open as you are, and, unfortunately, she knew as little. I don't think Ava confided in anyone, except maybe her sister, Jean. I hope to talk to Jean tomorrow."

"I never met Jean, but I can see that —

Ava spoke of her often and with great affection. Ava wasn't reticent, exactly. I'm having trouble putting my finger on the issue." She paused for a moment, and when she continued, she spoke with conviction. "Ava was warm and friendly, but she didn't encourage intimacy. Her friendliness was more polished than personal, like a diplomat or a party planner."

I decided to change tack and aim to gather more general information. With any luck, I'd find a way into Ava's world through the back door.

"How did you get involved in the book club in the first place?" I asked.

Olive laughed. "Through crew. Do you know Cara's grandson, Patrick?"

"Yes, indeed. Cara's brought him to several parties. He loves her to bits."

"He's a wonderful young man. My grandson, Kent, is the same, another great kid. It gives me hope for the future that we have young people like that, getting ready to lead." Olive looked down for a moment, her cheeks rosy, self-effacing and proud all at once. "Both Patrick and Kent row for Hitchens University. Cara and I attend the same regattas, and over time, we became friends. When a slot opened up in the book club, Cara introduced me to Diane as a potential candidate." She chuckled. "Diane runs a tight ship. I was invited to attend one meeting, then a second. After that, she invited me to attend as a guest for a year. I guess I passed muster, because after the year was up, she asked me to join permanently. I've been a member for three years now, four and a half, if you count my probationary period." Her smile disappeared. "I'm so sorry about Ava. I really am. I'm also sorry to think that something was troubling her and that she didn't tell me about it. If I could have helped, I would. I liked her very much, and I'm good at keeping secrets."

"That's quite a burden to bear."

"Only if you label it a burden. I call it a privilege."

"That's wonderful, and so true. Words matter. Thank you for talking to me."

Olive smiled and picked up her briefcase. "I'll look forward to seeing you at the tag sale!"

We went our separate ways. Olive drove toward town, toward the music school, and I drove home.

I always left a light on in my bedroom so I don't have to enter a dark house, and usually the soft golden glow cheered me. Not today. A maelstrom of upset, worry, and rage so caustic it threatened to eat through my carefully crafted insouciant facade held me in its grip. I felt drained and stultifyingly lonely. I wished Ty were home to comfort me.

"Oh, Ty," I murmured as I walked through the house turning on lights. The brightness helped a bit.

I lined up Sylvia's tomatoes on the counter in one long row. She'd given me eleven tomatoes. I picked the reddest, which was also the biggest, about the size of a Ping-Pong ball. I closed my eyes and transported myself back to a warm day in July. I was about ten. My friend Nina's mom had dropped me off after a play date, and I peeked into the backyard to see if Dad was there. He was. He wore navy blue shorts and a yellow collared T-shirt. He was watering the tomato plants, holding the hose high so the gentle spray rained down like a soft shower. He saw me and smiled, and spoke my name as if it were gold. "Josie! Come have a tomato!" He plucked two big tomatoes from the vine, and we rubbed them on our T-shirts. The first bite was heaven, sun-warm and sweet like candy. I rubbed Sylvia's tomato on my chest and bit in. I was ten again, loved, and cared for, and free.

I used another tomato in the salad I

prepared for dinner, and stuffed a third with herbs, breadcrumbs, balsamic glaze, olive oil, and honey. I knew all eleven would be eaten in just a few days, and with every bite, I'd think of my father.

I poured myself a Rouge Martini and settled into my favorite club chair to call Ty.

"I got you!" I said. "I was sure I'd get your voice mail."

"I was about to call you. I'm in for the night."

"Me, too. And it's not even six. Are you okay?"

"Just beat. Getting the lay of the land is always exhausting."

"Are you getting it? Or are you only slogging through muck?"

"A little of both. I'm making progress. And I have good news — I'll be home tomorrow for the weekend. If the weather holds, I'll be pulling in the driveway by six."

"Or even five thirty," I said, raising my glass in a private toast to my wish coming true, then sipped to seal the deal.

"That's probably overly optimistic."

"I miss you like you wouldn't believe."

"Me, too. Hard day?"

"Super hard. I spoke to Timothy. I'm probably in trouble with New York." I explained the situation, adding, "I'm so angry I'm having trouble maintaining objectivity. I talk to people and learn things, but nothing I learn seems to matter or help me find the Tiffany lamp, so I just get angrier and angrier."

"That confusion is pretty common in investigations, Josie. Think of all the times you've been hot on the trail of an antiques pedigree when out of the blue you get contradictory information and have to go back to the drawing board."

"That's true. And I hate it each time."

"Yet you always get the answers you need."

"Even if the answer is there is no answer," I said, thinking of Aunt Louise's remarkable globe desk. I told him how Fred was searching for the man who thought of the perfect gift for his girlfriend, Louise. "I doubt we'll find him, which means we'll never be able to verify provenance, but that's okay. We can authenticate the desk and charm the world with the story of Aunt Louise's mystery man." I placed the martini glass on a stone coaster. "The fake Ava haunts me, Ty. I can't get the way I was played out of my mind. It's the public humiliation. And I just hate the thought that my oversight might have landed Timothy in trouble with the network's lawyers and money people . . ." I let my voice trail off.

"You're being pretty hard on yourself, Joz. You don't have second sight or anything."

"I know." I raised, then lowered my shoulders. "If Edwin signs the release and I find the real Tiffany lamp, my mood will improve."

"He will and it will."

"You sound pretty certain."

"I know you."

"I think I'll take a bubble bath. I'm tense."

"What's for dinner?"

"Leftover spaghetti and meatballs. Garlic bread. Salad. With fresh tomatoes from Sylvia's garden. I told you about her — the Towsons' neighbor."

"Wish I was there."

"Me, too. What are you having?"

"A turkey sub."

"That's not dinner. That's lunch."

"I know, but I'm too tired to care."

"I'll make something special for you for tomorrow. What do you want?"

"Sliced tomatoes and corn on the cob."

"Done. What else?"

"Steamers and lobster."

"You got it."

"I love you, Josie."

"I love you, too, Ty."

After we hung up, I leaned my head against the cool twill fabric and closed my eyes. I felt better. Not good, but definitely better.

Wes called as I was running the water for my bubble bath. I turned off the faucet to take the call and sat on the edge of the tub, the leftover steam swirling around me.

"I can't believe you didn't give me your source," he said, fuming. "You know that reporters need to go to the original source. It's called verification."

"You can't believe I wouldn't reveal a source. Well, I can't believe you're indignant with me. And you're welcome. Did you find out anything?"

"I already knew about Jean's box. The cops got the skinny from that neighbor, Sylvia Campbell, when they first questioned her after Ava's murder. According to my police source, when they asked Jean about why she was carrying in a lamp box, she said it wasn't a lamp box, it was a shoe box."

"That's what I heard, too."

"Jean said she has so many shoes and boots she doesn't have room to store them all in her condo, so she brings them to her sister's house, where there's a spare cedar closet, switching out summer and winter clothes twice a year." He chortled. "Give me a break!"

"Everyone does that, Wes."

"Maybe, but everyone doesn't have so many shoes they can't store them in a three-bedroom condo — that they live in alone."

"True."

"The police saw the closet Jean used, and sure enough, it was filled with her winter clothes and a bunch of shoes and boots."

"Did the police examine the box itself?"

"It was long gone."

"So that's that." I stood and stared at my steamy reflection in the mirror. "I'll ask Edwin whether he knows anything about the avocados Sylvia brought over. Or the crate. And you'll keep me posted, right?"

"Don't I always?" Wes chuckled. "Don't answer that. I'll catch ya later."

I drained the now-cool water and refilled the tub. While I waited, I did a quick e-mail check. Ellis had sent an e-mail with a terse thank-you. I was in the doghouse; that much, at least, was clear.

CHAPTER TWENTY-TWO

I asked Sasha to lead our regular Friday morning staff meeting. My ability to focus was out the window.

I'd awakened certain that Jean's box hadn't contained shoes and boots. Who waits until summer is under way to retrieve her sandals? I needed to talk to her. Wes had asked if I thought Jean was on the lam with the lamp, and I'd said maybe, but I hadn't really meant it. It seemed so darn improbable. A well-off divorcée with a beautiful condo and a long-term boyfriend didn't just disappear. Or was it all a sham? For all I knew she was mortgaged to the hilt and glad to dump the boyfriend.

"I'm sorry to interrupt," I said, smiling at Gretchen, who was saying something about which temps had been trained and bonded, so they could work the cash register at tomorrow's tag sale. "Does anyone need me?" No one did. "There's a call I need to make, so I'll excuse myself."

I paused en route to say hello to Hank. He was lying in his basket, with one paw and his neck resting on the wicker rim, as if he'd attempted to get out but was just too exhausted. He was staring into space.

"Look at you," I said. "You had an errand, but you couldn't quite make it."

Hank looked up and mewed.

"Cara thinks you're bored. Are you bored, big fellow?"

I lifted him up and kissed the top of his furry little head. He snuggled up against my chest. I carried him upstairs. He settled into my lap and mewed imperiously, demanding jowlies. I put the phone on speaker so I had a hand available to do as he asked and dialed Jean. No answer. I nearly growled with frustration.

I called Wes and got his voice mail. "I'm wondering about Jean," I said. "It occurs to me I don't actually know much about her. Do you? Did you confirm that she's in as good financial shape as you thought? I mean, no kidding, Wes, is her boyfriend even real?"

I glanced at the time on my monitor — 9:10. I had more than two hours before I needed to drive to Towson's for my 11:45 A.M. meeting with Edwin. I brought up our master database and searched for clients who lived at the Grey Gull condo complex. Three names poppedup. Gary Datlin collected nineteenth-century political memorabilia; Marsha Korbin was always in the market for French cameo glass; and Penelope Hahn, who owned four world-class seventeenth-century Dutch cabinets, would love to add to her collection.

Our proprietary inventory system conducted an automatic search for clients who might be interested in an antique or collectible as soon as we entered the object's description into the database. Entering the keywords into the computer was one of Cara's jobs. If a name popped up, it got passed along to Sasha, who made the call herself, assigned it to Fred, or, for certain high-end antiques or special clients, passed it along to me. In addition, the software allowed for multiple-factor searches, so I could enter broad categories, like "political memorabilia," or narrow my search by adding a time period or keywords such as "President Lincoln" or "Confederate." Because of the automatic match function, I wasn't the least bit surprised that we had no inventory that might be of interest to any of them.

"What should I do, Hank?"

Hank was in heaven. He was sprawled across my lap as if he were lounging on a recliner, his eyes mere slits.

"You're not going to help me, are you, baby?"

I glanced around, waiting for inspiration. The love seat and matching wing chairs faced one another, creating a cozy conversation area. The butler's table I'd positioned between them was mahogany. So was the display cabinet at the end of the room. My roosters were mostly crafted of porcelain, but two were carved out of wood, and one was forged from pewter. Five black-framed photos covered the rest of that wall, candid shots of me and my parents during the happy times. On the long wall, I'd hung business-oriented objects, plaques and magazine covers and carefully posed photos of the staff, retouched so we all looked good. The framed certificate of appreciation I'd received from one of my favorite charities, New Hampshire Children First!, caught my eye. The charity was founded to fund innovative programs to help children with disabilities reach their full potential. I'd received the award last year at their annual volunteer lunch. I was their fund-raiser of the year.

"Bingo," I said.

I called the director, Helene Roberts.

"Where are we on funding the therapeutic horse-ride program?" I asked after we'd exchanged greetings.

"Close. We only need five thousand more to meet this year's goal."

"I have the program description you e-mailed last month. Has anything changed?"

"Nope. What's up your sleeve, Josie?"

"Only good things — I have a meeting with a potential donor. Wish me luck!"

She thanked me warmly as she always did and told me that she didn't know where the organization would be without me. There is no motivator as powerful as affirmation.

Gary's phone went to voice mail. I didn't leave a message. Marsha's just rang and rang. Penelope answered on the third ring.

"Penelope, this is Josie. Josie Prescott."

"Hi, Josie! Tell me you have a fabulous Dutch cabinet with burl walnut parquetry."

I laughed. "That's a very specific wish."

"I know. I was just going through a museum catalogue and saw one. I'm twitching with envy."

"I wish I had one for you. You know I'd call you right away."

"I count on it. What can I do for you?"

"I'm helping New Hampshire Children

First! raise money for a new program, and I was hoping I could stop by and tell you about it."

"By all means. I so admire their work. I'm heading out now but will be back at one. How's that?"

"Perfect," I said. *And that, ladies and gentlemen, is how you do that.*

I spent the next two hours reading reports and catalogue copy, responding to e-mails, and preparing the release form I hoped Edwin would sign.

"Time to go, Hank," I told him.

He ignored me until I lowered him to the ground. He meowed his complaint, but recovered quickly when he spotted a catnip mouse on the love seat. He pounced, picking it up in his teeth and shaking it the way his brethren in the jungle shake prey, then tossed it at my feet and mewed.

"Are you a good boy, Hank? You are. You're *such* a good boy." I picked up the mouse, and when we got to the bottom of the stairs, I threw it as far as I could into the center of the warehouse. Hank shot off after it like a cheetah in the savannah.

As I drove to my meeting with Edwin, I considered whether Ava's murder was as simple as it seemed. It was completely possible that Edwin was right: Ava had a falling-out with her partner, and he killed her. I supposed it was equally possible that two people set out to steal the Tiffany lamp, and when Ava walked in on them, they murdered her. All we knew for certain was that whoever was behind the theft knew enough about Edwin's background to pull it off. Who, besides Ava, and by extension Jean, was close enough to have learned the details?

Edwin swore he hadn't told a soul about his family history except Ava, and that only recently. Maybe he was wrong. Perhaps he'd mentioned it to someone years earlier, so long ago he'd forgotten. Or maybe he'd mentioned it casually after a few drinks and didn't remember doing so at all.

Edwin was a workaholic, spending most of his time at his company. Was he all business, as I'd assumed, or was there someone with whom he was close? Edwin was a tough boss. Everyone said so. Wes said that he was a slave driver, but no one cared because he paid them so much. Maybe. But I knew how seemingly minor slights could fester, chafing until your emotions are rubbed raw. Selling a Tiffany lamp meant you'd have the means to never have to see Edwin again. Whom had he offended or outwitted or fired?

Receptionists, I'd discovered over the years, knew everything about what really went on in a business. They knew who was seeing whom, who was angry at whom, who was working late, who was sneaking out early, who was the boss's favorite, and who was one error away from being canned.

Judi.

I arrived at Towson's at a quarter to twelve, as scheduled. Judi, at her regular place, greeted me with familiar warmth, ignoring my scrapes and scratches with studied detachment.

Miranda brought me back to Edwin's office and left.

"I can give you one minute," Edwin said.

"That should be enough for you to tell me about the avocados Sylvia dropped off while you and Ava were in Europe."

"What avocados?" he asked impatiently.

"Sonny helped Sylvia carry in a crate marked 'avocados.' Maybe it was just a vintage avocado crate she was using to transport something else. I need to track it down."

"Because maybe it held the lamp."

"It's possible."

Edwin tore a sheet from his memo pad

and scrawled for a moment. On a second sheet, he listed some numbers. He opened a mahogany box, a humidor, and extracted a key.

"Here," he said, handing everything over. "You now have the run of the house. I was going to call you next week, but today's as good a time as any. You said I could consign everything to you or sell it outright. I want to sell. Everything. Inside and out. I've already removed my clothes and a few other things that I want. How does it work?"

"We'll make a video recording so you and I both know and agree on the scope of the sale. We calculate how much we can offer, and if you say yes, we move everything to our warehouse."

"Good. Do it. You'll find an additional key in a fake rock by the kitchen door. I'll have Miranda call Tori, Sonny, and Merry, so they'll know what's going on. You may run into any of them — they're still working for me, and will be until the house is sold."

I picked up the two sheets of paper. The first was a note authorizing me and my staff to enter his house. The second was a seemingly random list of numbers.

"Is this the alarm code?" I asked.

"Yes."

"We'll get going on the video today. I

should have an offer in a few days. There's one more thing." I felt my cheeks redden. "The fake Ava signed a release authorizing me to use the Tiffany lamp on my TV show. The crew came up, and we filmed the episode." I slid the release across the desk. "Obviously, that release is null and void. I'm hoping you'll sign this one so we can use the footage."

Edwin read the form, then slipped it under a cut-glass paperweight. "If it airs, it may end up as part of a criminal investigation."

"It may anyway."

"If it's on television, the risk of bad publicity increases geometrically."

"We can run it anonymously."

"Not if the police get a court order."

I explained the potential value of association.

"You can't sell what you don't have, so considering potential value is a waste of time."

I knew when I'd reached the end of an argument. "Will you reconsider when we find the lamp?"

He stood up. "All I'll commit to now is that I won't reconsider unless you find the lamp."

"I understand," I said, and left.

It was eleven fifty. I'd stretched his one minute to five.

Without betraying either my disappointment and frustration that he wouldn't sign the release or my excitement at the prospect of acquiring a mansion full of objects, some antiques, others collectibles, and everything of the highest quality, I said good-bye to Judi.

Downstairs, I moved parking spots so I had a clear view of the exit but was not in anyone's line of vision. While I waited, I took photos of the two sheets Edwin had given me and e-mailed them to Gretchen, then called into work.

Sasha was on the phone, but Fred was available. I described what I wanted him to do at the Towsons' house, including letting me know the instant he located a vintage wooden avocado crate, explaining that he should take a copy of the authorization note and the alarm code, and where he could find the key.

"The whole houseful?" he asked, sounded dazed.

I grinned. "And the outside."

My call-waiting buzz sounded, and I glanced at the display. Wes. I ignored it.

"Why an avocado crate?" he asked.

"It's too long a story for the phone. If and

when you find it, don't touch it. Call me."

"Okay. Before I go, I'll tell Eric to cordon off a triple-wide section."

"Alert him to the possibility. At this point, all we're doing is making an offer."

"I know you. The offer will be fair, and therefore, it will be accepted."

I was touched. "Thank you, Fred."

We ended the call with his promise to keep me updated. Knowing the call to Timothy wouldn't get easier with age, I dialed his cell and got him.

"I don't have the release signed yet," I said, jumping in, "but neither did the owner refuse outright. He says he won't consider it until the lamp is found."

"I'll fly up today. I can be very persuasive."

"Thanks, but no. He's not a lukewarm sort of person. He was very clear. I'm sorry, Timothy. I don't want anything to put the show at risk."

"You and me both. Setting aside the lamp, the lawyers want to know whether your involvement in the theft and murder is likely to become a problem. I assured them it wouldn't, that your so-called involvement is simply a case of wrong place, wrong time. Tell me that's so."

"Of course!"

"Where are you with finding the lamp?"

"Doing everything I can."

"Give me odds."

"I can't."

"Give me an educated guess."

I rested my forehead on the steering wheel. Talking to Timothy was far harder than I'd anticipated, and I hadn't expected it to be easy.

"I'm hopeful."

"Really?" he asked, brightening.

I sat up. "Yes."

"Good. Let's go with that. Keep me posted."

I promised I would. After our call, I reviewed everything I was doing to find the lamp: the postings, the database alerts, and the coordination with law enforcement. Frustrated with the lack of progress, I made a fist and soft-pounded the steering wheel.

While I was on the phone with Timothy, Wes had left a message announcing that he had mega-news and I should call him right away.

"So the police decided to spread out their search for the fake Ava," he said as soon as he heard my voice. "Both Tori and Sonny have a woman of the right age and build in their lives. Tori's sister, Jennifer, is forty-five, but she lives in Jacksonville, Florida. I spoke to Jennifer's neighbor myself, and she confirmed that Jennifer hasn't been away in months. Sonny is married to a woman named Noreen who's also forty-five. She's a cafeteria worker at Rocky Point Hospital, and she was on duty both days when you met the imposter — and the morning Ava was murdered."

"Which means they're both eliminated. Did you find out anything about Jean's finances?"

"She's loaded. She got a sweet deal in her divorce. So . . . what do you have for me?"

"Nothing now."

Wes sighed to let me know my IOUs were stacking up. "When Jean was twelve and Ava was only eight, their parents were killed in a traffic pile-up. A drunk driver on I-95 heading the wrong way."

"That's awful!"

"I know. It really changed their lives. They moved in with a cousin in Wisconsin until Jean turned eighteen, at which point she became her sister's legal guardian. They left Wisconsin within days of her birthday, midway through her senior year in high school. Apparently, they hated living with the cousin. They chose Rocky Point because that's where they spent summers before their parents died. Jean finished high school here and got a gofer job working for a law firm. She attended night school to become a paralegal. She worked for the same firm until she married one of the partners. She sure knows how to take care of business, right? Meanwhile, Ava worked in a doctor's office while she went to school at night. She got her degree in English lit. She always loved to travel. She met Edwin while she was on vacation in Italy, some kind of foodie tour. Edwin was meeting with investors in Rome. They found themselves sitting next to one another at a café and got talking, and the rest is history. They married eight months later, at which point he moved his New York City–based company to New Hampshire."

"That's so romantic!"

"I guess. A year or so later, Jean's husband left her for a . . . wait for it . . . young paralegal in his office and moved to Miami. Jean got a fat settlement and maintains a six-figure balance in her checking account. She doesn't work, but she's active in a number of charities, blah, blah, blah. She's been dating an engineer named Shawn O'Boyle for nearly two years. Jean was serving brunch to him and another couple when she heard the news that her sister had been killed. Shawn had spent the night, so that confirms her alibi."

"What about the other couple?"

"They arrived around ten, so they can't say what she was doing before they got there."

"Thanks, Wes," I said.

He ended the call with his regular "Catch ya later."

CHAPTER TWENTY-THREE

Judi popped out of Towson's front door two minutes after twelve and walked to her car, shoulder-dancing to what looked like a jazzed-up hip-hop beat. I noticed earbuds.

Two minutes later, she set out south on Ocean Avenue. I counted ten before following. Once I made the turn, I could see her car, a blue Toyota, easily, so I slowed up. She drove steadily, and we passed a short street on the right named Richter that I knew ended at a scrub oak forest, the police station, and the dune where Wes and I often met. The sun angled into the car, and I lowered my visor. A Jeep turned onto Ocean between us, providing a welcome buffer. Just before we entered Rye, we passed a strip mall, and Judi took the next right. By the time I followed suit, she had parked in the lot that ran behind the stores. I idled at the curb watching until she started down a narrow passage that led back to Ocean

Avenue, and the shops.

I parked facing out, then walked slowly along Ocean, peering into each store's plate glass window. I passed a pizza joint, the front window decorated with red, white, and blue stenciled stars, and a tchotchkes tourist trap displaying Americana-themed baseball hats and fanny packs alongside bumper stickers and T-shirts emblazoned with New Hampshire's state motto, "Live Free or Die," before spotting her standing in the middle of the Clam Shack, a local beachside dive, popular with teens and surfer dudes. Her back was to me as she read the menu board mounted high above her head.

I hoped she was in a chatty mood.

The Clam Shack was paneled in rough-hewn wood, the kind you'd find in any of a thousand fishing shacks that dot the New Hampshire and Maine coastlines. It was decorated with fishing nets that drooped artfully from the ceiling, red and white buoys and used lobster traps affixed to the walls, and hurricane-style lamps overhead and on the tables. Also on the tables were red glass vases filled with red, white, and blue aluminum pom-poms.

I stepped inside and glanced around. The place was more than half full, with all but a handful of tables taken. Most stools at the counter were available, though, and that's where Judi headed.

She had her earbuds in place, and her shoulders were moving to the beat as I slid onto the stool next to her.

"Hey," I said, smiling.

Judi's eyes opened wide, and she pulled out an earbud. "Tell me this isn't one heck of a coincidence."

"It's not. I followed you." I smiled. "It's nothing urgent, but I wanted to talk to you privately, and this seemed the most efficient approach."

A waitress, about Judi's age, wearing cutoff jeans, a tie-dyed T-shirt, and Keds, sauntered over to us. I looked up at the board. Standard beachfront fare: lobster rolls, fried clams, burgers, hot dogs, and fries. Nary a salad in sight.

I turned to Judi. "Order anything you want — my treat."

She shot me a speculative look, more wary than appreciative, then turned back to the waitress. "A lobster roll, please, and a Coke."

"I'll have an iced tea," I said.

"No problem," the waitress said. She tapped the screen, entering our order.

"How come?" Judi asked, stuffing her earbuds into her purse.

"I don't mean to be mysterious. Here's the thing . . . I think someone has taken advantage of me — and of Edwin. Whoever it is got me to appraise one of Edwin's rare antiques under false pretenses. Their plan all along was to steal it and sell it for top dollar. Only someone who knew Edwin well could have pulled off such an elaborate hoax. My question to you is, who at work is close to him?"

"No one that I know. He's a great guy and all, but he's not the kind of person you get close to."

"Fair enough. Who has a grudge against him?"

"I have no idea. Why are you asking me? Why would you think I know anything?"

I smiled and leaned in close to whisper, "I was the receptionist at a big company for a summer after high school. By the time I left for college, I knew everything about that place. Who was friends, and who wasn't. Who goes to lunch with whom. You know what I'm talking about — it's part of the fun of the job. You're more in the know than the boss."

She giggled. "It's true."

"I know you don't know me well, but I also know you respect Edwin. If you have even a teeny hint of an idea that might point

244

me in the right direction, I sure hope you tell me. Even if all you have is a suspicion — I won't quote you. I just need a lead, a place to start. Don't you hate the thought that Edwin is being taken advantage of?"

"Of course . . . and what with his wife being killed . . . it's just awful."

"Let's be methodical. Is anyone desperate for cash?"

She scrunched up her face for a moment. "No one I know."

"Whoever is behind this scheme knew the antique's history, so it has to be someone who knew Edwin or Ava well. Is there someone he's especially close to? An old friend who pops in for lunch? Someone he's worked with forever?"

"Miranda, his assistant. I don't think they're close, but they've worked together for like fifteen years."

"Good. Thank you. How about someone who's mad at him? Maybe someone who got fired or demoted or something."

The waitress placed our drinks on the Formica counter. I sipped some tea.

Judi used her straw to stir the Coke. She lowered her voice. "You should talk to Tammy Perlow. She used to work at Towson's. She left about six months ago."

"What did she do?"

"She was brought in as a temp to scan in documents. We're going paperless."

"What happened?"

"It didn't work out. She left pretty abruptly, if you know what I mean. She was only there about three months."

"She was fired?"

"I'm not allowed to say."

"I understand. No problem. I asked for a hint, and you've given me one. I'm grateful."

"You promised you wouldn't quote me."

"And I won't." I lowered my eyes to my tea. "What's Tammy like?"

"She's beautiful. Like a model."

"Is she nice?"

"I guess." She stirred her Coke some more, spinning ice into the glass. "She and Edwin used to joke a lot."

"About what?"

"I don't know. I just saw them standing around laughing, you know?"

I nodded, reading between the lines. "Who else should I talk to?"

"I don't know . . . besides which, I'm really not supposed to talk about anyone or anything. I shouldn't have said as much."

"I'll never tell," I said, sipping my iced tea. "Do you know where I can find Tammy?"

She didn't, but that was okay. I had a name, and that was what I came for. I slid two twenty-dollar bills under my glass and stood up. Forty was probably ten too much, but it was way short of what anyone might mistake for a bribe. When Judi recalled our conversation, I wanted my generosity to be part of the mix.

"Thanks, Judi. Enjoy that lobster roll!"

I stopped at a deli three doors down and bought a premade spinach salad, the kind with three strips of grilled chicken on top. The clerk tossed a small plastic tub of ranch dressing into the bag, along with a napkin-wrapped plastic knife and fork. Once I reached my car, I levered the seat back so I had plenty of room, lowered the windows to catch the fresh, briny ocean breeze, and perched the salad on my lap.

Tammy was beautiful, like a model. Employed, then not, after only a few months. I considered the odds that Edwin had fibbed when he told me that he hoped his marriage would succeed. Based solely on what Judi hadn't said, I wondered if Tammy might be Edwin's mistress. Disappointed in his marriage, rich beyond most men's dreams, Edwin might have set Tammy up in a posh condo and given her a fancy car and endless credit cards. Everyone was happy until Ava got wind of it and raised all sorts of hell — especially since she'd just learned that she was pregnant. Maybe Ava confronted Tammy, saw a younger, prettier version of herself, and announced the gravy train had pulled out of the station. Perhaps Tammy decided not to go quietly, but rather to take out the competition.

People have killed for less.

CHAPTER TWENTY-FOUR

I breezed through Grey Gull security as if I owned the place.

The man working the guardhouse was younger and more affable than A. Henderson, the guard who'd refused to allow me in on Wednesday. This man's name tag read R. VORN. He handed me a laminated guest placard for my dashboard and told me how to find Penelope Hahn's unit.

Penelope's town house was tall and narrow, positioned to optimize the water view. The glossy admiral blue of her door contrasted nicely with the mellow red brick and the crisp white trim. A wreath made of sprigs of lavender and silvery gray dusty miller twirled through and around supple twigs hung from a silver hook. The lavender scent drifted toward me in the warm breeze. I pushed the buzzer.

Penelope opened the door, smiled warmly, and invited me in.

After I reassured her that my scrapes and nicks were nothing, just an unfortunate scuffle with a bush, she led the way into her country-farmhouse-style kitchen. I joined her for a cup of tea and nibbled on a chocolate chip cookie. We chatted easily about Dutch cabinetry, known for its dramatic floral and geometric marquetry ornamentations, the beautiful summer weather, and therapeutic horse rides. Half an hour later, I left with a $5,000 check payable to New Hampshire Children First! tucked in my tote and drove back toward the main entrance. Before reaching it, though, I turned right, then right again, and rolled to a stop behind the silver Lexus parked in Jean Cooper's driveway.

Jean's three-story town house also overlooked the pond, but the position and style were different from Penelope's. Jean's was built on a hill, and her front door was on the second floor.

I climbed the flight of stone stairs to the entry level and knocked. No answer. I pressed the doorbell and listened to the tinny chimes, then cupped my eyes to peer in one of the sheer-curtain-covered windows that flanked the door. Down the hall, past a bowl of oranges sitting on a kitchen counter, I could see out the back door and clear across the water to the library.

I returned to the driveway and glanced around. The complex grounds were fastidiously groomed. Bushes were neatly clipped. The plant arrangements — pink impatiens in the shady areas and rosy petunias in the sunny sections — were edged with gray bricks. The grass was mowed, the edges precisely trimmed. No one was in sight.

I walked to the other side of Jean's house. Hidden behind a ten-foot-tall Eastern pine, a six-foot-wide gravel passage gave access to the rear, separating Jean's end unit from the next row of town houses. I slipped past the tree, crunched my way along the path, sidestepped down a short, steep incline, and found myself on a pond-front swath of lawn. The pond was surrounded by wild growth, although it was possible, I supposed, that what appeared native and natural was cultivated and staged. Pussy willows and cattails grew in tangled abandon alongside tall grasses. I recognized wispy feather reed, soft red maiden, and yellowish northern sea oats. Mixed in were Boston and lady ferns, lilies of the valley, and riverbank grapes, the dark purple fruit hanging low, the tendrils twirling around Coral Fire mountain ash on their climb to the heavens.

Standing with my back to the water, I assessed Jean's unit. Sliding glass doors led to a ground-level room. The drapes were drawn. No sliver of light showed through. To the right, stairs led to a deck off the kitchen, and above it, on the third level, a Romeo and Juliet balcony jutted out from what I assumed was the master bedroom.

I tugged the sliding glass door, but it didn't budge.

I climbed the back staircase and peered through the window in the kitchen door. The bowl of oranges was directly in front of me. By angling my face and pressing my right eye into the glass, I was able to see sideways to the sink. Nothing. No dirty dishes. No coffee mug on the counter. No half-eaten muffin. I turned my face the other way, and with my left eye at the glass, I had a clear sight line into the dining room. A black and beige Michael Kors tote bag rested on the glass-topped table. A bone-colored shoe lay on its side by the china cabinet, the stiletto pointing toward me, toward my heart.

The shoe rested at an odd angle. I shifted my eye a half inch to the right. A leg.

I gasped and stumbled backward, lurching into the railing.

"Oh, my God," I whispered.

Jean could be injured, lying there, unable

to get up.

I flew back to the door and pounded on the frame. "Jean!" I hollered. "Jean!"

The leg didn't move.

I rang the bell, holding the button down, hearing the shrill, persistent buzz. The leg still didn't move, not even a twitch.

Using the butt end of my flashlight, I smashed the windowpane, reached around the jagged shards clinging to the putty, and unbolted the door. I dropped my tote and ran into the dining room.

It was Jean, or had been. Her raven black hair splayed out like a fan. Her ebony eyes stared at the ceiling. I knelt beside the body and took her icy hand in mine. I shivered as if a chill wind had blown in. There was no blood, no wound, no sign of how she died. I pressed my fingers against her wrist, hoping to feel a pulse. She lay in repose, as untroubled, unsurprised, and unconcerned as Ava had been. I kept my eyes on her face, waiting for the inchoate images and fractured recollections pinballing through my memory to resolve themselves into a single coherent image or thought. Nothing occurred to me except that she was dead, and that her death had to be related to Ava's.

I needed to call Ellis, to report the death. Before I could stand, a man's voice shouted,

"Don't move!"

I froze.

"Stay right where you are," he snarled. His tone became marginally more civilized as he continued talking. "It looks like we have a DOA. Call nine-one-one."

I recognized him from his voice — he was A. Henderson, the burly Grey Gull guard who hadn't let me knock on Jean's door — and I guessed he was reporting to a dispatcher or his boss. I stood up and turned to face him. He was talking into his collar mic while pointing a black matte-finish Glock .22 at my stomach, a cop's gun.

"I told you not to move," he growled.

"I can't believe Grey Gull security guards carry guns."

"It's my own. Properly permitted." His eyes narrowed for a moment as recognition dawned on him. "I remember you. You're the girl who tried to get me to let you into the complex even though Ms. Cooper wasn't home and didn't authorize it."

I don't like being called a girl, especially by a sixty-year-old security guard with delusions of grandeur and a gun.

"How'd you get into the complex?" he demanded.

I didn't reply. I couldn't think of a single question he might ask that I'd feel inclined to answer.

Sirens, faint but growing louder, sounded from somewhere nearby.

"Jean's security alarm was on," I said, "probably in home mode. When I broke the window, it alerted whoever monitors the system that a breach had occurred, and you came on the fly. Impressive response time."

Sirens blared.

"I asked you a question, missy."

I lowered my eyes to his weapon and kept them there.

The sirens abruptly stopped. Two minutes later, Ellis stepped into the kitchen, followed by Griff.

"Josie?" Ellis said, astonished. His gaze swept past me and fixed on Henderson. "I'm Rocky Point Police Chief Hunter. And you are?"

"Al Henderson, sir. Grey Gull security. I found the suspect kneeling over the body, sir."

"Lower your weapon."

Henderson did as he was told.

Ellis held out his hand. "I'll take it."

"I have a carry permit."

"Good. We'll take a look at it."

Henderson didn't want to turn over his weapon, and his dilemma was easy to read. Petulance and rebellion warred against a deeply engrained habit of following rules. Respect for authority won, and he handed over his weapon, butt first.

"Griff?" Ellis called without taking his eyes off Henderson's face.

"Yes, sir."

"Log this weapon into evidence."

"Evidence?" Henderson protested in what was close to a shout. "What the — ?" Henderson stopped himself, took a breath, and lowered the volume. "Evidence of what?"

Griff extracted a plastic evidence bag from his pocket, and Ellis slipped the weapon in.

"From where I stand, Mr. Henderson, it appears that I walked in on an assault with a deadly weapon. We're detaining you for questioning. Griff, escort Mr. Henderson out to a patrol car and take his statement."

"I caught this girl in the act and you're treating me like a perp?"

"In the act of what?"

"Checking Jean's pulse," I said, interjecting myself into their battle of wills and perception.

Ellis nodded. "That's what I figured." He jerked his head toward the door. "Get him out of here, Griff."

"This way, sir," Griff said, as unperturbed as ever.

Henderson stomped his way out, and

Griff pulled the door closed behind them.

"Are you okay?" Ellis asked me, his tone normal.

Apparently, I was forgiven for refusing to give him Mac's name as my source for the info about Orson Thompkins.

"Yes. Given the situation, I'm doing pretty well."

I stepped aside so he could see Jean's corpse.

He squatted beside her body, taking in details without touching anything, then stood again.

"What did you touch?"

"Her wrist. The rug. That's it."

"Why did you break in?"

"I saw her leg." I closed my eyes for a moment. "I knocked and rang the bell and shouted, and the leg didn't move. The guard got here less than a minute or two later, probably in response to the broken glass setting off a silent alarm." I glanced at Jean's body. "How did she die?"

"The ME will be here soon," he said, ignoring my question.

Daryl Lucher, the police officer who made killer barbecue, stepped into the kitchen.

"No one but the ME and the crime scene team gets in without talking to me first," Ellis told him.

"Got it," Daryl said.

I picked up my tote bag from where I'd dropped it in the kitchen, and we left.

"Your cuts seem to be healing nicely," Ellis said as we walked down the stairs.

"I got lucky."

"How's Ty doing in D.C.?"

It felt surrealistic to be chatting only steps away from a corpse. "Navigating the political landscape carefully. He'll be home for the weekend, thank God. We should have our July Fourth barbecue on Sunday."

"You're right. It's easy to put off stuff, then put it off again, then the next thing you know, you're buying your Thanksgiving turkey. I'll tell Zoë."

We walked up the gravel pathway to the front.

"I need to get the canvass and other things going," he said. "Can you stick around for a little?"

"Sure."

I took a seat on the second step of the front staircase, glad to have the sun on my face.

Dr. Graham, the medical examiner, pulled up in her official vehicle. She spoke to Ellis for a minute, not longer, then walked toward the back.

Two women came out of a town house

three doors down on the right and stood on the sidewalk, taking in the scene. One looked to be closer to eighty than seventy. She was short and thin with gray crimped hair, and she leaned heavily on a wooden walking stick. Her companion, a curvy blonde, was young enough to be her great-granddaughter.

Officer F. Meade rooted around the trunk of a patrol car for a few seconds until she located a roll of yellow and black crime scene tape. She began cordoning off the area, wrapping the tape around a silver birch near the curb, then heading to a light post in the neighbor's front yard.

Ellis read something on his BlackBerry, then started off toward Griff and Henderson. Henderson sat sideways on the backseat of a patrol car, his feet on the pavement. Griff leaned against the door frame, nodding at something Henderson said.

Another man, a stranger, hovered near the hood of Griff's police vehicle, maybe trying to eavesdrop. He looked about fifty. He was a little above average height and slender. His gray collared T-shirt was snug, not like it was too small, but like he cared about the way his clothes fit. He also wore black Bermuda shorts and black moccasins. The Grey Gull logo was embroidered in black over the shirt pocket.

He hurried toward Ellis.

"Are you in charge?" the stranger asked.

"Yes, I'm Police Chief Hunter. And you are . . . ?"

"Kirk Trevis, the manager on duty." His eyes were big with worry. "No one will tell me what's going on."

"We don't know what's going on yet."

"Is Ms. Cooper all right?"

"How do you know her?"

"She's lived here the whole time I've been a manager — five years. She's a wonderful woman. Always courteous to the staff, which is more than I can say about some residents."

Another car rolled to a stop, double parking. Detective Brownley stepped out. I could see how blue her eyes were from where I sat, a trick of the sun's angle, perhaps.

"When did you see Ms. Cooper last?" Ellis asked him.

"I don't know. Why? Please — tell me why you're here."

"We'll let you know what we can as soon as we can. I promise you that. When did you see her last?"

"Yesterday," Kirk said. "She stopped by the office to ask a question about renting out her condo. I gave her the forms. She was fine. We chatted about the weather. She was heading to the pool."

"When was she thinking about renting?"

"She didn't say. She was planning a long trip, that's all I know."

"Thank you." Ellis waggled fingers at Detective Brownley, calling her over. "Detective Brownley will take your preliminary statement."

"But I need to know about Jean!"

Detective Brownley led Kirk away.

An oversized black van pulled up. ROCKY POINT CRIME SCENE INVESTIGATION was painted on the sides in gold and white. Two men carrying pilot-style square black cases with the division's name stenciled on the sides in gold joined Ellis.

"Anything we need to know?" the older of the two asked Ellis.

"Dr. Graham's already inside." He pointed to the pass-through. "Behind that tree. Up the back stairs."

"Okeydokey," he said, and started off.

The younger man followed.

Ellis turned toward me, pressing the side of his hand against his forehead to shield his eyes from the sun's glare. "Any news about that missing Tiffany lamp?"

"No."

"Have you spoken to Edwin recently?"

"Just now. This morning. How come?"

"What about?"

"A couple of things. Mostly we talked about Prescott's buying the contents of the Garnet Cove house and grounds. We discussed the arrangements."

"Did he tell you anything about his plans?"

"He's moved into a hotel, if that what you mean. He's relocating his business to London."

"How about today? Did he discuss his plans for the day?"

"No . . . why?"

Ellis lowered his hand and squinted into the sun like a sheriff in an old Western. He surveyed the scene, his focus absolute.

After a minute, he turned back to me. "Because he's gone missing."

CHAPTER TWENTY-FIVE

Because of the incline, Ellis's and my eyes were level even though I was sitting on the second step of the stairway that led to Jean's condo and he was standing on the walkway.

"Edwin is missing? What do you mean, missing?"

"I sent Detective Brownley to bring Edwin in to talk about Jean. He wasn't at his company."

"I was just there. I talked to him."

"The receptionist saw him leave about noon. He's not answering his phone or responding to texts or e-mails, which, according to his assistant, is unprecedented. Where do you think he went?"

"Me? I have no idea. I barely know him."

"You were, it seems, the last person to speak to him. Your conversation was on a hot-button issue — selling all his worldly goods. How did he seem?"

"The same as always, impatient and annoyed. This time, I felt bad for him. What you call all his worldly goods were things his wife selected. He was pretty bitter about Ava's apparent betrayal, but who wouldn't be?"

Ellis cocked his head and narrowed his eyes. "What betrayal?"

"Selling the lamp out from under him. What else?"

"Chief?" Officer Meade called.

She lifted her phone above her head and moved it back and forth a bit — she wanted him to take a call.

"Wait here," he told me and strode off.

The two neighbors hadn't moved. Both women were watching the police like spectators at a tennis match, their gazes moving back and forth, keeping tabs on all the action. The police tape separated Jean's town house, the surrounding lawn, and the gravel passageway from the rest of the complex. I was inside the crime scene. Ellis stood with his back to me talking on Officer Meade's phone.

Edwin was missing.

I checked my phone. It was twenty after two. I had two voice mails, three texts, and eight emails. Zoë had called, saying she missed me and that she was excited our July Fourth barbecue was back on the schedule.

Lucky me, I thought, to have a friend like Zoë. The second voice mail was from Wes, along with two of the texts. The voice mail message was short and to the point: "Call me. Now." The first text, sent seconds after the call, read *Call.* The second text read *Josie. Call, URGENT.* The third text was from Ty telling me that he was on his way and that he loved me. I texted him: *Another woman is dead.* A minute later, I realized how cold and uninformative that must sound and sent a second text: *I'm so glad you're coming home. xxxxoooo.* All eight e-mails were work related; none required immediate attention.

Ellis, still on the phone, turned to face me, caught my eye, and raised his left index finger. "I'll just be a minute," the gesture communicated. I nodded, then called work.

"Oh, I'm glad you called in, Josie," Cara said. "Sasha would like to talk to you."

"Sounds good — but before you put her on . . . how are you doing?"

"Better. Thank you. Working helps."

"I'm glad to hear that. Is anything going on I should know about?"

She said no and transferred me to Sasha.

"The news from the marble expert is better than good. I spoke at length to Mr. Colby. The marble I thought might be a

Banded Oxblood Swirl — it is. For the last seventy years archaeologists have been digging at old glassworks sites in Germany, and a few examples have surfaced. As far as Mr. Colby knows, though, all of the examples have been damaged by the recovery process, or were discarded in the first place because they were marred during or after production."

"Could he date it?"

"Yes, 1850 to 1880."

"Do the typical factors that determine value apply here?"

"Yes, and all are in our favor. Not many Banded Oxblood Swirls of this size were made, so it's rare. Only a handful seem to have survived, so it's scarce. And it is highly prized by collectors."

"I'm sitting down — give me a number."

"Marketed properly, Mr. Colby thinks it might sell for as much as thirty thousand dollars."

Anyone looking at me must have wondered why my eyes and mouth opened wide. I took a breath, then said, "That's a good number. Didn't you say none has ever sold at auction?"

"That's right, but he cited two examples of other extremely rare marbles that had, and he thinks our marble will appeal to the same collector niche. For instance, a seven-eighth-inch split ribbon glass swirl Lutz marble, pink with green and oxblood lines — a color combination Mr. Colby says no expert had ever seen before — sold for more than twenty-five thousand dollars, the most ever paid for a marble smaller than one inch. The other example was what he described as a very rare opaque purple banded Lutz with a lavender core and a one-and-three-quarters-inch diameter. It sold for seventeen thousand dollars. Mr. Colby says everything seems to be in excellent condition, and that's the most important aspect. He thinks none will sell for less than a few hundred dollars."

"This is great news, Sasha. What's your next step?"

"If it's all right with you, I'd like to bring him in for two days to examine the marbles in person. He'll write the catalogue copy. His fee is within our expert consulting range. He doesn't want us to send them to him because he doesn't have a secure facility. He works out of his home office and keeps his own collection in a bank vault."

"I love that idea. Tell Gretchen I've approved it so she can arrange his travel. Any news from Fred about Aunt Louise's desk?"

"He's still at the Towsons', but he brought

me up to date earlier. The situation is complex. Karla, the archivist he's working with, has finished reviewing the News and Views photographs and has found fifty-seven that include a man with whom Aunt Louise seems particularly cozy. She's turned over the names to Fred. So far, he has confirmed that forty-two of them are deceased, no surprise given the timeline. Of the remaining fifteen, he's spoken to eight of them, all Aunt Louise fans, two of whom happily acknowledge having been her lover back in the day, but no one so far who knows anything about the desk."

"And we don't even know that anyone she met through her work is the buyer."

"Not good odds."

"No," I agreed. I thanked her for the update, then asked if anyone else needed me, and when she said no, we ended the call.

I was so fortunate in my staff. I'd discovered early on in my career that the secret to business success came from hiring the best people, ensuring they had the resources they needed to do their jobs, and staying out of their way.

The light breeze had dwindled to nothing, and the humidity had increased. I was sitting out in the open, and the sun beat down on me like fire. I fanned myself with my hand in a failed attempt to stir a cooling breeze. I stretched like a cat, stood up, and strolled across the lawn to the shade of a maple tree.

Ellis was still on the phone.

I glanced around. No one was paying any attention to me. Griff was still talking to Henderson. The two women were watching as the bevy of uniformed officers, F. Meade included, knocked on doors and chatted with whoever answered. Keeping one eye on Ellis, I called Wes.

Before I finished saying hello, Wes interrupted me, sounding both chagrined and suspicious.

"How did you get into the complex?" he demanded. After I explained, he added, "Go tell the guard to let me in. I'll be there in two minutes."

"Forget it, Wes. I'm inside the police line, waiting to be interviewed."

"Then take pictures. Lots of them. Record conversations. Be my eyes and ears."

"I'm hanging up now."

Twenty seconds later, my phone vibrated. It was a text from Wes. *Take photos.*

I thought about it for a minute, then walked slowly to the gravel walkway, acting as if I had no particular purpose and all the

269

time in the world. Using the tree as cover, I photographed the condo; the police canvass; Griff, as he shrugged in response to something Henderson said; and Ellis, who was still talking on the phone. I e-mailed Wes the photos, then waited some more. I turned my back to the street so I could see the pond and watched a duck dip its face into the cool water, shake off the excess, and paddle away. The water was glass-smooth, but only for a moment. Off to the left, concentric circles grew ever wider and fainter until they were nothing but a memory. A fish, probably, disturbing submerged duckweed or sea grass as it flitted through the water. Overhead, a bird chirped, la-oop, la-oop, a happy sound.

"Josie?" Ellis called.

I stuck my head out and waved, and he walked my way.

"Sorry about that," he said.

"No prob," I said.

He pulled his elbows back, arching his back, turning left, then right, loosening up, I guessed.

"Where were we?" he asked.

"You were telling me that Edwin has gone missing. Have you found him yet?"

"No. Have you thought of anything that might help us locate him?"

"No. You said you had him on camera in the parking lot. Then what?"

"He got in a red Mercedes and drove north on Ocean. That was at twelve fourteen. A camera mounted in a condo-complex parking lot picked him up about five miles from his company, continuing north. That's the last anyone has seen or heard from him."

"I thought he used a driver."

"Apparently he drives himself sometimes."

"Is the Mercedes Ava's?"

"Yes. What's north of here he might want to visit?"

"It has to be a person, not a place," I said. "He doesn't like New Hampshire. He's eager to get out. He's meeting someone."

"Who?"

"I have no idea."

The two women who'd been observing the police edged closer to the police tape, and their movement caught Ellis's eye. He turned toward Detective Brownley. She was leaning on her vehicle's hood writing something in a spiral bound notebook.

"Detective!" Ellis called.

The detective pivoted to face him. He jerked his head toward the women. She looked at them, then back at Ellis, and nodded. She flipped her notebook closed and

271

marched off toward the pair.

"Have the crime scene guys found the Tiffany lamp in Jean's condo?" I asked.

"Not yet or they would have called. It's not in plain sight. Will you help me look?"

"Of course."

He punched a number into his smart phone. "Can I bring someone in?" He listened for a moment, then said, "Will do." He tapped the END CALL button and slipped the unit into his pocket. "You'll wear booties and not touch anything. Nothing. If you want a drawer opened, tell me, and I'll open it. If you want to look under a table, you ask me before you get down on your hands and knees. Understood?"

"Yes."

We walked side by side down the gravel pathway.

"What are you doing here anyway?" he asked.

"I wanted to talk to Jean. I've tried calling for a while now without reaching her. I was in the complex for another reason and thought I'd try knocking on her door."

"What other reason?"

"Fund-raising."

"That's pretty convenient," he said, sounding skeptical.

"But true." I reached into my tote, found

Penelope's check, and held it up. "Ms. Hahn was very generous."

He gave the check a thorough viewing, not merely a glance. "What did you want to talk to Jean about?"

"The fake Ava. I'm still trying to find the stolen lamp and figure out who played me."

"What do you think she knew?"

"The truth? I think she was involved." I held up a hand. "No, I didn't expect her to confess, but I did think I might have been able to guilt her or frighten her into returning the lamp, no questions asked. Once I had the lamp secured, then I planned to turn everything I'd learned over to you."

"You're kidding, right? You thought she was simply going to hand over a stolen lamp worth more than a million smackers?"

"Little Miss Optimism, that's me."

"That's completely naive, not to say, foolish."

"I wasn't going to ask her about her sister's murder. Just about the lamp."

"What made you think Edwin would agree to a no-questions-asked-if-you-return-the-lamp deal?"

"He doesn't want the publicity that comes with a criminal investigation."

We climbed the back stairs. At the first landing, Ellis asked, "What makes you think

273

Jean was involved?"

"The thief referenced details about Edwin's family that only Edwin and Ava knew. I think Ava and Jean cooked up this plot together."

A technician greeted us at the door.

The booties were turquoise plastic, elasticized to fit snugly around the wearer's ankles. We paused at the archway that led into the dining room. Jean lay on her back, her gaze seemingly fixed on the ceiling. She appeared as attractive as ever.

"She hasn't been dead long," I whispered.

Ellis spoke in hushed tones, too. "A few hours, according to preliminary reports. The a/c is cranking, so it will take Dr. Graham a little time to confirm it."

"What killed her?"

"She was shot once in the back of her head, execution style."

I stared at the corpse, appalled. My heart stopped for a moment, then hammered against my ribs. "Could it be suicide?"

"No. No gun. The tech guys are fairly certain the weapon was a .45, though. Who do you know who has a gun of that caliber?"

"No one. I mean, I don't talk about guns with people."

"There's no sign of forced entry, no sign of a struggle, and no sign that anyone ransacked her condo. She had eighty-two dollars in her bag, which was on the dining room table, in plain sight. The security log indicates that her front door opened at nine thirty-two, then again at nine fifty-six."

"Who passed through the guardhouse around nine twenty-five?"

"Orson Thompkins."

"What?" I exclaimed.

"The security photo shows a woman wearing a big straw hat and big sunglasses. We can tell she's white."

"A woman." I lowered my eyes for a moment, then raised them to Ellis's face. "Did the cameras pick up a license plate?"

"Yes, but it was smeared with mud. The car was a white Impala."

"A rental."

"Maybe."

"Did the guard check ID?"

"No. He got the name and called Jean to get permission for her to enter. Jean gave it."

"So she was alive at nine twenty-five."

"Nine twenty-six, yes."

"When did the Impala leave?"

"Nine fifty-seven, through the back exit."

"The one with no guard."

"Right. The photos show the same person. A white woman in a floppy hat."

"You can't be certain it was a woman," I said.

"Nor can we be certain she was alone in the car."

"What about Jean's boyfriend?"

"Shawn O'Boyle. He's listed as one of Jean's emergency contacts, along with Ava. He's in Mexico City on business, been there for a week."

"And you'll be checking whether he flew in and out again."

"Of course. I bet he didn't."

"No bet. Why are you telling me all this? You're not usually so open."

"Everything I've just told you has already been released to the press." Ellis led me to the stairs that went down to the basement. "We might as well start at the bottom and work our way up."

CHAPTER TWENTY-SIX

The rooms in Jean's condo were spacious, the ceilings high, the fit and finishes top-of-the-line throughout. The basement was tricked out as a media room with a 100-inch TV mounted on the long inside wall, a butterscotch leather sectional couch in the middle of the room, and a popcorn machine in the corner. I walked closer. The machine had an "add butter" option. Ty loved popcorn, and I made a mental note to check out getting him a machine like this one for Christmas, then chastised myself for thinking such a thing while I was in a murder victim's house with the body lying overhead.

"It's freezing in here," I said, rubbing my upper arms.

"Yeah. Either Jean liked living in a meat locker or someone was trying to mess with the time-of-death analysis."

"Will it?"

"Maybe."

"Fingerprints on the thermostat dial?"

"It's a digital display, and it's been wiped."

"So it was the killer."

"Not necessarily. Look at this place."

"I see what you mean," I said. "I think the word for this is fastidious."

"Or compulsive. It would be like living in a museum."

I asked Ellis to open the built-in cabinet doors. The unit housed cable equipment, an old CD changer, racks of neatly organized CDs, mostly light rock, and a stack of puzzle magazines. I felt like a voyeur.

Back on the main level, the living room and den were furnished in ornate red, gold, and green tropical floral fabrics; heavy, dark walnut furniture; and lush Oriental rugs — a modern-day interpretation of British colonial furnishings. The kitchen, in contrast, was ultramodern, decked out in black granite, with a red glass backsplash and stainless appliances. Upstairs, the master bedroom evoked the Caribbean sea, the walls pale aqua, the drapes a delicate blue. The guest room was decorated in shades of crimson, yellow, and orange, like a sunset. All the rooms featured gleaming golden bamboo flooring except for one of the two walk-in closets in the master bedroom, which was carpeted in plush ivory wall-to-wall. The drapes throughout were heavy, with blackout linings. The light fixtures matched the decor: sleek red pendants hung in the kitchen; dark wood ceiling fans with built-in mushroom globes turned slowly in the living room; translucent sconces were mounted on the master bedroom wall; a pair of amber glass lamps with matching shades cast a golden glow in the guest room.

"Any thoughts?" Ellis asked, once we returned to the living room.

"I've seen more than one floor safe in a closet, and since that's the only space in the entire condo that's carpeted, it might be worth a peek."

"Good catch. Let's check."

We returned to the upper floor.

"Can I get on my knees?" I asked.

"I'll do it. Direct me."

Ellis extracted a neatly folded clear plastic minitarp from his pocket, shook it open, and knelt on it. With plastic-gloved hands, he peeled back a corner of the carpet, revealing the same golden bamboo hardwood flooring that was in the rest of the apartment. The carpet wasn't tacked down; it had been cut to fit and wedged in. He rolled the carpet up and laid it on the tarp, off to the side, out of the way.

I pulled my miniflashlight from my belt

and squatted as if I were doing a deep-knee bend to conduct an inch-by-inch search. In the far left corner, a triangular piece of wood with the grain running horizontally caught my eye. The grain on the rest of the floor ran vertically. Once seen, there was no missing it.

I pointed, aiming the light beam at the mismatched piece. "Do you see that triangular bit? It may be a latch. Push it."

Ellis leaned in and pressed down. A floor-board rose slightly.

"Do I push or pull?"

"Push, harder."

He did, and a 2' × 2' section of the floor slid up and back like an automated hatch, revealing an opening below. He touched the underside of the flooring section, and it raised effortlessly, revealing a cubbyhole. Inside, a stone-colored metal box, about 18" × 12", rested on the bottom.

Ellis called down for someone to come take photos, and also to bring him a jumbo-sized evidence bag. A minute later, the younger of the two technicians appeared and took an array of photos. Detective Brownley appeared in the doorway, a super-sized clear plastic bag in hand.

When the technician was done, Ellis eased the box out of the secret compartment and stood. The technician took photos of the empty cubbyhole.

As Ellis walked to the bed, he extracted a second plastic tarp from his pocket and spread it over the duvet. He lowered the box to the tarp. The technician continued taking pictures.

The box had FIREPROOF etched onto the hasp. It was unlocked. Ellis opened it. A folded sheet of paper partially covered stacks of rubber-banded hundred-dollar bills.

Ellis unfolded the paper and laid it on the tarp so the technician could get his shots. It was a receipt for a replica Tiffany wisteria lamp dated the day after Ava had closed her bank account. Jean had paid $44,500 to a New York City antiques dealer named Jonathan Swalling, including delivery charges. The lamp had been shipped via Malca-Amit, a top secure-transport company.

"May I take a picture?" I asked. "I'd like to follow up with Mr. Swalling."

"We'll make the call together. You know the questions to ask."

"I'd be glad to. Is that a no to the photo?"

"Yes, no. If and when it won't compromise the investigation, I'll see you get a photo. You can tell Wes I said so."

"I didn't mention Wes's name."

"I noticed that."

I didn't reply. My eyes dropped to the currency. I'd been right. Jean and Ava were in it together. Evidently, Edwin had been right, too — as soon as Ava learned she was pregnant, she came up with a plan to fund her new life by selling the Tiffany lamp. She couldn't wait for the prenup to expire, and she didn't want to deal with his complaints about how a baby would disrupt their jet-setting lifestyle.

Jean had overseen the acquisition of a replica good enough to fool him, not a hard task given his lack of interest in the details of his home. I considered how Ava might have justified the theft, whether she wanted the money to help ensure her baby would have the best possible life, or whether she thought she was entitled to it as compensation for her years of service. My mom once warned me that if you marry a man for his money, you earn every penny.

Jean brought the replica over to the Towson house the morning the fake Ava contacted me. They'd hired someone using the name Orson Thompkins to speak to me, pretending to be Edwin, then later to sell the genuine lamp. Once Ava was murdered, though, everything changed. Thompkins decided that discretion was the better part of valor and withdrew the ad. Perhaps they planned to relist it in a few months, once the brouhaha died down, or to try their luck in a different location, a place with a strong antiques market, Atlanta or Dallas or Chicago, or even overseas, in Japan, maybe, where the statute of limitations on stolen antiques was a mere two years. I wondered again, not for the first time, if Orson Thompkins was Ava's lover. I also wondered where Shawn O'Boyle, Jean's boyfriend, was in all this. Had he really been in Mexico the whole time? Might he have played the role of Orson Thompkins?

The clock radio on the bedside table read 2:51. "It's nearly three. May I leave?"

"I'll need you to stop by the station to give us an official statement."

"What with Ty coming in and all, can't it wait until Monday?"

"It shouldn't. Can you squeeze in half an hour tomorrow?"

"It's tag sale day."

"During your lunch break."

"You drive a hard bargain."

"Detective Brownley can come to you."

"Sold." I turned to the detective. "How's noon? I supply pizza on Saturdays, so come hungry."

She thanked me and said that noon would

work, then handed Ellis the evidence bag. "I'll walk Josie out."

The older technician stood in the dining room tapping something into a tablet. The corpse had been removed.

I paused on the stoop, glad to get out of the frigid air-conditioning and into the hot sun. A niggling suspicion that Edwin knew more than he was telling was with me like an itch I couldn't reach to scratch. Any man whose wife planned to sell a family heirloom to fund her escape from the marriage would feel betrayed. Some men would act out. Others would tough it out. Some would fall apart. Others would cope. A few might go all Machiavellian on her. I could easily see Edwin in that category. Whether Edwin was involved in the murders, or Shawn was, or neither, as far as I could see, there were no winners. Jean had lived alone, and she'd died alone. Her body had been found by a relative stranger — me. Everywhere I looked, I saw something sadder than the place I'd looked before. I hadn't even met Ava or Shawn, but my heart broke for them just as much as it did for Edwin and Jean. Ava must have felt like a big cat in a small cage. Edwin didn't know which way was up. Shawn was coming home from a business trip to nothing. Jean had only wanted to

help her sister.
Poor Ava.
Poor Edwin.
Poor Shawn.
Poor Jean.

CHAPTER TWENTY-SEVEN

I drove to the deserted stretch of beach where Wes and I often met and parked on the sandy shoulder. Jean's murder had left me shaken and fearful, and I needed to take a minute to let the roiling anxiety trilling through my veins dissipate. Whatever plot had been set in motion when the man calling himself Orson Thompkins asked me to appraise his Tiffany lamp wasn't over yet. Carrying only my keys, I climbed a low dune, then scampered down the other side and pushed past an unruly thatch of brambles and trailing wild roses until I came to soft sand. I took off my sandals, dropping them near a slick ribbon of bottle green seaweed. I placed my keys inside one shoe. The sand was searingly hot.

I ran for the water, stumbling on half-buried rocks, only stopping when I reached the cool wet sand. The ocean was calm. The tide rolled in with a soft swish. I dug my toes into the sand and stood still, letting the cold frothy water lap my ankles. A hundred yards from shore, a motorboat raced by. Gold stars shimmied across the blue ocean surface in its wake.

I needed to do something, but I couldn't think what. Ty would be home in a matter of hours, the only bright spot in an otherwise dark day. I was going to cook a feast for him: garlic-and-wine-infused steamers, lobsters stuffed with seasoned breadcrumbs and crabmeat, and all the trimmings, including sliced tomatoes and corn on the cob. It was only a little after three, though, so I had a good hour before I needed to drive to the Lobster Pot, where Marty, a third-generation fishmonger, stocked the freshest seafood on the coast.

A kayak swept by, shearing through the water like a knife through soft butter. A woman, digging deep. The sun was hot. When I was a kid, I'd sit in shallow water and dip my head backward. I wished I was in a bathing suit. I wet my hands and wiped the coolness on the back of my neck.

As I watched the gilt-tipped bobbing water, I considered my options. In five minutes, I had a plan.

I sat in my car with the air conditioner running and researched Tammy Perlow. The first two hits told me everything I needed to know to find her — where she worked and where she lived.

Tammy worked at Mandie's Candies, a Rocky Point landmark that served up salt-water taffy and easy-to-carry-to-the-beach favorite snacks, like chocolate ice-cream drumsticks and orange icicles. From her photo on the shop's "About Us" Web site page I could tell she was fully as beautiful as Judi had reported. Tammy had straight ice blond hair that fell below her shoulders, alabaster skin, big brown eyes that seemed to gaze at the world with guileless joy, and ruby lips. She was tall, probably just shy of six feet, and thin, not willowy, like Zoë, but slender and fit, like a long-distance runner. She must have towered over Edwin.

I found a bunch of photos on the Tarleton volunteer fire department's Web site. Tarleton, an old mill town west of Rocky Point, had been hurting big-time ever since the textile mills moved south in the 1950s, and there was no sign it was making a comeback. She and her mom, Peggy, had attended a charity event for the Tarleton volunteer fire department, a Mardi Gras casino night, and were listed in the hundred-dollar category called "Patrons." Peggy was a shorter, older, etiolated version of her daughter. In the photos, which were posted on the "Donate" page of the Web site, Tammy and Peggy wore countless strands of purple, green, and gold beads. One image showed Tammy holding a fifty-dollar bill leaning over a roulette table and hugging the wheel. Peggy was in the background applauding. The caption read "Gimme red every time!" Another photo showed Peggy sitting on a tall, thin man's lap, laughing. The man, who was about her age, looked embarrassed. This caption read "Come on, Uncle Hal! Loosen up!" A third photo showed a handsome man standing behind Tammy, encircling her in an embrace, his chin resting lightly on the top of her head. The pair smiled at the camera, relaxed, confident, content. The caption read "Life is good!"

Lots of people have given up their landlines, so I wasn't surprised that she wasn't listed in the Tarleton white pages. I tried general searches for her address without luck. I slid my tablet back into my bag and drove to Mandie's Candies.

I parked in the back row of the lot. On hot summer days Mandie's was packed, and today was no exception. I waited in line, and when it was my turn, I ordered a one-pound box of mixed flavored taffy from a short woman about my age. Her name tag said AMY. Tammy wasn't behind the counter, but that didn't mean she wasn't working. She could be in the back or on a break.

"Is Tammy here today?" I asked as she began filling the tissue-lined box.

"No. She'll be in tomorrow, though."

"Can you tell me where she lives?"

Amy's eyes narrowed. "Sorry, we don't give out that information."

I smiled sweetly. "I understand."

I paid and left.

I was tempted to give up, but I had one more lead, and forty minutes, so I decided to persevere. I turned right on Macaw, heading inland, and drove through Tarleton's desolate downtown. Boarded up storefronts nestled amid empty overgrown lots. Tumbles of frayed tires, battered furniture, and rusty old cars up on blocks covered most of the next block. A mile farther on, past deserted houses and fallow fields, I came to a well-lit and clean nineteenth-century brick firehouse. Its well-tended appearance seemed oddly out of place in the midst of such decay.

I parked off to the side and entered through a door painted glossy fire-engine red. A man in his early twenties sat at a card table playing solitaire. He was just as handsome as every firefighter I'd ever known. I often wondered if good looks was a requirement for the job.

"Great!" he said, grinning. "Gin or pinochle?"

"I wish I had time. I'm Josie."

He stood and offered a hand. "Chris. What can I do you for?"

I glanced around. A shiny red truck sat next to a white ambulance. Gray metal lockers lined one wall. Hoses hung in neat coils on the other side next to shovels and hatchets. Through an open door at the rear, I heard sounds of life, a pot clanging, a door opening, and footsteps.

"I'm looking for Tammy Perlow. You know her, right?"

"Sure. Her boyfriend is one of our volunteers. Did she tell you to meet her here?"

"No." I looked down, then back up. "I feel pretty dumb. I lost the slip of paper with her address and phone number on it. Knowing she hangs out here, I thought I'd take a chance and stop in."

"Don't feel dumb. I lose things all the time. She and Mark live in Seacoast Park, about a mile down on the right. Unit eighteen."

I gave him my 100-watt smile. "Thank you, Chris. You're the best!"

"Sure you don't want to try your luck at gin?"

"I'll take a rain check."

"Done!"

Chris stood at the door watching me back out. As I drove past the station, I gave a final wave, and he waved back.

Seacoast Park was a mobile home park. A sign on the left read:

WELCOME HOME!
Seacoast Park

Metallic red, white, and blue pinwheels attached to the sign with clear shipping tape spun merrily. A covey of kids ran through the small gardens that surrounded the trailers playing tag or chasing balls, and half a dozen adults, all women, sat on colorful woven-plastic lawn chairs alone or in pairs.

I drove to number 18, a nicely maintained double-wide mobile home. One parking slot was empty. A rusty old brown sedan was in the other slot, not the car of a rich man's mistress. If Tammy had ever been Edwin's mistress, I bet she wasn't now — not if she lived here and drove that car. I pulled into a parking spot.

I heard kids' squeals coming from inside the trailer. Moments later, two boys leaped from the stoop to the grass, each wielding a plastic sword, engaged in a ferocious galactic dual. One was slightly taller than the other. They looked to be about six or seven. I knocked on the screen door frame.

"Hi," I said when Tammy appeared at the door. "I'm Josie Prescott, an antiques appraiser from Rocky Point. I'm hoping you can help me."

She turned toward me, squinting into the setting sun, and cocked her head. "Antiques?"

"I know it seems kind of random, but it's not. I was working on an antiques appraisal with your former employer, Edwin Towson, when someone stole the object. My research suggests the theft was personal, that someone is out to get him."

Tammy snorted, an unladylike sound. "Couldn't happen to a nicer guy."

"What do you mean?"

Tammy stepped to the left. No lights were on, so despite the open door, she disappeared from view like steam in cold air. Two minutes later, just as I was about to knock again, she came outside carrying a folding stool, the kind people bring to tailgating parties, and a can of Dr Pepper. She used her left foot to kick open the stool and sat, leaning against the trailer, her eyes on the boys. She pressed the can against her forehead, rolled it along the back of her neck, then popped the top and sipped. She pulled a basil leaf from a bushy plant.

"I've worked retail since junior high, and I'm trying to get into office work, you know, to better myself. Mr. Towson didn't even give me a chance. He fired me before I could learn the job. You tell me that's fair."

The two boys whizzed by, swords flashing.

"Cute kids."

"Thanks," she said with the kind of smile that launches ships.

"I'm really sorry to hear you were fired. What happened?"

"I made too many *clerical errors*," she said, punctuating the words with air quotes. "Give me a break. I mixed up some papers. No one told me I needed to keep things in a certain order. What am I? A mind reader? I offered to do the job over, but Mr. Bigshot tossed me out flat. The bastard."

"And now you're back in retail."

"I'm not giving up, though. Our kids are getting older, you know? I need to show them that if you work hard, you get ahead."

" 'Our' kids?"

"Mark — that's my boyfriend. He's got a good steady job now. He's in construction. We're getting married in the fall. In Vegas.

My mom moved there last spring. She says the economy there is booming. She got a great job waitressing at the Venetian in about a minute and a half. Mark can work anywhere . . . so we'll see. If I can find something out there, we'll move. Why not, right?" She raised crossed fingers. "All you need is a good job."

"I have a feeling you're going to find a great job, Tammy. Not everyone is as determined as you are, and that counts for a lot. So can you think of anyone who might have it in for Edwin?"

"Besides me?" She gave a twisted grin. "Joke. Seriously, no way. Everyone wants him to live long and prosper. He's loved because he pays so much."

"How about someone at Towson's who needs extra money, despite the good pay?"

"You just described everyone. You start making more money, you start spending more money, so you need more money."

"That's for sure. I mean someone who's especially extravagant, though."

Tammy took a slug of Dr Pepper, then placed the can on the ground and stood up. I had to tilt my head back to meet her gaze.

"Like Mr. Towson?" she asked. "He spends a ton of money."

"On what?"

"He owns his own plane, can you imagine? One time, he and his wife flew to Paris for dinner. For real."

"That's amazing."

"He bought a beach house, too." She reached for the can and took a sip. "They call it a guesthouse, supposedly for company visitors." She lowered her voice. "Except visitors almost always stay at the Austin Arms."

"What do you think the guesthouse is really used for?"

"The truth?"

"Yes."

Tammy took a long swig. "I think Mr. Towson keeps a girl there."

"Really?" I let my jaw fall open and my eyes grow round.

Tammy giggled but didn't say anything else.

"Who? I'll never quote you. I promise."

"It's not like I've seen him doing the dirty or anything. But a guy like Edwin . . . come on . . . rich, middle-aged, likes to flirt. You do the math."

"Did he ever make a pass at you?"

One of the boys screamed, an angry screech. Tammy twirled toward the sound.

"Timmy!" she shouted. "Don't hit."

"Sorry!" a small voice called.

"Kids." She turned back to face me. "What did you ask?"

"Whether Mr. Towson ever made a pass at you."

"Not really, but I can read between the lines. If I'd shown any interest . . . let's just say, he made his intentions clear."

"Do you think that's why he fired you? Because you didn't show any interest?"

"I wondered about that." Her shoulders raised an inch, then lowered. "How can you tell?"

"It's like any kind of discrimination. It's not like they tell an older candidate, 'We don't want to hire someone over sixty.' They just don't hire him."

"Exactly."

"Do you know where the guesthouse is?"

"Sure. It's an easy address to remember. Number one Ocean Avenue, Rocky Point."

"That must mean it's near Rye."

"Right across the border."

The kids flew by, laughing, still fencing. She smiled as she watched them, proud and pleased.

"Any employees who gamble?" I asked.

"Sure," she said, turning back to face me. "There's an office pool every week."

"Anyone go overboard? Weekends in Atlantic City, that sort of thing?"

"Not that I know of. Everyone was nice. Work-till-you-drop types, a lot of them, but nice. Except Mr. Towson and the bitch who didn't train me."

"Who's that?"

"His bookkeeper, Lara Reisch. She's completely got a stick up her you-know-what."

"Not the warm and fuzzy type?" I asked with a sympathetic smile.

"Not hardly. She's the type who wants to know everything so she can make everyone else look stupid."

"That's awful."

"That's Lara."

"Do you have any other suggestions for me?"

"Sorry," Tammy said. "No."

I couldn't think of anything else to ask, so I thanked her for her time and the information, then left. I followed the road until I came to a small rotary. Heading back to the entryway, I noticed that the boys were still deep in their battle and Tammy was still watching them, her expression dreamy and distant.

Tammy hadn't asked me what was stolen. Either she wasn't curious — or she already knew.

CHAPTER TWENTY-EIGHT

After leaving Tammy's community, I drove back to Rocky Point. I parked in the Lobster Pot's oversized lot and checked messages. I had two, an e-mail from Wes and a text from Ty.

Wes wrote to ask if I had any tips, reminding me that the photos from Jean's condo complex weren't enough to equalize our balance sheet. I replied that while I didn't accept the premise of his statement, I did have a suggestion. I typed: *Ask the Towson bookkeeper, Lara Reisch, if anyone at Towson's is desperate for money. According to my source, she knows everything.* I smiled as I hit SEND. I figured it was better that Ms. Reisch shut the door in Wes's face, rather than mine, and there was always the chance he'd get lucky and learn something that would help.

Inside, I saw that Marty had added a dessert case, and I selected a small chocolate swirl cheesecake for tonight and a big cherry pie for my barbecue on Sunday. He'd also added a farm stand in a corner of his shop, a store-within-a-store arrangement, run by a local farmer, Al Montgomery, and his daughter, Bonnie. I bought so much, Al helped me carry the bundles to my car.

Time to cook for my fella. Time to turn off my brain, if I could.

As I was sealing an aluminum-foil-wrapped bundle of clams, the front door clicked closed, and I jumped, my heart shooting into my throat. I dropped the bundle on the counter and spun toward the front. Ty strolled into the kitchen.

"Oh, my God!" I grasped the counter, waiting for my fright to pass. "You startled me."

"Someone's on edge," Ty said.

I pressed my hand to my chest to quiet my pounding heart. "It was the aluminum foil — the crinkling. I couldn't hear you."

Ty spread his arms wide, and I ran into his embrace. I stood with my head resting on his shoulder. I closed my eyes and let the tension that had held me in its crushing grip like a vise evaporate. He kissed the top of my head. I leaned back so I could see his eyes.

He scanned my face. "You've healed nicely."

"Good as new."

"No sign of danger?"

"No. It's just like I told you — whoever shot at me didn't actually want to hit me. They wanted to stop me from entering the Towson house before they had an opportunity to steal the replacement Tiffany lamp."

"Any leads?"

"Not really. A lot of speculation and conjecture."

"Investigating something is a process." He sniffed, exaggerating the motion. "Just like cooking."

"I've made all your summer favorites. Sunday, we'll have burgers and dogs, just like we would have on July Fourth."

"I'm a lucky man."

"I'm the lucky one. How is it in D.C.?"

"Better than I expected. I'm making progress."

"In the investigation you can't tell me about?"

"What investigation?"

I play-punched his upper arm. "I thought I could get you to admit it."

"Ha. You underrate my powers of discretion."

I touched his cheek, drawing my finger down to his lips. "I underrate nothing about you. You're perfect."

"I love you, Josie."

"I love you, too, Ty."

"Now, cook, woman, cook! I skipped lunch so I could get here early."

"Yes, sir."

And I did. We ate the tomatoes and steamers on the patio and the baked stuffed lobster and corn at the picnic table on the lawn and the chocolate swirl cheesecake back on the patio, enveloped by the sweet scent of cherrywood burning in the fire pit. After dinner, we sat on a redwood-slat porch swing, built for two. I pushed off, setting the swing in motion. Katydids and crickets created a sound barrier, keeping the rest of the world at bay. Strings of Japanese lanterns illuminated our private oasis with a soft orange glow. It was a halcyon night, a perfect interlude.

"I don't want to go to work tomorrow," I said. "I want to stay here with you."

"Do it."

"I can't. It's tag sale day, and we didn't plan coverage."

"Leave early. Let's go to the beach."

"Sold."

Ty took my hand in his. "We should plan

a vacation. Where do you want to go?"

"I don't know."

"Do you feel like doing something active? Hiking somewhere beautiful? Or are you in a city mood, museums and fancy dinners and so on?"

I kept my eyes on the yellow flames, dancing in the light breeze. "I know! Let's go to New Orleans."

"Okay. How come?"

"I saw some photos today of a New Orleans–themed fund-raiser. It made me wish I was there. Have you ever been?"

"Once. A police chief conference long before I met you. You?"

"No, but I've always wanted to go. Did you like it?"

"Sure. What did Samuel Johnson say about London? 'When a man is tired of London, he's tired of life.' That's New Orleans."

"And New York."

"And Paris."

"And anywhere you are," I said, tilting my head to touch his shoulder. "What will I like best in New Orleans?"

"Sunday morning coffee and beignets at Café du Monde while reading *The New York Times* and listening to a sax player across the street in Jackson Square wailing sad.

We'll get there around seven, before the crowds."

"It sounds heavenly." A charred chunk of wood fell through the grate, landing with a soft thud. "I just quoted Samuel Johnson to Olive Winslow, one of the member's of Ava's book club."

"He's highly quotable."

"I liked her."

"You like most people."

"True," I said, and snuggled closer. "What percentage of time do witnesses lie?"

"Talk about a non sequitur! New Orleans to book clubs to liars. I don't know . . . Obviously it depends on the situation and the person. If we're talking criminals or witnesses with something to hide, even if their secret is unrelated to the case at hand, I'd estimate . . . ninety-nine, ninety-eight percent of the time . . . something like that."

I skewed around to better see his face. "You're saying people lie all the time."

"Pretty much. But not all lies are equal. A guy tells you a girl is a bitch. Maybe she's a bitch. But maybe he's calling her a bitch because he asked her out and she blew him off. The same woman tells you the guy's a creep. It's possible he's a creep, but maybe she's a stuck-up bitch. Since when does asking a girl out on a date make a guy a creep?

And that's a simple example. If a cop asks you an irrelevant, none-of-your-business question, is it better to challenge his right to ask or lie to make it go away?"

"I can't believe you're suggesting lying to a cop is ever okay."

"I'm not. This is the sort of thing we discuss in Homeland Security meetings where we're planning training. We have to train our investigators for reality, not some idealized version of reality. Why are you asking? Who do you think is lying?"

"Tammy." I filled Ty in, then added, "I took everything she said with a large grain of salt since hell truly does hath no fury like a woman scorned."

"I'll keep that in mind."

"Ha, ha. Tammy said she thought Edwin was keeping a girl at the corporate guesthouse. Tammy could have been that girl until she got the boot. Stealing the Tiffany lamp would be an elegant kind of payback."

"It's hard to imagine a young woman like you describe pulling off a heist like that."

"True, but we know she has a partner. Maybe her boyfriend Mark is pulling the strings."

"Does he look right?"

"Assuming he's the man in the photo with his arms around her, he's tall, thin, and white, which is all the description we have. So, yes, he looks right."

"Not such solid ground to walk on."

"Maybe Tammy told Ava what she and Edwin were up to, a kind of spiteful payback to Edwin after he dumped her. If so, that might have been the straw that broke Ava's back, thus setting the swindle organized by Ava and Jean in motion."

"I see what you mean about everything being conjecture and speculation."

"Tammy said something else that got me thinking. She talked about his extravagance. Maybe Edwin was doing a BMOC thing, you know, acting like the big man on campus, but actually, he's broke. Isn't it possible that Edwin orchestrated the theft of his own lamp? I mean, he flies to Paris for dinner and bought a beach house no one uses. He spends money like I drink water. But then I realized that's not logical. I made it clear to him that if he consigned his household goods, he'd earn double or more than if he sold them to us outright. He just wanted everything gone. If he'd needed the money, he would have accepted the consignment offer."

"Not if his need for cash was urgent."

"True."

"You should talk to Ellis."

"I will."

Ty raised my hand to his lips and kissed it. "But not tonight."

I nuzzled his hand with my cheek. "No, not tonight."

CHAPTER TWENTY-NINE

We all worked Saturdays, and our days were long. The tag sale ran from eight in the morning to six in the afternoon. Typically, I worked the entire day. Eric and Gretchen got in around seven and left around four. Fred and Sasha got in later and stayed later. Often, though, they all worked the whole day, too. Cara's hours varied. She was wonderfully flexible, helping us ensure we had phone coverage the entire day. Today, Fred was in by seven.

While Gretchen and Eric oversaw the final touches to the tag sale setup, Fred took me on a tour of the Towson furnishings.

"Any news on Aunt Louise's desk?" I asked on the way to the walk-in safe.

"Not yet. I'm still plugging away."

He punched in the code and pressed his finger against the access pad, then swung open the door. Toward the rear, balanced on a metal easel, was a small, softly colored neutral-hued landscape.

"Probably the most valuable object is the Nicholson, which, assuming it's genuine and the provenance checks out, will likely sell for about a quarter of a million dollars, followed by this Marie Bracquemond," Fred said. "It's called *Nu dans un intérieur, numéro deux.*"

I put my high school French to the test. *"Nude in an Interior, Number Two."*

"Mais oui."

I tilted my head, considering the painting. A woman stood next to a deep tub filled with steamy-hot water. Yellow petals floated on the surface. "It's her brushstrokes." I pointed to a bluish patterned background, wallpaper, I assumed, barely visible through the mist. "There's almost no paint here."

"It's an impression, right? Not a depiction."

"Which is why they call it Impressionism. If I remember right from the insurance listing, the Towsons acquired it at a Paris gallery about ten years ago."

"That's right. The provenance looks good."

"What's your estimate?"

"Somewhere around six thousand."

We never pay more than a third of our estimated value, to account for all the costs associated with running a business, including the risk that our estimate is wrong. With the arrangement I made with Edwin, I agreed to tally up our estimates for the entire lot and pay him outright. He didn't want to know any details.

"I forget . . . how much did they pay?"

"Including the buyer's premium, fifty-two hundred. Mr. Towson will be taking a hit on this one."

"The whole situation is sad."

Fred continued the tour by leading the way to the roped-off area. Hank came frisking over, wanting to play. I plucked a mouse from his collection — Gretchen kept him deep in mice — and lobbed it across the warehouse. He tore after it. The cordoned-off space held three rows of neatly labeled clear plastic tubs stacked twenty high, furniture organized by room, and wardrobe boxes containing Ava's gowns, designer outfits, and accessories.

"Did you find the avocado crate?"

"No."

"They probably threw it out. Rustic is not the Towsons' style."

"Not hardly. They sure have great taste, though. My overall estimate is somewhere around two million, plus or minus ten percent."

"A good day's work, then."

"There's great stuff here."

I grinned, pleased as much with Fred's thorough work as I was with the bottom line. Fred went to help Eric and Gretchen with the tag sale, while I climbed the stairs to my private office. As I started up the stairs, Hank came gamboling over, sans mouse.

"Where's your mouse, sweetheart?"

He meowed, explaining that he'd lost it somewhere.

"It's all right, sweetie. We'll find it later. Do you want a cuddle?"

He mewed. I picked him up and cradled him like a newborn, rubbing his tummy. He purred and cuddled in deeper.

"You're a good boy, Hank. A very, very good boy."

I kissed his cheek, and he licked my hand, then burrowed deeper into my arms. I got settled at my desk and turned on my computer. While I waited for it to boot up, I drew my nails gently along his spine. His eyes glazed over. He was rapturous.

I checked my e-mail. Everything could wait until Monday.

I swiveled to face my window. The sun hung low to the ground, partially hidden by gauzy streaks of silvery clouds. An orange glow permeated the forest that ringed my property. New Hampshire in summer was like I always imagined heaven must be — more Rembrandt than Renoir, fueled by warm briny breezes, and painted in colors as vivid as love.

Ten minutes later, I lowered Hank to the ground. He meowed angrily. If he had his druthers, I'd do nothing but pet him.

"Duty calls, Hank." I stood up, and he meowed again. "We'll have another cuddle later." I went down to the tag sale to go to work, and he sauntered off, annoyed.

Eric was standing three feet away from a vintage wooden printer's cabinet, the kind built to hold a printer's fonts when type was set by hand. He'd arranged some thimbles to showcase its decorative potential. His head was tilted and his lips were pursed, his standard position when thinking hard.

"It looks good," I said, assuming he was assessing whether his display was up to snuff.

I startled him. Eric was eager to please, sometimes too eager, and the omnipresent fear that he was failing made him edgy.

"Someone did yeoman's work in dusting all these minuscule cubbies," I added. "Was it you?"

He smiled, relaxing. "I gave it to one of the temps."

"Smart man."

He flushed a little. "I was thinking Grace might like it."

I pictured Eric's girlfriend, gentle, sweet Grace, studying to become an elementary school teacher.

"For a shadow box?" I asked.

"She's begun collecting miniatures, you know, small porcelain cats and birds and things."

"Cute. This might be perfect. What's her design style?"

"I'm not sure. She lives with her parents. Their house is . . . I don't know . . . I guess you'd call it contemporary."

"And you've never talked about it."

"No. I can ask her, I guess."

"Subtly, so she'll be surprised if you decide to get it. What's your style?"

"Me?" he asked, sounding astonished that someone wanted to hear his opinion.

Having met Eric's mother, with whom he lived, I understood. She was a difficult woman, domineering and unforgiving, a sharpened knife all too ready to prick. Yet having worked alongside him for a dozen years, I also knew that he was neither weak nor meek, merely reticent.

"Yes! Do you like contemporary furniture?"

"Not so much. I like the things we call country or farm style."

"So you must like this type case a lot."

"Yeah."

"I'd call it country rustic, if I were writing it up for a catalogue. Why don't you take it back to the warehouse? If you decide against it, we can put it out next week."

His smile widened. "Thanks."

Printer's cases were popular items, and we stocked them as often as we could find them. In excellent condition, like this one, they retailed for twenty-five dollars. After his employee discount, the cabinet would cost Eric twenty dollars, a more than fair price, but not an impulse purchase.

I glanced at the big round clock mounted over the front door. It read 7:53. My stint at Prescott's Instant Appraisal booth would begin at ten, but I liked to look around before we opened. We decorated the tag sale venue for every season or holiday. From mid-June until mid-August, when we morphed to a back-to-school, early autumn theme, we focused on Americana.

A series of 7″ × 3′ wooden signs were affixed to the wall about six inches below the ceiling, circling the entire space. The signs featured the Declaration of Independence, the First Amendment, and the Pledge of Allegiance, all written out in elegant black lettering over a folk-art-style flag. The signs were new but designed to look vintage, with muted paint and worn corners. Flag-inspired banners crisscrossed the space, ten feet overhead. Red, white, and blue burlap triangles hung from lengths of rope. The blue triangles were decorated with white stars. A carefully crafted and painted plaster of Paris eagle was mounted over the front door, just below the clock. The room looked perfect, not ostentatious but warm and welcoming — and uniquely American. I turned toward the entryway. Often there was a line waiting to get in, and I loved, loved, loved looking at the row of people so eager to have first dibs on our collectibles that they got there early. The ragged line seemed longer than usual, a good thing.

I joined Gretchen at the front. She was sitting on a stool at the cash register, looking more resplendent than ever.

"You look all excited-peppy," I said.

She glanced around to make sure she wouldn't be overheard and crooked her index finger, beckoning me closer. I gave her a questioning look before positioning my ear close to her mouth.

"Jack got recruited for a new job. We're so completely thrilled, I can't even tell you!"

My heart plummeted to my toes. A new job meant a new city. *What would I do without Gretchen?* My better self rose to the occasion, and I opened my eyes wide and smiled as if I were happy.

"Oh, Gretchen! That's wonderful! What is it?"

"Assistant director of research and development for Eliot Pharmaceuticals. I know I shouldn't think about money so much, but oh my God, he's going to earn thirty percent more than he is now. Thirty percent! Do you know what that means?"

"Eliot with one *l*?"

She blinked, focusing on what seemed to her an out-of-the-blue question.

"Yes. It's a branch of a big British firm, based just over the bridge in Maine. Why?"

I closed my eyes and gripped the counter, partially a genuine reaction to the relief that threatened to topple me, and partially for show.

"Because I thought for a minute you were going to relocate to somewhere like New Jersey or England or France. You know, big pharma."

Gretchen laughed and hugged me, nearly falling off her stool. "I'm never leaving

316

Prescott's. Not ever."

I hugged her back. "Never say never. Don't ever pass up a good opportunity, Gretchen. But talk to me before you commit to moving. I'll always try to beat someone else's offer."

Gretchen's eyes filled, and she winked tears away. "Thank you."

I touched her wrist. "Tell Jack congrats, okay?"

She nodded and wiped away a tear with the back of her hand, not yet trusting herself to speak.

"Do you mean that?" she whispered as I started away.

"You're the lynchpin here, Gretchen. Prescott's depends on you."

Her bottom lip trembled. I squeezed her hand, gave her a "see ya later" wave, and joined Fred at the front door. It was eight o'clock.

He swung the door wide and said, "Welcome to Prescott's! Come on in."

I stood off to the side, smiling and saying hello and how are you, silently counting the number of people who flooded the tag sale venue, early birds eager to start their hunt. Eighteen. I enjoyed a private *atta girl* moment. Eighteen was impressive, beating fourteen from last December, during the holiday season, our busiest time. It was a cloudy, foggy day, with the moist smell of rain in the air, good for business.

Once the initial crowd was in, I stepped out, circling the building to enter the office from the parking lot. I wanted a cup of coffee. I set Gretchen's wind chimes jangling as I entered the main office.

"She just stepped in," Cara said to someone on the phone. "Hold, please." She punched a button. "It's Hank's vet, Dr. Cross."

I took the call at the guest table. "Tell me you didn't misread Hank's test results, that he's as perfect as we think he is."

Peter Cross chuckled. "Nope. Hank is officially and scientifically perfect. Did Gretchen report that I thought Hank wasn't getting enough exercise? I recommended that you get him a playmate, someone to run around with, a companion. Well, I have one. She's about fourteen weeks old and cute as a bug."

"A cat?" I asked, stunned. I hadn't realized he was serious about Hank getting more exercise.

"A kitten. She's had all her shots. She's spayed. She's got a great personality, very outgoing and cuddly."

Cara was listening in, her eyes alight with

excitement.

"Where did you get her from?"

"A neighbor who adopted her only to discover her son is allergic."

"I don't know, Peter."

"What's your hesitation?"

I loved Hank. Hank was, to me, family, and when a newcomer arrives, family dynamics inevitably shift. I didn't want anything to change. I wanted Hank to continue to love me the way he currently did. *What,* I wondered, *if Hank loves the new girl more than me?* I bit my lip.

"I need to do what's best for Hank, and I trust your judgment. If you think we should adopt her, we will."

"I do. You'll love her, Josie."

"Gretchen will be there to pick her up sometime early this afternoon." I forced myself to smile, to act the part I needed to play. "We need to get set up for the new kid." After we ended the call, I swiveled to face Cara. "I gather you heard."

She clapped her hands softly. "We're getting a new baby. I'm thrilled! Hank will be so excited!"

"I hope so."

"He'll adjust quickly. Just you wait and see."

I stood up, my fake smile painted on like

makeup. "I'll go tell Gretchen the good news."

CHAPTER THIRTY

About eight thirty, Olive Winslow came into the tag sale venue. She scanned the space, then smiled and beelined for the display of porcelain near the back. She joined a younger woman and leaned down to peer into the cabinet. I walked over to join them.

"Olive!" I said. "Nice to see you again. On the hunt for more teacups?"

"Josie! Nice to see you, too! This is Charlotte, my daughter-in-law. She was here first thing, and when she saw what she thought was a hand-painted Sèvres cup and saucer, she called me. Naturally, I ran to the car. May I look at it?"

"Of course." I used my key to unlock the glass display cabinet and extracted the cup and saucer. A small tent card perched nearby read "Incised numbers and letters on both bases. Cup, 'S 74'; saucer, 'S 63.' Sèvres. Circa early 19th c. $75 for the set."

Charlotte and I watched as Olive assessed

the cup and saucer. The cup featured an elaborate landscape, an attractive young couple reclining on an ornate white iron bench in a formal garden. The multicolored painting was embellished with touches of gilt. The saucer included panels of red and yellow flowers with a gilt rim. There were no chips, cracks, spider-cracks, or signs of restoration, but the pieces didn't match, and the gilt on the saucer showed slight signs of rubbing, a minor imperfection to some, a knockout factor to most serious collectors. If it were a matched set in perfect condition, it would have been included in an auction and sold for hundreds or thousands of dollars.

"It's beautiful, isn't it?" Olive said, holding the cup up to the light, talking mostly to herself.

"Most of your collection is English bone china, isn't it?" Charlotte asked.

Charlotte was thin and petite, with short ash blond hair. She looked to be about thirty.

"Yes, and the truth is, I prefer it." She handed over the teacup and saucer. "I'm afraid I'm going to have to pass on this one."

"Too overwrought?" I asked as I returned the set to its place in the cabinet.

"Yes. It's just a bit too elaborate for my taste."

"And the saucer doesn't match the cup."

"To say nothing of the wear on the saucer rim," Olive said, smiling like a wily collector.

"There is?" Charlotte asked, leaning in to examine it.

"Just a little," Olive said.

"Just enough to make it undesirable to serious collectors," I added. "Condition is one of the most important considerations in assessing value and desirability, along with provenance, rarity, scarcity, popularity, and association."

"Provenance I know," she said, "because I'm a lawyer — clear title. What's the difference between rarity and scarcity?"

"Rarity is how many were created. Scarcity is how many are extant."

"And association?"

"Association looks at whether anyone intriguing owned it or used it or commented on it, or whether it holds any historical significance."

"Valuation is complicated," Charlotte said.

"Very. How about you? Do you collect anything?"

"Not really." She looked around for a moment. "While I was waiting for Olive, I peeked at the botanical prints. I'm going to take a closer look. I want one in green and yellow for the powder room."

"Any news about Ava?" Olive asked after Charlotte walked away.

"Not that I know of. Have you thought of anything else that might help?"

"Diane and I chatted a bit about it. We just can't imagine who would do such a thing." She clucked a bit, empathy mingled with unease. "I wish I could do more."

"Me, too."

"And now Ava's sister. It's just so horrific."

Charlotte was busily flipping through the art prints.

"Are you going to hold this quarter's meeting?"

"No. We decided to wait until September, when Diane is back from vacation."

Charlotte held up a plastic-encased botanical print, a lithograph created by Anne Pratt in 1860. "Look what I found! It's called *Common Daffodil, the Poet's Narcissus, Pale Narcissus, and Snowdrop*. I love it!"

"Anne Pratt is largely responsible for popularizing botanical prints," I said. "Sometimes prints this old have stains or tears. This one is in wonderful condition."

"But it's not rare," Charlotte said, her eyes alive with interest. "Or scarce."

I laughed. "True. And while they're always popular, they're not a hot item right now."

"No one famous owned it, either, so there's no association."

"You're a quick learner."

"You're a good teacher. Put it all together, and I understand why it's selling for fifty dollars, not five hundred."

I turned to Olive. "I sense a collector in our midst."

Charlotte lowered her eyes to the print. "You may be right. I certainly love this one."

Before I could respond, I felt eyes on me, a magnetic pull. I turned around. Ellis stood by the front door. He nodded, acknowledging contact, then jerked his head to the left, toward the door. I excused myself and threaded my way through the crowded aisles to reach him. The clock above his head told me it was 8:47.

"What's wrong?" I asked as I reached him.

"Let's step outside."

I had no idea what Ellis wanted, but I knew it could only be bad news. Police chiefs didn't stop by in the middle of murder investigations to chat.

CHAPTER THIRTY-ONE

Eric was manning the cash register, talking with an older man with a full head of starkly white hair. I called to him that I was stepping out for a minute. He glanced at Ellis, then me, and nodded.

Ellis pushed open the wood-and-glass door and held it ajar until I'd stepped through. The fog was, if anything, thicker than before. Without the sun beating down on us, it didn't feel steamy or sticky — just good. I could sense my pores opening up.

I walked a few steps away from the entryway, stopping beside a wooden slat-back bench I'd had Eric install at the beginning of the summer. We'd positioned it under a stand of birch trees in the middle of clusters of orange tiger lilies.

"I like the fog," I said.

"Zoë thinks it's romantic." Ellis inspected the area with narrowed eyes. "I need to talk — privately."

"My office?"

"We can go there later. I'll be taking your statement." He sent his eyes around. "Anywhere outside?"

I gave a little bow and swept open my arm toward the bench. "My outside office awaits."

"Josie!" a woman called. "Anything good today?"

I swung around. Elaina Lee, a serious collector of Victorian perfume bottles and a favorite customer, was coming up the flagstone pathway.

"Elaina! Hi! There's a ruby-glass beauty you're going to love."

"Cut glass?"

"Yes, with a silver neck and cap."

"Ooh! I'd better hurry!"

"Good luck!"

She nearly ran inside.

"If she's so hot on them, why didn't you hold it for her?"

"She has idiosyncratic taste. Some objects we think she'll love miss the mark. Others we're certain aren't right for her, she loves. We can't hold objects unless we're confident we know what a client is looking for. Don't get me wrong. I admire her conviction and commitment. I just don't understand what pushes her buttons. Also, she likes the hunt."

He smiled. "Which brings us back to the business at hand — hunting. If we sit in your outside office, I'm afraid customers will continue to interrupt us, so I guess we better go inside."

"If you don't mind standing, I know just the spot. Follow me." As we walked down the pathway toward the parking lot, I said, "I thought Detective Brownley was coming at noon to take my statement."

"She's tied up with something, and I had the time, so I volunteered."

"How did you know I was here?"

"Being a savvy detective, I looked out the window and saw your car was gone. Knowing it was tag sale day, I was optimistic I'd find you here."

I led the way to the weeping willow tree at the western edge of the parking lot. The tree soared thirty feet into the air and was nearly as wide. Pale yellow branches and slender green leaves swept the ground. I picked my way through the lacy curtain to reach the gnarled trunk. Ellis followed.

He did a slow 360, peering through narrow openings in the foliage.

"When I was a kid," I said, keeping my voice low, "we had a weeping willow in the backyard. One of the branches, about five feet off the ground, shot out sideways for a few feet, then turned upwards, a perfect perch for reading."

"When I was a kid, a man named Devon taught me how to track. He always said to look up as often as you look down."

"Because you might see a girl with a book?"

"He was thinking more about black bears, but yes."

"Who was he to you?"

"My Boy Scout leader."

"I have a suspicion you were a terrific Boy Scout."

One side of his mouth shot up. "Still am." After a moment of silence, he turned to face me. "I want to tell you something, but you've got to keep it confidential."

"Okay."

"Promise?"

"Yes. Of course."

"Ava was pregnant, and according to the medical examiner, Edwin isn't the father."

Both hands flew to my lips. "Oh, Ellis." I closed my eyes for a moment, reeling. As soon as I'd read that Edwin had had a vasectomy, I knew this was a possibility, but I hadn't wanted to believe it. I opened my eyes and lowered my hands. "Did you tell him?"

"Yes. Just before he disappeared. He said

he didn't even know she was pregnant."

"You don't believe him."

"I don't believe anyone."

"Thanks."

"Present company excepted, of course."

"Of course."

"Did you?" Ellis asked. "Believe Edwin when he talked about Ava?"

"Yes. My God. I think he was hoping to save his marriage."

"People who have a good reason to lie tend to do it well."

"You're saying that Edwin might have killed Ava, that he might have prerecorded the video conference, snuck out of his meeting, and mucked with the air-conditioning to confuse the medical examiner about the time of death."

"All the participants on the video conference, and I mean all of them, swear it wasn't staged. One man had to take an unexpected phone call, and the meeting went on hiatus for five minutes. Towson's records all calls and meetings to ensure no future misunderstandings, but we don't have enough evidence to get a court order for it, and Edwin won't give it up because of the confidential information that was covered."

"I can't imagine that Edwin has the technical wherewithal to pull off a scam like that, even without that unexpected hiatus."

"I agree."

"So he didn't kill her," I said.

"He's got the mother of all motives, so I'm not ready to give up on him. Maybe he arranged for someone else to kill Ava and got himself a world-class alibi."

"Maybe his mistress did it, if he has one." I felt the heat of Ellis's attention. "It's possible the woman on the Grey Gull security tape is his cookie."

The corner of his mouth shot up again. Ellis was amused, probably at my diction. "Maybe he's with her now."

"You still haven't found him?"

"No trace."

My throat closed as a terrifying thought came to me, and when I started to speak, I choked. I tried again. "Do you think he's dead?"

"I hope not."

"Oh God, Ellis, it's just awful. Ava, Jean, now this."

"There's no reason to suspect Edwin has been killed, Josie."

"Look at the timing — he disappeared right after we reached an agreement to sell his possessions and you told him about his not being the baby's father. Two horrific experiences coming right on top of one

331

another. Maybe he . . . you know . . . maybe he decided he couldn't . . ." I shuddered and hugged myself. "It happens, Ellis."

"Sales of ice cream cones go up in the summer, and so do incidences of rape, but no one thinks eating ice cream leads to rape."

I took in a deep breath and exhaled slowly. Ellis was right about ice cream and rape, but that didn't mean he was right about the potentially debilitating effect on a proud man of having humiliating bad news heaped on top of mortifying perfidy.

"Do you have any idea who Edwin's mistress is?" Ellis asked.

"No, and I don't know that he has one, but if he does, I could see her being white-hot angry. I mean, look at it from her side — Ava gets pregnant, and whether Ava knows the baby is Edwin's or not, that isn't the point. The point is that while Edwin is open about not wanting kids, he's a man who takes his responsibilities seriously, so he tells the cookie, now that he's about to be a papa, their relationship is over. From the cookie's point of view, Ava is about to screw up *her* future."

"So the lamp doesn't come into play in this scenario."

"Sure it could, if Edwin had previously

told the cookie about it."

"Are you certain you don't have any ideas about who she might be?"

I tapped a long-hanging strand of leaves, sending it swinging.

"What is it, Josie?"

"Have you spoken to Judi, Towson's receptionist?"

"Why?"

"Or Tammy, an employee who got fired?"

"Talk to me, Josie."

Muscles running along my shoulders tightened. I didn't appreciate Ellis's obdurate tone. I met his eyes. "I am."

He nodded, one crisp nod. "And I appreciate it. Why did you name those two women?"

I lifted, then lowered my shoulders. "I think they know things."

"Why did you talk to them?"

"Are you interrogating me?"

"Interviewing, informally."

"Why did you tell me about Ava's baby not being Edwin's child?"

"To get your opinion. You know Edwin better than most people."

"What are you talking about? I just met him."

"He has no friends. His employees, colleagues, and investors all have agendas. No one will tell me anything about him except that he's a smart, hard-nosed, straight-arrow businessman that they're proud to know."

"Maybe that's what he is," I said.

"True. For both gut- and fact-checking purposes, I need your help. Do you think Jean knew about Ava's baby?"

"Sure. Don't you."

"They seemed close. Do you think Jean helped Ava steal the lamp?"

"I don't think there's any doubt about that."

"Before Jean died, I asked her whether Ava was excited about being pregnant, and she told me she was, and that Edwin was, too."

"Someone's lying. Who's the baby's father, do you think?"

"Who do you think it is?" he asked.

"I have no idea. Can't you use DNA to trace him?"

"He's not in any DNA database, so he hasn't been convicted of a serious felony, or even, in some jurisdictions, arrested. He hasn't applied for a gun permit or a liquor license, and he hasn't served in the military."

"Is there any chance Ava conceived the baby on one of their trips?" I asked. "Maybe she had a fling on her walking tour in Wales."

"No, the timing is off. She was almost five months pregnant. Except for their recent trip to Europe, she was in Rocky Point full-time for the last six months. So in all likelihood, the baby's father was someone in her circle. A friend of hers. Or of Edwin's."

"Poor Edwin," I said. "He must be crushed. Just crushed."

"You think so? He doesn't strike me as the kind of guy who gets crushed."

"Come on, Ellis. Any man would."

"Some would. Others wouldn't."

"Maybe the father is the man we know as Orson Thompkins," I said.

"That's logical. We've scoured Ava's phone logs, e-mails, and social media accounts. Nothing stands out. Any other ideas about how we can find him?"

"No."

Ellis used the back of his hand to push aside enough willow branches and leaves to make a doorway.

"Okay, then," he said, "let's go make a video."

People change, I thought, as I walked across the lot to the front office. *An agreement you happily make in your twenties shackles you as forty comes into view.* My eyes filled as if it were me Ava had betrayed, not Edwin, and I blinked away the wetness.

CHAPTER THIRTY-TWO

Upstairs in my private office, sitting at my desk with Hank in my lap, I watched Ellis fuss with the tripod and camera he'd retrieved from his vehicle.

He flicked it on, stated the logistics of where we were and why we were talking, and thanked me for agreeing to talk to him. I didn't like that. There was a formality to his tone that I found disturbing. He started by asking me to recount why I'd been at the Grey Gull condo complex yesterday afternoon, moved on to why I'd knocked on Jean's door, then snuck in an unexpected question.

"Do you have any sense that Edwin Towson might have staged the theft of the Tiffany lamp?"

"No," I said, thinking that his question echoed my own speculation. I explained about consignment versus selling and the effect on the bottom line. "I understand that if he was desperate for cash, he might have thought that selling outright was his only option, but I have absolutely no sense that he was anywhere close to desperate."

Ellis spread his arms wide. "How about you? Your business seems great. Is it?"

My mouth opened, then closed, then opened again. "I think you just asked me if I switched out the genuine Tiffany lamp, maybe in cahoots with Ava and Jean, so that I could nab a chunk of a million-plus bucks for my personal coffers. Did I get that right?"

"I had to ask, Josie."

I'd asked Fred the same question, in almost the same way, and Fred had reacted in an almost identical fashion. I turned toward the camera, wanting to be certain that my answer was recorded, full face.

"No, you didn't."

"Indulge me. I know you wouldn't have done it unless there was an emergency. How many employees do you have?"

"Why?"

"That's a lot of mouths to feed."

"You're serious."

"I am."

When Fred answered, he'd had to restrain himself since I was his employer, but I didn't have to restrain myself at all. I cared

about Ellis the man, but I didn't give a flying hoot about Ellis the police chief.

"Bite me."

Ellis laughed. "Say again?"

"Yes, my business is doing great. We're in
the middle of our best year ever. No, I
didn't steal Edwin Towson's Tiffany lamp."

"Who else might have had an opportunity
to substitute a replica for the Towson lamp?"

His bland expression did nothing to
comfort me. The smoldering anger I'd
endured since I'd learned that I'd been
conned fired up anew, lit by fresh fuel. I
glared at him, my lips pressed together, my
arms crossed in front of my chest.

"Fred," I said, not trying to hide my
disdain. "And Eric. But neither one stole
it."

"How do you know?"

"I asked Fred, pro forma, and he told me
he didn't."

"That's it?"

"That's it?"

"What about Eric?" Ellis asked.

"He doesn't know anything is wrong."

"Why not?"

"I didn't want to upset him needlessly." I
shoved my chair back, preparing to stand.
"I need to go now. If you have any other
questions, feel free to contact me again."

"Thank you, Josie, for your cooperation." He tapped a button, and the camera's red light faded out.

I stood, not trying to hide the scorching disdain sparking from my eyes. I didn't say a word to him the whole way out, and he didn't say anything to me, either. We didn't need to speak for our mutual messages to be clear.

At the front door, he said, "Thanks! See you tomorrow."

I didn't reply. I stood at the window and watched him leave my property. He signaled a left turn, heading, no doubt, for the interstate. I glanced at the clock. It read 9:49. In eleven minutes, I was on duty at Prescott's Instant Appraisal booth, where I needed to be more than informative; I needed to be charming. Charm had deserted me. I doubted I could talk at all. I could barely breathe. I was so outraged at Ellis's implication that I — or a member of my staff — might be a thief, I was beside myself. How dare he?

My dad always said that sometimes in life you might have to eat dirt, but no one says you have to call it ice cream. I pulled a can of ginger ale from the minifridge and took a long swig, hoping it would quiet my agitation the same way it quiets nausea, and much to my surprise, it worked. By the time the can was empty, I was ready to assume my role as Prescott's charismatic leader.

First, though, I had to warn Fred and Eric that an ice floe had broken free and was heading their way.

I asked Sasha to cover for me at the instant appraisals booth for a few minutes and tracked down Eric. He was rearranging a collection of vases.

I asked him to join me in the warehouse, and his expression reflected his fretfulness at being singled out.

"I want to start by telling you that you did nothing wrong. The Tiffany lamp is a fake, and no one knows when it was switched out, so the police are investigating everyone who had any contact with it. That includes you."

"You always videotape antiques before we pack them up. I didn't do that."

"You're not supposed to. It's not your job. I shouldn't have let you go alone. This is all on me, Eric. I expect the police to call you to schedule an interview. Max — you know, our lawyer — will go with you."

"Okay."

"I'm sorry, Eric."

"It's no one's fault. None of us stole the lamp."

"That's exactly right, but it sure brings home the point about why we need to be so careful."

"I'm not worried about talking to the police, so I don't want you to worry about me."

I touched his arm. "Thank you, Eric." I asked him to send Fred in.

"Police Chief Hunter — Ellis — questioned me about the murders and the theft," I said to Fred, aiming for a neutral tone. "He asked me the same questions I asked you, about whether I stole it myself. I resented it the same way you did. I still do. Frankly, I'm steaming mad about it. One of his questions was who else had access to it, and I named you in addition to Eric. Do I need to explain why I gave him your name?"

"Of course not. I did have access to it, and our records reflect that, but regardless . . . we're truth tellers."

I smiled. "Always. Have you heard from Ellis yet?"

"No."

"You will, and when you do, I want you to bring Max Bixby, our lawyer. Okay?"

"Yes."

■ ■ ■ ■

At noon, Gretchen called to let us know she was about ten minutes away. I got Eric, and we met her at the loading dock. Together, the three of us carried in a new 9' × 12' rug. Gretchen explained that she chose seashell pink because the new kitty was a girl. She also bought two new litter boxes because Peter said that in multiple-cat families, it's best to have one per cat, plus an extra; porcelain pink and white zebra-print food and water bowls, along with a bubblegum pink place mat; and a brown, cushy kitty bed and a round wicker basket with a pale pink pillow, the same brands as Hank's. Hank's pillow was black, very manly. Also in the box were two packages of noisy, catnip-free mice, because Peter reminded her that the new kitten was too young for catnip, and two large bags of kitten food.

We unrolled the rug, aligning it with Hank's dark green carpet, placed the food and water bowls as far away from Hank's as possible, and positioned the kitty bed and basket so the edges touched Hank's.

"So they won't get lonely in the night," Gretchen said.

"What about a second kitty-condo?"

"It's on order. It should be here within a week." She giggled. "I ordered the one with perches big enough for two in case they feel like sharing."

"Let's hope Hank feels like sharing."

While Eric and I went to collect all the catnip toys scattered throughout the warehouse, Gretchen drove back to Peter's to pick up our new cat.

Cara, Gretchen, Eric, and I stood in the center of the pink carpet. Hank sat nearby, incensed yet curious.

Gretchen placed the kitty carry-bag in the center of the pink rug, unzipped the side flap, and laid it flat. Our new kitten stuck her face out and sniffed around. She meowed, then scampered out. She was all black except for a small white triangle on her breastbone, just below her neck. She had big eyes and big ears, and I thought that she was maybe the cutest thing I'd ever seen.

"Will we call her Carrie?" Gretchen asked. "That's what the woman whose son was allergic called her. That was only for a few days, though."

She didn't look like a Carrie.

Hank stood up, pinning her with a fiery glare. His back arched, and his tail puffed to twice its normal size.

She meowed again and started poking around, sniffing along the rug, finding her food and water, and walking into and out of the bed and basket. She batted a mouse, and the bells inside tinkled. She seemed comfortable and engaged. She stepped over the line and continued her sniffing on Hank's rug. He growled, a low steady message of discontent. She went right up to him and licked his side. He turned to look at her as if he couldn't believe what she'd just done. She licked him again before resuming her sniffing exploration.

"I guess Hank had a dirty spot," I said.

Gretchen giggled.

I reached down to give Hank a pat and a kiss, then knelt down and called to the new girl.

"Come here, little one," I said, holding out my hands, palms up.

She raised her head and turned toward me.

"Come here. Give me a whiff."

She walked toward me slowly. Hank turned around to watch her. She sniffed my palms, my wrists, and my knees. She placed a paw on my thigh. What a sweetie.

"Hello," I said. "I'm Josie." I pointed at Gretchen. "You know Gretchen."

"Yes, you do, don't you, darling?"

"This is Cara."

Cara leaned over to give her a little head pat. "You're precious, like a jewel." She stood up and turned toward me. "Maybe we should call her Jewel."

"Maybe." I opened my hand toward Eric. "This is Eric."

"Hi, kitty," Eric said.

"And this is Hank." Hank growled, just a little. "You can ignore that. He's just surprised to see you."

She licked my hand. "Thank you, baby. That's a very good girl." I picked her up. She was almost small enough to fit in the palm of my hand. Her purring machine whirred onto high, and her little eyes began to close. I used one finger to stroke the white fur on her chest. I looked up at Cara, Gretchen, and Eric, looking on with vicarious pleasure.

"Her name is Angela," I said, "because she has this little white spot. Angels wear white. Clearly this little girl is an angel."

"That's beautiful, Josie," Cara said. "An angel come from heaven to help us. To help Hank."

"She looks like an angel," Gretchen said. "Don't you, darling?"

Eric stared at the kitten, his head tilted. "Angela's a good name."

"Can I go tell Sasha and Fred?" Gretchen asked.

"Definitely. You and Eric can spot them so they can come meet our new little angel."

They left together. Cara kissed Angela on the top of her little head and set off toward the office. I lowered Angela to her kitty bed, and she yawned, stretched her bottom half, then her top half, and sauntered over to the water bowl as if she'd lived here forever. She took a long drink, paused, then drank some more. Hank looked at me.

"I know, Hank. She's gorgeous, isn't she?"

Angela walked back toward her bed, then changed her mind and crossed the line into Hank's domain. She went straight for his cat bed and sat down. Hank walked over and watched as she curled herself into a tight spiral. As her eyes closed, he began sniffing her from top to bottom, taking his time. When he was done, he meowed, and I picked him up.

I kissed him and whispered, "You're my original love bunny, Hank, and you always will be. It's your job to show Angela the ropes, okay?"

He mewed his begrudging agreement.

By the time Sasha and Fred arrived, Angela was solidly asleep. Her soft purr sounded like the hum of a high-performance engine. I'd placed Hank on his rug, and he stayed put, sitting near her, watchful but no longer growling.

"She's beautiful," Sasha said in a hushed tone.

Fred laughed. "So much for worrying about how she'd adjust to her new surroundings."

Hank came to me and rubbed my calf while arching his back, his way of asking to be cuddled. I scooped him up again and held him close.

After they left, I stayed where I was for a while longer, hugging and kissing Hank, and watching our new little angel sleep.

"You're awfully quiet," Ty said.

It was Sunday morning around eleven. I slid the last plate from our late breakfast into the dishwasher and positioned two cutting boards on the counter, one near the sink for Ty, the other near the fridge for me.

"I guess I'd label how I feel as subdued. Would you get the dishwasher started? I'll cut the potatoes."

He poured the soap into the receptacle. "How come you're feeling subdued?"

The dishwasher hummed to life, a comforting sound. "The last time I made potato salad, Ellis got a call that Ava had been murdered."

Ty leaned against the counter. I felt his eyes on my face, but I didn't look up. I opened the refrigerator and started extracting the ingredients for my mother's potato salad: boiled new potatoes, celery, mayonnaise, a lime, and Dijon mustard.

"I don't think you're subdued. I think you're pissed off."

"Feeling subdued and angry aren't mutually exclusive."

"What did I do?"

My eyes flew to his face, and I laughed. "Nothing. I'm not mad at you."

He opened his palms, his fingers spread apart, silently asking, *Well, then, who?* I didn't want to talk about it, but I didn't want to fence Ty out, either.

"If you want the truth, I'm furious at Ellis." I sliced a cold boiled potato into large chunks. "He had the audacity to ask me if my business was in trouble, thinking maybe I switched out the Tiffany lamp myself, you know, to get some cash. Overnight, it occurred to me that what he was really wondering about was whether Ava caught on somehow and I killed her. I'm fuming."

"And getting madder by the minute, it sounds like."

"Can you blame me?"

"Blame doesn't come into it. You feel as you feel. The question is what to do to relieve the pressure, to manage the situation."

"I'm handling things just fine," I said, laying into a second potato.

"You should call Max."

I spun to face him. "What? You think I need a lawyer?"

"Yes. You've just been questioned — on camera — about your possible involvement in a major art theft, which may relate to a murder."

I laid the knife on the counter. "What are you saying?"

"Can't do any harm."

"You're saying it's not my imagination, that I'm really a suspect."

"I doubt Ellis considers you a suspect for real, but he's a by-the-book cop, and there's nothing that excludes you. Motive — he's supplying one. Means — the weapon was available. Opportunity — sure. You don't have to prove a negative — that you didn't do it — but you should be ready if he circles back for another go at you."

"By calling Max, I'm taking charge of the situation, not simply allowing Ellis to call the shots."

"Which means you won't feel like a victim."

"I gave Ellis Fred's and Eric's names, too. I already told them that Max will go with them when they're questioned." I turned back to the potatoes. "Thank you, Ty."

"You're welcome."

I chopped another potato. "You're a smart man."

"You're a smart woman. And beautiful. And a helluva cook." He walked toward me. "I'm about to hug you, so I'd appreciate it if you'd put the knife down."

I laughed and placed the knife on the cutting board. Ty took my hands in his and gently pulled me into his arms. He hugged me tight. I leaned my head against his soft cotton T-shirt, and in that moment, I knew everything would be just fine.

Almost a week late, we were about to celebrate our independence. I'd switched out the orange Japanese lanterns for July Fourth–themed red, white, and blue ones, laid in a supply of sparklers, and loaded patriotic tunes on my iPhone, from country favorites like Charlie Daniels's "In America" and Waylon Jennings's "America" to show tunes like "76 Trombones" and "The Yankee Doodle Boy."

Ellis was either a superb actor or far better than I was at compartmentalizing. At the barbecue, he was as genial and as witty as ever. No one watching his performance would think there was any ill will between us. From his point of view, maybe there wasn't. His attitude reminded me why he was my friend. From what I could tell, he wanted to at least create the appearance of normalcy, and one of his tactics had him saying things that required responses.

"I can't believe the fog burned off overnight," he said.

"It's good to see the sun again."

"Great martini, Josie! What do you call it?"

"A Rouge Martini."

"I love it."

"Zoë gets the credit. She came up with the idea."

It was exhausting, but it served to whisk away the worst of my impotent fury. There's something to be said for civility. Courtesy tempers rage.

I couldn't sleep. I wound myself up in the blanket like a tangled strand of yarn. I wasn't upset, exactly. It felt as if a memory were just out of sight, a thought just out of reach. I couldn't put my finger on it. Around four thirty, I gave up trying to sleep and went downstairs.

I made coffee and booted up my computer. The *Seacoast Star* featured a rehashing of old news about the murders. The only new-to-me information was that Jean's will left her entire estate to her sister, and in the event Ava predeceased her, to a variety of local charities; and Shawn O'Boyle had been in Mexico the whole time he said he was. Wes published a photo of him. He was short for a man, about five-four, at a guess, and bald. He and the man in the pharmacy security photo were definitively not one and the same. Shawn O'Boyle was not Orson Thompkins.

After I finished reading Wes's article, I relocated to the kitchen. I sat on the section of bench that faced the meadow, sipping coffee and thinking about motives for stealing and motives for murder until the sun came up over the trees sometime around twenty after five. Merry had seen Jean with a box in her hands while playing ball with Eleanor in the backyard. Sylvia had heard Edwin and Ava fight through an open window. I wondered whether Sonny, the Towsons' handyman/gardener, had heard Edwin talking about his family's history with the Tiffany lamp while he was watering plants or pulling weeds. His wife had been eliminated as the fake Ava, but as far as I knew, no one had taken a look at whether Sonny was the fake Edwin. I couldn't recall Sonny's last name, although I knew I'd heard it or read it.

I moved back to my office. The *Seacoast Star*'s archives were searchable, and by using the advanced function, I could limit the search window to a certain time frame, in this case starting the day before Ava's murder to now. I found the reference I'd recalled in his article about the sketch. They'd shown it to Sonny Russo, among others.

No Sonny Russo lived in the seacoast region, but Sonny, I knew, was often a nickname. I tried Salvatore Russo, then Santino Russo, without finding him. I brought up the white pages and navigated to "Russo," searching for a first name that began with *S.* Third down was Sandro. Sandro Russo. Sonny Russo.

I gasped.

Sonny Russo lived at 29 Sonille Road in Portsmouth — only a few houses down from the house that Orson Thompkins used as a mail drop. Surely Sonny could have observed that his neighbor was often gone for extended periods.

I Googled his name and clicked on a link that took me to Rocky Point Hospital's December newsletter. On page 3, an article touted the employees' food drive. Noreen Russo, a cafeteria worker, was a volunteer, and her husband, Sonny Russo, was helping out by delivering all the canned goods to a local food pantry. The photo showed the couple standing among a clutch of other volunteers next to Sonny's loaded pickup. Sonny was tall and thin. The truck was blue. I'd seen it before, and I'd seen Sonny. He'd backed out of a driveway in the Grey Gull complex, but he hadn't left. He'd driven deeper into the complex. Maybe to Jean's condo. If Jean needed a handyman, surely she would have asked Ava for a recommendation. I wondered if the police had cleared him of involvement. It was possible I hadn't heard his name mentioned because he had an unassailable alibi. I needed to talk to Wes.

I glanced at the time log on my monitor. It was 5:43. Too early to call, so I e-mailed him: *What do you know about Sonny? Alibi?*

As I walked back to the kitchen to get more coffee, an idea came to me, and I ran back to my computer. I brought the white pages back up and jotted down Sonny's phone number. Many day laborers start work early, some as early as seven, and I wanted to try to reach him before he left for the day. I decided to call at six thirty.

I heard rustling overhead. Ty was awake. I poured him a cup of coffee and brought it upstairs.

"I wish you didn't have to leave," I said.

"Me, too."

"When will you be back?"

"Friday."

"I miss you already."

He kissed me, and I kissed him back.

Ty left at six, and I left ten minutes later. Max wouldn't be in until eight at the earliest, which meant I had at least two hours before I could talk to him. While I waited for the a/c to kick on in the car, I considered what I should do with the time. I smiled as I recalled my mother shaking her head anytime someone said they had time to kill, as if time itself were the enemy, a demon to exorcise. I tapped on the steering wheel, thinking.

Ten seconds later, I nodded, knowing how to best spend my time. I wanted to see the Towson Company guesthouse. Maybe it was empty — but maybe it wasn't.

CHAPTER THIRTY-THREE

Just before Rye, the town north of Rocky Point, I came to the address Tammy had given me — 1 Ocean Avenue. It was a beautiful cottage with a rose-covered trellis, a wraparound porch, and an ocean view. There was a blue Lexus in the driveway, parked in front of the attached garage.

I parked around the corner on a street called Mallery facing Ocean, diagonally across from the cottage. The roar of the surf was thunderous, even today, when the sea was calm. On a stormy day, it must sound like the wrath of God.

I got out of my car and looked around. This stretch of Ocean Avenue was lined with stately homes. From where I stood at the intersection of Mallery and Ocean, facing the beach, no other house was visible on the beach side of the street. Across from the beach, there were two properties, one on each side of Mallery. A meticulously trimmed eight-foot-tall boxwood hedge enclosed the northernmost property; the other was surrounded by a six-foot-high fieldstone wall. I walked to the southwest corner of Mallery and Ocean and stood with my right side pressed against the rough surface of the stone wall.

I wanted to know if anyone was living in the cottage, and if so, whom. The Lexus indicated someone was there now, but that didn't tell me much. Maybe the Lexus belonged to a real estate agent taking photos in preparation of putting the house on the market. With Edwin's plans to relocate his company to London, he had no need for a guesthouse.

The Towson property was marked by a four-foot-high cypress hedge. A latticework bower was twined with white, pink, and red roses. The porch was unscreened and wide. The wood siding was salt-flecked brown. The house was perfectly situated for both serenity and privacy.

Using the telescopic setting on my camera, I snapped a photo of the Lexus's license plate and dashed back to my car to call Dowd Investigations, the company we used to conduct background checks. I punched through their interactive menu to reach the person on off-hour duty. I gave my company's account number, answered two security questions, and had the information five seconds later — the Lexus was registered to the Towson Company.

At six thirty, I called Sonny Russo. A woman answered.

"Hi," I said. "I hope I'm not calling too early. This is Josie Prescott calling about some gardening work. Is Sonny there?"

"Hold on."

A moment later a gruff-sounding man said, "Hello?"

"This is Josie Prescott. I understand you do gardening."

"That's right."

"I need some new bushes planted. Can you come take a look and give me an estimate?"

"Where are you?"

"In Rocky Point, not far from the interstate."

"I could come later today. Sometime in the afternoon."

"I'll call you around noon if my schedule opens up. What's your cell phone number?"

He gave it to me, a 603 number. Local.

I tapped it into my computer, just in case, but I doubted I'd need it — I'd never spoken to Sonny before, which meant he wasn't the fake Edwin. I thanked him and ended the call.

He might not be the fake Edwin, but that didn't mean he wasn't a killer.

I resumed my study of the Towson guesthouse. The windows were open. White sheer curtains fluttered in the mild breeze. If I lived there, I'd use the porch with the ocean view, not the one facing the street. I was about to make my way down Ocean to a beach access path when I noticed that the red mailbox flag was up.

I sprinted across the street, and, with my heart thudding so hard I thought it might break my ribs, opened the mailbox. There was only one envelope inside. It was white with delicately rendered butterflies printed on the back, a greeting card. It was addressed to someone named Alli Rheingold in Ann Arbor, Michigan. The return address read Clover Avenue in Los Angeles. The sender's name was Coco Tully. I photographed both sides of the envelope, shut the mailbox, and scurried away down Ocean toward the path that led to the beach.

Turning into the sandy alley that ran from Ocean Avenue to the dunes, I glanced over my shoulder. No one was following, and I paused, leaning gingerly against a rickety picket fence, willing the adrenaline rush to pass. I couldn't believe I'd just peeked inside a stranger's mailbox. I closed my eyes and concentrated on the ocean's roar and rumble. The waves cracked with lightning-bolt fervor, then ebbed into shore with purling calm. My hands were trembling. After a while, a familiar and welcome serenity replaced my agitation, and I continued down the path.

When I reached the beach, I stuffed my sandals inside my tote bag and set off south, placing the Towson cottage at my back. The shifting sand was littered with shiny twirls of dark green seaweed and countless clam and mussel shells. A hundred yards down the empty beach, I came to a long, twisted branch of silvery gray driftwood. After being blown into the ocean during a storm and moiled in the turbulent water for years, the bark fell away and the wood was sanded to a silky finish, until finally, a confluence of fierce winds, powerful waves, and high tide tossed it onto shore. I stretched out beside it, lying on cold, hard sand. I peered through a crook in the branch. A tall, thin woman somewhere in her thirties was on the porch, sitting on an Adirondack rocker, facing the ocean, drinking from a blue mug and reading something on a tablet. She had short auburn hair. She wore a silky, tangerine-colored maxigown and an ivory fine-knit sweater. After a moment, she placed her mug and the tablet on a nearby table and walked to the railing. She stared out over the ocean.

I raised myself up on one elbow and took three photos, wishing she would gaze in my direction so I could capture her full face. After a few minutes, she walked back to the rocker and sat down again. I was ready and took three more shots. After another minute watching, with my neck cricked and my foot tingling as if it were about to go to sleep, I said, "Enough."

I stood, turned my back to the cottage again, brushed off the sand that clung to my skin and dress, then walked slowly back to the beach access passageway. I still had some flyers for New Hampshire Children First! in my tote bag. Funding therapeutic horse rides would serve as a logical reason for me to knock on her door. Once I was back on Ocean, I picked my way along the shoulder until I reached the cottage drive-way.

Circling around the Lexus to reach the porch steps, I raised my shoulders to my ears, then lowered them, three times, then turned my head as far as I could to the right, then to the left, surefire relaxation techniques. The garage door had three big windows, and as I passed, I glanced in. A red Mercedes was parked inside. The license plate read MYLV.

I gawked, frozen like a mime.

It looked like I'd discovered the reason for Edwin's sudden disappearance — he was hiding out with a beautiful woman named Coco.

CHAPTER THIRTY-FOUR

My paralysis was short-lived. I was way out of my depth, no matter why Ava's car was in the Towson Company guesthouse garage. I backed away from the garage, raced all the way to Mallery, caroming off the wall as I took the corner. My chest heaving, I somehow got myself into my car. Leaning my head against the cool hard plastic steering wheel, I took a few moments to breathe, to think. Three minutes later, when I was able to hold out my hand without trembling, I started the engine and brought up the photos on my phone.

Coco Tully, assuming that was the woman I'd seen, was lovely, ethereal, and a little bohemian. Her features were delicate, her skin rosy. In addition to the flowy dress and delicate sweater, she wore turquoise strappy sandals, turquoise and silver dangling earrings, and three strands of turquoise beads.

I slid my phone into my bag and pulled a

U-turn. I drove along Mallery to the intersection of Main, then turned into a strip-mall parking lot. To avoid the awkward questions I was certain Ellis would ask, I e-mailed him instead of calling. I wrote:

Hi Ellis,
I happened to see Ava's Mercedes at the Towson Company guesthouse at One Ocean Ave. Maybe Edwin didn't disappear so much as relocate. Photos attached.

Josie

I selected two images to send, one a profile, the other full face.

While I thought about how much I should tell Wes, I Googled "Coco Tully." None of the images matched the woman I'd seen at the Towson cottage. There was no Coco Tully in New Hampshire that I could find. My abilities to research people paled in comparison to Wes's. It was time to call in the big gun. My dash clock read 7:20. Early, but that wouldn't bother Wes.

"Did you get my e-mail?" I asked as soon as he was on the line.

"Yeah. I was about to call you. Whatcha got?"

I reported my findings, that Sonny Russo

lived on the same street as Cal Miller, that I'd seen him at the Grey Gull complex, which meant he might know Jean, and that I'd spoken to him.

"You're certain he's not the fake Edwin."

"A hundred percent. But he could still be the killer. Does he have an alibi?"

"I'll check. This idea is better than that Lara Reisch lead you gave me. What a bust."

"She wouldn't talk, or she had nothing to say?"

"She wouldn't even admit she worked for Towson's. Win some, lose some."

"I have other news," I said, and recounted what I knew about Coco Tully. "I'll send you photos, but you can't publish them yet. I sent them to Ellis, too, and if he sees them in print, he'll know you got them from me."

"I'll think about it," he said as if he were doing me a favor.

"Forget it, Wes. If you want them, you have to promise. I'm sending them to help you learn who she is and what's she's doing here — that's all."

He sighed and agreed. I e-mailed him the same two photos I sent Ellis.

"Got them. Holy hottie! She's a babe. Do you think Edwin's getting a little nookie with this hot tomato?"

I shook my head. Wes had his own way of

expressing himself.

"That's what I'm hoping you'll find out."

"Wicked cool, Joz!"

"We didn't find the avocado crate among the Towson property," I said. "Did you hear anything about it?"

"Yup — it's nothing. According to the police, that neighbor, Sylvia, uses old crates to carry stuff. She pickles her own cucumbers and brought some jars over to the Towsons."

"Did the police find the crate?"

"Nope, but they found the pickles."

"Another dead end."

"Maybe this Coco gal is a live one. Anything else?"

"No.

"Catch ya later."

I was relieved Sylvia was out of it. She hadn't mentioned that she'd been one of the people who'd entered the Towson house, but that was natural. When you try to recall what other people did, you forget all about yourself. She might be eliminated as a suspect, but Sonny wasn't.

I cruised past the Towson house in Garnet Cove. It looked empty, as if the building itself had a soul.

Sylvia was watering the tomatoes. I waved

and parked in front of her house. I reached around to the backseat and found her basket.

"Those tomatoes were among the best I've ever had," I said, handing her the basket. "Thanks again."

"You didn't need to bring the basket back! How about if I refill it for you?"

"Do you have enough?"

She laughed. "I could go into business, I have so many."

"What do you do with them?"

"I put up sauce, make tomato relish, and freeze individual portions of ratatouille, which I must say tastes pretty darn good come January."

"I bet it does."

Sylvia assessed each tomato to ensure it was ready to be picked before plucking it from the vine and placing it in the basket. There was love in every move.

"Do you drink, Sylvia?"

She laughed again. "You bet! I love a good gin and tonic."

"Do you have a favorite brand?"

"I'm not that knowledgeable. I just know enough to not buy the cheapest ones. Headache city, my husband used to say, may he rest in peace."

She handed me the basket.

"You're a wonderful woman, Sylvia."

"It takes one to know one."

I thanked her again and placed the basket on the front seat, protected from jiggling by my tote bag.

As I pulled away, I saw Sylvia back at work, weeding.

I drove out the Hastings exit and parked at the dead end of the short street.

It was cooler today, and hazy, but the sun was fighting through the clouds, burning the gloom away as it rose. I felt pretty gloomy, too, frightened and perplexed.

I stood on the precipice watching the ocean surge toward shore. Waves broke fifty feet out, leaving bubbly white foam in their wake. The water rolled toward land with frothy ripples until it hit the boulders that lay against the sheer granite wall. Jets of swirling water shot twenty feet into the air, spraying everything in sight with a soft, sea-scented rain.

I stopped at Sweet Treats Bakery & Tea Shoppe in downtown Rocky Point and picked up a pair of cinnamon lattes, then walked the four blocks to Max's office.

Max Bixby, who knew about the law, was a rock and a comfort. He never pushed. He explained, then waited for me to make decisions.

I pushed open the bright red door and stepped into what used to be the entry hall of a sprawling four-story mansion on the Piscataqua River. Max owned the building and rented out one- and two-room office suites to therapists, insurance agents, financial advisers, and the like. His small law firm was located on the ground floor.

Max was standing in the center of the hall staring at a radiator grate. He was approaching forty and had thickened a bit around the waist since the last time I saw him. He wore a 1940s-style blue and white striped seersucker suit, a pale blue shirt, and a dark blue bow tie. My eyes followed his gaze.

"You're thinking of replacing steam heat with electric and wondering what to do about the radiators," I said.

"Josie!" he said, extending his hand for a shake. "No, there's something rattling around in there, and I don't like it."

"I don't even like the sound of it. What do you think it is? A mouse?"

"Or a rattler."

My eyes opened wide. "There aren't rattlesnakes in New Hampshire."

"Sorry to be the one to break it to you, but the timber rattlesnake is native around these parts. They're rare nowadays, but I don't like the sound I'm hearing."

I lowered my eyes to the grate as a low-pitched, tinny rattle sounded. It was loud and echoed throughout the open hallway.

"Are they dangerous?" I asked.

"Extremely."

"What are you going to do?"

"I'm waiting on the snake man. You have to get a special service because the snakes are a protected species. You can't kill them."

"Fancy that." I handed over a paper cup. "Have a latte."

"Thanks. I will. Is this a business call?"

"Yes. Hopefully a brief one."

"Come on in and tell me what's going on."

"How's Babs?" I asked, following him down a short hall.

"My better half is fabulous. Gorgeous, smart, and sensible."

I laughed. "That's quite a tribute."

"And well deserved. I love my wife."

Max's office was as big as Edwin's, yet in style and tone, it was as different as the two men themselves. Max's office was contemporary. Edwin's was traditional. Max was warm and personable. Edwin was cold and cerebral. It would be an interesting study, I thought, to try to correlate taste in interior design to personality. I followed Max across the cushy charcoal gray carpet to the glass-topped conference table positioned near the windows. The sun had broken through, and glints of gold dotted the fast-moving river. The walls were pale gray with a blue tint. Bursts of color came from the paintings, abstracts featuring explosions of red and purple.

I asked if he was familiar with the double murder case, and he said he was. He'd also heard a little about the stolen Tiffany lamp, so I didn't need to spend any time bringing him up to date about the basic facts of the case. Instead I told him about my sending Eric for the lamp, which meant we hadn't properly video-recorded it; my asking Fred the same questions Ellis asked me, my concern that Eric would feel intimidated by a police interrogation, and Ellis's outrageous implications about me and my company.

"When Ty heard that Ellis asked if I needed money, he thought I ought to touch base with you. I understand why Ellis had to ask, but I'm still hot as a firecracker about it."

"I don't blame you. Ty was right. It sounds like a routine question, but I recommend that you don't talk to the police without me."

"I want to cover Eric and Fred's lawyers, too. Can you represent all three of us, or will that be a conflict of interest?"

"As it stands now, I can represent you all in my role as your corporate attorney. If a conflict arises, I'll make sure you know about it before it becomes an issue. Tell Eric and Fred to call me pronto. And not to talk to the police without me."

I extracted two business cards from the Plexiglas stand in the center of the table. "One for each of them." I stood up. "Thank you, Max."

When we stepped back out into the hall, the rattling sound started up again, loud and persistent.

"I hope that's not an omen," I said.

"You mean you hope it's not a *bad* omen."

"True."

"Great news. Rattlers are good luck symbols."

"You're making that up."

"Am not."

"Well, I hope you're right. You can use some of that good luck getting rid of it."

"Relocating it — if it's a rattler." We shook again, and he added, "Thanks for the latte."

"You're welcome." I paused with my hand on the doorknob and looked back at him. "I'm kind of scared, Max."

"Don't be. You're on solid ground. So are Eric and Fred. Ellis is just casting a wide net."

His words lightened my load a little. "Really?"

"Truly."

I smiled. "Thanks."

Fred was at work when I arrived just before nine. "You're in at the crack of dawn," I said.

"I know, and it's painful. But duty calls. I have a nine thirty call with a curator from the Philadelphia Museum of Art, nine thirty P.M., his time. He's in Hong Kong." Fred grinned and pushed up his glasses. "He thinks he has information about Aunt Louise's desk."

"Get out of town! How did you connect with him?"

"I sent out photos of the globe desk to museums with important colonial furniture collections, and he responded. He thinks it was loaned to the museum as part of an exhibit in 1973."

"Well done, Fred! Anything from the remaining *News and Views* names?"

"It's slow going, but it's going. Three more say they have no information. I'm still tracking the other four."

"It's amazing that you've had as much success as you've —" I broke off as Gretchen's chimes sounded.

We all turned toward the door. Sasha came in followed by a stranger, a man. I stood up.

Sasha was flushed, almost smiling. Knowing her as I did, I could tell she was nonplussed.

The man who followed her in looked like Santa Claus. He was about five-eight and tubby, with a well-groomed full white beard and neatly trimmed short white hair. His complexion was ruddy, his eyes twinkled, and his smile was broad. I half expected him to call out, "Ho, ho, ho!" He wore a light tan summer-weight suit, a white shirt, and a green and tan striped tie.

"This is Franklin Colby," Sasha said, "our marble expert, in from Oklahoma to help us out with the O'Hara collection."

"Howdy!" he said, raising his arm and slightly rocking his palm like a king greeting an adoring crowd.

I glanced around. Everyone was smiling. I was charmed, but I understood why Sasha felt awkward — Frank was as gregarious as Sasha was reserved. I stepped forward and extended my hand.

"How do you do, Mr. Colby. I'm Josie

Prescott. Thanks for coming all this way."

"My pleasure, my pleasure. Please, call me Frank." He smiled at Sasha. "I was just telling this young lady that this is my first trip to the East Coast, and only my second east of the Mississippi. That one took me to Akron. That's a town in Ohio. Have you ever been to Akron?"

"I don't think so."

"How about you, young lady?" he asked Sasha.

She tucked her hair behind her ear. "No, but I bet I know why you went. The toy marble museum."

"A magnificent place! What a week that was!"

"There's a toy marble museum?" Cara asked.

"It's a wondrous thing."

Fred stood, introduced himself, and leaned back against his desk. "Do you blow glass, too?"

"Now that's an interesting question, young man. I tried it once when I first got the glass-collecting bug. I learned that making things requires a different skill set than collecting them. Have you ever tried it?"

"Yes — I took a class in college, actually."

"You did?" Sasha asked.

"My thesis was on the fifteenth-century

artist Paolo Uccello. There's some speculation that he designed one of the first stained glass windows."

Sasha nodded. "For the Florence Cathedral."

"Exactly. His thing was perspective. He used the concept of a vanishing point to add depth to his designs, unlike other artists of his day, who used perspective to tell multiple stories." He pushed up his glasses. "Anyway, I got interested in the process. I dabble."

"What kind of things have you done, Fred?" Gretchen asked.

"I replaced a small piece of cobalt glass in one of the Congregational church's windows. It got chipped somehow." He grinned. "Matching the color, texture, size . . . now that was a challenge."

"I'm so impressed!" Cara said.

"Thanks. What it comes down to is that Frank and I share an admiration for glasswork."

"There's nothing to equal it," Frank said. He turned to face Sasha. "I'll tell you one thing, young lady — I can't wait to get a gander at those marbles."

"Frank, we're going to do everything we can to make sure you're comfortable while you're here," I said. "Can we get you a cup of coffee or tea?"

"That's most kind of you. I would like some coffee."

I nodded at Cara, and she stood up. "I'll bring some gingersnaps, too. Fresh made."

"Good." To Frank, I said, "Cara is famous for her gingersnaps. Let's get you checked in. As you know, our insurance company requires a background check, which you passed with flying colors. All we need to do now is check your ID and scan in your fingerprints to confirm you are who you said you are."

"Very sensible, very smart. You never know who may be prevaricating, for reasons sly or mighty."

I pointed to a chair at the guest table. "Have a seat. Sasha will take it from here."

Out of Frank's line of vision, I gave Sasha a thumbs-up, then turned toward Fred. "Can I have a minute, Fred?" He stood up. I turned to Gretchen. "Would you ask Eric to meet me by Hank's area?" I laughed. "Hank and Angela's area."

She smiled and reached for the phone.

Fred and I walked side by side across the warehouse. Neither of us spoke until we reached a worktable near where Hank and Angela were playing with a mouse, the purple one with the green feathery tail.

Angela batted it toward Hank. He used his teeth to pick up the mouse and shook it as if he wanted it dead. As soon as Hank got the mouse, Angela lost interest; instead, she focused on Hank's tail. She went low to the ground and circled to his rear. Pausing to line herself up, she gave a little wiggle-bum and pounced. Hank dropped the mouse and looked over his shoulder. She pounced again, and he lashed his tail aside.

"I've seen cats chase their own tails, but never someone else's," I said.

"Hank has a very attractive tail."

"Obviously."

"He's pretty patient. Some guys would have a different attitude."

"Hank is a perfect boy, aren't you, darling?"

He mewed, his tail flicking, as Angela continued to stalk it.

We watched them play for a minute, until Angela got tired. She yawned and climbed into Hank's basket. He went for water.

Eric came from the loading dock, his work boots clapping against the concrete floor.

"You wanted to see me?" Eric asked.

"I wanted to see you both." I extracted Max's cards from my pocket and handed them over. "Max is expecting to hear from you. As I told you, this is corporate business, so the company will pay his fee."

Eric stuffed the card into his shirt pocket. Fred read it carefully, taking his time.

"I don't know why I'm not nervous," Eric said, "but I'm not."

"Maybe it's because you did nothing wrong," I suggested.

Eric smiled. "That's never stopped me from feeling anxious before."

I laughed. "A sign of maturity, then."

"I'll tell Grace you said so. Is there anything else?"

"No, thanks, Eric. I'm really sorry for this mess."

"All in a day's work."

"I hope not. I hope this is unique."

Eric turned and left, retracing his steps.

"The only time I've ever spoken to a lawyer," Fred said, his eyes still glued to Max's card, "is at a cocktail party." He slid the card into an inside slot in his wallet. "I don't own a house — I rent. I'm not married, and I don't have any kids, so I have a do-it-yourself will. Suzanne and I are talking about getting married, though, so I figured, you know, we'd sit down with a lawyer and go over stuff."

"Oh, Fred! That's wonderful news. I love Suzanne!"

"Thanks." He pushed up his glasses. "I

guess my first experience talking to a lawyer will be as a suspect in a series of felonies."

"I don't think you're any more of a suspect than I am."

Fred laughed. "Which, if I may say so, isn't particularly reassuring."

I smiled, although I wasn't really amused.

CHAPTER THIRTY-FIVE

Both cats followed me upstairs. Hank sat by the love seat. Angela tried to bat his tail. As soon as he sensed her presence, he whisked his tail away. She leapt on his tail, trying, it appeared, to capture it. Hank stood up, shook her off as if she were a feather, and sat back down. From his expression, I could tell that he thought of her the way I perceive a gnat, annoying but not the least bit threatening. He turned toward the stairs, choosing, I conjectured, to nap in his basket rather than on the love seat. Once he'd passed out of Angela's field of vision, she lost interest and began to clean herself, licking a paw, then wiping her face, over and over again.

"Are you doing cleanies?" I asked. "What a good girl!"

Up until now, I'd focused on who could have learned enough about the lamp's history to pull off the scam. I hadn't considered the logistics, that just as the fake Ava had to have known that the Towsons were out of town, the man who called himself Orson Thompkins had to have known Cal Miller's travel schedule. If we could find someone who knew both Cal Miller and one or both of the Towsons, then we had a likely suspect.

I called Wes and got him. I asked to meet, and he agreed. We settled on the Rocky Point Diner at ten.

In the ten minutes I had available before I needed to leave, I checked all the stolen art and antiques databases we subscribed to, hoping against hope to see an inquiry from some dealer somewhere asking whether anyone had information about a Tiffany lamp he was considering buying. Sure, we'd posted call-for-sighting alerts everywhere — but people are human, and notices get missed or forgotten all the time. Nothing.

"Darn!" I said aloud.

I was fed up to my eyeballs with passively waiting for a posting that would lead to the lamp. I wanted to do something, to make something happen. If only I could come up with a plan.

While I waited for a plan to germinate, I tackled an unpleasant responsibility and e-mailed Timothy. *No news re: the lamp. But no news is just that — no news. It's not bad news. I remain hopeful.*

He replied almost immediately. *Thx, J! I'm working the room on this end. Don't get me started about lawyers. Issue #2: Any update re: murders?*

My reply reflected my appreciation for Timothy's unwavering support and was designed to give him a sound bite he could take to the lawyers.

Thank you, Timothy. No news re: murders, but I would have no reason to know anything since I'm not involved.

His final reply was short and oh, so sweet.

You rock, girlfriend.

I got to the diner ahead of Wes, snagged a small booth by a window, and ordered coffee. Wes joined me a few minutes later and ordered a club soda with an orange slice.

"Most people ask for lime or lemon," I said, "not orange."

"I like oranges."

"Me, too." I waited until his club soda was delivered, then asked, "Any news about Sonny?"

"The police questioned him straight off but have put him off to the side. He has an alibi. He was installing a custom-made closet system. It took him all morning. He picked up the units at the cabinetmaker's at seven thirty, then went straight to his client, arriving about eight ten."

"He didn't kill Ava."

"And he didn't pretend to be Edwin." Wes sipped some soda noisily, like a little boy, his eyes bright with news. "The best part is that he's not Ava's baby daddy."

It took me a few seconds to respond. "You're saying the police thought Ava might have been sleeping with the gardener?"

Wes chuckled. "It's been known to happen."

"Not all things are possible."

"He volunteered his DNA. He's officially out of it."

"Ick. All right, then . . . Sonny's not involved. Have the police found out who it is?"

"Nope. He's flying below the radar. Do you still think it's that Orson guy?"

"Who doesn't seem to exist. Yes, I do. It's logical. I'm assuming it's a made-up name, and that if we could figure out who knew Cal Miller well enough to know his schedule *and* Edwin or Ava well enough to know Edwin's family history, we've got him."

"But how can we?"

"I don't know."

Wes poked at the orange slice with his straw. "Do you think Orson — whoever he is — killed Ava and Jean?"

"It's possible. I mean, think about it, Wes. Jean must have known what was going on. It didn't occur to me at the time, but when she came to my office, she was scared and confused. At the time, I just focused on the confusion. I assumed she was in shock about Ava's death. Now I think she was terrified that her partners would kill her next — and that's exactly what happened."

"Sure, but that doesn't help us any."

"I know." I pushed my mug aside, frustrated. "Any news about why Edwin was at the beach house?"

"None. The police asked him to come in and talk to them about it, and he refused."

"I didn't know you were allowed to refuse."

"Sure you are. You know that."

I thought of all the times when I'd been called in by the police and Max had reassured me that I was a good citizen cooperating with the authorities, not a suspect under investigation. Edwin was choosing not to cooperate, and I wondered why.

"You're right," I said. "Of course."

"I found Alli Rheingold, the woman that Coco Tully sent the card to. She's a nurse, and she won't even admit knowing Coco Tully."

"That's bizarre. What do they have to hide?"

"Edwin told the chief that a desire for privacy shouldn't imply guilty knowledge."

"That's true, too."

"Who knows? Coco isn't talking either. The Clover Avenue address on the envelope goes to a nice house in a nice neighborhood in West L.A. near the Santa Monica line. No one is home. The neighbors don't know anything except that a couple moved in recently. The house is owned by a big law firm, and you can forget trying to get information from a law firm."

"Maybe Coco is a nickname."

"For what?"

"Charlotte. Colleen. Caroline."

"Really?"

"It's possible."

Wes slid out of the booth. "Anything else?"

"No."

He placed two dollars on the table. "Catch ya later!"

I waved good-bye and sat, watching Wes. He walked so fast, he nearly ran. He was always in a hurry.

Window boxes packed with fuchsia and white petunias rested on ornate brass supports. Hints of sunlight touched the parking lot. I tried again to bring up an image of the fake Ava. The sketch artist, Bryan, and Ellis were hopeful that more pieces of the picture would find their way to my consciousness, adding to the integrity of the image. Then, without warning, a different memory surfaced. The elusive idea I'd been chasing overnight came to me: Ava had been on her high school reunion committee.

Rocky Point High School was housed in a long brick building overlooking Old Mill Pond, not far from the library. From the rear, rolling lawns led to nicely groomed athletic fields, stainless steel spectator stands, and the Pond. A boathouse sat near a long dock.

"Which way to the library, please?" I asked the guard, a portly man long past traditional retirement age.

He asked for my ID, then checked a printed list. When he saw my name wasn't on it, he said he'd need to call someone.

I waited off to the side. Two people who looked like parents passed through. So did a man with a sample case. All three were on the appointment list.

About five minutes later, a young woman wearing a mint green sweater set, a white skirt, and white low-heeled sandals spoke to the guard. Her ID badge hung from a yellow lanyard. She nodded at something the guard said, then turned to me.

"Hi! I'm Edie Bradovich, the assistant librarian. Mr. Peterson said you want to visit our library — is that correct?"

"Yes, for what I hope will be an easy request. I'm an antiques appraiser, Josie Prescott. In connection with an appraisal I'm working on, I need to consult an old yearbook."

I could tell Edie wanted to ask me for more details, not because she needed to know but because she was curious. I put my patient mask on and smiled. My dad always said that the trick to negotiation was to challenge the premise of any question you didn't want to answer, answer those that passed muster truthfully and simply, and never volunteer information.

"Sure, come on back."

After the guard wrote my name down on his list, I passed through the security checkpoint and followed Edie to the library. The expansive room looked its age in the best possible way, with wood paneling, dentil crown molding, and oak wood flooring, burnished to a lustrous gold. There was a small checkout stand near the entry door, a large reference desk, rows of carrels, and angled stacks of periodicals and books.

Thirty or so students were scattered around.

I followed Edie to the reference desk, where a woman sat reading something on her computer monitor. A black and white sign told me her name was Ms. S. Schaeffer. She was a little older than me, with short, shaggy brown hair and a big smile.

"This is Josie Prescott," Edie whispered. "She wants to look at an old yearbook."

Ms. Schaeffer looked up. When she spoke her tone was hushed, too. "Sure! I'm Sydney, the head librarian. Follow me."

We crossed the room to a corner shelf. "What year are you looking for?"

"Nineteen ninety-seven."

"Oh, no! We only keep them here for ten years. We have such limited space we have to make hard decisions. After that period, they go to the archives."

"Where is that?"

She smiled. "A storage unit."

I laughed. "Can you access it for me? Or if you're short-staffed, I don't mind doing the hunt."

"Sorry, no. Library staff only. You'll have to complete a requisition form. We're pretty quick. It will only take us a few days to retrieve it."

"Do you know of anywhere else that might have a copy I could get my hands on today?

The alumni office, maybe?"

"We don't have an actual alumni office. All that sort of thing is run through the principal's office." She paused for a moment, thinking. "You might try the public library. I think they have a full set of yearbooks."

I thanked her, told her I might be back, and drove straight to the library.

Sydney was right — the Rocky Point library housed a full set of Rocky Point High School yearbooks. I eased the 1997 edition from the shelf and sat at a large wooden table near the reference desk to go through it. An older man sitting across from me was reading the *New York Times.* A young woman on my side of the table was writing something on a yellow legal pad.

As soon as I turned to the class entries, I realized I didn't know Ava's maiden name. I read every name until I found her entry. Her maiden name had been Collier.

Ava Collier's photo was pretty typical for a high school yearbook. The background was pale blue. Her brown hair was cut in short layers. Her smile looked forced, not as if she were uncomfortable but as if the photographer told her to say "cheese," then snapped the shot before she got into position. She listed her after-graduation goal as "travel."

I continued turning pages, pausing again when I came to Diane Hawkins, the librarian who ran Ava's book club. Her maiden name was Lerner. Her photo was better than Ava's. She looked sweet and starry-eyed. I recognized her prom date from the photo on her office wall. His name was Mitch Montley. He was a fireplug of a young man, short and squat with a shock of dark red hair. He liked fishing.

I continued flipping pages. Phillip Wilcox had been Ava's prom date. I touched his handsome face. He'd been a football player and had planned to join his dad's car dealership as a sales associate after graduation. I used my smartphone to Google him. Evidently, Phillip had done well. He was now the president of Wilcox Car Emporium. I'd passed their lot on Route 1 a thousand times. His dad was listed as the chairman of the company.

I navigated to Rocky Point's community blog and scrolled down until I found the photo where Ava posed with the chair of the high school reunion committee. The chair's name was Janet Chirling. I turned back to the *C*'s in the yearbook and found Janet's listing. Either Janet hadn't married or she'd kept her maiden name. She was a mousy-looking young woman, with buck teeth and a too-wide nose. She wore a white blouse that washed out her olive complexion. From LinkedIn, I learned she was an emergency room nurse at Rocky Point Hospital, and that she loved her work. I Googled her name and found she lived in a single-family house on Strawberry Hill, the oldest section of town.

I slid the yearbook back onto the shelf and left. Walking across the parking lot to my car, I wondered what someone looking at my high school graduation photo would think. I went to the prom with T. J. Matthews, one of the cool kids in my class. We stayed in touch the summer after graduation, while he was working at his grandparents' farm in Maine and I was waitressing in Boston, but then we drifted apart. I went to college in New York. He went to school in Boulder.

High school. When I first moved to Rocky Point, a typical "nice to meet you" question was where I went to school. Having lived in big cities all my life, I was surprised to learn they were asking where I went to high school, not college. My stock answer evolved to "In a suburb of Boston, where I was one of a thousand students." For some of the folks I met during those first years, typically the star athletes, high school represented the zenith of their lives. For others, high school was a nightmare of not fitting in, of failure, real or imagined, a nadir, not easily overcome. For most of us, though, Ava and me included, high school was merely a step along the way.

Janet Chirling wasn't on duty and wasn't expected back until Wednesday. Her regular schedule had her working the 3:00 P.M. to 11:00 P.M. shift, Wednesday to Sunday. I drove to the address on Strawberry Hill.

Her Cape Cod–style house was located on a winding road about halfway up the hill. Positioned to capture the ocean view, she had a large garden in the front, protected from deer and other critters by chicken wire. I recognized peppers, lettuce, zucchini, pumpkins, and two kinds of tomatoes, cherry and beefsteak. The cherries were an early harvest breed. One look at those plump red beauties and I started salivating.

She answered the door in a purple and yellow floral-patterned short-sleeved bath-robe.

"Oh, no!" I said. "I woke you up."

"Not a bit. I'm just having a lazy day."

Her hair was now chin length and wavy, a

good style for her, and she'd had work done on her teeth and nose. She'd never be a beauty, but she was no longer homely. She wore tortoiseshell-framed glasses.

"Sounds wonderful! I'm Josie Prescott, and I —"

"I know who you are! I'm one of the volunteer wranglers for the therapeutic horse-ride program. You were honored at last year's volunteer luncheon."

"Isn't it a terrific organization?"

"Absolutely. Can I get you a cup of coffee?"

"Thanks, but I only have a minute. I just have one quick question. In connection with an antiques appraisal, I need to know who's on your high school reunion committee."

"You need to know who's on . . ." She pressed her hand to her mouth. "This is about Ava, isn't it?"

I smiled, aiming for casual and reassuring. "Actually, no. I know it sounds odd, but it's about an object I'm appraising. How many people are on the committee?"

"Six of us, five, now that Ava's passed on. I don't mind telling you the names."

She named them, two women besides her, and Phil Wilcox.

I thanked her, and left. She stood at the door until I drove around a curve and passed out of sight. From her wrinkled brow, I could tell she thought my question was about as weird as any she'd ever been asked.

I drove down the hill toward Route 1, determined to get a look at Phil Wilcox. I was confident he was the man I knew as Orson Thompkins.

CHAPTER THIRTY-SIX

Multicolored flags attached to crisscrossing rope lines flew high above the cars that filled the Wilcox Car Emporium lot. A six-foot-tall inflatable Uncle Sam bounced around overhead. He held a sign announcing a GRAND JULY 4TH SALE. Three men in summer-weight suits, salesmen, stood around, waiting for customers. I pulled into a grocery store parking lot across from the dealership and rolled to a stop against the low barricade that separated the lot from the sidewalk. From my position, I had an unobstructed sight line into the showroom. A shiny red car was parked inside. Phil Wilcox stood chatting to a woman in a sundress. She nodded at something he said and walked into a back office. Through the glass wall, I could see her settle in behind a small desk.

Phil Wilcox was just as good-looking now as he had been in high school. He hadn't gained weight, his hair was neatly trimmed, his clothes looked expensive, and he walked with an athlete's confidence. I wondered what would happen if I popped in and called him Orson. Instead, I called Wes and asked him to get the lowdown on the man and his emporium.

"Why?" he asked.

"I'll tell you, but you can't follow up until I say so. Promise?"

After our familiar back-and-forth, he agreed.

"I think he might be Ava's baby's father."

Wes low-whistled. "That means he might be Orson Thompkins."

"Exactly."

"What's your plan?"

"I'm not ready to talk about it yet."

"But you're thinking."

"So hard, it hurts."

Wes promised to call me back ASAP. I continued to watch Phil Wilcox work the room. He patted an inside salesman heartily on the back. He walked outside, smoothing his hair, then joked around with the three salesmen. There was something pathetic about his joie de vivre in the face of no customers.

"You never know who may be prevaricating, for reasons sly or mighty," Sasha's marble expert, Frank Colby, had said. We routinely verified identity in our work, which meant I was well equipped to scam a scammer. As I sat across the four-lane highway, my eyes taking in Phil Wilcox's smooth moves, the plan I'd hoped for began to evolve. Ten minutes later, as disparate elements began to gel, Wes called back.

"This was easy-peasy," he said. "Phil is up to his ears in debt, and so is the dealership. They were profiled in *New Hampshire Business* last spring, and I just checked with a banking source to confirm it. It seems that Phil replaced his dad three years ago as president and began what the magazine called a 'too-rapid expansion.' He opened two additional locations, one in Newington and the other in Dover, but those cities aren't big enough to support a dealership, and by opening them, he cannibalized on the flagship location's business, so now all three are in trouble."

"How bad?"

"Bankruptcy looms."

"Expansion is tricky. Is he married?"

"Yup — and he has four kids between two and thirteen."

"That makes his financial situation dire."

"Which means he had a motive to steal the lamp. But how is he involved?"

"I'll tell you everything, Wes, but not now."

"Josie!"

I glanced at the dash clock. It was almost noon. "I'll be in touch later this afternoon. I promise."

I pushed the END CALL button and backed out of the parking spot. I hoped Max was in his office and available to talk.

Ellis sat across from me at Max's conference table, listening with riveted focus as I described my idea. Max sat at the head of the table taking notes.

When I finished, Ellis tapped the side of his nose. "Why Fred? Why can't we use an undercover police officer? Maybe Dawn LeBlanc. You've worked with her before."

"A couple of times. She's good. Sure, I could write up a script, but anyone selling a multimillion-dollar object is going to ask a gazillion questions, some of which she — or any antiques novice — wouldn't how to answer. I can anticipate some, but not all, of them. It's one thing to pretend to be a customer so you can sneak GPS devices into containers.* It's another thing altogether to pretend to be an antiques appraiser of some repute."

* Please see *Dolled Up for Murder.*

"Give me some examples of questions Dawn would struggle to answer."

"How can you know this lamp is real? You say that as part of your appraisal, you're going to tap the glass in the lampshade — won't that break it? How many pieces of glass are there in the shade? Didn't Tiffany use a variety of marks? How many wisteria pattern lamps are extant? Did Clara Driscoll design it? And those are only the questions I thought of off the top of my head. There would be a trap around every corner."

"You know the answers to those questions?"

I smiled, an impish one. "To confirm authenticity, we test the materials, research the marks, and confirm provenance. No, tapping the glass won't shatter it. We use specific techniques and tools so the shade won't be damaged in any way. There are about two thousand pieces of glass, each one individually selected and cut. No one knows how many lamps are extant. Clara Driscoll did design most of the lamps, so it's likely she designed this one, too."

"I'm impressed, and I get that you can't do it because you're known to them, but why Fred? Why not an outside expert?"

"We could get someone from outside, but that would require a delay while we think of someone, vet them, get them here, and get them up to speed. With Fred we can begin today." I soft-pounded the table with my fist. "Right now."

"What makes you think he'll agree? Two people have been killed. You were shot at. That would give many people pause."

"Maybe he'll say no, but I bet he agrees. He doesn't scare any more than I do. He's cool under fire, knowledgeable as all get-out, and as angry as I am that we got duped."

Ellis transferred his gaze from my face to the far wall. After several moments, he looked back at me. "I can't see a downside. Worst case, it doesn't work. Best case, it flushes them out. The room will be wired for sound and video. I want a police officer in the room. Who would accompany Fred?"

"He could have an assistant."

"Good. I'll call Dawn's department and see if she's available."

Max laid down his pen. "We need to spell out the liability limitations before we proceed."

"I'll ask an ADA to take care of that with you," Ellis said. "I'll also call Detective Brownley and ask her to help with the logistics." To me, he added, "Call Fred and get him here. Let's get this party rolling."

Ellis made his calls from where he sat at the table. I stood by the window to make mine.

The ADA, Ellis said, would join us in half an hour. Detective Brownley would arrive sooner. Fred was already en route. For the moment, there was nothing to do. Ellis and Max were chatting about the recently renovated Little League field. I couldn't fathom chatting. The more I listened in on their friendly, mundane conversation, the more agitation settled on me like fog in a valley.

"I'm going to stretch my legs for a few minutes," I said. "I'll be back."

It was still chilly, and the clouds were blowing in from the west. I walked fast, up Bow Street, down Thistle, keeping the river in sight. The water was dark, nearly black, moving fast, and churning. I saw Victor's Liquor Shop a block ahead and stopped in. Victor was behind the counter. Victor had helped me select wines for cooking and wines for drinking. He was of average height and thin, wearing jeans and a red collared T-shirt with VICTOR'S embroidered over the pocket.

After we exchanged greetings, I explained I wanted to send a bottle of Bombay Sapphire gin with a note.

"You got it. What's the occasion? Birthday? Wedding? Anniversary?"

"It's a thank-you gift."

"Nice!"

He handed me a small ecru note card and matching envelope. The words *Thank you* were embossed in silver script.

I wrote:

Dear Sylvia,
Thank you again for the tomatoes. Thank you also for your company. I've enjoyed our conversations!

I recommend you keep this gin in the freezer — it gets all creamy and yummy that way. Add lemon!

Warm regards,
Josie

Thinking of Sylvia sipping gin put a smile on my face, just as she had smiled as she handed over the baskets of luscious tomatoes.

It took about two minutes to get Fred excited about the plan; an hour to persuade John Navarro, the seasoned ADA assigned to oversee the operation, to jump on board; another hour to gain the cooperation of the Austin Arms' general manager; and the rest of the day to map out an online presence that would persuade skeptical people that the persona we were inventing was a real person. Figuring out the logistics took even longer than that.

Fred settled into a corner of Max's office to begin drafting the script he'd use on the telephone. Mr. Navarro and Max went into his conference room to hammer out the details of our agreement. The hotel agreed to let the police wire up the Presidential Suite — and the lobby, hallway, and elevator. Katie, the IT gal, designed an elegant Website for Fred under the name of his brand-new limited liability corporation, Harrison R. Endicott LLC, while I created a comprehensive backstory for him. The LLC was Max's idea. If Orson Thompkins checked the domain name ownership records and questioned why Endicott's Web site was new, he had a good answer: His consulting firm was so successful, he was now dealing with larger and more prestigious organizations, the kind that don't do business with individuals, only companies.

We took some photos of Fred. In one he posed with his head back a bit, the better to look down his nose. In another he looked sideways into the camera, his expression aristocratic. In a third, he rested his chin on his laced fingers, staring into the camera with the arrogance that comes from being the scion of a family as old as the Endicotts. If I didn't know we were inventing it all, I'd be convinced that Harrison was no one to toy with.

We determined we should all park at the police station, on the remote chance someone might recognize one of our personal cars, plotted out who would be stationed where and when, were fitted with bulletproof vests, and agreed not talk to the press until the operation was over and arrests were made — or not.

On Tuesday morning, Fred and I met Katie in her office to help her organize the Web site content. Our goal was to create a credible portfolio stretching back five years, so that anyone vetting Harrison R. Endicott would see a distinguished résumé and engaging information, including comments on important antiques appraisal issues of the day, updates on his projects, and photographs of several art and antiques appraisals he'd been involved with. We also included several references to his family's compound in ritzy Kennebunkport, Maine. The disposable phone the police had bought for Fred to use had a 207 area code, and since his cover story had him based in Chicago, we needed to justify the out-of-state phone.

At noon, Sasha called and asked if there was any way I could get back to the office.

"Frank is done with his assessment. He was hoping to say good-bye before he left."

"Hold on a sec." I lowered the phone and looked at Fred. "Are you okay to finish up without me?"

"I'm almost done," Katie said, her eyes on her monitor, her fingers flying across the keyboard.

"Good." I went back to the phone. "Please tell Frank I'll be there in about fifteen minutes. Will I be happy?"

"Yes."

I grinned. "Excellent!"

"Are we still looking to make the initial call at three?" I asked Ellis as I passed his office.

He looked up from a bound report he was reading. "Yes." He smiled, a wise and wily gleam in his eyes. "This is a good idea, Josie."

I smiled back. "I know."

"What a treat this was!" Frank said. "You have some fine examples, young lady. Some very fine examples."

"This is wonderful news, Frank. Did you find any surprises?"

He rubbed his hands together joyously. "You own a large peppermint ribbon marble." He explained that its 1 and 19/32;" diameter made it extremely rare. He held up a clear plastic bag containing the marble. It was creamy white with red and green swirls. "Notice the uniform spacing between the twists and how deep and consistent the color saturation is, more indicators of value. Using the standard marble-grading scale, ranking condition from one, valueless, to ten, perfect, I scored this marble an award-winning nine-point-seven." He lowered the bag to Sasha's desk.

"What did it lose points for?"

"An incomplete swirl tip on one of the red lines."

"Oh."

"Tell her the estimate," Sasha said, her eyes radiating pleasure.

"That's the best part — I can't. No peppermint ribbon marble of this size and quality has ever gone to auction. One rated a nine-point-one sold for $15,200 four years ago. Nothing even close has been offered since then."

The marble was shiny and smooth, made by a master. "And it's beautiful."

"It's magnificent!"

"Can we take you to lunch, Frank, before

you head out?"

"Thank you, young lady. Sasha made the same offer. I'm going to decline, with thanks. I don't want to miss the opportunity to visit the Peabody Museum. Marbles aren't my only interest — I love everything glass, from bottles to inkwells, including flowers."

"That's one of my favorite museums. Seeing those glass flowers when I was young — I'd never seen anything so beautiful. Will you have time? Are you going back to Oklahoma today?"

"Tomorrow. I decided to treat myself to a night in Boston. I want to try some real New England clam chowder. I mustn't dally! You can tell I have plans and am eager to be on my way."

I extended my hand. "Thank you again, Frank. It was a real pleasure meeting you."

"I'll walk you out," Sasha said.

Frank said his final good-byes and thank-yous to everyone, and the ill-assorted pair left. I watched through the window as they walked slowly across the parking lot. Sasha was talking, gesturing broadly. At his rental car, she went up on tiptoes to kiss his cheek. He hugged her, and she hugged him back. She stood in the middle of the lot as Frank got situated behind the wheel, and stayed there as he drove away, turning left out of the lot toward the interstate. He raised his left hand and gave a cheery wave. Sasha waved back. She stood there for a moment longer, then turned and walked slowly back to the building.

"What a nice man," Cara said.

"Very," I agreed.

"He's a funny one," Gretchen said. "I mean that as a compliment."

"He's not a marble guy," I said. "He's a glass guy."

Gretchen giggled.

Sasha walked in. Her eyes were moist.

"That went well," I said.

"Better than well," she said, smiling through fresh tears. She sniffed and looked aside. "He reminds me of my dad."

"Oh!" Cara said. "That's lovely, Sasha."

Sasha flashed a brief smile, then quickly slid behind her desk and began typing.

A loud meow caused all of us to turn toward the warehouse door. Cara, who was closest, pushed it open. Angela sashayed in, wondering why the door wasn't left open for her convenience.

"My goodness," I said, picking her up, "that's a very big noise coming from such a little girl."

She purred and snuggled into the crook

of my neck. I kissed the top of her head. Another meow, this one imperative, echoed from behind the door.

"Hank," I said.

Cara pushed open the door, and Hank ran through. He pressed his cheek against my calf, complaining that he didn't like to be left alone in the warehouse when everyone was in the office, and by the way, he was hungry.

"I'll take her," Gretchen said.

"PTK!" I said as I passed her over. "Pass the kitty!"

I scooped up Hank and cuddled him for a moment. "I know, baby, I know," I whispered, "but don't you fret. Not ever. Angela is a good girl, but you're my best little boy." He started purring. I kissed his cheek and stroked his tummy, and he settled in against my chest. After another minute, I told him, "I need to go now, sweetheart. You be a good boy." I lowered him to the ground.

Spending time with cats before entering the fray is like stocking up on essentials during the calm before a hurricane — your survival depends on it.

"Tell me again," I said, "how do people live without cats?"

CHAPTER THIRTY-SEVEN

At three o'clock, Ellis, Fred, Detective Brownley, Officer Dawn LeBlanc, and I sat around the old wooden table in Interview Room One. The human-sized cage loomed large, a warning and a promise. The fluorescent lighting was harsh, coloring the world with a faint green tinge. Red pinpricks of light showing on the three wall-mounted video cameras indicated they'd been activated. A small projectile was attached to the right side of Fred's cell phone, a wireless recording device. That light was amber. We each had a set of wireless headphones in front of us so when the time came, we could listen in.

"Tell me my phone number again," Fred said.

Ellis called it out, and Fred wrote it down on his notepad.

I put my headphones on. "Let me try it." I punched the number into my phone.

Seconds later, Fred's phone rang. His ringtone was one of Bach's Brandenburg Concertos. He tapped the screen, and the music stopped.

"This is Harrison Endicott. And you are?"

"Josie Prescott."

He ended the call.

"Your tone is perfect," I said.

"Ready?" Ellis asked Fred.

"Yes," Fred said.

Fred stood up and shook out his hands, an actor's relaxation technique I recalled from an Intro to Theater course I'd taken as an elective in college. He reoriented his chair so his back was toward us. He consulted his notepad and punched in the number Orson Thompkins had given in the *Antiques Insights* ad. The call went to voice mail immediately. The message was the default, the automated robotic female-sounding voice stating the phone number and nothing else.

"This is Harrison R. Endicott," Fred said in an appropriately haughty tone, a little nasal and a lot brusque. He stated his phone number. "I'm calling in reference to the wisteria-patterned Tiffany lamp you offered for sale. I represent a major museum that might be interested in acquiring it. I understand you withdrew the ad. I hope that doesn't mean it's already sold. If you would like to hear more about the museum's interest, I'd be most pleased to discuss it with you. I will be here for another hour. If you can't return the call during that period, perhaps you'd leave me some time options when you'll be available. That way we can, I hope, avoid phone tag." He repeated his phone number, then ended the call.

We sat in silence for a moment, then Ellis said, "That was excellent. You sounded like . . . like . . . I don't know what."

"A prig," I said.

"A snob," Ellis said.

"A priggy snob."

"A snobby prig."

"No one calls him Harry," I said.

"No one wants to call him Harry."

"All of that," Fred said, "and more."

"Now we wait," Ellis said.

Ellis reminded us we were welcome to boot up our computers or do whatever we wanted as long as we stayed in the room. Detective Brownley would also stay. He would be in his office and would come on the run the minute Orson called back, if he did. He had his hand on the doorknob ready to leave when Harrison's phone rang.

We all looked at Fred. We all got our headphones in place.

Fred answered on the third ring. "Harrison Endicott speaking."

"I got your message," Orson said, sounding even younger than I recalled. "Who are you exactly?"

"I'm an antiques appraiser and art consultant. I've been retained by a museum to advise them on whether this Tiffany lamp would be an appropriate addition to their permanent collection."

"Which museum?"

"I'm not at liberty to reveal that information."

"Why not?"

"If they wanted it known they were in the market for a Tiffany lamp, they wouldn't have hired me. Why did you withdraw the listing?"

"Life got a little complicated on our end, and we realized we couldn't pay as much attention to the sale as we should. We figured waiting a few months would give us a breather, let our personal situation sort itself out."

I admired his answer. It was simultaneously unprovable and vague, yet it held a ring of truth. Clearly, asking follow-up questions would be crass. Ellis slid a slip of paper in front of me. *Do you recognize his voice?*

I nodded and jotted *Yes.*

"How did you know to call me?" Thompkins asked.

"I got your details while the ad was still up. It took my client a while to authorize the purchase. He needed board approval. From the listing, I see you have an appraisal in hand. If you would e-mail it to me, and everything seems in order, I'll fly in tomorrow to examine the lamp. I'm based in Chicago."

"Chicago? The phone ID lists your number as originating in Maine."

"Yes, I bought the phone last summer. I spend time in Kennebunkport. Are you able to send the appraisal?"

"Sure. I can do that."

Fred gave him the e-mail account that linked to the "Contact" page of the Web site we'd created, and Thompkins said he'd e-mail it right now.

"Give me a few minutes to read it," Fred said, and Thompkins said that was fine.

"How certain are you that's the same voice?" Ellis asked me once the call ended.

"A hundred percent. That's the man who called me pretending to be Edwin Towson."

Fred downloaded the appraisal. As expected, it was mine. My blood began heating up, a slow burn certain to ignite. Orson Thompkins was going to be sorry he tried to involve me in his con.

We waited half an hour; then Fred called Thompkins back, saying the documents seemed in order and he'd make the trip.

"My assistant booked a suite at the Austin Arms — do you know it? The weather looks good, so I expect my flight will be on time. Can you meet me at the hotel tomorrow at two?"

"Two will work."

"Bring the lamp. I'll arrange its transport back to Chicago."

"That's getting a little ahead of the curve."

"I meant for the appraisal."

"What are you talking about? You've seen the appraisal."

"I've seen *an* appraisal. I need to verify that the appraisal you sent me is for *this* lamp."

"Which is why I'll bring it with me."

"Appraisals take time and specialized materials and equipment. I can't do it in a hotel room."

"What kind of materials and equipment?"

"Chemicals to test that what seems to be wax is. Equipment to assess electric currents. As examples."

"You can't take it out of the hotel. No way."

"I'll give you a receipt."

"Anybody can write a receipt."

Fred sighed impatiently. "Look me up. I have a peerless reputation."

"I did. You look fine. But this lamp is worth millions."

"I don't know about value yet, but the museum would be willing to put up a reasonable sum as earnest money. We would be fine with depositing it in escrow with your lawyer or CPA."

"How much are you talking?"

"Fifty thousand dollars."

"A hundred thousand."

"That can be arranged," Fred said superciliously. "If, when I look at the lamp, it seems genuine, I'll authorize the deposit via wire transfer. As you know, such transfers are essentially instantaneous."

Thompkins agreed and said he'd e-mail his lawyer's escrow account information, and they ended the call.

"Well done, everyone," Ellis said. "We'll meet here at eight tomorrow morning, all except Fred and Dawn, who will be renting a car at Logan and driving up." He turned to Fred. "You'll arrive at the hotel at ten."

"Right — but isn't that kind of overkill? Why don't I just drive my own car?"

"If Thompkins wants to carry the lamp to your car," I said, "and makes a note of the license plate so he can check up on you later, we want him to learn it's a rental issued to Harrison, not a car owned by some guy named Fred."

"Fair point," Fred said. "And our fake IDs will be ready in time?"

"They should be here now," Detective Brownley said. "Let me check."

She slipped out of the room. We waited silently.

The IDs were ready. Harrison had an Illinois driver's license, a Platinum American Express card, a debit card, and a membership card from the International Art and Antiques Appraisers Association. Dawn, using the name Veronica Brooks, had a driver's license, a Visa card, and a debit card.

"What should I wear?" Fred asked.

"Something artsy?" Ellis asked, looking at me.

"Something sharp," I said. "You're a sharp dresser in general, Fred, so I'd just go with one of your Italian suits."

"With enough room for a bulletproof vest. We can get you a loaner if you need one."

"I probably will." Reacting to the surprise apparent on Ellis's face, he added, "I buy the slim fit."

"Let me make a phone call."

I turned to Dawn. "You should dress for

418

your pay grade. You're an assistant."

Dawn was short and stocky, with short layers of chestnut brown hair, dark brown eyes, and a sprinkling of freckles across her cheeks and nose. "I go by Ronnie. I'd wear trousers and a blouse."

"Even in this weather?" I asked.

"Everything is air-conditioned."

"Each of you bring a suitcase," Ellis said. He stood up. "Any other questions?"

No one had any. Fred walked with Ellis to his office to see about the suit, and I left.

Wes called around six asking what was up.

"My police scanner is buzzing, but no one is saying anything. The technical team is to meet tomorrow morning at eight. Ellis and the ADA are meeting tonight. You're co-operating, but they don't say how. What gives?"

I couldn't tell him anything, and I didn't feel like fencing. "I need to go, Wes," I said, and hung up.

I was willing to bet I wouldn't sleep a wink, not one single wink, all night.

I was wrong. Now that the sting was under way, I was cloaked in crisis-calm, and I slept like a cat.

CHAPTER THIRTY-EIGHT

It was noon on a steaming hot Wednesday, and we were eating from room service wheel-in tables. I was dressed for work in jeans and a collared T-shirt. My hair was up, my bee spears in place. I'd selected a grilled cheese and tomato sandwich on white — comfort food. The tomatoes were standard restaurant fare: pink, hard, and flavorless, neither grown nor harvested with love.

Harrison's suite at the Austin Arms comprised two bedrooms, each with its own bathroom, and a spacious living/dining area. The main room was nicely furnished, decorated in various shades of orange and green. One of the attached bedrooms was staged as Harrison's sleeping room. Fred's suitcase was on the mahogany luggage rack at the foot of the bed, and a toothbrush and tube of toothpaste, provided at the last minute by the hotel, were on the marble vanity. If

Thompkins asked to use the restroom, he'd be directed there. The other bedroom, where we were holed up, was decorated in cool blues and grays.

Besides Ellis, Dawn, and Katie, there were five of us packed into the room. Fred and I were the only outsiders. The other three were police officers, two I knew, F. Meade and Daryl Lucher, and one I didn't, a medium-sized man who looked like he'd lifted a lot of weights in his day, named Stan Rogers.

Fred and I sat on one of the two queen-sized beds, our food spread out on a bath towel, a makeshift picnic.

"Anything from Hong Kong?" I asked.

"All good. The man I spoke to is the curator of the museum's furniture collection. His name is Vincent O'Reilly. He recognized Aunt Louise's desk from the exhibition catalogue. According to notes written by the curator at the time, Jerry Ross, Aunt Louise loaned her desk to the museum after a friend of hers, Peter Gerstein, introduced her to his friend, the curator. The exhibit was called 'British Colonial Keepsakes: Cherished Artifacts from Around the World.' Mr. O'Reilly is a punctilious sort, very thorough and well informed. He conferenced in his assistant to our call. She'll be photocopying all of Mr. Ross's notes and sending us a copy of the catalogue. While she was on the phone, she read the notes so I could get a sense of what we can expect. Aunt Louise got the desk as a gift from a man named Ferdinand Locke. Interestingly, he was not on the archivist's photo list. Upon inquiry, Mr. Locke gave Mr. Ross a copy of his purchase receipt. He bought the desk from Universal Antiques and Auctions for twelve hundred and eighty dollars, delivered. The delivery address was Aunt Louise's apartment."

Fred paused to take a bite of his Cobb salad.

"This sounds very promising, Fred."

"Universal was acquired by another firm in the mid-1980s." He grinned. "Want to guess?"

"Are you going to make my day?"

"Oh, yeah. Frisco's."

I soft-clapped. "Send me the particulars, and I'll call my friend."

"You don't need to. I called a guy I know in the Furnishings Department. They've computerized all Universal's records. The desk comes with a perfect — and I mean perfect — paper trail. Universal bought the desk as part of an estate sale, Melinda Trent of Saddle Brook, New Jersey. The desk had been in the Trent family since it was custom-made for Bernard Trent, a British envoy who served in India from 1799 to 1804. The cabinetmaker was none other than Thomas Sheraton."

"Sheraton." My smile grew.

"It was in the Trent family for more than a hundred and fifty years."

"Whoever buys it will be only its third owner in more than two centuries. Did Sheraton make many desks with hidden compartments?"

"Yes."

"The museum association will add to the value. Are you ready to name a number yet?"

"Not definitively. I should think it will be somewhere in the eighty-thousand-plus range."

"Way to go, Fred!"

He grinned again and went back to his salad.

Ellis walked over to the bed. "I don't like your being here."

"Why?"

"It's dangerous." He glanced at Fred. "I don't like you being here either."

"It's too late to turn back now," I said. "Thompkins is expecting Harrison Endicott. Who's going to play that role? You?

Daryl? And I'm the only person who can ID the fake Ava."

"If he brings her."

"She'll be here. If I had an interest in a one-point-five-million-dollar lamp, I'd be Johnny-on-the-spot before letting my partner hand it over to a stranger."

"No offense intended," Fred said, "but there have to be at least a dozen people who know what we're up to. More if you add in the team from the DA's office. I'd worry more about that than gunplay. Thompkins wants money, not trouble. Loose lips sink ships and all that."

"No offense taken, but we're a pretty discreet lot."

"Plus I bet you're watching Phil Wilcox, aren't you?" I asked. "Just to make sure he doesn't slip away."

Ellis grinned. "From a distance. We don't want to spook him."

"Thanks for lunch," Fred said as he stood up. Fred's suit looked bulky on him. "I'm going back to the big room and review my notes."

"I'll come, too," Dawn said.

Two officers wheeled the food tables out and away from our room. Everyone dispersed, moving to their assigned places. Ellis and I sat in straight-back chairs in front of a split-screen monitor. We each wore headphones and a bulletproof vest. Katie, who'd been assigned the role of tech project manager, sat in front of an array of listening, viewing, and recording equipment. Her headphones were bigger than ours. Officer Meade stood near the door that led to the corridor in case she had to intercept someone coming or going in the hall. Detective Brownley, wearing a pink sundress, oversized sunglasses, and a floppy straw hat, was positioned in the lobby as a lookout. Her glasses were equipped with a video hookup, streaming live to one quadrant of the monitor in front of me. Two of the other sections showed different views of the suite. One showed the corridor, including the suite's entry door. Other police officers, also dressed in civvies, sat in unmarked cars, ready to follow anyone at a moment's notice.

"Officer LeBlanc, please walk around for me," Katie said into a mic attached to her headset. "Talk in a normal voice. Sit on every chair. Go into the bathroom."

This was Katie's fifth run-through.

On the monitor, Dawn cruised around. She sat on the couch, at the table, and on the easy chairs. She stood facing the window, and a wall. Katie confirmed she had audio and video contact no matter where Orson Thompkins might go, including the bathroom.

"We're good to go," Katie said just after one.

My job was to watch the lobby video. People came and went. I recognized no one.

We waited, drinking coffee, not talking. The tension in the room was intense, and growing.

At 2:00 P.M. on the button, a tall white man about twenty-five, wearing khakis and a pale green collared short-sleeved shirt, crossed the lobby. He glanced around until he found the house phone.

At 2:01, the phone in Fred's suite rang.

Fred answered with a stern "Harrison Endicott." He listened for a moment, then added, "Eight-fourteen."

Ellis texted Detective Brownley: *Target entering elevator now.* I watched as the man stepped into the elevator.

"That can't be him," I said. "Something's wrong."

"What are you talking about?" Ellis asked.

"That's not Phil Wilcox."

His eyebrows lifted. "Who is it?"

"I have no idea. Besides which, he's way too young to pull off something like this."

At 2:04, I heard a faint knock on the door

and watched Fred walk across the room. I turned my attention back to the lobby feed.

"Mr. Thompkins? Come in. I'm Harrison Endicott." Fred turned toward Dawn. "This is my assistant, Ronnie."

"You're from Chicago?" the young man asked Fred as he entered the room, looking in all directions at once, alert, concerned, guarded.

I recognized his voice, except that he sounded less confident now than he had during our initial phone conversation.

"Right. Where's the lamp?"

"I thought we ought to talk first, before I hand it over."

"Talk about what?"

"Money."

"The earnest money is a phone call away. The museum will wire the money into your lawyer's escrow account on my word."

"How does it work?"

"I have a letter of agreement — or I should say, Ronnie does. If I don't return the lamp as promised, you keep the money. The document empowers you to use all means to recover it." Fred pointed at an orange patterned club chair. "Have a seat." I turned to the suite monitors. Fred sat across from him and crossed his legs, his right ankle resting on his left knee. "Tell me about the lamp."

Ronnie perched on a nearby ottoman, a notepad at the ready.

"It's terrific."

"How do you come to own it?"

"It's been in my family forever."

"Forever since when?"

"You read the appraisal. What else do you want to know?"

"Lots of times, people remember details in the days or weeks after recounting a story. The more information I get from you, the easier — and quicker — my appraisal will be."

"I just had it appraised. Don't you think the one done by Prescott's is good enough?"

"Prescott's is a very well respected house, but no one pays more than a million dollars without conducting their own appraisal. No one."

"The price is two million."

"Where's the lamp?"

"In my car."

"Let's hope your car hasn't been stolen."

"I left someone with it."

Ellis texted Detective Brownley and the plainclothes officers sitting in their vehicles, cc'ing me, alerting them to be ready: *Lamp & accomplice in car.*

Detective Brownley read a message on her

phone, then ambled outside, checking her watch, looking for all the world like a woman waiting for a ride.

Fred spread his arms and flipped his palms. "So? Bring it up."

"First, the money."

"No way. Not until I look at it."

"Money first, or no lamp."

Fred stood up. "There's a difference between prudence and paranoia. Do you want to do business or not?"

Thompkins stared at Fred for a long time, a minute or more, assessing him using some private metric.

Downstairs, under the hotel's front portico, Detective Brownley turned a slow circle, stretching and yawning, taking her time. She sank onto a wooden bench positioned near a standing ashtray. No one could enter or leave through the lobby's main entrance without passing her.

Thompkins extracted his phone and walked to the window. He had a brief conversation in a voice that was almost too low to make out. I pressed the earphones against my head so I could hear his side of the conversation.

"He insists . . . I know . . . I tried . . . No . . . I did . . . Uh-huh . . . I can't . . . Okay . . . Okay . . . Come up to eight-fourteen."

Two minutes later, a woman carrying a lamp box came into view, walking from the left side of the building. She was big-boned but not fat. Sturdy. Strong. Handsome. Her shoulder-length hair was medium brown with bold, brassy highlights. She wore more makeup than I use in a year — neon blue eye shadow and Marilyn Monroe–red lipstick. Her dress was turquoise, as were her glasses. She didn't look at all like the woman I knew as Ava Towson. Except that she did. Sort of. The set of her chin. Her posture. The line of her neck.

I texted Ellis and Detective Brownley: *That may be her.*

"She's coming," Thompkins told Fred.

"Good."

The woman entered the elevator. No one spoke. No one moved until a knock sounded on the door. Fred opened it, and the woman I'd seen downstairs stepped into view.

"This is Moira," Thompkins said.

Moira slid the box onto the coffee table. She undid the flaps, and Thompkins lifted the Tiffany lamp clear.

Ellis texted us all: *Get ready — on my signal.*

"It's magnificent," Fred said. "Would you hold it sideways for me? I want to see the bottom."

"Sure."

Fred examined the underpart of the base, using a small silver flashlight. "*Tiffany Studios New York, one-eight-one.* Thanks. You can put it down."

Thompkins eased the lamp back into the box and tucked the flaps in.

"Okay?" Thompkins asked.

"Yes, indeed. I will arrange the lamp's secure shipment to Chicago and let you know as soon as I've finished my appraisal."

"How long?" Moira asked, her dialect more Brooklyn than New England.

"I don't know. There are too many variables for me to predict."

"We've got to set an end date," she said. "A week?"

Fred shook his head, then pursed his lips. "No way. Six weeks."

"Forget it. Two weeks."

"Let me call Prescott's," Fred said. "I should be able to give you a more realistic estimate based on what I learn from them."

"All right," Moira said. "I want this settled now."

Fred turned to Dawn. "Get Josie Prescott on the phone."

By the time Dawn spoke to Cara at my company, learned I wasn't there, and left a voice mail asking me to call her back about the Tiffany lamp appraisal I'd just completed, Detective Brownley had entered our room from the hallway. She tossed her hat and purse on the bed, kicked off her strappy sandals, put on sensible running shoes, and zipped up her bulletproof vest. She stood by the door, her weapon by her thigh, pointing down.

Ellis called out orders, his voice low and urgent. Officers Lucher and Meade were to stay in the outside corridor, ready to intercept the suspects if they got that far. He, Detective Brownley, and Officer Rogers were ready to storm the living room.

Ellis turned to me and whispered, "Stay back."

Katie remained uninvolved, listening in on her headphones, checking her controls, part of the team but separate. Officer Rogers joined Ellis and Detective Brownley at the connecting door.

He mouthed, "One . . . two . . . three," and whipped open the door.

The police charged in and fanned out. Officer Rogers blocked the door that led to the corridor. Dawn drew her weapon and aimed it at Moira. Detective Brownley aimed hers at Thompkins.

"Don't move," Ellis said, his eyes ablaze.

"Either of you. You're under arrest."

"Grab the lamp and follow me," Moira yelled to Thompkins, her eyes on Ellis.

"Don't be stupid," Ellis said to her. "There are four of us here and more outside. You can't get away."

When Thompkins didn't move, Moira screeched, "Do it!"

Moira backed up toward the door that connected the living area to the bedroom where Katie and I now sat. Thompkins licked his lips, snapped up the box containing the lamp, placed it in front of him like a shield, and darted toward her. I stood up, not knowing what I should do.

"Any of you move," Moira said, "and he slams the lamp against the wall. Got that, Orson?"

Thompkins didn't speak. He looked terrified, his eyes round, his mouth agape. No one moved. Moira's gaze was unwavering, focused solely on Ellis.

I pressed against the wall, wishing I could disappear.

It didn't work. The instant they entered the room, they spotted me. Two steps brought Moira to my side, and she latched on to my arm with a marauder's grip. She yanked me from the wall by my left arm. I faux-fainted, a dead weight. She didn't let go. She dragged me across the carpet. The rug rasped my skin raw. I heard scraping sounds, then a clunk. Katie hurtling out of her chair, maybe, and knocking it over, mixed with pounding footsteps.

I couldn't think. My arm felt like it was being ripped from its socket. I didn't know what to do. Then all at once it came to me. I bounced back to life, dragged the protective tip from one of my bee hairpins, and thrust the dagger-sharp point into her thigh.

Moira shrieked and shook me off, giving Ellis an opportunity to pounce. I rolled into the bed frame, panting. Ellis wrestled Moira to the bed and snapped on handcuffs, then flipped her over. He grasped her upper arm and held fast.

Thompkins continued backing away toward the corridor door. "Moira?" he said, turning her name into a plea and an admonition.

"Don't make a bad situation worse," Ellis told him, his demeanor serious but calm. "Put the box down — gently."

"Screw him!" Moira shouted, thrashing around. "Hurl it."

Thompkins lowered his arms, as if he intended to follow Ellis's instructions, but stumbled over something, or maybe nothing but air and fear, and the box tottered and nearly spun out of his grasp. He righted himself, and the box stabilized.

With my heart slamming against my ribs and my lips parchment-dry, I sat up.

"Please," I said. "Don't hurt the lamp."

With Moira screaming and thrashing and everyone else frozen in place, Thompkins lowered the box to the ground and stepped back, raising his hands over his head, a full surrender.

Ellis and Officer Meade flew at Thompkins, shoving him facedown onto the bed, then cuffing him.

I slid the box along the rug into a corner on the far side of the bed.

Moira howled like a wounded animal.

Ellis hauled Thompkins up from the bed, threw him against the wall, and patted him down.

I sat on the bed, my chest heaving.

"Call for a bus," Ellis told Dawn, his eyes moving from Moira's thigh to the rug-burn scrapes that colored my arm and shoulder. "Two."

A rivulet of blood ran down Moira's leg. I looked away. My hairpin lay on the rug near where I'd attacked. The tip was by the bed. I picked both parts up. I raised my eyes. Ellis was looking at me.

"Lay them on the bedside table," Ellis told

me, and I did.

My French twist had loosened. I removed the remaining hairpin and tucked it into its pouch. I ran my fingers through my hair.

Ellis picked up Moira's purse from where it had fallen, opened it, and emptied it on the bed. In addition to a phone, a key ring, a wallet, and a clear plastic makeup case packed with cosmetics was a large silver gun.

"You have a gun?" Thompkins hollered, flabbergasted. "Are you crazy?"

Moira continued shrieking.

Thompkins collapsed against the wall, trembling. "I had no idea . . . ," he said to no one, his eyes on Moira, his voice trailing off.

Ellis took three evidence bags from an inside pocket. He placed the weapon in one, everything else from her bag in the second, and the hairpin and protective tip in the third.

Fred stepped into the doorway and leaned heavily against the jamb. He looked exhilarated.

"Buses on their way," Dawn told Ellis.

"Thank you," Ellis said. "Come help Officer Lucher hold the prisoner."

Dawn reached for one of Moira's arms.

I took a deep breath, willing myself to

calm down. I took stock. My scraped arm and neck were stinging and throbbing. My wrenched shoulder ached. I wanted this to be over. No one spoke for several seconds.

"We did it," Fred said to me, talking over Moira's continuing yowls.

I smiled as best I could. "You were terrific, Mr. Endicott."

He bowed.

"Detective Brownley, Officer Meade — please remove the male prisoner."

Faint sounds of sirens penetrated the solid walls.

Detective Brownley grasped Thompkins by the arm and led him away, with Officer Meade running interference.

Officer Rogers was told to stay in the corridor to ensure no housekeeping or room service staff decided it was time to clean up.

Fred removed his bulletproof vest. "Am I done here?"

"Yes," Ellis said. "We need a statement. I'll ask one of the plainclothes guys to give you a lift to the police station."

"Should I return the rental car first?"

"Dawn will take care of it. Give her the keys."

Fred handed over the keys, then started to leave, pausing at the door to the corridor. "It looks like you got the worst of it, Josie.

Are you okay?"

"I'm fine, thanks. How about you?"

He grinned. "Never better." His smile faded. "I don't like the look of those bruises of yours, though. Are you sure you're all right?"

"You bet! Really, Fred, you did a great job."

"Thanks." He semi-saluted. "See ya."

Ellis called down and asked Griff to drive to the front of the hotel and pick up Fred; then he turned to me. "I'll send Daryl to the hospital with you."

"I don't need to go to the hospital."

"I saw Moira dragging you by your arm. Someone should look at your shoulder. Those rug burns look like they could use some attention, too. After you get an all-clear, Daryl will bring you to the station. You can pick up your car and, if you're up to it, give your preliminary statement." He turned to Katie. "You got knocked over. Are you okay?"

"It was a controlled fall to get out of harm's way. I'm fine."

"Good. Can you finish up by yourself?"

"Yup. I'm all set. I'll call for the guys to pack up the equipment. By the time they get here, I'll be done with my backups."

I walked to join him in the center of the

room. I looked at Moira, rolling back and forth, davening, mewling, her eyes shut. "We were expecting the fake Ava and Phil Wilcox, not this woman and that stranger. Who are these people?"

"I don't know. Yet."

I pointed to Moira's hair. "That looks like a wig. Can we remove it?"

He stared at me for a moment, then turned toward Moira, assessing her hair. Ten seconds later, he said, "Officer Le-Blanc, the prisoner may be hiding a weapon under her wig. Please remove it."

Moira's eyes shot open. "Don't touch me!" Moira said in an icy tone as Dawn reached for her hair. "You have no right!"

Daryl and Ellis held her fast, Ellis holding her legs in place, Daryl pushing her shoulders into the bed. Moira squirmed and kicked and tried to bite. Dawn grabbed a hank of hair and pulled. The wig came off easily. Dawn got her fingers under the wig cap and tugged it off, too. Moira's own hair sprang free. Her hair was short and black. She growled in impotent fury as the detective wrestled away the glasses, and then I knew.

"Oh, my God," I whispered, clutching Ellis's arm. "It's Diane."

"Diane?" he asked.

"The librarian. The book club." I stared at her. "Diane is the fake Ava."

CHAPTER THIRTY-NINE

It was nearly five o'clock. I was sitting on a hard wooden bench in the Rocky Point police station lobby waiting for I wasn't sure what.

Fred had already given his preliminary statement and left. After giving me a thumbs-up, he crossed the lobby with a bounce in his step. Intrigue agreed with him.

I'd called work on the drive to the emergency room to let everyone know I wouldn't be in today but would be there in the morning. I was in and out of the hospital in less than an hour. It wouldn't have taken that long, but I had to wait for a radiologist to read the X-ray of my shoulder. I was, the doctor told me, perfect. At his words, the last remnants of fear dissipated like the tide. Daryl said Diane was also treated and released quickly.

Ellis came out of his office and stood in front of me. "How are you?"

"Fit as a fiddle."

"Good. While Diane and Thompkins are being processed, let's look at the lamp."

He held open an unmarked door off the main corridor, and I passed through into a small anteroom. The door in front of us was labeled with large signs warning that only authorized people were allowed inside. There were security cameras mounted on the ceiling and both a number keypad and fingerprint pad next to the door.

"This is a secure facility," I said.

"I can't get anything past you."

"I'm a smart girl."

Ellis punched in a code. A luminescent blue glow appeared on the fingerprint pad, and he inserted his left index finger into the slot. A click sounded, and he pushed open the heavy door.

"I'm accompanied by Josie Prescott," he said to no one I could see.

The blue light illuminated again.

"Left index finger," he told me.

"Why that finger?" I asked as I placed my finger into the slot. Our system used thumbprints.

"It changes periodically. You either know the correct finger to use or you don't."

The light turned off, and I withdrew my finger. "That's pretty intense."

"It's called multilevel authentication."

I followed Ellis into an isolated area I hadn't known existed. There were secondary doors labeled LAB, EVIDENCE, LOST AND FOUND, and TECHNICAL. In the main area, sitting on a stainless steel table, was the Tiffany lamp box.

"I've been worried about it," I said.

"I'll be glad to see it's intact."

"Is everything we're doing being recorded?"

"Yes."

"Good."

I lowered the box to the floor, unlatched the folded cardboard flaps, and eased the lamp out. I circled the table, assessing the lamp from all sides.

"I think it's fine. What a relief." I had Ellis lift it and hold it sideways so I could confirm the mark. "Thank you. You can put it down. Based on the mark, I can attest that this is probably the same Tiffany lamp I appraised for the fake Ava Towson. According to Edwin Towson, that one was the Tiffany lamp recovered from his great-grandmother's attic."

"Probably?"

"I'm not a metallurgist, but it's possible, I suppose, that someone ground down the original serial number and remarked it."

"Do you test for that?"

"No, not when we're appraising an object for insurance purposes for an owner."

"Would the fabrication you're describing be easy to detect?" he asked.

"Not to the naked eye. I suspect techniques like X-raying would reveal it, though."

"Do you have any reason to suspect this lamp was manipulated in that way?"

"No."

"The ADA will want to know what it will take to confirm it's the same, not a fake someone marked up."

"A separate company should conduct a proper appraisal so we can compare that one with the one I did. Then we'll know. If there's any concern that the mark has been tampered with, you'll need to ask them to check the materials for consistency, among other factors."

"Thank you, Josie. Pack up the lamp, please."

We went through another multilevel authentication process to access the evidence room. Ellis slid the lamp into a padded cubbyhole plenty big enough, then closed the Plexiglas door and locked it. The box went into a second cubby.

"Will I get my hairpin back?"

"Yes, but I don't know when." He locked the second door. "Can you stay for a while after you give your statement? In case questions come up about the lamp or their plans to sell it?"

"Sure."

Detective Brownley took my preliminary statement, then led me to the narrow observation room.

"Chief Hunter will be in shortly," she said.

"Thanks."

One-way windows provided views of Interview Rooms One and Two. Orson Thompkins sat in Room One, his elbows on the table, his head on his hands. The cage was to his right. Officer Meade sat in a wooden slat-back chair pushed up against the wall. Diane Hawkins stood against the outside wall in Room Two, her hands crossed against her chest. Her eyes flashed with dragon fire. Her lips were pressed tightly together. She tapped her foot. The puncture wound on her thigh was protected by a Band-Aid. Daryl sat in a corner on a dinged-up metal chair. The operation was over, and arrests had been made, which meant there was nothing stopping me from telling Wes what was going on. I wrote him:

Hi Wes,

Tip: Diane Hawkins, the librarian, is the fake Ava. She's in the police station now, under arrest. So is Orson Thompkins. Details to follow. You're welcome.

Josie

Knowing Wes, I bet his first question would be to ask if I took photos.

I was just finishing writing an e-mail to Ty when Ellis entered the room. I added *xo* and sent it off.

"Hey," he said.

"Hey." I turned toward Room Two, where Diane continued to fret and fume. "You can tell a lot from body language."

He gazed into each room for a minute, then said, "Which is why I'll let Diane stew for a while longer." He faced me. "You ready?"

"Yes."

He ensured the audio settings were correct so I could hear but not be heard, reminded me to text him anytime, and left. Two minutes later, he entered Room One. My phone buzzed. It was Wes. As expected, his text read *Thanks, Joz! Take photos.*

"Sorry to keep you waiting," Ellis said to Thompkins.

At his words, Thompkins lifted his head.

If anything, he looked even more frightened now than he did in the hotel room when I'd noticed him trembling.

Ellis sat at the head of the table, directly opposite Orson Thompkins.

"Let's get the logistics out of the way." He read the Miranda warning, which Thompkins signed without comment; explained that video cameras were recording their conversation; recited who was in the room, the date, and time; then asked, "Can we get you anything? A glass of water? Some coffee."

"I'm okay."

"You have a commercial driver's license with a hazmat endorsement. To get it, you had to submit your fingerprints. That's how we know you're Calvin Miller."

My mouth opened, then closed. Cal Miller. Orson Thompkins used Miller's address. It was such a simple idea — use a different name and your own address — yet it never occurred to me.

"Who is Diane Hawkins to you?"

Cal swallowed and his Adam's apple bobbed. "My half sister."

"She asked you to help her steal the lamp?"

"What? No! We weren't stealing a lamp. I was helping her sell it."

Ellis sat back at his ease. "Really . . . Tell me about it."

"Diane bought it at a garage sale thinking it was a cheesy replica — then realized it might have real value."

"Connect the dots for me. Why did she need you to pretend to be Edwin Towson?"

"She said that if she tried to sell the lamp with no history, she'd get pennies on the dollar, but if she went in with a solid and real story, she'd get what it was worth. No one would ever know. No one would get hurt. The lamp was real and honestly acquired. She just needed the story."

"And she learned about Towson how?"

"She's a librarian, you know? Good at research. She got the info from some article in a business journal. Towson's a famous finance guy, so he gets written up all the time."

I texted: *Not true. The lamp's history has never been published.*

Ellis's phone vibrated. He tapped the screen and read for a moment. Message received.

"What did you think of Ava Towson?" Ellis asked.

"The wife? I never met her."

"How about the house. It's something, isn't it?"

Cal looked confused. "I never saw it."

"How about Jean Cooper?"

He flipped open his palms. "I've never even heard of her."

"Why did your sister use you at all? Why didn't she just make the call herself pretending to be Ava?"

"The article was clear — the lamp had been in Edwin's family, not Ava's. Diane said any antiques appraiser, especially one as high-level as Prescott's, would find the same article, know who the real owner was, and want to talk to him. She needed a man."

I saw Diane's point. There was no article, but since the history actually related to Edwin's family, not Ava's, if my only contact had been Ava, I would have worried that a wife was trying to sell a valuable object out from under her husband's nose, and I would have insisted on talking to him directly. The last thing Diane wanted was an antiques appraiser tracking down the real Edwin Towson to ask him about his Tiffany lamp.

Ellis rat-a-tat-tatted a steady beat with his pen against the table edge. "We have a serious situation here, Calvin. Ava Towson was murdered."

Miller jerked forward, his jaw dropping, grasping the table as if he might fall over without holding on. "What?"

"You didn't know?"

"No. I've been on the road for more than a week. I just got back. Murdered?"

"Jean Cooper was her sister. She was killed, too."

Cal stared at him, stunned into silence.

"Jean was killed with a .45," Ellis said. "Just like the gun Diane had in her bag."

"I didn't even know Diane had a gun."

"I thought you two were close."

Cal lowered his eyes to his hands. "I thought we were, too."

"Did she promise you a cut when the lamp sold?"

"That's not how she put it, but sure. She said we were family."

Ellis waited for more. When it didn't come, he asked, "Did you grow up together?"

"I didn't know she existed until about five years ago."

"So you would have been eighteen. You're fifteen years younger than she is."

"Right."

"How did you connect?"

"She called me." He raised his eyes from his hands to Ellis's face. "I was shocked to hear from her. I had no idea she existed."

"What did your dad say about it?"

"He died of a heart attack when I was

seventeen. My mom died a couple of years before that, of breast cancer, so all I know is what Diane told me. She said she never saw him after he left when she was three. Her mom was plenty bitter." He paused for a moment, thinking of what he wanted to say, or maybe trying to find the right words. "Diane always had this fantasy that the reason Dad never got in touch with her was that he traveled all the time. Then, after her mom died, she learned that it had all been a lie. Her mom told her that her dad had moved to Santa Monica and left no forwarding address. The truth is he was here in Portsmouth, one town over from Rocky Point, the whole time and she never knew it. He paid alimony and child support every month. Her mom used a PO box so Diane would never catch on."

"That's cold."

"Brutal."

"How did she figure it out?"

"She discovered an envelope marked 'Deceased: Return to Sender' among her mother's papers. Inside was a nasty letter her mother had written to Dad demanding her alimony. That gave Diane his last known address — Portsmouth."

"That's a pretty sad story."

"I'll say. It'd do something to you, to learn

all that after the fact. She couldn't even confront her mother because she was dead, too."

"So Hawkins is Diane's married name?"

"Right. Until then, she went by Lerner. She said her mom jettisoned the Miller name along with the Miller man. Lerner had been her mother's maiden name."

"Her dad never mentioned you to her?"

"Not once. I didn't even know he'd ever been married before."

"Are you an only child?"

"Uh-huh. My folks thought they couldn't have kids, then, surprise! Here I came."

"Finally, you have a sister, and now you learn she's been lying to you for months."

"I know." He kneaded the back of his neck for a moment. "I don't know what to think."

"What's Diane like?"

"I don't know. I mean, I thought I did, but now . . . I just don't know."

"You said you didn't know she had a gun — is that right?"

"Hell, no! She's anti guns. She used to tease me about going hunting, telling me that until you give deer guns, it's not a fair fight." He lowered his eyes again and resumed studying his hands. "Did Diane kill those women?"

"Looks that way."

He raised his eyes and looked around as if he might find answers in the room's corners. "What happens now?"

"Once you and I are done talking, I'll meet with the ADA."

"He's the person who decides what charges to bring against me."

"Yes."

"Would you tell him that I didn't know? That I didn't understand?"

Diane was out for bear. The minute Ellis stepped into Interview Room Two, she snapped, "About time! I've been waiting for hours."

"I apologize for the delay. I needed to talk to Cal first."

"Cal?" she said, fire still smoldering in her eyes.

"Your brother . . . or rather, your half brother." He pointed to the chair nearest to where she stood. "Have a seat. Let's get the logistics out of the way."

She didn't move. Her glare was contemptuous.

Ellis repeated the same spiel he gave Cal, with different results.

She placed her hands on her hips. "Forget it. I'm not signing anything."

"Here's a written statement of your rights.

Read it, please." Ellis eased a single sheet of paper from his folder and slid it across the table. "All your signature says is that it was given to you and you understand it."

She shoved the paper aside without even glancing at it. It skittered off the table and fell to the ground.

Ellis didn't move to retrieve it. Neither did she.

"I can't talk to you unless you sign it."

Diane placed her hands on the chair back and leaned forward, flirtatiously showcasing her bosom. "What a shame . . . I was so looking forward to getting to know you better."

"You're a great actress, Diane. For real. I've seen you in *Gypsy, Annie Get Your Gun,* and *Chicago.* You've got major league pipes. My wife was a Broadway dancer, so I've been to a thousand shows. You could have competed in the big time."

"Flattery will get you nowhere."

"No flattery."

"You're good. Very good. But it's all for naught." She sat down, relaxed and smiling. "I want a lawyer."

Ellis rejoined me in the Observation Room.

"Now what?" I asked.

"You go home with the thanks of a grateful police chief."

"And come back when?"

"Tomorrow. I don't know when."

"What's going to happen?"

Ellis turned toward the now empty Room Two. "We hope Cal gets himself a good lawyer."

I followed Ellis's gaze. Our reflections shimmered on the glass that separated us from the empty, dark room. It was a terrible thing to take advantage of someone's innocence. It takes a special kind of evil to betray family.

"I heard from Olive, one of the book club members, that Diane has vacation plans," I said.

"A three-week trip to Indonesia."

"Bali?"

"And Jakarta."

"How do you know?"

"E-mail confirmations. We checked her phone first thing to see if she had additional accomplices."

"Did you find any?"

"No."

"We have no extradition treaty with Indonesia. Jean was going somewhere, too. Remember? Kirk Trevis from her condo said she asked about subletting."

"Cape Cod. She rented an oceanfront cottage for August through the end of the year."

"I wonder why."

"Grief, maybe. Some people like to be alone."

"Perhaps." I turned away from the darkened window.

"The ADA is going to want to talk to you as well."

I ripped a sheet of paper from the small spiral-bound notebook I carry in my tote bag and wrote down Max's name and phone number under the heading *The best lawyer in Rocky Point.* I handed it to Ellis. "Would you give this to Cal?"

Ellis read it. "I can't."

"He needs a good lawyer. You said so."

"True, but as the police chief, I can't tell him so."

"He's a kid."

"He's an adult."

"Can he have visitors?"

"Not yet."

"Can't you see he gets this? Somehow?"

"I'm sorry, Josie. If he has a note in your handwriting . . . you're an aggrieved party . . . can't you see the traps looming in front of us?"

I crumpled the paper and tossed it in the trash can.

He patted my arm. "You have a good heart."

"I just want him to get a fair shake."

"He will."

Ellis walked me out. I waved good-bye and left. Outside in the fresh, salty air, I stretched, arching my back. A warm breeze was blowing in from the west. The weatherman had predicted rain by evening, but the storm seemed to have passed us by. To the west, the still-thick clouds were backlit with pink and yellow streaks from the setting sun.

I had thought that once I knew who was behind the theft and murders, I would feel a sense of relief, that I would feel good, but I didn't. I felt sad. From what Cal said and what Diane didn't, she betrayed him for money. The Bible doesn't say that money is the root of all evil. It says the love of money is the root of all evil, and you only had to witness Diane's final performance to see the truth in that.

CHAPTER FORTY

I crossed the street and climbed a dune.

The ocean was midnight blue laced with riffles of chop running on the diagonal.

I reached Edwin at his office.

"We found the lamp. It's safe."

"Where?"

I told him, the two-minute version.

"That's quite a story."

"I'm just glad the plan worked. I have to ask . . . Now that the lamp is back safe and sound, would you reconsider allowing it to be featured on my show? Anonymously, of course."

"I'll think about it. I have a call I need to take."

And he was gone.

I was tempted to call Timothy, but I didn't want to deliver half a story and get his hopes up. He'd hear the news, though, so I needed to update him. I opted for e-mail.

The lamp has been found intact. Yay! Edwin

has agreed to think about letting us use it. I'll keep you posted.

There was nothing more I could do, and I knew it.

Wes called me at home on Thursday morning. I glanced at the oversized clock mounted above the refrigerator, a Chessman original.

"Wes, I can't believe you're calling me so early! It's not even seven in the morning!"

"Early bird, Joz. That's me. Listen . . . I'm pitching an article to *Drop a Dime,* you know it, don't you? The monthly that runs those exposés of the rich and famous? Anyway, my hook is the Tiffany lamp, natch. I'm listing you as a primary source, with an exclusive. When can we meet so you can give me a couple of quotes? How's now?"

"First, I think you just called me a worm. Second, you can't have an exclusive. Third, I'll be glad to give you a few quotes. Fourth, now is good. I'll buy you breakfast at Ellie's."

"What do you mean I can't have an exclusive?"

I chuckled. Wes was so predictable.

"See you soon," I said, and hung up.

I knew how our breakfast would go. Wes would position his demand for an exclusive

459

as fair and reasonable. When I still refused to agree to his terms, he'd sigh to his toenails, making his profound disappointment in me obvious. I'd remain unmoved. Then he'd get to work. He'd ask smart questions, and I, knowing the kind of tantalizing quotes he needed to land the assignment, would make certain he got them.

Before I left, I checked my e-mail. Timothy had replied with characteristic wit and business acumen.

You are a steely-eyed wonder woman. Can we use the rescue story in the episode? (I bet the owner says yes.)

"The whole idea was simple," I said, after savoring a bite of Ellie's impossible-to-replicate ham and cheese crêpe, "not just Diane's disguise. Ava and Jean planned it together. Ava didn't want to risk Edwin discovering that she switched the lamp. She was smart about that. Edwin is a brilliant businessman and hard as granite. One whiff that he'd been conned and he would have been relentless in pursuing her. So they organized everything down to the smallest detail, and they were super cautious. This plan of theirs was in the works for months, ever since Ava learned she was pregnant. We know the timeline since we know when Cal bought the disposable phones in Boston. Ava gave Jean the hundred and twenty-five thousand she got when she closed out her bank account. Jean bought the replica lamp and brought it over to Ava's house the Monday morning I was scheduled to examine the original. They knew I'd take the real lamp away to do the appraisal, so the replacement had to be ready to go."

Wes nodded as he jotted a note. "Right, and we know this because of the voice mails and texts the police recovered when they picked up those disposable phones."

"Exactly. Pretty much, that's all we know. The rest is speculation, but it all fits. The day I returned the genuine lamp after appraising it, Jean picked it up and brought it to her condo. Merry said she saw Jean in the living room with the box that supposedly contained shoes and boots. Why was she in the living room? The cedar closet is upstairs. That's why she asked Merry not to mention it to the police, to avoid their getting . . . ha-ha . . . sidetracked. It seems to me their plan would have worked except that Diane got greedy. Jean gave her twenty-five thousand dollars to split with Cal. Cal said Diane gave him five thousand dollars, which was fine for the little bit he had to do. On the one hand, if you have nothing, twenty-five thousand seems like a lot of money, and so does five thousand. On the other hand, when you find out there's likely to be more than a million dollars on the table, suddenly twenty-five thousand seems like an insult. Everything is relative."

"Then she knifes him in the back by tricking him into committing a felony. Nice. For five G's."

"Do the police have any evidence that Diane actually got the twenty-five thousand dollars?" I asked.

"Yup. Cal told them where to find his five thousand, and they found the remaining twenty thousand in Diane's house."

"Really? I would have thought she would have used it to pay for the trip to Indonesia."

"She charged the trip," Wes said, "and the bills haven't come due yet."

"And it's hard to stash cash in a bank. You can't just open an account and keep depositing amounts under the ten-thousand-dollar reporting threshold because that's a crime, too. It's called 'structuring.' "

Wes stared at me for a moment. "And you know this . . . how?"

I laughed. "No, I'm not trying to hide cash. I just know things. I read a lot. Any fingerprints?"

"Uh-huh. They've got Diane dead to

rights on the money. Both Ava and Jean's fingerprints are all over the bills — along with Diane's. Not Cal's, though, which will help him at trial time."

"Why aren't his prints on his cut?"

"Diane put the money in an envelope — he never even opened it."

"That's good, because I wouldn't put it past Diane to try to put the murders on Cal."

"She already is," Wes said. "She took the story he told the police and turned it around, saying he was the one who found the lamp at a garage sale, and she was helping him out."

"But the bulk of the money was found at her place."

"She was holding it for him. The five thousand he kept was — she said with a straight face — walking-around money."

"What a witch!"

"She's some piece of work, all right. So you think Diane went to Ava's house demanding a bigger cut, and when Ava refused, she grabbed the frying pan and killed her?"

"It's logical. I doubt we'll ever know for sure, since the last I heard, Diane isn't talking and there's no forensic evidence." I laid my fork down and looked straight at Wes. "I thought there was a chance Edwin killed Ava."

"So did I."

"We were wrong, showing that anyone can use facts to prove the truth they want to believe."

"People do it all the time."

"Usually not on purpose — I hope." The waitress refilled our coffee cups. "What else have you learned?"

"They found a professional makeup kit and a bunch of wigs and eyeglasses. Strands of Diane's own hair are in the wigs and wig caps, including the ones used by the fake Ava, the gal who gave her name as Orson as she passed through the Grey Gull condo complex security booth, and the one she used at the Austin Arms. They also found the Gucci horsebit loafers and Picasso bracelet Diane wore when she was the fake Ava in Jean's closet. Evidently, Jean lent them to her. There's something I don't get. I understand why Ava and Jean needed someone to pretend to be Ava — the real Ava was out of the country making certain Edwin didn't muck up her plans. What I don't understand is why they chose Diane."

"Really? I think Diane was a smart choice — she was both a good friend and a talented actress." I sipped some coffee. "Cal was a good choice, too. Neither one of them has a criminal record, so they'd never be on the cops' radar. Another smart thing they did — both Jean and Diane planted suggestions that Edwin was violent, exaggerating so the police would think he had a motive. Sylvia told the truth as she knew it. Jean and Diane used facts to tell a lie. Sophistry."

"Why didn't Jean report Ava's actual scheme as soon as Ava was killed?" Wes asked. "After all, that Ava intended to steal the lamp to fund a new life because she was having another man's baby gives Edwin one heck of a motive."

"At a guess, because Jean was the buyer of record of the reproduction Tiffany lamp, so any revelation she made about Ava's intentions would implicate herself. Plus, Jean would have had to reveal the rest of the plan, and that would incriminate Diane and Cal, and she had to know that Cal at least would have turned on her without blinking. It's one thing to keep a secret about what Cal thought was a white lie designed to help his sister. It's another to keep that secret when doing so means you go to jail, especially when your cut is a measly five thousand dollars."

"It was all about money."

"It's more complicated than that. I think

465

it was about living your dream. Diane longed for travel, for adventures, for grand passion. Money was merely the means to that end. The lamp was her ticket out."

"What do you long for?"

"Community. I want to fit in. To belong."

"Don't you feel as if you belong?"

"Sometimes. How about you? What do you long for?"

Wes grinned, a cocky one. "A Pulitzer."

"I believe in you, Wes. You'll get there."

"You do? You believe in me?"

"Yes." I patted the back of his hand. "I really do, Wes. I really do."

I gave Wes two killer quotes for his proposal, one about how Cal had been betrayed by Diane, his newfound family, the other about Diane's longing for adventure and love. I knew they'd resonate with Wes, the *Drop a Dime* editor, and the publications' readers because I've learned over the years that facts are far less compelling than emotions. Steer toward the pain and you reach the truth.

CHAPTER FORTY-ONE

Ellis called as I was driving to work and asked me to stop by the station. As soon as I sat down at the guest table, he placed a photograph in front of me.

"Do you recognize this person?" he asked.

I was staring at the fake Ava. The hair and glasses were the same as in the other photos and in the sketch, but this time everything was right.

"This is the fake Ava," I said. "Bryan did an incredible job." I raised my eyes to his face. "How did you get Diane to pose for the photo?"

"We didn't. We used an image from the theater's Web site."

"Clever." I slid the photo back toward him. "With my ID, you can prove Diane perpetrated a fraud. Can you get her for murder?"

"Looks that way. The ADA is going to try her for Jean's murder first since that's the strongest case. It's all about the weapon. Diane bought it at a gun show in Augusta, Maine, last month. She charged it, so there's no question of ownership. She had it with her at the Austin Arms, so we have it in her possession. The bullets match those that killed Jean."

"That sounds pretty cut and dried. She doesn't have an alibi, does she?"

"Nope. And our canvass turned up a neighbor who saw a woman place a cardboard box of the right shape and size in her trunk and drive away. She can't ID her, but we have the car. Her description of the vehicle matches the white Impala they recorded at the security gate, which just happens to be the kind of car Diane rented that morning."

"Was Diane's own car in the shop?"

"Nope."

"Is the witness reliable?"

"She's old, but sharp as a tack, from what I hear."

"We saw her at the crime scene," I said. "An older woman stood just outside the police line watching you work. She was with a young woman, a girl, really."

"I remember her."

I gazed out the window toward the dunes. "Diane killed Jean to steal the genuine

Tiffany lamp."

"Which makes it a capital crime. And let's not forget that Diane tried to kill you, too."

"Yeah . . . that's not something I'll forget anytime soon. Objectively, I understand why she did it. She and Jean couldn't let me appraise the replica lamp. If I did, their entire plan would unravel. I suspect the break-in was Jean's idea. Probably Jean offered Diane a huge chunk of money to do it, maybe as much as half the proceeds of the sale."

Ellis nodded. "That's what I think, too. Better to have us investigate a brazen theft than discover a motive for murder."

"Diane saw her travel dreams draw closer. Her intention was to smash a window, knowing that would trip the alarm, figuring she could get in and out with the lamp in the two or three minutes she had before the police arrived. Desperate times require desperate acts. Then she saw me and shot at me. She still would have tried to recover the replica lamp — but Eric arrived, and then sirens sounded, and the whole idea was foiled."

Scuffling noises came through the open door, followed by shouts and angry voices, a babble of protest. I turned to see what was going on. Ellis rose at the first sounds and strode to the lobby. I followed, standing just inside the office. I could see and hear but was away from the skirmish.

A gaggle of reporters was queued up along one wall. Wes was among the several who were trying to move forward, to work their way closer to the reception desk and the internal corridors that led to the interrogation rooms and jail cells.

Detective Brownley stood facing them, her hand raised like a traffic cop, telling them, "Stay back. You heard me — stay back. You cannot block the door or access to the hallways."

No one seemed to be listening to her. Daryl came out from behind the reception counter on the run just as Ellis charged into the melee.

"That's it!" Ellis boomed.

I wasn't surprised that the fracas died down on the spot. The power and authority Ellis brought to those two words would have stopped a charging elephant in its tracks.

"Stay back or stay outside. Your choice."

"Chief," Wes said, pivoting on a dime, "ADA Navarro announced he'll be indicting Diane Hawkins for the murder of Jean Cooper. What about Ava Towson?"

Officer Meade appeared from the corridor on the left, her hand grasping Diane's arm. Diane wore a red sheath with a black and red striped bolero jacket and black pumps. Her hands were cuffed behind her back. Her chin was up. Her hair was styled as I'd seen it at the library, chic and modern. She seemed poised and confident. As soon as she saw the reporters, she raised her chin a bit higher and angled her head to the right, presenting, I gathered, her best side. Cameras flashed. Questions were shouted and ignored. Ellis stood facing them, keeping them at bay.

Detective Brownley took her other arm, and the two women marched Diane past the gauntlet. As they passed Ellis's door, Diane saw me and stopped.

"You should have died," she said.

"I almost did."

The detective propelled her out the door, with the reporters following close behind.

Ellis walked toward me. I backed up.

"Are you okay?" he asked.

"Did you see her eyes when she saw me? She's filled with hate." I sat back down at the guest table. "I feel so bad for Cal — with a sister like that."

"He'll be okay."

"How can you say that? She got him in six kinds of trouble."

"He's going to walk."

"Really? How so?"

471

"Cal is eager to testify against Diane and clear his own name."

"He negotiated a plea deal."

A corner of Ellis's mouth lifted. "At first, he agreed to plead guilty to criminal impersonation. You know that statute, right? That's what they use to prosecute identity theft. He would have served a year. But then he got a lawyer who put the kibosh on that deal. They were at it most of the night, negotiating the terms. Cal is getting full immunity on all charges relating to the theft in return for his testimony. Even the record of his arrest will be expunged."

"Oh, that's terrific news, Ellis. Who's his lawyer?"

"Max Bixby."

"You're a good guy, Ellis."

"Me? What makes you think I had anything to do with it?"

"I can't imagine."

Footsteps echoed from the lobby. I skewed around to peek and saw Phil Wilcox striding across the lobby to the reception desk. A short bald man in a dark blue suit followed a pace behind him.

"That's Phil Wilcox," I said. "Is he Ava's baby's father?"

"It looks that way. We're trying to persuade him to take a paternity test."

"Why would he?"

"To help the ADA make his case. Ava's pregnancy is crucial to proving motive."

"You'd have to be very civic-minded to put yourself through that."

"The press are already onto him. Wes found the hotel room where he took Ava — he charged it."

"I feel terrible for his wife."

"Who's already left him."

"Who can blame her?"

"Not me. His dad fired him, too. From what I hear, he'll be filing for personal bankruptcy protection within days."

"What about Edwin? Does he know?"

"Edwin gave us a blood sample, and he's been ruled out as the father — and yes, he knows."

"What a mess." I stood up, preparing to leave. "I'm really glad about Cal."

Ellis smiled. "Me, too."

CHAPTER FORTY-TWO

I got into work just before ten. Cara was preparing our mailing list for a midsummer promotional flyer. Sasha was on the phone thanking someone for something. Eric, Cara told me, was polishing furniture, and Gretchen was changing Hank and Angela's water. I poured myself a cup of coffee.

"That was a nice call," Sasha said. "A man named Dylan Locke returned Fred's call. Since Fred isn't in yet, I took it. He's Ferdinand Locke's grandson, and he has all of his grandfather's papers. Among the dozen love letters Aunt Louise wrote Ferdy — which is what she called him — is one where she thanks him for the desk."

"Way to go, Fred!" I said, giving a small air pump. "He's going to be over the moon!"

"Dylan will be scanning in the letter and e-mailing it to us today."

"Great. Did you hear from Frank? What did he think of the Peabody? How was his clam chowder?"

Sasha's cheeks grew rosy. "He loved both."

"If you talk to him again, give him my regards," I said, turning toward the front door in response to the wind chimes jingling.

Edwin stepped into the office. With one quick glance he took in the office and my staff. "Do you have a minute?" he asked me.

"Of course. Let's go to my private office. Would you like some coffee?"

"No, thanks."

Upstairs, Edwin perched on the edge of the love seat. I sat in the wing chair and waited for him to speak.

"I wanted to say good-bye and thank you."

"You're leaving for London."

"Yes. Chief Hunter called on me last evening. He gave me a comprehensive update."

"It's all pretty shocking."

"Shock wears off and life goes on." He tapped the love seat's arm with his index finger. "Chief Hunter asked me why I was staying at the guesthouse. I inferred that he thought I was having an affair. I assured him I wasn't. On the off chance you might think the same thing, I want to repeat my assurance."

"You don't need to explain anything to me."

"I want the respect of people I admire. You are in that category."

"Thank you, Edwin. I'm honored by that."

"The woman staying there is Uma Young, a consultant specializing in helping hospitals expand their fund-raising efforts."

"I'd heard her name was Coco Tully."

"Coco is a nickname. Tully is her married name, which she doesn't use in business. Her full, legal name is Uma Corcoran Young Tully. In her personal life, she's known as Coco Tully. Professionally, she goes by Uma Young."

"Her husband is a lawyer, and they just relocated to Los Angeles."

Edwin's eyes narrowed. "How did you know that?"

"I was curious about her. I should apologize to you about that, for intruding in your business."

"Did you consider whether I stole the Tiffany lamp myself?"

"Not seriously."

"The police did."

"They have to look at everything, I guess. They asked me if I stole it, too."

"A waste of time and resources," Edwin said, his voice laden with contempt. "Not that it's anyone's business, but I brought Ms. Young in to help Ava's pet charity."

"So not only were you *not* having an affair with her —"

"Or with anyone," he said, interrupting me.

"Or with anyone . . . you were trying to help Ava succeed."

"Grief is a funny thing," he said, meeting my eyes. "I had just authorized you to sell everything in the house. I was grieving more than I wanted to admit, not just for my wife, but for the loss of . . . I guess you would call it . . . a dream."

"After we met, you went to the guesthouse to ask Ms. Young to stay and help the hospital, as a kind of tribute to Ava."

"Yes." He paused for several moments. "I felt sick, really ill, as if only then did the reality set in. I went upstairs to lie down for a few minutes. I don't recall ever feeling so weary. I slept for ten hours and stayed for days. I was just so damn sad." He stood up. "If you're ever in London, I hope you'll contact me."

I thanked him and walked him out.

Outside, he turned back, reached into an inside pocket, and handed me a sheet of paper. I unfolded it. It was the authorization form, signed.

"Oh, Edwin . . . thank you."

He nodded once and resumed his march to London.

I stood on the stoop watching until the long black limo turned the corner and was lost behind the trees. I wondered what would have happened had Ava told Edwin the truth, whether he would have stuck to the prenup, or whether he would have tried to work something out with her.

Upstairs again, I scanned in the signed authorization form and e-mailed it to Timothy. I inserted a happy face emoticon in the e-mail, figuring that one icon said it all.

I called Max.

"I hear you got a killer deal for Cal Miller, and I wanted to tell you that I think it's wonderful. The poor kid."

"Any deal that might or might not be in the works has not yet been officially announced."

"Understood. So what was that rattling sound?"

"A rattler."

I gasped. "You're kidding, right?"

"Nope. The snake handler has never seen a rattler in this urban an area, nor has he any idea how it got into the duct. He assures me the snake will live a long and happy life in a distant part of the state."

"I thought you were going to tell me it was a baby's rattle that somehow got into the a/c system and every time a certain gizmo moved, it rattled."

"The lesson is that often things are just what they seem to be."

"Like Cal just seems to be a young man who stepped into a sinkhole his sister dug and covered up with Astroturf. What's going to happen to Diane?"

"Off the record?"

"Of course. Everything we discuss is off the record."

"I think she's going to be convicted of capital murder, and I think she'll get the death penalty."

"I'm completely conflicted about Ava."

"So is Babs. Men aren't. Women see her as a kind of Madonna trying to protect her child. Men see her as a manipulative gold digger."

"That's funny."

"That's what makes the world go round."

"Ellis did a great job on this case."

"Ellis is maybe the best police chief ever."

"Why do you say that?"

"He follows the Siren call of justice."

I smiled. "I like that allusion."

"I like you, Josie."

"I like you, too, Max."

After catching up with e-mails, and voice mails, and my staff, I decided I needed a good dose of hard work, so I headed to the warehouse to help Fred with his preliminary assessment of the Towson household goods. As I entered the warehouse, Eric was leaving it, carrying the printer's case.

"The printer's case," I said. "It's going to the tag sale this week after all."

"Nope. I'm bringing it to Gretchen to ring up. Grace likes country rustic a lot."

"You two have a lot in common."

His cheeks turned a rosy pink. "I know."

"Are you giving it to her now?"

"I'm going to save it for Christmas. As a gift for our new house."

"What? You're moving in together?"

His flush reddened. "No. Not yet. She's still in school and all. But we talk about the future sometimes. We talk about getting married."

"And this will be for your shared future. I think that's incredibly romantic."

He looked down, then up. "You won't tell anyone, will you?"

I drew an *X* on my heart and raised my right hand. "True blue and never stain."

Angela came running over and tried to

climb my leg. I picked her up and kissed her cheek.

Eric smiled awkwardly, thanked me, and pushed through into the office.

I carried Angela to the cordoned-off Towson area.

"Do you want to keep me company, little girl?" I asked her. She mewed and licked my neck. "Thank you, little one."

Fred wasn't around. I figured he was in the office. I placed Angela on my shoulder and used one hand to check the computer record so I'd know where Fred left off. He'd recorded boxes 1 through 18. Still working with only one hand, I set a video recorder on a tripod and opened the clear plastic tub labeled BOX 19, AVA TOWSON DESK. I flicked the camera on.

I started with a set of heavy bookends. I placed them side by side on a closed tub.

"This is a set of heavy bookends," I said to the camera, creating an annotated video recording, as per Prescott's protocol. We would do it for every object. I talked as I recorded all sides and angles. "The design is reminiscent of Greek columns. The set is probably made of copper alloy. No marks. In excellent condition. Not worth appraising." I set them aside. "The rest of this box contains books." I hit PAUSE.

"Angela, I'm sorry darling, but I'm going to be bending over a lot, and I need both hands. I'll give you a proper cuddle later, I promise." I lowered her to the floor, and she scampered off as if she'd just recalled an urgent errand.

I extracted a set of four brown leather-bound duodecimo volumes. I examined the title and copyright pages, recording them one at a time, in numerical order, for the camera. "This is a four-volume set of *The Farmer's Tour Through the East of England,* published in 1771 in London by W. Strahan. Marbled paper-covered boards, numerous folding copper-engraved plates throughout. At first glance, the set appears to be a reading copy, and as such, it is in only fair to good condition. The boards are scuffed, rubbed, and edge-worn. The joints are worn and beginning to crack, although the boards are firmly attached. We should appraise it to confirm it's the complete set, that all illustrations are in place, and determine value."

I lowered the books into the tub.

The next book on the pile was *The Lantern.* "Oh, wow," I whispered. "Ava's copy of the book club selection." I opened it. It was a contemporary copy of the recently published book, a first edition. I was turning to the title page when two sheets of paper spilled out. I stared at them for a moment before picking them up.

One sheet showed a Grey Gull Condo Association–issued floor plan. A hand-drawn star was in the upper corner along with the words *IT'S AVAILABLE!* handwritten in all caps. Evidently Ava had been considering moving into her sister's condo complex.

The other was a handwritten draft of a Dear John letter.

Dear Edwin,

~~I love you.~~ I hope you know how much I've loved you, but I can't stay with a man who is so insensitive to my needs. You ignore my wishes, insisting you know what's best, not listening to me at all. ~~You've never believed me when I've told you how much I want a baby, that it's almost like a phantom limb.~~ I told you a long time ago that I wasn't interested in children, but you know that's no longer the case. ~~Now it's in my mind all the time.~~ Now when I think of having a baby, it's almost like a phantom limb, present and vital.

~~I've always honored my vows.~~ I've suffered in silence, determined to honor my vows, and I did so until I ran into my high-school boyfriend, Phil Wilcox. Phil is married, too, and neither of us has any interest in a long-term relationship. I simply succumbed to a tidal wave of desire, and my sin turned into a blessing because I got pregnant.

I understand that leaving you now and under these circumstances means I won't get any ~~alimony~~ money, but I would rather go back to work than give up this dream. This baby may not be reared in ~~luxury~~ affluence, but it will be reared with love and without rancor.

~~Do you think you can forgive me?~~ Can you understand? Can you forgive me?

I stood for longer than a minute, thinking of loss and desire, of the hidden costs of finding what you yearn for. After I surfaced from my trancelike reverie, I wondered if Ava had ever really planned to go back to work. I doubted it. Her noble-sounding statement was just a cover story, a smoke screen intended to help hide her motive should the theft of the Tiffany lamp ever come to light.

I called Ellis to come get the documents, then took photos for Wes.

Timothy wrote back: The lawyers are happy.
 Wait until I told him about Aunt Louise's
desk. He'd love it.

Fred didn't come into work all day, but I
wasn't worried. After the stress and exhila-
ration of yesterday, I figured he'd collapsed
and was still asleep.

CHAPTER FORTY-THREE

At ten Friday morning, Gretchen asked, "Has anyone spoken to Fred?"

No one had.

"I knew he needed a good night's sleep, but this is pushing it!" I said, trying to make light of the situation.

At noon, I succumbed to worry and called him. His cell phone, his only phone, went straight to voice mail. I texted: Are you okay?

At two, with no reply, I called the Blue Dolphin to see if his girlfriend, Suzanne, knew where he was.

The longtime hostess, Frieda, answered with a welcoming "Blue Dolphin, how may I help you?"

"Frieda, it's Josie, Josie Prescott."

"Hi, Josie. Are you looking to come in tonight?"

"Actually, no. I'm calling for Suzanne. Is she there?"

After a too-long pause, she said, "No. I'm

sorry, Josie. Would you like to leave a message?"

I thanked her, said no, and ended the call. I found Suzanne's phone numbers — home and cell — in my contact list and dialed both. No answer.

Something was very wrong.

I couldn't decide what to do, but I needed to do something. Fred was responsible, courteous, and professional. No way would he have simply vanished without a word unless he was in trouble. Or unless he had a compelling reason to do so. Remembered facts fell into place like dominoes.

Ellis had asked if the Tiffany studio mark could be falsified.

Fred knew how to work with stained glass.

Fred had accessed the walk-in safe after Eric had stored the lamp.

Fred knew enough about the antiques black market to use the system for his own benefit.

"No," I said aloud.

I didn't believe it.

Trust, I thought, silently repeating the familiar mantra, *but verify.*

I accessed my security company's digital files, entered the date I wanted to view, clicked on the walk-in safe camera file, and entered the time range.

Fred opened the safe, looked at the lamp, and locked it back up.

"There," I said, relaxing. "See? I knew it."

I closed the files, then swiveled so I could see out the window. The sun tinted everything with a warm wash of color. I gazed into the forest, comparing the different shades of green, my mind racing, thinking ugly thoughts. I heard myself sigh.

Viewing the security tape hadn't proved a thing. I'd confirmed that Fred hadn't switched out the lamp during that visit to the safe, but that didn't mean he hadn't done it another time. Or perhaps he didn't need to switch lamps here. He could have been working with Jean all along. He could have helped her locate the replica, then, later, during an examination of the genuine lamp, switched it for the one he manufactured using our appraisal as a design checklist. With skill and determination, he could have created a fake lamp that would appear to be identical to the original.

I simply couldn't envision Fred in the role I was assigning him, but the fact remained that he could have acted as I'd laid out — and he was missing. If Fred didn't surface soon, I would have to reveal my concerns to Ellis, but I didn't have to do it now.

I forced myself to work.

While I caught up on accounting reports, with Hank sitting in my lap, happy-padding, and Angela crouching on the floor, swiping at his tail, I turned on Rocky Point's local radio station. Hank ignored her, lashing his tail up when she touched it, then lowering it again. She was having a blast.

"Angela! Leave Hank's tail alone or I'm going to rename you Devila."

She ignored me.

The weekend weather was going to be perfect, eighty-five with low humidity. Our Little League team won against Newington, five to three. The Seacoast Garden Club was hosting a workshop called "Organic Gardening." The Rocky Point Yacht Club was sponsoring a fund-raiser, also on Sunday, to raise money for college scholarships. It was open to the public. The highlight was an afternoon regatta among ten regional colleges, including Hitchens.

I reached around Hank for the phone and called the yacht club. I bought six tickets, certain that Ty, Zoë, Ellis, and the kids would like to come to the regatta, too.

At four, after trying Fred's and Suzanne's

numbers again, I went downstairs. I'd put it off long enough. I was going to have to talk to Ellis.

Before I could tell Cara I was leaving, the door opened, setting the wind chimes jingling.

Fred walked in. For one moment, no one said anything; then everyone exploded into talk at once.

"Are you all right?" Cara asked.

"It's so good to see you," Gretchen said.

"You're okay," Eric said.

"Hi," Sasha said.

Fred turned to me. "Sorry."

"We were worried."

"I have no excuse about not calling. I just forgot."

I laughed. "You forgot to call your job to say you weren't coming in for two days? Did I hear you right?"

"I had other things on my mind." He held up his left hand and pointed with his right index finger to a shiny gold band. "Suzanne and I eloped."

I stood, disbelieving, amid the cacophony of oohs and aahs and best wishes and congratulations and where and when and why from Cara, Gretchen, Eric, and Sasha.

"After the kind of life-and-death experience we went through during that sting,"

Fred said, his eyes still on mine, "I realized that life is short. As soon as I left the police station, I drove straight to the Blue Dolphin and asked Suzanne to marry me." He grinned. "She said yes. We made an eight o'clock flight to Vegas, got in around eleven, found an all-night chapel, and were married by one." He turned his wrist to check the time. "Today. This morning." He chuckled. "We had a helluva champagne breakfast to celebrate and caught a five A.M. flight back."

"I can't believe you didn't stay for the weekend!" Gretchen exclaimed.

"We thought about it . . . but we didn't want to. We'll take a proper honeymoon later. All we wanted to do was get married, and we did."

"Sounds like we better start planning a party," I said.

"I really am sorry, Josie."

"You're forgiven. Any time you elope, you should feel free to blow off work."

Cara clapped her hands. Gretchen giggled. Eric looked thoughtful. Sasha smiled.

I walked toward Fred, my arms open. He hugged me, and I hugged him back, and then I hugged him again, relief weakening my knees and making me smile so broadly, it hurt.

■ ■ ■ ■

On the ride home after a relaxing hour sitting on a blanket listening to Academy Brass play an array of familiar patriotic tunes, Ty surprised me by telling me he was going to grill me a steak. He made the turn that led to my house and away from the grocery store.

"Aren't we stopping at the store?" I asked.

"I have everything packed in a cooler in the back. This is a surprise I've had planned on a theoretical basis for a few weeks now."

"You don't say."

"It's a celebration."

"I love celebrations."

"I know you do."

"What are we celebrating?"

"The successful completion of my D.C. assignment."

"Completion? As in, it's done?"

"My boss texted me this morning. I'm done. While you were in the shower, I hotfooted it to the grocery store."

"You devil, you."

"Crafty like a fox, that's me."

I reached out a hand to touch his shoulder. "You don't have to leave tomorrow! I'm so excited!"

Ty stopped at a light and turned toward me. Our eyes locked, and for that moment, we were alone in the world.

He smiled, the one that no one but me ever gets to see, and said, "Me, too."

Once he passed through the intersection, I said, "Now that it's over, can you tell me about your investigation?"

"What investigation?"

I laughed, then he laughed, and we didn't stop until he rolled to a stop in the driveway.

"Watch the grill for a minute, okay?" Ty said.

He handed me the tongs, and I used them to stir the mushrooms Ty had simmering on one side of the grill. The orange light cast by the Japanese lanterns added a magical sheen to the soy-marinated mushrooms. I listened to nature's music, focusing on the familiar, "Who-who-WHO-whooo, who-who-WHO-whooo" from the barred owl who lived in the forest on the far side of the meadow.

"Look this way."

I turned toward Ty's voice. He was holding up a dirt-smeared gray plastic flower pot containing a three-foot-tall tomato plant. I laid the tongs down on the side counter.

"You bought me a tomato plant."

"Two. The other one is still in the truck. This one is called Fourth of July because it has an early harvest. See? Some of the tomatoes are already turning red. The other one is a Big Boy. It'll take us into fall."

"Sylvia grows Fourth of July tomatoes. They're incredible. I'm going to plant them now."

While Ty went back to the truck for the other plant, I grabbed my gardening gloves and a small shovel from the mudroom and started digging in a small patch of dirt under the kitchen window. I had the first plant in the ground and was pressing down the dirt by the time Ty got back from his third trip to his SUV, this time carrying stakes and chicken wire. Ty removed the mushrooms from the grill while I dug the second hole. I got the twine from my everything drawer in the kitchen. Ten minutes later the tomatoes were staked, fenced in, and well watered. I leaned back on my haunches to admire my handiwork.

"Done!" I said, standing. "Yay!"

"You're a model of efficiency."

"And cute as a bug."

"Cuter."

Ty laid the steak on the grill and set the timer. In four minutes, he turned it, and four minutes after that, he set it aside to rest.

As he worked, I poured myself a Rouge Martini and told him about Fred and Suzanne and Eric and Grace.

"I love Fred's spontaneity," I said, "and I think it's so completely sweet that Eric bought Grace a decorative piece for their someday-home. It's kind of like those promise rings they used to have."

"I think I saw one of those in an old Sandra Dee movie. Did Sandra Dee ever make a movie set in New Orleans?"

"I don't think so."

Ty took my hand. "When do you want to go to New Orleans?"

"The first weekend in November."

He laughed. "That's very specific. Why?"

"It's before we get busy for the holidays, but after October, which is maybe my favorite time of year in New Hampshire."

"I thought you liked summer best."

"I do. Except for October."

"And spring."

"That, too."

"The first weekend in November is good. I'll make us reservations."

"You're a wonderful man."

Timothy called on Monday, just before

noon to tell me the *Josie's Antiques* regular shooting schedule was set. We were going to resume filming in early August. He needed a list of the antiques I wanted to focus on.

I grabbed a sheet of paper and began making notes. We already had the Tiffany lamp film in the can. We could use the fake one, for comparison. Aunt Louise's desk, of course. Some Disney animation cells we'd just acquired. A nineteenth-century Chinese opium box with a gorgeous orange patina. My pen flew across the page. It wasn't until Hank came into the room and meowed, wanting attention, that I looked up. An hour had passed. Angela pushed past him, romping across the floor. My phone buzzed. It was a text from Ty: Let's go to my place tonight. Xo

Sure, I wrote back.

I turned to Hank, waiting for me to reply to his demand.

"I love you, Hank. Come here, baby."

He walked across the room as if he were in no hurry, which he wasn't, and arched his back. I picked him up and settled him in my lap. Angela pounced on a pink felt mouse.

I loved my office. I loved my company. I loved Rocky Point. I loved my life. I was in a place where I belonged.

CHAPTER FORTY-FOUR

The day before we left for New Orleans, I went for a walk on the beach. Each fall, I selected a piece of driftwood to serve as the star of my Christmas table decoration. A winter chill was in the air. I wore my favorite bone-colored Irish knit sweater, fitted enough around the neck for warmth, yet loose enough around the hips for comfort. My eyes swept the ground from the dunes to the water in a steady, hypnotic back-and-forth motion.

"Ms. Prescott!"

I looked up. Merry and Eleanor were jogging toward me, sand spewing as they ran. Eleanor's apricot fur was less finely groomed than I recalled. She was almost smiling, her tongue lolling, her tail wagging.

"Merry!" I called.

They slowed to a stop.

"It's good to see you, Merry. You, too, Eleanor. How are you?"

"Good. I don't know if you heard, but Mr. Towson moved to London." She reached down and gave Eleanor a little head-patty. "He gave Eleanor to me. My lucky day!"

Eleanor raised her head as if she understood and lapped Merry's hand.

"Eleanor looks like she thinks it was her lucky day, too."

"We're a good pair. Well, we better finish our run!"

They set off, heading north, and I resumed my hunt.

A length of driftwood that might work was half hidden by sand. It was long, but not too long, smooth and silky, with appealing knots and crooks so I could wedge in candles, berries, and boughs of holly. I smiled.

I reached for it, brushed off the sand that clung to hidden damp spots and little nubs, and considered it from all angles. It was perfect.

I was sitting in the aisle seat. Ty was at the window. He'd treated us to first class. A tall, thin flight attendant with a big smile wove through the line of boarding passengers to offer us a choice of magazines and newspapers. Her name, Bev, was embroidered on the dark blue apron that protected her red uniform. I eased the *Financial Times* out from the middle of the fanned-out options. Ty chose *The Boston Globe*.

"The captain says it's going to be a smooth and sunny flight the whole way to New Orleans," Bev said, her eyes sparkling. "I mention it because we made a batch of Dark 'n' Stormies, in case you're interested. I promise it won't jinx the flight!"

Ty and I both laughed and took her up on the offer, and when the drinks arrived, we clinked glasses.

"I can't believe we're flying first class," I said.

"Nothing but the best for you."

"We went to the Bahamas a few years ago, and we flew coach."

"You made those reservations."

"You know what that means, right? I'm never making a plane reservation for us again."

I was deep in an article about mobile advertising when my phone buzzed. It was a text from Sasha: *Lot 18 sold for $1.85 m.* I stared at the display for several seconds, then turned back to the article, but I couldn't seem to focus on the words. I glanced at Ty. He was reading about the Red Sox.

I reread Sasha's text and, with my eyes

still on the message, asked, "May I interrupt?"

"Sure."

"We sold the Towson Tiffany lamp for nearly two million dollars, a record."

"Congratulations!"

"Yeah."

"You don't seem very happy."

"Two women died because of that lamp. It feels like blood money."

"Your success in selling an object for top dollar is unrelated to their murders."

"I know."

Ty patted my hand. "You'll process it in your usual methodical way. Then you'll be ready to celebrate."

I leaned back against the leather headrest and smiled, my tension dissipating. "Thank you."

A conga line of seven travelers semi-danced by, the last of the passengers to board. From what I could tell from their joyful banter as they passed our row, they were the New England branch of a mostly Louisiana-based family on their way to a reunion.

We finished the last sips of our Dark 'n' Stormies as the boarding door closed. Bev came by and picked up our empty glasses.

Ty stuffed his paper into the seat-back pocket.

"I have something for you," he said.

I was certain I was about to get a temporary tattoo, probably a butterfly, maybe a heart. I touched my neck, remembering the four-leaf clover I got at a carnival last May. Ty thought it was sexy.

He reached into his shirt pocket and came out with a gold ring. A round-cut diamond, maybe as large as a karat, sat atop a simple mounting.

"It's beautiful."

"It was my Aunt Trina's.* When I was a little kid, I used to sit on her lap and play with it. She left it to me when she died, and I've kept it in a drawer all these years, until today."

"I wish I could have met her."

"You would have liked her, and she would have liked you." The plane started rolling backward from the gate, and Ty glanced out the window, then turned back to me. "So . . . I know we're not ready to get married . . . but will you marry me?"

My heart began thudding in a staccato beat. My throat didn't close exactly, but for a few seconds it felt as if I couldn't breathe.

* Please see *Deadly Appraisal.*

A moment later, my pulse steadied and my breathing returned to normal.

"What makes you think we're not ready to get married?"

Ty stared into my eyes as if he could see into my soul. "Are we?"

"Aren't we?" I held out my left hand and smiled. "Yes. I'll marry you."

He slid the ring onto my finger and leaned over for a kiss.

We held hands the whole way to New Orleans.

CHAPTER FORTY-FIVE

I woke up early on Sunday morning, rolled over, and tried to go back to sleep. At six, I gave up. I was tempted to wake Ty, but he was sleeping solidly, so I left him be. I tiptoed around the room, getting ready. I wrote a note saying I was going to toddle around the French Quarter and would end up at Café du Monde at seven.

It was cool and humid outside, with dew-laden fog drifting along the Mississippi River, and it was quiet. The antiques stores along Royal Street were dark, but the plate glass windows that fronted the street were ungated and open for window shopping.

A few minutes before seven, I was ensconced at a table by the river with a café au lait, an orange juice, an order of beignets, and *The New York Times.* Just as Ty had told me, a sole sax player stood across the street near the iron fence that surrounded Jackson Square. He wore dark jeans and a black short-sleeved shirt and flip-flops. I didn't recognize the song, but I didn't need to. I could have sat there all day.

Ty swung into a chair right at seven.

"Trouble sleeping?" he asked.

"Just excited to be here."

The saxophonist picked up the beat with a shoulder-dancing, foot-tapping, finger-snapping rendition of Billy Strayhorn's "Take the 'A' Train." Thirty seconds into the song, Ty stood up and held out his hand, his hips swaying. We started dancing, just us two, in the corner by the river, and I thought that this had to be the pinnacle, that surely no one had ever been happier than this.

ACKNOWLEDGEMENTS

Thanks to G. D. Peters for his assistance with this novel.

Special thanks go to my literary agent, Cristina Concepcion of Don Congdon Associates, Inc. Thanks also go to Michael Congdon, Katie Kotchman, and Katie Grimm. I'd also like to thank Cara Bellucci.

The Minotaur Books team also gets special thanks, especially those I work with most closely, including executive editor Hope Dellon; former associate editor Silissa Kenney; assistant editor Hannah O'Grady; publicist Sarah Melnyk; director of library marketing & national accounts manager (Macmillan) Talia Ross; copyeditor India Cooper; and the original edition's cover designer David Baldeosingh Rotstein.

ABOUT THE AUTHOR

Jane K. Cleland once owned a New Hampshire-based antiques and rare books business. She is the author of several previous Josie Prescott Antiques mysteries, is the winner of an Agatha Award and two David Awards for Best Novel, and has been a finalist for the Macavity and Anthony Awards. Jane is the former president of the New York chapter of the Mystery Writers of America and chairs the Wolfe Pack's Black Orchid Novella Award. She is part of the English faculty at Lehman College and lives in New York City.